The
Garden
of
Evening Mists

Also by Tan Twan Eng

THE GIFT OF RAIN

The
Garden
of
Evening Mists

a novel

TAN TWAN ENG

NEW YORK   BOSTON

Reprint excerpts from the following printed material are used with permission. "Winter" by N.P. Van Wyk Louw, anthologized in the three-volume *Groot Verseboek*, edited by Andre P Brink and published in 2008 by NB Publishing, Cape Town, South Africa

Richard Holmes' *A Meander through Memory and Forgetting* from *Memory:An Anthology*, edited by Harriet Harvey Wood and A.S. Byatt and published in 2009 by Vintage Publishing, a division of Random House.

Japanese Death Poems, compiled by Yoel Hoffmann and published in 1998 by Tuttle Publishing, North Clarendon, Vermont.

The author commentary on p. 336 is reprinted from The Guardian (UK).

Hachette Books
Hachette Book Group
1290 Avenue of the Americas, New York, NY 10104
hachettebooks.com
twitter.com/hachettebooks

First Edition: September 2012

Hachette Books is a division of Hachette Book Group, Inc. The Hachette Books name and logo are trademarks of Hachette Book Group, Inc.

The publisher is not responsible for websites (or their content) that are not owned by the publisher.

The Hachette Speakers Bureau provides a wide range of authors for speaking events. To find out more, go to www.hachettespeakersbureau.com or call (866) 376-6591.

Library of Congress Cataloging-in-Publication Data has been applied for.

ISBNs: 978-1-60286-180-0 (paperback), 978-1-60286-181-7 (e-book)

Printed in the United States of America

LSC-C

20   19   18   17   16   15

Praise for

THE GARDEN OF EVENING MISTS

"This novel uses fine art as its major theme and, in the process, becomes a work of fine art itself."

—*The Washington Post*

"[A] sumptuous . . . thoughtful . . . heartbreaking tale . . . . How to excise trauma . . . how to inscribe it on the present without tainting the world itself: these are the grand issues of this novel. With each one of its sentences, *The Garden of Evening Mists* poses a beautiful answer to these questions."

—John Freeman, *The Boston Globe*

"Enchanting."

—*The New Yorker*

"This story of a Japanese garden created in honour of a Japanese victim-of-war is sternly paced to match its subject. One of us likened its beauty to those of slowly clashing icebergs. The gardener is one of the most memorable characters in all the 30,000 pages we read this year."

—Man Booker Prize judging panel, *The Telegraph*

"[A] strong quiet novel [of] eloquent mystery."

—Dominique Browning, *The New York Times Book Review*

"Tan writes with breath-catching poise and grace . . . *The Garden of Evening Mists* also offers action-packed, end-of-empire storytelling . . . His fictional garden cultivates formal harmony—but also undermines it. It unmasks sophisticated artistry as a partner of pain and lies. This duality invests the novel with a climate of doubt; a mood—as with Aritomo's creation—of 'tension and possibility.' Its beauty never comes to rest."

—*The Independent* (UK)

"*The Garden of Evening Mists*, Tan Twan Eng's second novel, continues Eng's exploration, begun in *The Gift of Rain*, of the mystery that is memory, how remembrance never proceeds in anything like a straight line, and how its gaps are as crucial as silence is to music . . . Beautifully written . . . Eng is quite simply one of the best novelists writing today."

—Frank Wilson, *The Philadelphia Inquirer*

"As intricately designed as a Japanese garden, this deceptively quiet novel resonates with the power to inspire a variety of passionate emotions . . . A haunting novel certain to stay with the reader long after the book is closed."

—*Booklist*

"The unexpected relationship between a war-scarred woman and an exiled gardener leads to a journey through remorse to a kind of peace. After a notable debut, Eng (*The Gift of Rain*) returns to the landscape of his origins with a poetic, compassionate, sorrowful novel set in the aftermath of World War II in Malaya . . . Grace and empathy infuse this melancholy landscape of complex loyalties enfolded by brutal history, creating a novel of peculiar, mysterious, tragic beauty."

—*Kirkus Reviews* (starred review)

"Tan Twan Eng's superb *The Garden of Evening Mists* is . . . a gripping read. A new favorite."

—Nick Harkaway, *The Daily Beast*

"Like his debut, *The Gift of Rain*, Tan's second novel is exquisite . . . Tan triumphs again, entwining the redemptive power of storytelling with the elusive search for truth, all the while juxtaposing Japan's inhuman war history with glorious moments of Japanese art and philosophy. All readers in search of spectacular writing will not be disappointed."

—*Library Journal* (starred review)

"A complex and powerful narrative . . . . . .[a] sophisticated and satisfying novel."

—*The Sunday Times* (UK)

"The descriptions of nature in this heartfelt novel are so powerful, so sensitively handled that a palpable feeling of having seen the garden and the surrounding mist-shrouded hills is engendered . . . an outstanding prose writer."

—Ed Voves, *California Literary Review*

"Once again, Eng transports the reader to a world that few people know about and reveals the complicated humanity of its inhabitants."

—*BookPage*

"Tan's second novel is exquisite. . . . [He] manages to intertwine the redemptive power of storytelling with the elusive search for truth. . . . His is a challenging balancing act, and yet he never falters, intimately revealing his stories with power and grace."

—Terry Hong, Bookslut.com

For my sister
and
Opgedra aan A. J. Buys—sonder jou sou hierdie boek
dubbel so lank en halfpad so goed wees.
Mag jou eie mooi taal altyd gedy.

There is a goddess of Memory, Mnemosyne; but none of Forgetting. Yet there should be, as they are twin sisters, twin powers, and walk on either side of us, disputing for sovereignty over us and who we are, all the way until death.

RICHARD HOLMES,
A Meander Through Memory and Forgetting

The
Garden
of
Evening Mists

CHAPTER ONE

On a mountain above the clouds once lived a man who had been the gardener of the emperor of Japan. Not many people would have known of him before the war, but I did. He had left his home on the rim of the sunrise to come to the central highlands of Malaya. I was seventeen years old when my sister first told me about him. A decade would pass before I traveled up to the mountains to see him.

He did not apologize for what his countrymen had done to my sister and me. Not on that rain-scratched morning when we first met, nor at any other time. What words could have healed my pain, returned my sister to me? None. And he understood that. Not many people did.

Thirty-six years after that morning, I hear his voice again, hollow and resonant. Memories I had locked away have begun to break free, like shards of ice fracturing off an arctic shelf. In sleep, these broken floes drift toward the morning light of remembrance.

The stillness of the mountains awakens me. The depth of the silence: that is what I had forgotten about living in Yugiri. The murmurings of the house hover in the air when I open my eyes. *An old house retains its hoard of memories*, I remember Aritomo telling me once.

Ah Cheong knocks on the door and calls softly to me. I get out of bed and put on my dressing gown. I look around for my gloves and find them on the bedside table. Pulling them over my hands, I tell the housekeeper to come in. He enters and sets the pewter tray with a pot of tea and a plate of cut papaya on a side table; he had done the same for Aritomo every morning. He turns to me and says, "I wish you a long and peaceful retirement, Judge Teoh."

"Yes, it seems I've beaten you to it." He is, I calculate, five or six years older than me. He was not here when I arrived yesterday

1

evening. I study him, layering what I see over what I remember. He is a short, neat man, shorter than I recall, his head completely bald now. Our eyes meet. "You're thinking of the first time you saw me, aren't you?"

"Not the first time, but the last day. The day you left." He nods to himself. "Ah Foon and I—we always hoped you'd come back one day."

"Is she well?" I tilt sideways to look behind him, seeking his wife at the door, waiting to be called in. They live in Tanah Rata, cycling up the mountain road to Yugiri every morning.

"Ah Foon passed away, Judge Teoh. Four years ago."

"Yes. Yes, of course."

"She wanted to tell you how grateful she was that you paid her hospital bills. So was I."

I open the teapot's lid, then close it, trying to remember which hospital she had been admitted to. The name comes to me: Lady Templer Hospital.

"Five weeks," he says.

"Five weeks?"

"In five weeks' time it will be thirty-four years since Mr. Aritomo left us."

"For goodness' sake, Ah Cheong!" I have not returned to Yugiri in almost as long. Does the housekeeper judge me by the increasing number of years from the last time I was in this house, like a father scoring another notch on the kitchen wall to mark his child's growth?

Ah Cheong's gaze fixes on a spot somewhere over my shoulder. "If there's nothing else . . ." He begins to turn away.

In a gentler tone, I say, "I'm expecting a visitor at ten o'clock this morning. Professor Yoshikawa. Show him to the sitting room verandah."

The housekeeper nods once and leaves, closing the door behind him. Not for the first time I wonder how much he knows, what he has seen and heard in his years of service with Aritomo.

The papaya is chilled, just the way I like it. Squeezing the wedge of lime over it, I eat two slices before putting down the plate. Opening the sliding doors, I step onto the verandah. The house sits on low stilts and the verandah is two feet above the ground. The bamboo blinds creak when I scroll them up. The mountains are as I have always remembered them, the first light of the morning melting down their flanks. Damp withered leaves and broken-off twigs cover the lawn. This part of the house is hidden from the main garden by a wooden fence. A section has collapsed, and tall grass spikes out from the gaps between the fallen planks. Even though I have prepared myself for it, the neglected condition of the place shocks me.

A section of Majuba Tea Estate is visible to the east over the fence. The hollow of the valley reminds me of the open palms of a monk, cupped to receive the day's blessing. It is Saturday, but the tea pickers are working their way up the slopes. There has been a storm in the night, and clouds are still marooned on the peaks. I step down the verandah onto a narrow strip of ceramic tiles, cold and wet beneath my bare soles. Aritomo obtained them from a ruined palace in Ayutthaya, where they had once paved the courtyard of an ancient and nameless king. The tiles are the last remnants of a forgotten kingdom, its histories consigned to oblivion.

I fill my lungs to the brim and exhale. Seeing my own breath take shape, this cobweb of air that only a second ago had been inside me, I remember the sense of wonder it used to bring. The fatigue of the past months drains from my body, only to flood back into me a moment later. It feels strange that I no longer have to spend my weekends reading piles of appeal documents or catching up with the week's paperwork.

I breathe out through my mouth a few more times, watching my breaths fade away into the garden.

My secretary, Azizah, brought me the envelope shortly before we left my chambers to go into the courtroom. "This came for you just now, Puan," she said.

Inside was a note from Professor Yoshikawa Tatsuji, confirming the date and time of our meeting in Yugiri. It had been sent a week before. Looking at his neat handwriting, I wondered if it had been a mistake to have agreed to see him. I was about to telephone him in Tokyo to cancel the appointment when I realized he would already be on his way to Malaysia. And there was something else inside the envelope. Turning it over, a thin wooden stick, about five inches long, fell out onto my desk. I picked it up and dipped it into the light of my desk lamp. The wood was dark and smooth, its tip ringed with fine, overlapping grooves.

"So short-*lah*, the chopstick. For children is it?" Azizah said, coming into the room with a stack of documents for me to sign. "Where's the other one?"

"It's not a chopstick."

I sat there, looking at the stick on the table until Azizah reminded me that my retirement ceremony was about to begin. She helped me into my robe and together we went out to the corridor. She walked ahead of me as usual to give the advocates warning that Puan Hakim was on her way—they always used to watch her face to gauge my mood. Following behind her, I realized that this would be the last time I would make this walk from my chambers to my courtroom.

Built nearly a century ago, the Supreme Court building in Kuala Lumpur had the solidity of a colonial structure, erected to outlast empires. The high ceilings and the thick walls kept the air cool even on the hottest of days. My courtroom was large enough to seat forty, perhaps even fifty people, but on this Tuesday afternoon the advocates who had not arrived early had to huddle by the doors at the back. Azizah had informed me about the numbers attending the ceremony but I was still taken aback when I took my place on the bench beneath the portraits of the *agong* and his queen. Silence spread across the courtroom when Abdullah Mansor, the chief justice, entered and sat down next to me. He leaned over and spoke into my ear. "It's not too late to reconsider."

"You never give up, do you?" I said, giving him a brief smile.

"And you never change your mind." He sighed. "I know. But can't you stay on? You only have two more years to go."

Looking at him, I recalled the afternoon in his chambers when I told him of my decision to take early retirement. We had fought about many things over the years—points of law or the way he administered the courts—but I had always respected his intellect, his sense of fairness and his loyalty to us judges. That afternoon was the only time he had ever lost his composure with me. Now there was only sadness in his face. I would miss him.

Peering over his spectacles, Abdullah began recounting my life to the audience, braiding sentences in English into his speech, ignoring the sign in the courtroom dictating the use of the Malay language in court.

"Judge Teoh was only the second woman to be appointed to the Supreme Court," he said. "She has served on this Bench for the past fourteen years . . ."

Through the high, dusty windows I saw the corner of the cricket field across the road and, further away, the Selangor Club, its mock-Tudor facade reminding me of the bungalows in Cameron Highlands. The clock in the tower above the central portico chimed, its languid pulse beating through the walls of the courtroom. I turned my wrist slightly and checked the time: eleven minutes past three; the clock was, as ever, reliably out, its punctuality stolen by lightning years ago.

". . . few of us here today are aware that she was a prisoner in a Japanese internment camp when she was nineteen," said Abdullah.

The advocates murmured among themselves, observing me with heightened interest. I had never spoken of the three years I had spent in the camp to anyone. I tried not to think about it as I went about my days, and mostly I succeeded. But occasionally the memories still found their way in, through a sound I heard, a word someone uttered, or a smell I caught in the street.

"When the war ended," the chief justice continued, "Judge Teoh worked as a research clerk in the War Crimes Tribunal while waiting for admission to read law at Girton College, Cambridge. After being called to the bar, she returned to Malaya in 1949 and worked as a deputy public prosecutor for nearly two years . . ."

In the front row below me sat four elderly British advocates, their suits and ties almost as old as they. Along with a number of rubber planters and civil servants, they had chosen to stay on in Malaya after its independence, thirty years ago. These aged Englishmen had the forlorn air of pages torn from an old and forgotten book.

The chief justice cleared his throat and I looked at him. "Judge Teoh was not due to retire for another two years, so you will no doubt imagine our surprise when, only two months ago, she told us she intended to leave the Bench. Her written judgments are known for their clarity and elegant turns of phrase . . ." His words flowered, became more laudatory. I was far away in another time, thinking of Aritomo and his garden in the mountains.

The speech ended. I brought my mind back to the courtroom, hoping that no one had noticed the potholes in my attention; it would not do to appear distracted at my own retirement ceremony.

I gave a short, simple address to the audience and then Abdullah brought the ceremony to a close. I had invited a few well-wishers from the Bar Council, my colleagues and the senior partners in the city's larger law firms for a small reception in my chambers. A reporter asked me a few questions and took photographs. After the guests left, Azizah went around the room, gathering up the cups and the paper plates of half-eaten food.

"Take those curry puffs with you," I said, "and that box of cakes. Don't waste food."

"I know-*lah*. You always tell me that." She packed the food away and said, "Is there anything else you need?"

"You can go home. I'll lock up." It was what I usually said to her at the end of every court term. "And thank you, Azizah. For everything."

She shook the creases out of my black robe, hung it on the coat stand and turned to look at me. "It wasn't easy working for you all these years, Puan, but I'm glad I did." Tears gleamed in her eyes. "The lawyers—you were difficult with them, but they've always respected you. You listened to them."

"That's the duty of a judge, Azizah. To listen. So many judges seem to forget that."

"Ah, but you weren't listening earlier, when Tuan Mansor was going on and on. I was looking at you."

"He was talking about my life, Azizah." I smiled at her. "Hardly much there I don't know about already, don't you think?"

"Did the *orang Jepun* do that to you?" She pointed to my hands. "*Maaf*," she apologized, "but . . . I was always too scared to ask you. You know, I've never seen you without your gloves."

I rotated my left wrist slowly, turning an invisible doorknob. "One good thing about growing old," I said, looking at the part of the glove where two of its fingers had been cut off and stitched over. "Unless they look closely, people probably think I'm just a vain old woman, hiding my arthritis."

We stood there, both of us uncertain of how to conduct our partings. Then she reached out and grasped my other hand, pulling me into an embrace before I could react, enveloping me like dough around a stick. Then she let go of me, collected her handbag and left.

I looked around. The bookshelves were bare. My things had already been packed away and sent to my house in Bukit Tunku, flotsam sucked back to sea by the departing tide. Boxes of *Malayan Law Journals* and *All England Law Reports* were stacked in a corner for donation to the Bar Library. Only a single shelf of *MLJs* remained, their spines stamped in gold with the year in which the cases were reported. Azizah had promised to come in tomorrow and pack them away.

I went to a picture hanging on a wall, a watercolor of the home I had grown up in. My sister had painted it. It was the only work of hers I owned, the only one I had ever come across after the war. I lifted it off its hook and set it down by the door.

The stacks of manila folders tied with pink ribbons that normally crowded my desk had been reassigned to the other judges; the table seemed larger than usual when I sat down in my chair. The wooden stick was still lying where I had left it. Beyond the half-opened windows, dusk was summoning the crows to their roosts. The birds thickened the foliage of the angsana trees lining the road, filling the streets with their babble. Lifting the telephone receiver, I began dialing and then stopped, unable to recall the rest of the numbers. I paged through my address book, rang the main house in Majuba Tea Estate, and when a maid answered asked to speak to Frederik Pretorius. I did not have to wait long.

"Yun Ling?" he said when he came on the line, sounding slightly out of breath.

"I'm coming to Yugiri."

Silence pressed down on the line. "When?"

"This Friday." I paused. It had been seven months since we had last spoken to each other. "Will you tell Ah Cheong to have the house ready for me?"

"He's always kept it ready for you," Frederik replied. "But I'll tell him. Stop by at the estate on the way. We can have some tea. I'll drive you to Yugiri."

"I haven't forgotten how to get there, Frederik."

Another stretch of silence connected us. "The monsoon's over, but there's still some rain. Drive carefully." He hung up.

The call to prayer unwound from the minarets of the Jamek Mosque across the river to echo through the city. I listened to the courthouse empty itself. The sounds were so familiar to me that I had stopped paying attention to them years ago. The wheel of a trolley squeaked as someone—probably Rashid, the registrar's clerk—pushed the day's applications to the filing room. The telephone in another judge's chambers rang for a minute, then gave up. The slam of doors echoed through the corridors; I had never realized how loud they sounded.

I picked up my briefcase and shook it once. It was lighter than usual. I packed my court robe into it. At the door I turned around to look at my chambers. I gripped the edge of the door frame, realizing that I would never again set foot in this room. The weakness passed. I switched off the lights but continued to stand there, gazing into the shadows. I picked up my sister's watercolor and closed the door, working the handle a few times to make sure it was properly locked. Then I made my way along the dimly lit corridor. On one wall a gallery of former judges stared down at me, their faces changing from European to Malay and Chinese and Indian, from monochrome to color. I passed the empty space where my portrait would soon be added. At the end of the passageway I went down the stairs. Instead of turning left toward the judges' exit to the car park, I went out to the courtyard garden.

This was the part of the court buildings I loved most. I would often come here to sit, to think through the legal problems of a judgment I was writing. Few of the judges ever came here and I usually had the place all to myself. Sometimes, if Karim, the gardener, happened to be working, I would speak with him for a short while, giving him advice on what to plant and what ought to be taken out. This evening I was alone.

The sprinklers came on, releasing the smell of the sun-roasted grass into the air. The leaves discarded by the guava tree in the center of the garden had been raked into a pile. Behind the courts, the Gombak and Klang rivers plaited together, silting the air with the smell of earth scoured from the mountains in the Titiwangsa range up north. Most people in Kuala Lumpur couldn't bear the stench, especially when the river was running low between the monsoon seasons, but I had never minded that, in the heart of the city, I could smell the mountains over a hundred miles away.

I sat down on my usual bench and opened my senses to the stillness settling over the building, becoming a part of it.

After a while I stood up. There was something missing from the garden. Walking over to the mound of leaves, I grabbed a few handfuls and scattered them randomly over the lawn. Brushing off the bits of leaves sticking to my hands, I stepped away from the grass. Yes, it looked better now. Much better.

Swallows swooped from their nests in the eaves, the tips of their wings brushing past my head. I thought of a limestone cave I had once been to, high in the mountains. Carrying my briefcase and the watercolor, I walked out of the courtyard. In the sky above me, the last line of prayer from the mosque drifted away, leaving only silence where its echo had been.

Yugiri lay seven miles west of Tanah Rata, the second of the three main villages on the road going up to Cameron Highlands. I arrived there after a four-hour drive from Kuala Lumpur. I was in no hurry, stopping at various places along the way. Every few miles I would pass a roadside stall selling cloudy bottles of wild honey and blowpipes and bunches of foul-smelling *petai* beans. The road had been widened considerably since I last used it, the sharper turns smoothed out, but there were too many cars and tour buses, too many incontinent lorries leaking gravel and cement as they made their way to another construction site in the highlands.

It was the last week of September, the rainy season hovering around the mountains. Entering Tanah Rata, the sight of the former Royal Army Hospital standing on a steep rise filled me with a sense of familiar disquiet; Frederik had told me some time ago that it was now a school. A new hotel, with the inevitable mock-Tudor facade, towered behind it. Tanah Rata was no longer a village but a little town, its main street taken over by steamboat restaurants and tour agencies and souvenir shops. I was glad to leave them all behind me.

The guard was closing the wrought iron gates of Majuba Tea Estate when I drove past. I kept to the main road for half a mile before realizing that I had missed the turn-off to Yugiri. Annoyed with myself, I swung the car around, driving more slowly until I found the turning, hidden by advertisement boards. The laterite road ended a few minutes later at Yugiri's entrance. A Land Rover was parked by the roadside. I stopped my car next to it and got out, kicking the stiffness from my legs.

The high wall protecting the garden was patched in moss and old water stains. Ferns grew from the cracks. Set into the wall was a door. Nailed by the doorpost was a wooden plaque, a pair of Japanese ideograms burned into it. Below these words was the garden's name in English: EVENING MISTS. I felt I was about to enter a place that existed only in the overlapping of air and water, light and time.

Looking above the top of the wall, my eyes followed the uneven tree line of the ridge rising behind the garden. I found the wooden viewing tower half-hidden in the trees, like the crow's nest of a galleon that had foundered among the branches, trapped by a tide of leaves. A path threaded up into the mountains and for a few moments I stared at it, as if I might glimpse Aritomo walking home. Shaking my head, I pushed the door open, entered the garden and closed it behind me.

The sounds of the world outside faded away, absorbed into the leaves. I stood there, not moving. For a moment I felt that nothing had changed since I was last here, almost thirty-five years before— the scent of pine resin sticking to the air, the bamboo creaking and knocking in the breeze, the broken mosaic of sunlight scattered over the ground.

Guided by memory's compass, I began to walk into the garden. I made one or two wrong turns but came eventually to the pond. I stopped, the twisting walk through the tunnel of trees heightening the effect of seeing the open sky over the water.

Six tall, narrow stones huddled into a miniature limestone mountain range in the center of the pond. On the opposite bank stood the pavilion, duplicated in the water so that it appeared like a paper lantern hanging in midair. A willow grew a few feet away from the pavilion's side, its branches sipping from the pond.

In the shallows, a gray heron cocked its head at me, one leg poised in the air, like the hand of a pianist who had forgotten the notes to his music. It dropped its leg a second later and speared its beak into the water. Was it a descendant of the one that had made its home here when I first came to Yugiri? Frederik had told me that there was always one in the garden—an unbroken chain of solitary birds. I knew it could not be the same bird from nearly forty years before, but as I watched it, I hoped that it was; I wanted to believe that by entering this sanctuary the heron had somehow managed to slip through the fingers of time.

To my right and at the top of an incline stood Aritomo's house. Lights shone from the windows, the kitchen chimney scribbling smoke over the treetops. A man appeared at the front door and walked down the slope toward me. He stopped a few paces away, perhaps to create a space for us to study one another. *We are like every single plant and stone and view in the garden*, I thought, *the distance between one another carefully measured*.

"I thought you'd changed your mind," he said, closing the space between us.

"The drive was longer than I remembered."

"Places seem farther apart, don't they, the older we get."

At sixty-seven years old, Frederik Pretorius had the dignified air given off by an antique artwork, secure in the knowledge of its own rarity and value. We had kept in touch over the years, meeting up for drinks or a meal whenever he came down to Kuala Lumpur, but I had always resisted his invitations to visit Cameron Highlands. In the last two or three years his trips to KL had tapered off. Long ago I had realized that he was the only close friend I would ever have.

"The way you were watching that bird just now," he said, "I felt you were looking back to the past."

I turned to look at the heron again. The bird had moved farther out into the pond. Mist escaped from the water's surface, whispers only the wind could catch. "I *was* thinking of the old days."

"For a second or two there I thought you were about to fade away." He stopped, then said, "I wanted to call out to you."

"I've retired from the Bench." It was the first time I had said it aloud to another person. Something seemed to detach from inside me and crumble away, leaving me less complete than before.

"I saw it in yesterday's papers," said Frederik.

"That photograph they took of me was dreadful, utterly dreadful."

The lights in the garden came on, dizzying the flying insects. A

11

frog croaked. A few other frogs took up the call and then more still until the air and earth vibrated with a thousand gargles.

"Ah Cheong's gone home," said Frederik. "He'll come tomorrow morning. I brought you some groceries. I imagine you haven't had time to go to the shops yet."

"That's very thoughtful of you."

"There's something I need to discuss with you. Perhaps tomorrow morning, if you're up to it?"

"I'm an early riser."

"I haven't forgotten." His eyes hovered over my face. "You're going to be all right on your own?"

"I'll be fine. I'll see you tomorrow."

He looked unconvinced but nodded. Then he turned and walked away, taking the path I had just come along, and disappeared into the shadows beneath the trees.

In the pond, the heron shook out its wings, tested them a few times and flew off. It circled the area once, gliding past me. At the end of its loop the bird opened its wings wide and followed the trail of stars that were just appearing. I stood there, my face turned upward, watching it dissolve into the twilight.

Returning to my bedroom, I remember the plate of papaya Ah Cheong brought me. I make myself eat the remaining slices, then unpack my bags and hang my clothes in the cupboard. In the last few years I have heard people complaining that the highlands' climate is no longer as cool as it used to be, but I decide to put on a cardigan anyway.

The house is dark when I emerge from my room, and I have to remember my way along the twisting corridors. The *tatami* mats in the sitting room crackle softly when I walk on them, parched of oil from the press of bare soles. The doors to the verandah are open. Ah Cheong has placed a low, square table here, with thin rattan mats on each side of it. Below the verandah, five dark gray rocks, spaced apart, sit on a rectangular bed of gravel covered in leaves. One of the rocks is positioned further away from the others. Beyond this area, the ground slopes gently away to the edge of the pond.

Frederik arrives, looking unhappy about having to sit on the floor. He drops a manila folder onto the table and lowers his body

into a cross-legged position, wincing as he makes himself comfortable on the mat.

"Does it feel strange to be back here?" he asks.

"Everywhere I turn, I hear echoes of sounds made long ago."

"I hear them too."

He unties the string around the folder and arranges a sheaf of
papers on the table. "The designs for our latest range. This one
here"—a forefinger skates a sheet across the table's lacquered surface to me—"this is for the packaging."

The emblem used in the illustrations is familiar; what initially
appear to be the veins of a tea leaf transform into a detailed drawing of the valleys, with Majuba House mazed into the lines.

"From the woodblock print Aritomo gave Magnus?" I say.

"I'd like to use it," Frederik says. "I'll pay you, of course—
royalties, I mean."

Aritomo had bequeathed Yugiri and the copyright in all his literary and artistic works to me. With rare exceptions I have never
allowed anyone to reproduce them. "Use it," I say. "I don't want
any payment."

He does not hide his surprise.

"How is Emily?" I cut him off before he speaks. "She must be
what, eighty-eight?" I strive to remember how old his aunt was
when I met her all those years ago.

"She'll have a fit if she hears that. She turned eighty-five this
year." He hesitates. "She's not well. Some days her memory would
shame an elephant's, but there are also days . . ." His voice tapers
away into a sigh.

"I'll see her once I've settled in." I know that Emily, like so many
older Chinese, places great importance on having a younger person
visit them first, to give them face.

"You'd better. I've told her you're back."

I wave a hand out to the garden. "Your workers have been taking good care of Yugiri."

"Judges aren't supposed to lie." The smile on Frederik's face
sinks away a second later. "We both know my boys don't have the
skills to maintain it. And besides, as I keep telling you, I honestly
don't have the knowledge—or the interest, or the time—to make
sure they do their work properly. The garden needs your attention."

He stops, then says, "By the way, I've decided to make some changes to Majuba's garden."

"What kind of changes?"

"I've hired a landscape gardener to help me," Frederik says. "Vimalya started her gardening service in Tanah Rata a year ago. She's very much a fan of indigenous gardens."

"Following the trend." I do not bother to sieve the disdain from my voice.

His face twitches with annoyance. "We're going back to everything nature intended. We're using plants and trees native to the region. We'll let them grow the way they would have done in the wild, with as little human assistance—or interference—as possible."

"You're removing all the pine trees in Majuba? And the firs, the eucalyptuses . . . the roses, the irises . . . the . . . the strelitzias?"

"They're alien. All of them."

"So is every single tea bush here. So am I. And so are you, Mr. Pretorius. *Especially* you."

It is none of my concern, I know, but for almost sixty years, ever since Frederik's uncle Magnus established Majuba Tea Estate, its formal gardens have been admired and loved. Visitors have been coming from all over the country to enjoy an English garden in the tropics. They walk among the meticulously shaped hedges and voluptuous flower beds, the herbaceous borders and the roses Emily planted. It pains me to hear that the garden is to be transformed, made to appear as though it forms part of the tropical rain forest crowding in around us—overgrown and unkempt and lacking any order.

"I've told you before, a long time ago—Majuba's gardens are too artificial. The older I get, the more I don't believe in having nature controlled. Trees should be allowed to grow as they please." Frederik swings his gaze to the garden. "If it were up to me, all of this would be taken out."

"What is gardening but the controlling and perfecting of nature?" I am aware my voice is rising. "When you talk about 'indigenous gardening,' or whatever it's called, you already have man involved. You dig out beds, you chop down trees, and you bring in seeds and cuttings. It all sounds very much planned to me."

"Gardens like Yugiri's are deceptive. They're false. Everything here has been thought out and shaped and built. We're sitting in one of the most artificial places you can find."

Sparrows rise from the grass into the trees, like fallen leaves returning to their branches. I think about those elements of gardening Frederik is opposed to, aspects so loved by the Japanese— the techniques of controlling nature, perfected over a thousand years. Was it because they lived in lands so regularly rocked by earthquakes and natural calamities that they sought to tame the world around them? My eyes move to the sitting room, to the bonsai of a pine tree that Ah Cheong has so faithfully looked after. The immense trunk the pine would have grown into is now constrained to a size that would not look out of place on a scholar's desk, trained to the desired shape by copper wire coiled around its branches. There are some people, like Frederik, who might feel that such practices are misguided, like trying to wield heaven's powers on earth. And yet it was only in the carefully planned and created garden of Yugiri that I had found a sense of order and calm and even, for a brief moment of time, forgetfulness.

"Someone is coming to see me this morning," I say. "From Tokyo. He's going to look at Aritomo's woodblock prints."

"You're selling them? Are you short of money?"

His concern touches me, cools my anger. In addition to being a garden designer, Aritomo was also a woodblock artist. After I admitted, in an unguarded moment during an interview, that he had left me a collection of his woodblock prints, connoisseurs in Japan tried to convince me to part with them, or to put them on exhibition. I have always refused, much to their resentment; many of them have made it clear that they do not see me as their rightful owner.

"Professor Yoshikawa Tatsuji contacted me a year ago," I say. "He wanted to do a book on Aritomo's prints. I declined to speak to him."

Frederik's eyebrows spring up. "But he's coming here today?"

"I've recently made inquiries about him. He's a historian. A respected one. He's written articles and books about his country's actions in the war."

"Denying that certain things ever took place, I'm sure."

"He has a reputation for being objective."

"Why would a historian be interested in Aritomo's art?"

"Yoshikawa's also an authority on Japanese woodblock prints."

"Have you read any of his books?" Frederik asks.

"They're all in Japanese."

"You speak it, don't you?"

"I used to, just enough to get by. Speaking it is one thing, but reading it . . . that's something else."

"In all these years," Frederik says, "all these years, you've never told me what the Japs did to you." His voice is mild, but I catch the seam of hurt buried in it.

"What they did to me, they did to thousands of others."

I trace the lines of the leaf on the tea packaging with my finger. "Aritomo once recited a poem to me, about a stream that had dried up." I think for a moment, then say, *Though the water has stopped flowing, we still hear the whisper of its name.*

"It's still hard for you, isn't it?" Frederik says. "Even so long after his death."

It never fails to disconcert me whenever I hear someone mention Aritomo's "death," even after all this time. "There are days when I think he's still out there, wandering in the mountains, like one of the Eight Immortals of Taoist legend, a sage making his way home," I say. "But what amazes me is the fact that there are still people who keep coming here, just because they have heard the stories."

"You know, he lived here for—what, thirteen years? Fourteen? He walked the jungle trails almost every day. He knew them better than some of the forestry guides. How could he have gotten lost?"

"Even monkeys fall from trees." I try to recall where I have heard this, but it eludes me. It will come back to me, I think, trying to reassure myself. "Perhaps Aritomo wasn't as familiar with the jungle as he thought he was." From within the house I hear the bell ringing as someone pulls the rope at the gate. "That should be Yoshikawa."

Frederik presses his hands on the table and gets up with an old man's grunt. I remain seated, watching the marks his palms have left on the table fade away.

"I'd like you to be here, Frederik, when I speak to him."

"I have to rush. Full day ahead of me."

Slowly I unfold my body until I am eye to eye with him. "Please, Frederik."

He looks at me. After a moment he nods.

CHAPTER TWO

The historian has arrived precisely at the appointed time, and I wonder if he has heard of how I dealt with advocates who appeared late in my court. Ah Cheong shows him to the verandah a few minutes later.

"Professor Yoshikawa," I greet him in English.

"Please call me Tatsuji," he says, giving me a deep bow, which I do not return.

I nod toward Frederik. "Mr. Pretorius is a friend of mine."

"Ah! From Majuba Tea Estate," Tatsuji says, glancing at me before bowing to Frederik.

I indicate that Tatsuji should take the customary seat for an honored guest, giving him the best view of the garden. He is in his mid-sixties, dressed in a light gray linen suit, a white cotton shirt and a pale blue tie. Old enough to have fought in the war, I think, an almost subconscious assessment I apply to every Japanese man I have met. His eyes roam the low ceiling and the walls and the wooden posts before looking to the garden. "Yugiri," he murmurs.

Ah Cheong appears with a tray of tea and a small brass bell. I pour the tea into our cups. Tatsuji looks away when I catch him staring at my hands. "Your reputation for refusing to talk to anyone in our circles is well-known, Judge Teoh," he says when I place a teacup before him. "To be honest, I was not surprised when you refused to see me, but I *was* taken aback when you changed your mind."

"I have since discovered your impressive reputation."

"'Notorious' would be a better description," Tatsuji replies, looking pleased nonetheless.

"Professor Yoshikawa has the habit of airing unpopular subjects in public," I explain to Frederik.

"Every time there is a movement to change our history text-

18

books, to remove any reference to the crimes committed by our troops, every time a government minister visits the Yasukuni Shrine," Tatsuji says, "I write letters to the newspapers objecting to it."

"Your own people . . . ," Frederik says, "how have they reacted to that?"

For a few moments Tatsuji does not speak. "I have been assaulted four times in the last ten years," he replies at last. "I have received death threats. But still I go on radio shows and television programs. I tell everyone that we cannot deny our past. We have to make amends. We *have* to."

I bring us back to the reason for our meeting. "Nakamura Aritomo has been unfashionable for so long. Even when he was still alive," I say. "Why would you want to write about him now?"

"When I was younger, I had a friend," Tatsuji says. "He owned a few pieces of Aritomo-*sensei*'s *ukiyo-e*. He always enjoyed telling people that they were made by the emperor's gardener." The historian kisses the rim of his cup and makes an appreciative noise. "Excellent tea."

"From Majuba estate," I tell him.

"I must remember to buy some," Tatsuji tells Frederik.

"Ooky what? The stuff Aritomo made?" Frederik says.

"Woodblock prints," Tatsuji replies.

"Did you bring them?" I interrupt him. "Those prints your friend owned?"

"They were destroyed in an air raid, along with his house." He waits, and when I do not say anything he continues. "Because of my friend, I became interested in Nakamura Aritomo. There is nothing authoritative written on his artworks, or his life after he left Japan; I decided to write something."

"Yun Ling doesn't just give anyone permission to use Aritomo's artworks, you know," Frederik says.

"I'm aware that Aritomo-*sensei* left everything he owned to you, Judge Teoh," Tatsuji says.

"You sent this to me." I place the wooden stick on the table.

"You know what it is?" he asks.

"It's the handle of a tattooing needle," I reply, "used before tattooists switched to electric needles."

"Aritomo-*sensei* produced a completely different type of artwork, one he never disclosed to the public." Tatsuji reaches across the table and picks up the handle. His fingers are slender and his nails, I notice, manicured. "He was a *horimono* artist."

"A what?" Frederik says, his cup halted halfway to his lips. His hand has a slight tremor. When was it that I began noticing these little signs of age in people around me?

"Aritomo-*sensei* was more than the emperor's gardener." Tatsuji shapes the knot of his tie with his thumb. "He was also a *horoshi*, a tattoo artist."

I straighten my back.

"There has always been a close link between the woodblock artist and the *horimono* master," Tatsuji continues. "They dip their buckets into the same well for inspiration."

"And what well is that?" I ask.

"A book," he says. "A novel from China, translated into Japanese in the eighteenth century. *Suikoden.* It became wildly popular when it was published."

"Like one of those fads that regularly drives your schoolgirls into a frenzy," Frederik remarks.

"It was much more than that," Tatsuji says, raising a forefinger at Frederik before turning to me. "I prefer that we speak in private, Judge Teoh. If we can arrange to meet another time . . ."

Frederik moves to get up, but I shake my head at him. "What makes you so certain that Aritomo was a tattoo artist, Tatsuji?" I say.

The historian glances at Frederik, then looks at me. "A man I once knew had a tattoo on his body." He stops for a few seconds, gazing at emptiness. "He told me it had been done by Aritomo-*sensei*."

"And you believed him."

Tatsuji stares into my eyes and I am struck by the pain in them. "He was my friend."

"The same friend who had the collection of Aritomo's woodblock prints?" I ask. Tatsuji nods. "Then you should have brought him here with you today."

"He passed away . . . some years ago."

For an instant I see Aritomo's reflection on the surface of the table. I have to restrain from turning around to see if he is standing behind me, looking over my shoulder. I blink once, and he is gone. "I agreed to see you on the matter of Aritomo's woodblock prints," I remind Tatsuji. "Are you still interested in them?"

"You will let me use his *ukiyo-e*?"

"We'll discuss which of his prints will go into your book once you've finished examining them. But there will be no mention of tattoos supposedly created by him." I hold up my hand as Tatsuji is about to interrupt. "If you breach any of my terms—any of them— I will make sure all copies of your book are pulped."

"The Japanese people have a right to appreciate Aritomo-*sensei*'s works."

I point to my chest. "*I* will decide what the Japanese people have a right to." I get to my feet, wincing at my rusting joints. The historian stands up to assist me, but I brush his hand away. "I'll get all the prints together. We'll meet again in a few days' time for you to look through them."

"How many pieces are there?"

"I have no idea. Twenty or thirty perhaps."

"You have never looked at them?"

"Only a few."

"I am staying at the Smokehouse Hotel." The historian writes down the telephone number on a piece of paper and gives it to me. "May I see the garden?"

"It hasn't been properly looked after." I ring the brass bell on the tray. "My housekeeper will show you out."

The day is turning out to be cloudless, with a strong, clear light pouring into the garden. The leaves of the maple tree by the side of the house have begun to turn, soon to become heavy with red. For some inexplicable reason this maple has always defied the lack of changing seasons in the highlands. I lean against a wooden post, my knuckles kneading the pain in my hip. It will take me a while to get used to sitting in the Japanese style again. From the corner of my eye I catch Frederik watching me.

"I don't trust that man, whatever his reputation," he says. "You should let other experts look at the prints as well."

"I don't have much time here."

"But I'd hoped you'd stay for a while," he says. "There's our new tearoom I want to show you. The views are magnificent. You can't leave again so soon." He looks at me and a slow realization slackens his face. "What is it? What's wrong?"

"Something in my brain, something that shouldn't be there." I pull my cardigan tighter over my body. I sense him waiting for me to explain. "I've been having problems with names. There were occasions when I couldn't think of the words I wanted to use."

His hand brushes the air. "I have those moments too. That's just age catching up with us."

"This is different," I say. He looks at me, and I wonder if I should have kept quiet about it. "Sitting in court one afternoon, all of a sudden I couldn't make head or tail of what I had written."

"The doctors, what did they say?"

"The neurosurgeons ran their tests. They told me what I had suspected. I'm losing my ability to read and write, to understand language, any language. In a year—perhaps more, probably less—I won't be able to express my thoughts. I'll be spouting gibberish. And what people say, and the words I see—on the page, on street signs, everywhere—will be unintelligible to me." For a few seconds I am silent. "My mental competence will deteriorate. Dementia will shortly follow, unhinging my mind."

Frederik stares at me. "Doctors can cure anything these days."

"I don't want to discuss this, Frederik. And keep this to yourself." My palm stops him, my palm with its two stubs. A moment later I close my three fingers and draw them back, holding them tight in a bud. I feel as though they have captured something intangible from the air. "The time will come when I lose all my faculties . . . perhaps even my memories," I say, keeping my voice calm with an effort.

"Write it down," he says. "Write it all down, the memories that are most important to you. It shouldn't be difficult—it'll be like writing one of your judgments."

I glance sidelong at him. "What do you know about my judgments?"

He gives me an embarrassed smile. "My lawyers have instructions to send a copy to me, every time the *Law Reports* publish them. You write well—your judgments are clear and engaging. I can still remember the case about the cabinet minister who used black magic to murder his mistress. You really should compile them into a book." The lines on his forehead deepen. "You once quoted an English judge. Didn't he say that words are the tools of a lawyer's trade?"

"Soon I won't be able to use those tools anymore."

"I'll read them to you," he says. "Whenever you want to hear your own words again, I'll read them aloud to you."

"Don't you understand what I've been trying to tell you? By then I won't be able to know what anyone says to me!" He doesn't flinch from my anger, but the sorrow in his eyes is unbearable to look at. "You'd better go," I say, pushing myself away from the post. My movements feel slow, heavy. "I've already made you late."

He glances at his watch. "It's not important. Just some journalists I have to show around the estate, charm them into writing something complimentary."

"That shouldn't be too difficult."

A smile skims across his face, capsizing an instant later. He wants to say something more, but I shake my head. He takes the three low steps down from the verandah, then slowly turns around to face me. All of sudden he looks like an old, old man. "What are you going to do?"

"I am going for a walk."

Ah Cheong hands a walking stick to me at the front door of the house. I shake my head, then take it from him. The stick has a comfortable heft. I look at it for a moment and then return it to him. Three or four steps later I stop and glance back over my shoulder. He is still standing there in the doorway, looking at me. I feel his eyes pinned on me all the way until I reach the opposite side of the pond. When I look back across the water, he has gone back inside the house.

The air is clean, as if it has never been breathed by any living thing. After the clammy heat of Kuala Lumpur, the change is welcome. It is almost noon, but the sun has slunk behind the clouds.

Lotus pads tile the surface of the pond. There are too many of them; I had not noticed it the previous evening when I arrived. The hedges on the opposite side of the pond had originally been shaped to resemble the waves of an ocean surging to the shore, but they have not been properly clipped and their lines are blurred. The pavilion's roof beams are sagging. The entire structure seems to be melting, losing the memory of its shape. Leaves and dead insects and bark peelings cover its floor. Something slithers among them and I step back.

The track leading into the garden is paved with rings of slate cut from drill cores discarded from the gold mines of Raub. Each turn in the path reveals a different view; at no point is the entire garden revealed, making it appear more extensive than it actually is. Ornaments lie half-hidden among the overgrown lallang grass: a granite torso; a sandstone Buddha's head with his features smoothed by mist and rain; rocks with unusual shapes and striations. Stone lanterns, their eaves curtained with tattered spiderwebs, squat among the curling ferns. Yugiri was designed to look old from the first stone Aritomo set down, and the illusion of age he had created has been transformed into reality.

Frederik's workers have been looking after the place, following the instructions I have given them. The garden has been maintained by untrained hands: branches that should have been left to grow pruned away; a view that should have been obscured opened up; a path widened without consideration to the overall harmony of the garden. Even the wind streaming through the shrubs sounds wrong because the undergrowth has been allowed to grow too densely and too high.

The omissions and errors are like the noise generated by a collection of badly tuned musical instruments. Aritomo once told me that of all the gardens he created, this one meant the most to him.

Halfway in my walk through the garden, I stop, turn around and head back to the house.

The fourteenth-century bronze Buddha in the study has not grown older; his face is unmarked by the cares of the world. Ah Cheong has opened the windows to air the room all day, but the smell of mildew from the books on the shelves ages the twilight filling up the house.

The feeling that something was wrong with me surfaced five or six months ago. I was often awakened by headaches in the night, and I began to tire easily. There were days when I could not summon up any interest in my work. My concerns sharpened into fear when I began to forget names and words. It was not merely the unfolding of age, I suspected, but something more. I was frail when I emerged from the slave-labor camp, and my health has never recovered completely. I forced myself to pick up the life I had known before the war. Being an advocate, and later on, a judge, gave me solace; I found enjoyment in working with words, in applying the law. For over forty years I succeeded in staving off this exhaustion of the body, but I always feared that a day would come when there was nothing left to be depleted from me. What I did not expect was how soon, how swiftly that moment would arrive.

I have become a collapsing star, pulling everything around it, even the light, into an ever-expanding void.

Once I lose all ability to communicate with the world outside myself, nothing will be left but what I remember. My memories will be like a sandbar, cut off from the shore by the incoming tide. In time they will become submerged, inaccessible to me. The prospect terrifies me. For what is a person without memories? A ghost, trapped between worlds, without an identity, with no future, no past.

Frederik's suggestion that I write down the things I do not want to forget has rooted itself into the crevices of my mind. It is futile, I know, but a part of me wants to make sure that, when the time comes, I will still have something that gives me the possibility, however meager, to orient myself, to help me determine what is real.

Sitting at Aritomo's desk, I realize that there are fragments of my life that I do not want to lose, if only because I still have not found the knot to tie them up with.

When I have forgotten everything else, will I finally have the clarity to see what Aritomo and I have been to each other? If I can still read my own words by then, with no knowledge of who had set them down onto the page, will the answers come to me?

Outside, the mountains have been drawn into the garden, becoming a part of it. Aritomo was a master of *shakkei*, the art of Borrowed Scenery, taking elements and views from outside a garden and making them integral to his creation.

A memory drifts by. I reach for it, as if I am snatching at a leaf spiraling down from a high branch. I have to. Who knows if it will ever come back to me again?

During the Emergency, some of the people who were given a private tour of Majuba Tea Estate would also ask to see Yugiri. And sometimes Aritomo allowed it. On such occasions, I would be waiting for them at the main entrance. Most of the visitors were senior government officials taking a holiday with their wives in Cameron Highlands before going back to waging war on the communist terrorists hiding in the jungles. They had heard about the garden in the mountains and wanted to see it for themselves, to boast to their friends that they had been one of the privileged few to have walked in it. Murmurs of anticipation would warm the air as I welcomed the group. "What does 'Yugiri' mean?" someone—usually one of the wives—would ask, and I would answer them, "Evening Mists."

And if the hour was right and the light willing, they might even catch a glimpse of Aritomo, dressed in his gray *yukata* and *hakama*, raking out lines on white gravel, moving as if he were practicing calligraphy on stone. Observing the expressions on the visitors' faces, I knew that some, if not all of them, were wondering if their eyes had made a mistake, if they were seeing something that should not have been there. That same notion had entered my mind the first time I saw Aritomo.

He never accompanied these people on the tour of his garden, preferring that I entertain them. But he would stop what he was doing and talk to the visitors when I introduced him to them. I was certain that the questions had all been asked before, over the long years since he had first come to these mountains. Nevertheless, he would answer them patiently, with no hint of weariness that I could detect. "That is correct," he would tell them, prefacing his answers with a slight bow. "I was the emperor's gardener. But that was in a different lifetime."

Invariably, someone would inquire as to why he had given it all up to come to Malaya. A puzzled look would spread across Aritomo's face, as though he had never been asked that particular question before. I would catch the flit of pain in his eyes and, for a few moments, we would hear nothing except the birds calling out in the trees. Then he would give a short laugh and say, "Perhaps someday, before I cross the floating bridge of dreams, I will discover the reason. I will tell you then."

On a few occasions one of the visitors—usually someone who

had fought in the war, or, like me, had been imprisoned in one of the Japanese camps—would grow belligerent; I could always tell who these would be, even before they opened their mouths to speak. Aritomo's eyes would become arctic, the ends of his mouth curving downward. But he would always remain polite, bracketing all his answers with a bow before walking away from us.

Despite the intrusive questions, I had always felt there were times when Aritomo liked to think that he, too, was one of the reasons people came to visit Yugiri, that they hoped for a sight of him, as though he were a rare and unusual wild orchid not to be found anywhere else in Malaya. Perhaps that was why, in spite of his dislike of them, Aritomo had never stopped me from introducing the visitors to him, and why he was always dressed in his traditional clothes whenever he knew a group would be coming to see his garden.

Ah Cheong has already gone home. The house is still. Leaning back in the chair, I close my eyes. Images fly across my vision. A flag flutters in the wind. A waterwheel turns. A pair of cranes take off over a lake, hauling themselves with beating wings higher and higher into the sky, heading into the sun.

The world seems different, somehow, when I open my eyes again. Clearer, more defined, but also smaller.

It will not be very much different from writing a judgment, I tell myself. I will find the words I require; they are nothing more than the tools that I have used all of my life. From the chambers of my memory I will draw out and set down all recollections of the time I spent with Aritomo. I will dance to the music of words, for one more time.

Through the windows I watch the mists thicken, wiping away the mountains borrowed by the garden. Are the mists, too, an element of *shakkei* incorporated by Aritomo? I wonder. To use not only the mountains, but the wind, the clouds, the ever-changing light? Did he borrow from heaven itself?

CHAPTER THREE

My name is Teoh Yun Ling. I was born in 1923 in Penang, an island on the northwest coast of Malaya. Being Straits Chinese, my parents spoke mainly English, and they had asked a family friend who was a poet to choose a name for me. Teoh is my surname, my family name. As in life, the family must come first. That was what I had always been taught. I had never changed the order of my name, not even when I studied in England, and I had never taken on an English name just to make it easier for anyone.

I came to Majuba Tea Estate on the sixth of October, 1951. My train was two hours late pulling into the Tapah Road station, so I was relieved when I glimpsed Magnus Pretorius from the window of my carriage. He was sitting on a bench, a newspaper folded on his lap, and he stood up as the train came to a stop. He was the only man on the platform with an eye-patch. I stepped down from the carriage and waved to him. I walked past the Wickham Trolley carrying the two soldiers manning the machine guns mounted on it; the armored wagon had escorted the train from the moment we had left Kuala Lumpur. Sweat plastered my cotton blouse to my back as I pushed through the crowd of young Australian soldiers in khaki uniforms, ignoring their whistles and the looks they gave me.

Magnus scattered the Tamil porters mobbing me. "Yun Ling," he said, taking my bag. "Is this all your *barang*?"

"I'm only staying a week."

He was in his late sixties, although he looked ten years younger. Taller than me by half a foot, he carried the excess weight so common in men his age well. He was balding, the hair around the sides of his head white, his remaining eye mired in wrinkles, but startlingly blue.

"Sorry you had to wait, Magnus," I said. "We had to stop for endless checks. I think the police were tipped off about an ambush."

"*Ag*, I knew you'd be late." His accent—the vowels flattened and truncated—was distinct even after forty-odd years in Malaya. "The stationmaster made an announcement. Lucky there wasn't an attack, hey?" I followed him through a gate in the barbed-wire fence surrounding the train station, to an olive-green Land Rover parked under a stand of mango trees. Magnus swung my bag into the backseat; we climbed in and drove off.

Above the limestone hills in the distance, heavy clouds were gathering to hammer the earth with rain later in the evening. The main street of Tapah was quiet, and the wooden blinds of the Chinese shophouses—painted with advertisements for Poh Chai indigestion pills and Tiger Balm ointment—were lowered against the afternoon sun. At the junction turning into the trunk road, Magnus stopped for military vehicles speeding past: scout cars with gun turrets, boxy armored personnel carriers and lorries packed with soldiers. They were heading south, toward Kuala Lumpur.

"Something's happened," I said.

"No doubt we'll hear about it on the evening news."

At a security checkpoint just before the road tipped upward to the mountains, a Malay special constable lowered the metal barrier and ordered us out of the car. Another constable behind an embankment trained a Bren gun on us, while a third searched our car and pushed a wheeled mirror under it. The constable who had stopped us asked to see our identity cards. I felt a spurt of anger when he searched me but left Magnus alone. I suspected that his hands were less intrusive than they usually were as they patted my body: I was not the typical Chinese peasant they were used to, and the presence of Magnus, a white man, was probably a deterrent.

Behind us, an old Chinese woman was ordered off her bicycle. A conical straw hat shaded her face and her black cotton trousers were stiff with dried rubber latex. An SC rooted around inside her rattan basket and held up a pineapple. "*Tolong lah, tolong lah,*" the woman pleaded in Malay. The policeman pulled on the top and bottom sections of the pineapple and the fruit came apart in half. Uncooked rice concealed in the hollowed-out fruit streamed to the ground. The old woman's wails became louder as the constables dragged her into a hut by the roadside.

"Clever," Magnus remarked, nodding at the mound of rice on the road.

"The police once caught a rubber-tapper smuggling sugar out of his village," I said.

"In a pineapple?"

"He mixed it in the water in his canteen. It was one of the first cases I prosecuted."

"You've done a lot of cases like that?" he said as the SC raised the barrier and waved us through.

"Enough to receive death threats," I said. "One of the reasons I resigned."

Less than half a mile further we stopped behind a line of lorries, their tarpaulins peeled back. Scrawny Chinese attendants sat on gunnysacks of rice, cooling themselves with tattered bamboo fans. "Good. I was worried we had missed the convoy," Magnus said, switching off the engine.

"We'll be crawling up the mountain," I said, looking at the vehicles.

"Can't be helped, *meisiekind*. But at least we'll be escorted," Magnus said, pointing to two armored scout cars at the head of the line.

"Any recent attacks in Cameron Highlands?"

Three years had passed since the Malayan Communist Party had launched its guerrilla war against the government, forcing the high commissioner to declare a state of emergency. The war showed no signs of ending, with the communist terrorists—which the government referred to as "CTs" or, more commonly, "bandits"—keeping up regular attacks on rubber estates and tin mines.

"They've been ambushing buses and army vehicles. But last week they showed up at a vegetable farm. Torched the buildings and killed the manager," Magnus said. "You haven't exactly picked the best of times to visit us."

The sun reflected off the vehicles in front. I wound down my window but that only let in a rush of heat shimmering off the road. More cars had stopped behind us while we were waiting. Fifteen minutes later we were moving again. For security reasons, the undergrowth along the road had been hacked away and the trees felled, leaving only a narrow field of stumps. Far back from the road, beneath what had once been the cool shadows of trees, an aboriginal longhouse stood high on stilts, like an ark that had been washed up by a flood. An old woman in a sarong squatted on a tree stump and watched us, her breasts exposed, her lips painted bright red.

Groves of bamboo leaned into the road, filtering the light into weak yellow patches. A lorry, overloaded with cabbages, careened down from the opposite direction, pushing us against the rock face on the side of the road; I could have reached out and pulled a clump of ferns growing on it. The temperature continued to drop, the air warmed only in the short stretches where the road dozed in the sun. At the Lata Iskandar waterfall, the sprays opened its net of whispers over us, rinsing the air with moisture that had traveled all the way from the mountain peaks, carrying with it the tang of trees and mulch and earth.

We arrived in Tanah Rata an hour later, the road entering the village watched over by a red-brick building perched on a rise. "You might want to explore the area," Magnus said, "but remember the village gates close at six."

Mist washed the lorries in front of us into gray, shapeless hulks. Magnus switched on his headlights, turning the world into a jaundiced murk. Visibility improved once we left the main street. "There's the Green Cow," Magnus said. "We'll go there for drinks one evening." We picked up speed, passing the Tanah Rata Golf Club. Looking at Magnus from the corner of my eye, I wondered how he and his wife had coped in the Japanese Occupation. Unlike so many of the Europeans living in Malaya, they had not evacuated when the Japanese soldiers came, but had remained in their home.

"Here we are," he said, slowing down the car as we approached the entrance into Majuba Tea Estate. The granite gateposts were gouged with empty sockets where the hinges had once been set, like teeth that had been pulled out. "The Japs took the gates. I haven't been able to replace them." He shook his head in disgust. "The war's been over for, what, six years already? But we're still short of materials."

Tea bushes clad the hillsides, shaped into box hedges by decades of picking. Moving between the waist-high bushes, workers plucked the leaves with voracious fingers, throwing fistfuls of them over their shoulders into rattan baskets strapped to their backs. The air had a herbal undertone, more a flavor than a scent.

"It's the tea, isn't it?" I said, inhaling deeply.

"The fragrance of the mountains," Magnus replied. "That's what I miss most, whenever I'm away."

"The place doesn't look as if it suffered *too* much damage in the Occupation."

Hearing the bitterness in my voice, Magnus's face tightened. "We had to put in a lot of work to rebuild after the war. We were lucky. The Japs needed us to keep production running."

"They didn't intern you and your wife?"

"*Ja*, they did, in a way," he replied with a touch of defensiveness. "The senior army officers moved into our home. We lived in a fenced-off compound on the estate." He sounded his horn, sending a tea picker who had strayed onto the road skipping back onto the grassy verge. "Every morning we were marched to the slopes to work alongside our coolies. But I have to say, the Japs were kinder to us than the English were to *my* people."

"So now you've been a prisoner twice," I said, recalling that he had fought in the Boer War. He would have been only about seventeen or eighteen then. Almost the same age I had been when I was interned.

"And now I'm in the middle of another war." He shook his head. "Seems to be my fate, doesn't it?"

The road took us further into the estate, winding uphill until we came to a long driveway lined with eucalyptus trees. The driveway funneled open at a circular ornamental pond, a line of ducklings on the water smearing the reflection of the house. The barbed-wire fence protecting the grounds reminded me of my internment camp.

"It's a Cape Dutch house," Magnus said, misreading the uneasiness on my face. "Very common where I came from."

A Gurkha hurried out from the guard post to open the gates. A pair of large brown dogs loped alongside the car as Magnus drove around the house to the garage behind. "Don't worry, they won't bite." He pointed to the darker strip of fur along their spine. "Rhodesian ridgebacks. That one's Brolloks; the smaller one's Bittergal."

The two dogs looked equally big to me, their cold, wet noses sniffing at my shins as I got out of the Land Rover. "Come, come," Magnus said, hefting my bag. At the front lawn he stopped, swept out an arm and said, "Majuba House."

The walls of the one-story house were plastered in white, setting off the black thatch of river reeds combed down the roof. Four wide windows, spaced generously apart, took up each flank of the front door. The wooden shutters and the frames were the green of algae. A holbol gable with a plasterwork of leaves and grapes capped the porch. Tall stalks of flowers that I later found out were called stre-litzias grew by the windows, their red and orange and yellow flow-ers reminding me of the origami birds a Japanese guard in my camp had so loved to fold. I pushed the memory away.

On the roof, the wind pulled at a flag, the broad stripes of orange, white, blue, and green unfamiliar to me. "The Vierkleur," Magnus said, following my gaze. "The Transvaal flag."

"You're not taking it down?" The hoisting of foreign national flags had been prohibited the year before, to prevent the flying of the Chinese flag by supporters of the Malayan Communist Party.

"They'll have to shoot me first."

He did not remove his shoes before going inside, and I followed his example. The walls in the hallway were painted white, the yel-low wood floorboards buttered by the evening sun through the windows. In the living room, a row of paintings on a wall caught my attention, and I went in for a closer look. They were scenes of a mountainous landscape, barren and stretching to the horizon. "Thomas Baines. And those lithographs there of the fever trees— they're Pierneef," Magnus said, looking pleased at my interest. "From the Cape."

A reflection spilled into the frame; I turned around to face a Chi-nese woman in her late forties, her graying hair pulled back into a bun. "My Lao Puo, Emily," Magnus said, giving his wife a kiss on her cheek.

"We're so happy you're here, Yun Ling," she said. A loose beige skirt softened the lines of her thin figure, and a red cardigan was caped over her shoulders.

"Where's Frederik?" Magnus said.

"Don't know. Probably in his bungalow," Emily said. "Our guest looks tired, Lao Kung. It's been a long day for her. Stop showing

off your house and take her to her room. I'm off to the clinic—
Muthu's wife was bitten by a snake."

"Have you called Dr. Yeoh?" Magnus asked.

"Of course-*lah*. He's on his way. Yun Ling, we'll talk later?" She
nodded to me and left us.

Magnus led me down the hallway. "Frederik's your son?" I
asked; I could not recall having heard anything about him.

"My nephew. He's a captain in the Rhodesian African Rifles."

The house was filled with reminders of Magnus's homeland—
ocher-colored rugs woven by some African tribe, porcupine quills
sticking out of a crystal vase, a two-foot-long bronze sculpture of
a leopard in pursuit of an unseen prey. We passed a little room in
the eastern wing at the back of the house, not much larger than a
linen closet. A radio set took up half of a narrow table. "That's how
we stay in touch with the other farms. We got them after the CTs
cut down our phone lines too many times for our liking."

My room was the last one in the passageway. The walls—and
even the Bakelite switches—were painted white, and for a few seconds I thought I was back in the Ipoh General Hospital again. On
a table stood a vase of flowers I had never seen in the tropics before,
creamy white and trumpet shaped. I rubbed my wrist against one
of the flowers; it had the texture of velvet. "What are these?"

"Arum lilies. I had bulbs sent over from the Cape," Magnus said.
"They grow well here." He set my bag down by a teak cupboard
and said, "How's your mother? Any improvements?"

"She's lost in her own world. Completely. She doesn't even ask
me about Yun Hong anymore." I was glad in a way, but I did not
tell him that.

"You should have come here to recuperate, after the war."

"I was waiting for a reply from the university."

"But to work for the War Crimes Tribunal—after what had happened to you?" He shook his head. "I'm surprised your father
allowed it."

"It was only for three months." I stopped, then said, "He had
heard no news of me or Yun Hong all through the war. He didn't
know what to make of me when he saw me. I was a ghost to him."

It was the only time in my life that I had seen my father cry. He
had aged so much. But then, I suppose, so had I. My parents had

34

left Penang and moved to Kuala Lumpur. In the new house he took me upstairs to my mother's room, walking with a limp that he had never had before the war. My mother had not recognized me, and she had turned her back to me. After a few days she remembered I was her daughter, but each time she saw me she began asking about Yun Hong—where she was, when she was coming home, why she had not returned yet. After a while I began to dread visiting her.

"It was better for me to be out of the house, to keep myself occupied," I said. "He didn't say it, but my father felt the same way."

It had not been difficult to be hired as an assistant researcher—a position that was nothing more than a clerk, really—at the War Crimes Tribunal in Kuala Lumpur. So many people had been killed or wounded in the war that the British Military Administration had faced a shortage of staff when the Japanese surrendered. Recording the testimonies of the victims of the Imperial Japanese Army affected me more seriously than I had anticipated, however. Watching the victims break down as they related the brutalities they had endured, I was made aware that I had yet to recover from my own experience. I was glad when I received my letter of admission from Girton.

"How many war criminals did they actually get in the end?" asked Magnus.

"In Singapore and Malaya together, a hundred and ninety-nine were sentenced to death—but only a hundred were eventually hanged," I said, looking into the bathroom. It was bright and airy, the floor a cold chessboard of black and white tiles. A claw-footed bathtub stood by the wall. "I attended only nine of the hangings before I left for Girton."

"*My magtig.*" Magnus looked appalled.

For a while we were silent. Then he opened a door next to the cupboard and asked me to follow him outside the room. A gravel path ran behind the house, taking us past the kitchen until we came to a broad terrace with a well-tended lawn. A pair of marble statues stood on their own plinths in the center of the lawn, facing one another. On my first glance they appeared to be identical, down to the folds of their robes spilling over the plinths.

"Bought them ridiculously cheap from an old planter's wife after the planter ran off with his fifteen-year-old lover," said Magnus. "The one on the right is Mnemosyne. You've heard of her?"

"The goddess of Memory," I said. "Who's the other woman?"

"Her twin sister, of course. The goddess of Forgetting."

I looked at him, wondering if he was pulling my leg. "I don't recall there's a goddess for that."

"Ah, doesn't the fact of your not recalling prove her existence?" He grinned. "Maybe she exists, but it's just that we have forgotten."

"So, what's her name?"

He shrugged, showing me his empty palms. "You see, we don't even remember her name anymore."

"They're not completely identical," I said, going closer to them. Mnemosyne's features were defined, her nose and cheekbones prominent, her lips full. Her sister's face looked almost blurred; even the creases of her robe were not as clearly delineated as Mnemosyne's.

"Which one would you say is the older twin?" asked Magnus.

"Mnemosyne, of course."

"Really? She looks younger, don't you think?"

"Memory must exist before there's forgetting." I smiled at him. "Or have you forgotten that?"

He laughed. "Come on. Let me show you something." He stopped at the low wall running along the edge of the terrace. Pinned to the highest plateau in the estate, Majuba House had an unimpeded view of the countryside. He pointed to a row of fir trees about three-quarters of the way down a hill. "That's where Aritomo's property starts."

"It doesn't look far to walk." I guessed it would take me about twenty minutes to get there.

"Don't be fooled. It's further than it looks. When are you meeting him?"

"Half past nine tomorrow morning."

"Frederik or one of my clerks will drive you there."

"I'll walk."

The determination in my face silenced him for a moment. "Your letter took Aritomo by surprise . . . I don't think he was at all happy to receive it."

"It was *your* idea for me to ask him, Magnus. You didn't tell him that I had been interned in a Japanese camp, I hope?"

"You asked me not to," he said. "I'm glad he's agreed to design your garden."

"He hasn't. He'll only decide after he's spoken to me."

Magnus adjusted the strap of his eye-patch. "You resigned even before he's made up his mind? Rather irresponsible, isn't it? Didn't you like prosecuting?"

"I did, at first. But in the last few months I've started to feel hollow . . . I felt I was wasting my time." I paused. "And I was furious when the Japan Peace Treaty was signed."

Magnus cocked his head at me; his black silk eye-patch had the texture of a cat's ear. "What's that got to do with the price of eggs?"

"One of the articles in the treaty states that the Allied Powers recognize that Japan *should* pay reparations for the damage and suffering caused during the war. However, because Japan could not afford to pay, the Allied Powers would waive all reparation claims of the Allied Powers and their nationals. *And their nationals.*" I realized that I was near to ranting, but I was unable to stop myself. It was a relief to uncork myself and let my frustrations spill out. "So you see, Magnus, the British made certain that no one—not a single man or woman or child who had been tortured and imprisoned or massacred by the Japs—none of them or their families can demand any form of financial reparation from the Japanese. Our government betrayed us!"

"You sound surprised." He snorted. "Well, now you know what the *fokken Engelse* are capable of. Excuse me," he added.

"I lost interest in my work. I insulted my superiors. I quarreled with my colleagues. I made disparaging remarks about the government to anyone who would listen. One of them who heard me was a reporter for the *Straits Times*." Thinking about it brought back a flood of bitterness. "I didn't resign, Magnus. I was sacked."

"That must have upset your father," he said. Was there a mischievous—even malicious—glint in his eye?

"He called me an ungrateful daughter. He had pulled so many strings to get me that job, and I had made him lose face."

Magnus clasped his hands behind his back. "Well, whatever Aritomo decides, I hope you'll stay with us for a while. A week's too short. And it's your first time here. There are plenty of nice places to see. Come to the sitting room later, say in an hour's time. We have drinks before dinner," he said, before returning into the house through the kitchen.

The air became colder, but I remained out there. The mountains swallowed up the sun, and night seeped into the valleys. Bats squeaked, hunting invisible insects. A group of prisoners in my camp once caught a bat; the ravenous men had stretched its wings over a meager fire, the glow showing up the thin bones beneath its skin.

On the edge of Nakamura Aritomo's property, the failing light transformed the firs into pagodas, sentinels protecting the garden behind them.

CHAPTER FOUR

I left Majuba House at half past six the next morning. Even after more than five years the routine of the camp had never left me, and I had been awake for the past two hours. I had slept fitfully, worried about how I would be received by the Japanese gardener. In the end I decided I would not wait until half past nine to see him but go as soon as there was enough light in the sky.

Tucking a roll of papers under my arm, I shut the front door quietly and walked to the gate. The air stung my cheeks and the clouds from my mouth seemed to make my breathing sound louder than usual. The Gurkha outside was sharpening his *kukri* and he slid the curved blade into its sheath before unlocking the gate for me.

It was Sunday, and the tea fields were deserted. In the valleys, the points of light from the farmhouses were as faint as stars behind a weave of clouds. The smells of the nearby jungle transported me back to the prison camp; I had not expected that. I stopped and looked around me. The moon was retreating behind the mountains, the same moon I had seen at almost every dawn in the camp, and yet it seemed altered to me. So long after my imprisonment, there were still moments when I found it difficult to believe that the war was over, that I had survived.

I thought back to my conversation with Magnus at the bar of the Selangor Club a month before, when I was still a deputy public prosecutor. Returning to my office after I had finished a case, I had cut through one of the narrow lanes behind the courts. Turning a corner, I found my way blocked by a crowd. Men in white singlets and black pants were setting up paper effigies of Japanese soldiers, the life-sized figures shown being disemboweled by the demons of hell. I had heard of these rites but had never witnessed one. They were held to soothe the spirits of those killed by the Japanese, spirits now wandering namelessly for all eternity.

Standing at the back of the crowd, I watched the Taoist priest in his faded black robe ring his bells and write invisible amuletic words in the air with the tip of his sword. The effigies were then set ablaze, the heat from the flames pushing the crowd back. All around me people wailed and keened as the ashes rose to the sky, leaving behind a charred odor in the air. Perhaps the spirits were appeased, but I felt only a renewed sense of anger when the crowd dispersed. Knowing that I would not be able to concentrate on my work for the rest of the day, I decided to go to the Selangor Club's library. I had not seen Magnus in eleven or twelve years, but I recognized him in the foyer—I remembered his eye-patch—and I called out to him. He was with a group of men surrendering their guns to the clerk, and he had looked at me, trying to remember who I was. A smile sprawled over his face when I reminded him, and he insisted on buying a round of drinks. We sat at a table on the verandah overlooking the cricket *padang* and the court buildings. "Boy!" he called for the waiter—an elderly Chinese—and ordered our drinks. The ceiling fans rattling at full speed above our heads did nothing to dispel the humidity. The clock above the courthouse rang out across the *padang*. It was three o'clock and the usual crowd of planters and lawyers would not show up for at least another two hours.

Magnus told me he was in KL to get money from the Chartered Bank for his workers' payroll, which he did once a month. "I heard your parents are living in KL now," he said. "I never thought your father would ever consider leaving Penang. Your mother . . ." Magnus had lowered his voice and looked at me intently. "How is she?"

"She has good and bad days," I replied. "Unfortunately the bad days seem to be happening more often."

"I tried to visit her, you know. It was just after you went to England. But your father wouldn't allow it. I don't think he lets anyone see her."

"It upsets her too much when someone she doesn't recognize speaks to her," I said. "And she has trouble recognizing most people."

"I heard what happened to your sister. Terrible," he said. "I only met her once. She was keen on gardening, I remember."

"She always dreamed of building her own Japanese garden," I said.

He studied me, his eye sweeping down to my hands before rising up to my face again. "Build it for her." His finger stroked the strap of his eye-patch. "You could make it a memorial for her. I'm not sure if you remember, but my neighbor's a Japanese gardener. He was the *emperor's* gardener, would you believe? He might be willing to help you out. You could ask him to make a garden for—yes, ask Aritomo to design a garden for your sister."

"He's a *Jap*," I said.

"Well, if you want a Japanese garden . . . ," Magnus said. "Aritomo wasn't involved in the war. And if it hadn't been for him half my workers would have been rounded up and taken down to some mine or worked to death on the railway."

"They'd have to hang their emperor first before I'd ask for help from any of them."

His stare disconcerted me; it was as though the power of his lost eye had been transferred to his remaining one, doubling its acuity. "This hatred in you," he said a moment later, "you can't let it affect your life."

"It's not up to me, Magnus."

The waiter returned with two frosted mugs of Tiger Beer. Magnus emptied half of his in one swallow and wiped his mouth with the back of his hand. He continued to stare at me. "My father was a sheep farmer. My mother died when I was four. I was brought up by my sister, Petronella. My older brother, Pieter, was teaching at the Cape. When the war broke out—that's the Boer War I'm talking about, the second one—I joined up. I had just turned twenty. I was captured by the English less than a year later and shipped out to a POW camp in Ceylon."

He had brought his mug to his lips again but then, without drinking from it, put it down heavily on the table. "I was away fighting the English when Kitchener's men showed up at our farm one morning," he said. "Pa was at home. He put up a fight. They shot him, then burned down our farmhouse."

"What happened to your sister?"

"She was sent to a concentration camp in Bloemfontein. Pieter tried to get her out. He had an English wife, but even he wasn't allowed to visit the camp. Petronella died of typhoid. Or perhaps not—survivors later said the English had mixed powdered glass into the prisoners' food."

He gazed across the *padang*; the grass was dry, the heat warping the air. "Coming home after the war to find out all this about my family . . . well, I couldn't live in that part of the country again— not where I had grown up. I went to Cape Town. But still it wasn't far enough for me. One day—in the spring of 1905, I'd guess—I bought a ticket for Batavia. The ship was forced to dock in Malacca for repairs and we were told it would take a week to complete. I was walking in the town when I saw an abandoned church on a hill—"

"St. Paul's."

He gave a grunt. "*Ja, ja.* St. Paul's. In the church grounds, I came across gravestones three, four hundred years old. And what do I find there, but the grave of Jan van Riebeeck." Seeing the blank expression my face, he shook his head. "The world is not made up of only English history, you know. Van Riebeeck founded the Cape. He became its governor."

"How did he end up in Malacca?"

"The VOC—the Dutch East Indies Company—sent him there, as punishment for something he had done." Memory softened his face, seeming to age him at the same time. "Anyway, seeing his name there, carved into that block of stone, I felt I had found a place for myself here in Malaya. I never returned to my ship, never went on to Batavia. Instead I made my way to Kuala Lumpur." He laughed. "I ended up in a British territory after all. And I've lived here for— what . . ." His lips moved soundlessly as he counted. "Forty-six years. Forty-six!" He sat up in his chair and looked around for the waiter. "That calls for champagne!"

"You've forgiven the British?"

He subsided into his seat. For a while he was silent, his gaze turned inward. "They couldn't kill me when we were at war. And they couldn't kill me when I was in the camp," he said finally, his voice subdued. "But holding on to my hatred for forty-six years . . . *that* would have killed me." His eye became kindly as he looked at me. "You Chinese are supposed to respect the elderly, Yun Ling, that's what that fellow Confucius said, isn't it? That's what my wife tells me anyway." He managed a sip of his beer at last. "So listen to me. Listen to an old man . . . Don't despise all Japanese for what some of them did. Let it go, this hatred in you. Let it go."

"They did this to me." Slowly I raised my maimed hand, protected in its leather glove.

He pointed to his eye-patch. "You think this fell out by itself?"

Three weeks after that meeting with Magnus at the club, I was sacked. His idea of building a garden for Yun Hong had stayed with me; in fact it had grown more insistent. In the camp, she had often talked to me about the garden she would build once the war was over and our lives were returned to us again.

On my last day at work, I sat down to clear my desk. Packing away my personal things, I stopped when I saw the news article I had clipped from the *Straits Times*. The photograph accompanying the article showed a group of Japanese men in tailcoats standing behind their prime minister, Yoshida, as he signed the Japan Security Treaty with the Americans. Staring at the photograph, I thought about the camp. And I thought about Nakamura Aritomo, recalling the first time I had heard about him, all those years ago. I had never forgotten his name; it had followed me wherever I went. It was time I visited him. Creating a garden was something I had to do for Yun Hong, something I owed her.

Taking out a blank sheet of paper, I uncapped my fountain pen and wrote a letter to Magnus, asking him to arrange a meeting with the gardener for me. When I had finished, I sealed it in an envelope and asked the clerk to post it for me as I left my office for the last time.

The world was growing brighter, bleaching away the moon and stars. Halfway down to the bottom of the valley, I found the path separating one division of tea bushes from another. The track was tramped hard by generations of tea pickers. This shortcut would take me to Yugiri, Magnus had informed me at dinner the night before. "There's no fence on this side," he had said, "but you'll know where Yugiri starts when you come to it."

The fir trees in the distance rose higher as I came nearer to Yugiri. The path wound between the trees and continued into a thicket of bamboo, their poles knocking gently against each other, as if transmitting the news of my arrival through the garden, passing the message from tree to tree.

It began to drizzle. Wiping the blisters of rain from my face, I walked beneath the bamboo and emerged into another realm.

The silence here had a different quality; I felt I had been plumbed with weighted fishing line into a deeper, denser level of the ocean. I stood there, allowing the stillness to seep into me. In the leaves, an unseen bird whistled, deepening the emptiness of the air between each note. Water dripped off the leaves. Not far away, the edge of a red-tiled roof could be seen through the treetops. Setting off toward it, I soon came to a long rectangle of round, white pebbles. I crouched and picked one up. It was about the size of one of the leatherback turtles' eggs my mother had sometimes bought at the Pulau Tikus market.

About fifty feet away to my left stood two round targets. Set on low stilts to my right was a simple wooden one-story structure with an attap roof. Putting down the stone, I went closer to it. The front of the structure was open, the bamboo chicks rolled up to the eaves. A man was standing at the edge of the platform, dressed in a white robe and a pair of gray pantaloons that just showed his white socks. He appeared to be in his early fifties, his hair just starting to turn gray. In his right hand he held a bow. He did not acknowledge my presence, but somehow I knew that he was aware of me.

I had not seen a Japanese nor spoken to one in nearly six years, but I would always be able to recognize them. It had been easy enough to write to Nakamura Aritomo, but I had been a fool to think I could just stroll in here and talk to him. I was not ready to do this; perhaps I never would be. The urge to turn around and leave the garden took hold of me. But when I looked at the roll of documents in my hand, I knew that I had to speak to the gardener, I had to tell him what I wanted from him. I would do it, and then I would leave. If he chose to accept my offer, we would communicate through the post. There would be no need for me to talk to him in person again.

Raising his bow, the man drew back the bowstring, his arms stretching in opposite directions until he reached a point where he seemed to be floating just above the floorboards. He stood there with his tautened bow, an expression of complete peace spreading across his face. Time had stopped: there was no beginning, there was no end.

He released the arrow. The bowstring sliced a sharp sound from the air. The man remained unmoving, one arm still extended, keeping the center of the bow where he gripped it level with his eyes. He looked at the target for a moment longer before lowering the bow. The arrow had struck well away from the center.

I took the three low steps up to the platform, the gleaming cypress floorboards creaking beneath my feet. "Mr. Nakamura?" I said. "Nakamura Aritomo? We were supposed to meet later today—"

"Take off your shoes!" he said. "You bring the problems of the world inside."

Glancing behind, I saw sand and shreds of grass smeared across the floorboards. I stepped down from the range. The man returned the bow to its stand, his white socks leaving no mark on the floor. I waited as he put on his sandals.

"Go around to the front of the house," he said. "Ah Cheong will take you to the sitting room."

A Chinese manservant led me through the house, sliding open the doors that partitioned off each room and then closing them behind us. I had the impression of moving through a series of boxes, each one opening up to reveal another box, and then another. The servant left me in a sitting room. The doors were opened to the verandah, where a low square table was positioned.

On the lawn below the verandah, string tied to four bamboo splints marked out a rectangle; the top layer of grass had been peeled away, exposing the moist, dark soil beneath. Beyond the rectangle, the ground sloped gently away to the edge of a depression, wide and empty as a salt pan. Mounds of earth and gravel were piled up at its side.

The drizzle had stopped, but water continued to drip from the eaves, drops of congealed light falling to earth. The servant came out with a tray bearing two small celadon cups, a teapot and a small teakettle, its spout steaming weakly. The archer joined me a few minutes later. He had changed into a pair of beige-colored trousers and a white shirt, matched with a gray linen jacket. He sat in the traditional manner on one of the mats, his legs folded, the weight of his body pressing down on his heels. He indicated that I should sit on the other side of the table. I looked at him for a second and then followed his example, putting the roll of documents next to my knee.

"I am Nakamura Aritomo," he said, placing an envelope on the table. I recognized my handwriting on the front, addressed to him. I told him my name and he said, "Write it out in Chinese," his fingers scribbling over the table.

"I went to a convent school, Mr. Nakamura. I was taught Latin but not Chinese. I only picked up a little of it after the war."

"What does 'Yun Ling' mean?"

"Cloud Forest."

He considered it for a moment. "A beautiful name. In Japanese you would be called—"

"I know what I'd be called."

For a few seconds he stared at me. Then he emptied the teapot into a bowl and threw the still-steaming tea over the verandah. I thought it odd but said nothing. He refilled the teapot with hot water from the kettle. "I thought we had agreed to meet at nine thirty."

"If it's inconvenient for you now, I'll come back later."

He shook his head. "How old are you? Thirty-three, thirty-four?"

"I'm twenty-eight." I was aware that I had been aged beyond my years by the deprivations in the camp; I thought I had come to accept it but the sudden jab of shame surprised me. "You're making a pond?" I said, looking to the shallow pit at the bottom of the slope.

"I am merely changing its shape, making it bigger." Lifting the teapot, he filled the cups with a translucent green liquid and slid one toward me as if it was a piece on a chessboard. "You were a guest of the emperor."

This time his arrow had found its mark. "I *was* a prisoner in a Japanese camp," I said, wondering how he had known.

"When I was building this house, Magnus gave me a watercolor your sister had painted," Aritomo said. "He reminded me about it when he brought your letter."

"Yun Hong used to exhibit her paintings with some artists."

"That is not surprising. She has a lot of talent. Does she still paint?"

"She was with me in the camp." I shifted my body, unknotting the pain in my ankles; it had been a long time since I had last sat like this. "She died there."

Aritomo caught my left hand as I was reaching for my cup. A guarded look sheathed his face the instant his fingers closed around my wrist. I tried to pull away, but he tightened his grip, his eyes compelling me not to struggle. Like an exhausted animal caught in a trap, my hand stopped moving, became inert. He turned it over and touched the stitches where the last two fingers of the glove had been cut off. I withdrew my hand and placed it beneath the edge of the table.

"You want me to design a garden for you."

From the moment I had sent my letter off to the gardener, I had been going over what I would say when I met him. "Yun Hong . . . my sister . . . she heard about you eleven years ago," I said, searching for the right words. "You had just moved to Malaya. This was sometime in 1940."

"Eleven years." He turned to stare at the empty pond, his face barren. "Hard to believe that I have been living here for so long."

"Yun Hong was fascinated by Japanese gardens even before we heard about you. Before you came to Malaya," I said.

"How did she know about our gardens?" he said. "I doubt there were any in Penang in those days, or in the whole of Malaya. Even today, mine is the only one."

"My father took all of us to Japan for a month. In 1938. Your government wanted to buy rubber from him. He was busy with his meetings, but the officials' wives showed us around the city. We visited a few of the temples and the gardens. We even took the train to Kyoto." The memory of that holiday—the only time I had been overseas till then—made me smile. "I'll never forget how excited Yun Hong was. I was fifteen, and she was three years older than me. But on that holiday . . . on that holiday she was like a little girl, and I felt I was the elder sister."

"Ah . . . Kyoto . . . ," murmured Aritomo. "Which temples did you see?"

"Joju-in, Tofuku-ji, and the Temple of the Golden Pavilion," I said. "When we returned home, Yun Hong read all the books she could find on Japanese gardens. She wanted to know—she was obsessed with knowing—how they were created."

"You cannot learn gardening from books."

"We soon found that out," I said. "She tried to make a rock garden behind our house. I helped her, but it was a failure. My mother was furious that we had ruined the lawn." I paused. "When Yun Hong heard about you living here, she wanted to see your garden."

"There would have been nothing to see. Yugiri was not completed at that point."

"Yun Hong's love of gardens kept us alive when we were in the camp," I said.

"How did it keep you alive?"

"We escaped into make-believe worlds," I said. "Some imagined themselves building the house of their dreams or constructing a yacht. The more details they could include, the better they were insulated from the horrors around them. One Eurasian woman—the wife of a Dutch engineer at Shell—this woman wanted to look at her stamp collection again. It gave her the will to go on living. Another man recited the titles of all of Shakespeare's plays again and again, in the order they had been written, when he was being tortured." My throat dried up and I took a swallow of tea. "Yun Hong kept our spirits up by talking about the gardens we had visited in Kyoto, describing even the smallest details to me. 'This is how we'll survive,' she told me, 'this is how we'll walk out of this camp.'"

The sun was breaking free of the mountains. Over the distant treetops, a flock of birds unspooled into a black wavering thread, pulling across the sky.

"One day, a guard beat me for not bowing properly. He wouldn't stop, but just kept hitting me. I found myself in a garden. There were flowering trees everywhere, the smell of water . . ." I paused. "I realized that where I had been was a combination of all the gardens I had visited in Kyoto. I told Yun Hong about it. That was the moment we started to create our own garden, in here," I said, tapping a finger on the side of my head. "Day by day we added details to it. The garden became our refuge. Inside our minds, we were free."

He touched the envelope on the table. "You mentioned that you worked as a researcher for the War Crimes Tribunal."

"I wanted to ensure that those who were responsible were punished. I wanted to see that justice was done."

"You think I am a fool? It was not all about justice."

"It was the only way that I would be allowed to examine the court documents and official records," I said. "I was searching for information about my camp. I wanted to find where my sister was buried."

His eyes narrowed. "You didn't know where your camp was located?"

"We were blindfolded when the Japs—when the Japanese—transported us there. It was somewhere deep in the jungle. That was all we knew."

"The other survivors from your camp, what happened to them?"

A butterfly trembled over the cannas by the verandah. It finally alighted on a leaf, its wings closing together in prayer. "There were no other survivors."

"You were the only one?" He looked at me as though I was trying to deceive him.

I held his stare, not swerving away from it. "I was the only one."

For a while we did not speak. Pushing the tray to one side, I untied the twine around the tube of papers I had brought with me and unrolled it on the table, weighing down the edges with our cups. "My grandmother left a piece of land in KL to Yun Hong and me. It's about six acres." I pointed to the first document, a map from the Land Office. "It's a short walk up the hill from the Lake Gardens. The climate is too hot and humid for an authentic Japanese garden, I know," I added quickly, "but perhaps we can use the local flora instead. Here, I've taken photographs of the place. You can have some idea of what the terrain looks like, what needs to be done."

He gave only a cursory glance at the map and the photographs. "Your sister was the one who dreamed of creating gardens, not you."

"Yun Hong lies in an unmarked grave, Mr. Nakamura. This is for her, a garden in her memory." I foraged among my thoughts for the words to persuade him but found none. "This is the only thing I can do for her."

"It makes me uncomfortable—the fact that you are asking me to do this because of what happened to your sister—and to you."

"It shouldn't, if you weren't involved in the Occupation." I spoke more sharply than I had intended.

The line of his jaw became accentuated. "If I had been, would I not have been hanged? Perhaps by you even?"

"Not every guilty Japanese was charged, much less punished."

Some element in the air between us changed, as though a wind that had been blowing gently had been come to an abrupt stillness.

"British soldiers came here one day, not long after the surrender," he said. "They dragged me out of my house and made me kneel on the ground, there. Just there." He pointed to a patch of grass. "They clubbed me. When I fell over and tried to get up, they kicked me, again and again. Then they took me away."

"Where to?"

"The prison in Ipoh. They locked me in a cell. They never charged me with anything." He stroked his cheek with the back of his hand. "There were other prisoners there, Japanese officers, waiting for their sentences to be carried out. Some of them wept when they went to their execution. One by one they were taken away, until I was the only one left. And then, one evening, the guards came for me." He stopped stroking his cheek. "They took me out of my cell. I thought I was going to be hanged. But they let me go. Magnus was waiting for me at the prison gates. I had been inside for two months."

The butterfly flew off, its wings flashing black and yellow semaphores. The gardener drummed the table with his fingers. Eventually he rose to his feet. "Come, I will show you part of the garden."

"Our tea will get cold." I had hoped to get a decision from him and he had not given me any indication of whether he would accept my offer.

"We are not likely to run out of tea in this part of the world," he said, "are we?"

He collected an old solar topi from a hat stand by the front door and led me outside. We skirted the edge of the unfilled pond; I noticed that the bottom was already lined with hardened clay. Further into the garden, a Tamil coolie was stacking rocks coated in a batter of mud and broken-off roots into a wheelbarrow. *"Selamat pagi, Tuan,"* he greeted Aritomo. The gardener examined the man's work and shook his head, his irritation obvious. The Tamil spoke barely any English and Aritomo was unable to tell him exactly what he wanted done. I stepped between them and translated his instructions into Malay. Aritomo gave me more detailed directions to convey to the man, interrogating him until he was satisfied that he was understood precisely.

"He will still make a mess of things," Aritomo said as the Tamil pushed the wheelbarrow away.

"How many workers do you have here?"

"I used to have nine," Aritomo replied. "When the war ended they went to Kuala Lumpur. Now I have only five of them working for me. They have no interest or ability in gardening. And as you have seen, they cannot understand my instructions."

"You've been here eleven years," I said, gazing around us. "I would have thought that the garden would've been completed by now."

"I am making some changes to it," he replied. "The soldiers who came for me took pleasure in wrecking my garden. For a long time I wondered if there was a point to my restoring it. I did not want another group of soldiers to destroy it again. I put off the repairs until a few months ago."

"These changes, how long will it take to finish them?"

"Probably another year." He stopped to examine a row of heliconia flowers. "There are some new ideas I want to realize."

"That seems a long time just to finish a garden."

"Then it is clear that you know very little. Rocks have to be dug up and moved. Trees have to be taken out and replanted. Everything has to be done by hand—*everything*." Aritomo snapped off the twigs of some low-hanging branches. "So you see, I cannot accept your commission."

I was wracked by bitter disappointment. "I'm willing to wait a year," I said eventually. "Even two years, if that's what you need."

"I am not interested in your proposal." He strode to a large boulder hulking by a hedge; I followed him a second later. The stone came up to my hips. Set into its flat surface was a hollow the size of a small washbasin. Water trickled from a bamboo flume, filling the hollow before overflowing down the sides. A bamboo dipper lay beside the natural basin. Aritomo scooped it into the water and drank from it, passing it to me when he was done. I hesitated, then took it from him.

The water was icy, tasting of moss and minerals, of rain and mist. Bending to replace the dipper, my eyes were drawn across the water's surface to a gap in the hedge, through which a solitary mountain peak in the distance could be seen. The sight of it was so unexpected, so perfectly framed by the leaves, that my mind was momentarily stilled. The tranquility in me drained away when I straightened up, leaving me with a sense of loss.

"A tea master horrified his pupils by planting a hedge in his garden, blocking the view of the Inland Sea for which his school was famous," I said, half to myself. "He left only a gap in the hedge and set a basin before it. Anyone drinking from it would have to bend down and look at the sea through the hole."

"Where did you hear that story?"

For a moment I considered telling him that Yun Hong had read about the tea master in a book, but somehow I knew he would not believe me. "A Jap told me," I said. "In the camp."

"A soldier?"

"He wasn't in the army. At least I never saw him in uniform. I never knew what he was. His name was Tominaga. Tominaga Noburu. He told me that story."

Something flickered in Aritomo's eyes, fleeting as a moth risking a candle flame; it was the first time I had seen any hint of uncertainty in him. "I have not heard his name in years," he said.

"You know him?"

"That tea master was his great uncle," he said. "Why do you think he planted the hedge to block out the famous view?"

"Tominaga explained it to me," I said. "But I've only just really understood it now—the effect of seeing the view is much more powerful than if the sea has not been obstructed."

He observed me for a few moments, then nodded.

We were approaching his house when the housekeeper came out with a tall, sandy-haired European. "Afternoon, Mr. Nakamura," the man said. He turned to look at me. "And you must be Yun Ling. I'm Frederik." His accent was unlike his uncle's, more English. I guessed him to be about two or three years older than me. "Uncle Magnus sent me to drive you home. He's worried there might be trouble."

"Has something happened?" asked Aritomo.

"You haven't heard? It's been on the news all morning—the high commissioner's dead. The CTs killed him."

Aritomo glanced at me. "You must go."

At the weathered door of the front entrance Frederik stopped and said, "Oh, Mr. Nakamura—Magnus asked me to remind you about his party. Why don't you come with us? We'll wait for you."

"I have work I must finish," Aritomo said.

He unlatched and opened the door. I hung back, letting Frederik squeeze past me to his Land Rover parked across the road. Aritomo bowed to me but I did not return it: it brought back too many memories of the times when I had been forced to do it, how I was slapped when I did not bow quickly or low enough.

I opened my mouth to speak, but Aritomo shook his head. I stepped through the doorway and then turned to look at him. He bowed to me one more time and shut the wooden door. I stood there for a moment longer, staring at it. I heard the latch drop and the key turn in the lock.

Chapter Five

Every child longs for a larger-than-life uncle, and because I had
none, Magnus Pretorius became a figure of fascination to me,
although he was hardly anything more than a vague presence in my
life when I was growing up. What I knew of him I heard from my
parents and from the things they left unsaid, the broken-off twigs
of conversations I picked up whenever I walked in on them, and
from what Magnus told me after I got to know him better.

Arriving in Kuala Lumpur from Cape Town in 1905, Magnus
worked as an assistant manager in one of Guthries's rubber estates
in Ipoh. He liked to tell people that he had been employed only
because the interviewer discovered he could play rugby. It was during this period that he became friendly with my father. They went
into business together, buying up a rubber estate, acquiring a few
more over the years.

Outstation planters lived in isolation among the rubber, with the
nearest European neighbor usually twenty miles or more away.
Growing up in Penang, I had heard stories of planters drinking themselves to death, or dying from snakebite or malaria or a variety of
other tropical diseases. Hemmed in by the neat, unending lines of rubber trees, Magnus came to hate the life and began searching for better prospects. Drinking at the FMS Bar in Ipoh one weekend, he
overheard a government official talking about a plateau three thousand feet high on the Titiwangsa mountain range. The man spoke of
plans to turn it into an administrative center of government and a hill
station resort for senior officials of the Malayan Civil Service.

Magnus, who had once hiked up one of the mountains in that
region, saw the potential of the plans immediately. A week later he
obtained a concession of six hundred acres in the highlands from
the government. He sold off his shares in the rubber plantations to

my father just before the Great Slump, an act that my father would always hold against him.

A government surveyor, William Cameron, had mapped out the highlands in 1885. He had come upon the endlessly unfolding misty mountains and valleys while traversing the ranges on his elephants, charting the borders of Pahang and Perak. "Like Hannibal crossing the Alps," I would often hear Magnus tell visitors during my stay in Majuba.

Magnus brought in seeds and tea plants from the hills of Ceylon. Laborers were shipped in from southern India to clear the jungle. In the space of four, five years, the slopes and hillsides in his estate were covered with tea bushes. The tea trees eventually became stunted from the workers' constant picking, like the bonsai trees maintained by generations of Japanese nobility. A few years after he started planting, two other rival tea estates were also established in Cameron Highlands, but by that time the Majuba label had taken root in Malaya.

It was the only brand of tea my father prohibited in our home.

Frederik tried to engage me in conversation on the short drive back to Majuba House, but my thoughts were on Aritomo and on my failure to convince him to design a garden for me. Staring out of the window, I paid scant attention to the terraced slopes of the vegetable farms outside Majuba, or the occasional bungalow we passed. It was only when the Gurkha at Majuba House opened the gates for us that I noticed the cars parked in the driveway.

"What's happening here?"

"Magnus's *braai*. He has one every Sunday," Frederik said. "Starts at eleven in the morning and usually goes on till seven, eight at night. You'll love it." I vaguely recalled Magnus telling me about the *braai* the night before, but I had forgotten all about it.

In the passageway outside the kitchen, we nearly collided into Emily scurrying out with a tray of strange-looking tubes. "*Aiyoh*, we were so worried about you-*lah*," she scolded me. "Everyone's outside already." She nudged her chin at the back of the house. "Go and join them. No, not you, Frederik! You come and help me. Take these out to Magnus." She pushed the tray to me. The glistening tubes, I saw, were coils of uncooked sausages, each one about an inch thick and one and a half feet long.

Fifteen to twenty people were gathered on the terrace garden behind the house, a mix of Chinese, Malays and Europeans. Some lounged in rattan chairs while others stood talking in small groups, a drink in their hands. The day was bright and windless, but the atmosphere was somber. A woman laughed, then stopped abruptly and glanced around. Plates and cutlery and casseroles of food took up a long table at one end of the terrace. Curries simmered over charcoal stoves and sunlight winked off the tuberous bottles of Tiger Beer planted in a tub of ice. In the shade of a camphor tree, Magnus watched over a barbecue grill that had been made from an old oil drum cut in half lengthwise and laid on a trestle. The ridge-backs lazed at his feet, scratching themselves and looking up at me as I approached.

"Ah, you've been found!" Magnus said. "Knew you'd be at Yugiri when you didn't show up for breakfast."

"I've never seen these at the Cold Storage," I said, handing the tray of sausages to him.

"*Boerewors*. Made them myself."

"They look like something Brolloks and Bittergal might leave behind," I said. The dogs glanced up at the sound of the names, their tails flattening the grass.

"*Sies!*" Magnus grimaced. "Put them on the *braai*. You'll soon see how *lekker* they taste."

The sausages were flecked with coriander seeds and other spices Magnus refused to divulge. "It's my *ouma*'s recipe," was all he would say. They gave off the most wonderful aroma when they began cooking over the coals and I realized suddenly that, except for the tea I had drunk with Aritomo, I had consumed nothing all morning.

"Before you think I'm being disrespectful"—Magnus tilted his bottle of Tiger Beer at the people scattered across the lawn—"by the time we heard about Gurney's death, it was too late to cancel." He took another swig from his bottle. "You get what you wanted from Aritomo?"

"He turned me down."

"*Ag*, shame. But stay here. For as long as you want. The air will do you a world of good." His eye searched the crowd. "Didn't Frederik remind him about the *braai*?"

"He has work to do," I said. Magnus picked up a pair of metal tongs. "Were there reprisals against him when the Occupation ended?"

"By the anti-Japanese guerrillas?" He wiped his lips with his hand. "Of course not."

"He told me he was arrested."

"Well, the Brits couldn't charge him with anything," Magnus replied. "And I vouched for him." He turned the *boerewors* over and fat dripped into the coals, sending up a cloud of fragrant smoke. "He made sure we weren't sent to the camps. At one point in the war he had more than thirty people working for him. All of them—and their families—survived the war."

"We should have come here to wait out the war."

He stopped rearranging the sausages on the grill and looked at me. "Weeks before the Japs attacked, I told your father to bring all of you here."

I stared at him. "He never said anything about it."

"He should have listened to me. I wish he had."

The noise of the party behind me seemed to recede into the distance. I felt a sudden fury at my father's obdurate pride. Magnus was right—things would have turned out differently: I would be unharmed, my mother would not be lost inside her mind, and Yun Hong would still be alive.

"You knew early on that the Japanese would attack us?" I asked, watching him carefully.

"Anyone with half a brain looking at a map would have realized that," Magnus replied. "China was too big for Japan to swallow— all it could do was nibble at the edges. But these smaller territories in the southern seas were easier meat."

Frederik came out with another tray, this one filled with lamb chops. "Buy a donkey," Magnus said to him.

"Buy a what?" I wondered if I had heard him correctly.

"I'm trying to make this young man here speak more Afrikaans," Magnus said. "He's been mixing with the English for so long he's forgotten his own language. Tell her what it means."

"*Baie dankie*," Frederik said, and I asked him to spell it out for me. "It means 'Thank you.' I've been taking lessons in Malay too," he added. "It's funny, how many words they both share: *pisang, piring . . . pondok*."

"It's because of the slaves taken from Java to the Cape," said Magnus. He poured his beer into the coals and asked the two of us to follow him. He introduced us to the guests. In spite of the chill in the air, I was the only one wearing gloves.

"Meet Malcolm," Magnus announced. "He's the Protector of Aborigines. Be careful of what you say when he's around—this man speaks Malay and Cantonese and Mandarin and Hokkien."

"Malcolm Toombs," the man said with a warm smile. He was in his late forties, with a guileless face I immediately took to. It probably helped in his work, looking after the welfare of the Orang Asli.

"Not a grave person, in spite of his name," Frederik whispered to me.

We piled our plates with food from the buffet table and were about to start eating when Toombs asked us to stand in a loose circle. Magnus's mouth tightened, but he said nothing. We closed our eyes in a minute's silence in memory of the high commissioner. Only now did the full import of Gurney's death strike me. Despite what the government had been telling us, things were getting worse.

"How's the *boerewors*?" Magnus asked once everyone had sat down and begun eating.

"They taste much better than they look." I chewed, swallowed and said, "How did Gurney die?"

"Terrorists ambushed his car and shot him. Happened yesterday afternoon on the road up to Fraser's Hill," Magnus said. "They were going on holiday, apparently—he and his wife. Traveling in an armed convoy."

"And yet they managed to kill him," said Jaafar Hamid, the owner of the Lakeview Hotel at Tanah Rata. He pulled his chair closer to us.

"Why was the bloody news kept back until today?" Magnus asked.

"Everything's censored these days," I said. "But, by now, there'll hardly be a wireless anywhere in the world that isn't broadcasting what has happened. They must have already killed him when you were bringing me here from the station. That's why there were so many army vehicles on the road."

"That's possible . . . ," Toombs said quietly. "It's quite a coup for the Reds. They'll be dancing and singing in the jungles tonight, I'm afraid."

"Gurney's wife?" I said, looking at Magnus.

"The wireless said the CTs fired at the vehicle in front first. When they started shooting at his Rolls, Gurney got out from the car and walked away from it."

"That was reckless of him," one of the European women spoke up.

Magnus corrected her immediately. "He was drawing fire away from her, Sarah."

"Poor woman . . . ," said Emily.

Magnus squeezed his wife's shoulder. "I think it'll be good for us to look at our security measures again, come up with some suggestions to improve them."

"There's not much more we can do, is there?" a middle-aged man said. Earlier he had introduced himself to me as Paul Crawford, telling me that he owned a strawberry farm in Tanah Rata and that he was a childless widower. "We've put up fences around our homes, trained our workers to be sentries, and formed a Home Guard in the kampongs. But we're still waiting for the special constables we asked for."

When the war ended, I had hoped I would never have to experience something like that again. But here I was, in the heart of another war.

"Those few weeks after the Japs surrendered," Emily said, "we kept hearing about the communists killing the Malays in their kampongs, and the Malays taking their revenge on the Chinese. It was frightening."

"The Chinese squatters I've spoken to still believe that it was the communists who defeated the Japs," Toombs remarked.

"My first week in Malaya," Frederik said, "a soldier told me he had been with the first batch of troops coming back to take control of the country. He thought the communists had won the war. Every town his regiment drove through had buntings and posters celebrating the communists' victory against the Japs."

"Malaya, Malaya," Hamid grumbled. "None of you find it strange that what you English so carelessly named 'Malaya'—my *tanah-air*, my home—didn't *officially* exist until only recently?"

"This is my home too, Enchik Hamid," I said.

"You *orang* China, you're all descendants of immigrants," Hamid retorted. "Your loyalty will always lie with China."

"That's nonsense," I replied.

"Oh, I'm sorry. You're a *Straits* Chinese, aren't you? Even worse! The whole lot of you think home is England—a place few of you have ever seen." Hamid rapped his chest with his fist. "We Malays, *we* are the true sons of the soil, the *bumiputera*." He looked around at us. "Not one of you here can be called that."

"Please-*lah*, Hamid," Emily said.

"Old countries are dying, Hamid," I said, keeping a grip on my anger, "and new ones are being born. It doesn't matter where one's ancestors came from. Can you say—with absolute certainty—that one of *your* forebears did not sail from Siam, from Java, or Aceh, or from the islands in the Sunda Straits?"

"What do you mean, that Malaya didn't exist until recently?" This was Peter Boyd, the assistant manager of a rubber estate; he had only arrived from London a few weeks before to take over from his predecessor who had been killed by the CTs.

"It's always been a convenient name for the ragtag collection of territories the British had obtained control of," I explained before Hamid could reply. "First there were the Federated Malay States, each one headed by a governor and situated on the west coast." It shocked me that such ignorance among the Europeans sent out to administer Malaya was still common; no wonder the Malays had had enough and wanted the *Mat Sallehs* out. "Then there were the Non-Federated Malay States," I continued, "ruled by their sultans with assistance from British advisers. And then there were the Straits Settlements—Malacca, Penang and Singapore."

"And all stolen from us Malays," Hamid said.

"Who were too lazy to have done anything with it," Emily said. "You know very well, Hamid, that we Chinese built up the tin industry. We established towns, and we brought in commerce. Kuala Lumpur was founded by a Chinese! Don't pretend you didn't know."

"Hah! We were far too clever to want to spend our days slaving for the *Mat Salleh* in the tin mines, unlike you *orang* China." Hamid leaned forward with his plate. "Eh, Emily, some more of your *belachan* please."

The discovery of tin in the Kinta Valley in the eighteenth century had compelled the British to ship indentured coolies from southern China to work the mines, as the Malays preferred to remain in their kampongs and till their own fields. The Chinese immigrants came with the intention of returning to their homeland after making their fortune. Many had stayed on, however, preferring the stability of life in a British colony to the wars and upheavals in China. They established families and fortunes in Penang, Ipoh and Kuala Lumpur, and opened the way for more of their countrymen from the southern ports of China. These immigrants soon became part of Malaya. I never wondered about it, just as I never thought it strange that I should also have been born beneath the monsoon skies of the equator, that with my first breath I would inhale the humid, heated air of the tropics and feel immediately and forever at home.

Magnus rubbed his one good eye with his knuckles. "I remember a couple of years ago I was sitting in my study, listening to the evening news," he said. "What I heard made me despair." He turned to Crawford and Toombs. "Your Mr. Attlee, giving official recognition to that fellow Mao's government in China, while the communists were killing hundreds of us in Malaya every month."

"Don't forget there's an election in a couple of weeks," Crawford said. "We might get Winston back." Magnus simply grimaced, looking singularly uninspired by the prospect.

"If you do," said Frederik, "he'll inherit Mao on this side of the world and Mau Mau in Africa."

"You're terrible-*lah*," said Emily, covering her laugh behind her hand.

"What Yun Ling mentioned just now, about old countries dying—well, she's right," Magnus said. "There isn't one that's older than China, and look at it now. A new name, and a new emperor."

"Emperor Mao?" said Frederik.

"In all but name."

"For goodness' sake," Emily said. "Let's talk about something else, can we not? Has anyone here read that new book by that Han Suyin? She came here for a visit last year, you know. Eh, Molly, is it true, they're going to make a film of it? With William Holden?"

Lunch was winding down when one of the servants came out from the house and whispered to Magnus. He got up from his seat and went in through the kitchen, the ridgebacks padding after him. He looked troubled when he returned to join us a few minutes later.

"That was one of my assistant managers on the telephone," he said, looking around at all of us. "CTs torched a squatter village in Tanah Rata an hour ago. Chopped the headman up with a *parang*. They forced his wife and daughters to watch. I'm not trying to get rid of you lot, but a six o'clock curfew's been put into place."

Enchik Hamid sprang to his feet, crumbs scattering from his lap. "*Alamak!* My wife is alone at home."

The others got up too, and I realized that the high commissioner's murder had frightened them more than they cared to admit. Magnus and Emily showed the guests out while I remained in the garden. I walked past the statues of the two sisters and stopped at the low stone balustrade, leaning over it. On the terrace below lay a formal garden where oak leaves were scattered on the lawn like pieces of an uncompleted jigsaw puzzle. A peacock chased its mate across the grass and their tail feathers raked over the leaves. To one side of the lawn was a rose garden, the bushes planted in a spiral pattern.

At first I thought the noise was coming from a lorry struggling up a steep road somewhere over the next ridge. It grew louder within seconds, exploding into a bone-penetrating rumble as an airplane flew over Majuba House, circling the tea fields.

"A Dakota," Frederik said, coming out from the house to join me.

The door near the plane's tail opened and a brown cloud spilled out from it, breaking into pieces an instant later. For a second I thought the aircraft was disintegrating, its body flaking away. "What's that?" I asked.

"Safe conduct passes and notices, urging the CTs to surrender," Frederik said. "Hell of a mess to clean up when the wind blows them over the tea, Magnus says. The coolies complain bitterly."

The Dakota banked around a hill, the noise of its passage gradually sputtering away. Sheets of paper eddied toward the house. I went to the far end of the lawn and plucked one from the air. I had heard about these notices issued by the Psychological Warfare Department, but I had never seen one till now. Printed on it was a pair of photographs, placed side by side. The first showed a bandit at the moment of his surrender, scrawny and malnourished and dressed in rags, his face all cheekbones and buckteeth. "*Comrades, my name is Chong Ka̱ Heng. I was once a member of the Fourth Johor Regiment,*" I read aloud. The other photograph was of the same man, grinning and well fed, looking like an office clerk in a smart white shirt and black pressed trousers, his arm around the waist of a plain but smiling young Chinese woman. "*The Government has treated me well since I surrendered. I urge you to think of your family, of your mother and father, who all miss you. Give up your struggle, and return to the people who miss you.*" The offers of amnesty and rewards were repeated in Malay, Chinese and Tamil. The paper was thin and light brown in color, as though it had been soaked overnight in the dregs of tea. "Odd choice of color to use," I said.

"It's deliberate. Makes it less conspicuous for a bandit to pick it up." Frederik cleared his throat. "Magnus lets me use one of the bungalows. It's on the other side of the estate." He added, after a pause, "Come and have a drink?"

"The curfew's on."

"We're already inside the estate."

"Not today, Frederik," I said, crumpling up the notice. "But thank you, for driving me back this morning."

Pain started up in my left hand when I returned to my bedroom, throbbing in time to my pulse. My fury at Aritomo, which had abated during the party, resurfaced. The nerve of the man, making me come all the way from KL only to turn down my offer so quickly and with hardly any serious thought given to it. Bloody Jap. Bloody, *bloody* Jap!

Opening the bedside drawer, I took out my notebook. It was heavy, thickened by the newspaper clippings I had pasted in it. I turned the pages without really looking at them; I knew their contents by heart. When I had worked as a research assistant in the war crimes trials, I had collected newspaper reports about the trials in Tokyo and other countries the Japanese had occupied. I knew intimately the offenses the Japanese officers were charged with, but I still read the clippings regularly, even though I had long ago accepted that there wasn't a name that I recognized or a familiar face in a photograph. There was never any mention of the camp where I had been imprisoned.

Inserted between the pages at the back of the notebook was a pale blue envelope, the address written in Japanese and English. It was light as a leaf when I held it up. The envelope marked the page where I had recorded the last conversation I had had with a convicted war criminal, a week before I left for Cambridge. I remembered the promise I had made to the man, the promise that I would post his letter for him.

Slowly, the pain in my hand subsided. But it would return. The servants' voices came faintly from somewhere in the house. One of the peacocks called to its mate. I slotted the envelope back between the pages, closed the notebook and went out to the terrace.

I stood there for a long time, looking toward Yugiri. I stood there until evening submerged the foothills of the valleys and Aritomo's garden sank away from sight.

Chapter Six

Following the high commissioner's murder, Magnus and Frederik went about supervising the workers as they repaired the fence protecting the house. They set up a pair of spotlights along the fence, facing them outward. Having heard from someone at the Tanah Rata Golf Club about an incident in Ipoh where CTs had lobbed a hand grenade into the dining room of a rubber estate manager's bungalow as his family was sitting down for lunch, Magnus decided to have the windows covered in a thin wire mesh.

"Emily said you haven't seen our clinic," Magnus said while I helped him nail a sheet of wire netting over my bedroom windows. The netting made the room gloomy, and I switched on the light. Two days had passed since Aritomo had turned me down, but I was still resentful about it. "Go take a look," Magnus went on. "Our nurse quit last year—said it was too dangerous to work here. Emily decided to run it herself. She trained as a nurse, you know, before she saw the light and married me."

I was reluctant to visit the clinic, but I knew I had to, if only to give Emily face. The whitewashed bungalow was a short walk from the workers' houses. A Tamil man slouching on a chair grinned at me when I entered the waiting room. Emily sat behind a low counter, her lips moving soundlessly as she counted out pills into a bottle. Through an open doorway I saw a room with two beds behind a partition. The bare legs of a woman were sticking out from one of the beds.

"That's Letchumi," Emily said, glancing at me.

"She's the one bitten by the snake?"

Emily tilted her head to one side. "Oh, yes, it was the night you arrived. She's doing fine now. Dr. Yeoh gave her an injection. Maniam, eh, Maniam! *Ambil ubat.*"

The coolie in the chair stood up and came to collect the bottle of pills from her. She made him repeat her dosage instructions in Malay before she let him leave. Turning back to me, she pointed at the boxes of medicines stacked in a corner. "These came in today. I ordered more, in case the CTs attack us." She shook her head. "Ironic isn't it, that Gurney was killed by them?"

"In what way?"

"That man sat on his *ka-chooi* for days after the CTs attacked that estate in Sungai Siput. He did nothing."

"He *did* declare a nationwide state of emergency."

"Only because the planters made him do it. Magnus got everyone here to sign a petition. You people living in the cities"—she hawked a derisive noise up her throat—"I don't think you even realize there's a war going on." There was some truth in her allegations. "One thing I'm happy about," she went on, "at least Magnus no longer wastes his Sundays running around in the mountains with his friends."

"What do they do, hunt wild boar?"

"Have you not heard the stories? They say that the Japs in Tanah Rata buried a pile of gold bars somewhere in these mountains before they surrendered."

"That's just a rumor, surely."

"They're like schoolboys-*lah*, looking for buried treasure. If you ask me, I think they just like being away from their wives." She opened a cupboard and began packing away boxes of sanitary napkins. Waving a box at me, she said, "I hope you don't think I'm a busybody, because I'm not. But I've always been curious—how did you cope, when you were a prisoner?"

"Many of us stopped menstruating."

"It happens. The terrible conditions, not enough food."

"Even after I was released, my blood didn't flow for two, three months. And then one day when I was in my office, it came back, just like that." It had caught me unprepared and I had had to ask my secretary for something. But I remembered the relief I had felt afterward. I could finally accept the fact that the war was truly over. My body was free to return to its own rhythms again.

The smell of disinfectants in the clinic raked up the beginnings of nausea in me; it must have been obvious because Emily looked concerned. "You want some Tiger Balm or not?" she asked.

"This place, the smells . . . they remind me of hospitals."

"*Sayang*," she said, shaking her head regretfully. "I was hoping you could help out here."

"I won't be staying here for long."

I left the clinic, glad to get out into the sun and fresh air again. Returning to Majuba House, I found a rolled-up bundle of papers on my dressing table: the maps and photographs I had left at Yugiri for Aritomo to look at.

The siren calling the workers to muster was sinking away when I left the house the next morning. I stood outside the garage, rubbing my hands. The world was gray and damp. The sound of steady crunching on the gravel came to me a minute later, and then Magnus emerged from the mist, the ridgebacks close behind. On the previous evening I had asked him to show me around the estate but he still looked surprised when he saw me. "I didn't think you'd be able to wake up this early," he said, opening the back door of the Land Rover for his dogs. I caught the glimpse of a revolver in a holster under his jacket.

"I don't need much sleep," I replied.

On the short, rattling drive to the factory, he gave me a quick explanation of how the estate was run. "Geoff Harper's my assistant manager," he said. "We have five European junior assistants watching over the *keranis* in the office."

"And out in the fields?"

"The estate's divided into thirty-five divisions. Each division's supervised by a *kangani*—the conductor. Below him are the *mandors*—the foremen. They're responsible for their work gang: the pickers, weeders, sweepers. Watchmen make sure there's no thieving or idling. And I've posted Home Guards to watch over them."

"There were some children outside the factory when I went past it yesterday."

"The workers' children," Magnus said. "We pay them twenty cents for every bag of caterpillars they catch in the tea bushes."

The factory was the size of a wharf-side godown. The coolies were already lined up outside. *Kretek* cigarettes cloyed the air with the scent of cloves. Magnus greeted them and a senior *kangani* called out their names, marking them off against a list on a clipboard. It reminded me of roll call in the camp.

Magnus consulted with the assistant manager Geoff Harper, a short, burly man in his fifties with a pair of rifles slung over his back. "All the workers showed up today?" Magnus asked.

Harper nodded. "Rubber price was low."

"Let's hope it stays that way."

"We had an ambush last night on the road going into Ringlet. A Chinese couple," Harper said. "The bastards—pardon me, miss, the CTs—left their bodies hacked into bits all over the road."

"Anyone we know?"

"They were visitors from Singapore. They were driving back from a wedding dinner."

The tea pickers marched off to the slopes. I trailed behind the workers entering the factory. "Grinders, rollers and roasters," Magnus said, pointing to the huge, silent machines lined up inside. The smell of roasting leaves dusted the air; I felt I had pried open a tea caddy. Workers wheeled out racks of tin trays covered with withered leaves curled up like insect larvae. The machines started up a second later, pounding the factory with their racket. Magnus beckoned me back outside.

We went onto a track between the tea bushes. The dogs trotted ahead, noses to the ground. "What has the price of rubber got to do with your workers?" I asked.

"Geoff checks it on the radio every evening. If it goes up, we know some of our workers will leave to work in the rubber plantations. Most of those who left before the Occupation have returned, but we're always shorthanded."

"You employed them again, after they deserted you?"

He turned to look at me, then resumed walking. "When the Japs came, I told my workers that they were free to leave. Their old jobs would be available to them once the war was over. I told them I'd keep my promise if I were still alive."

The ground steepened sharply, straining my calves. Tendrils of steam uncurled off the tops of the bushes. Glancing behind at me, Magnus shortened his stride, which only made me push myself harder to keep up. I was breathing hard when we reached the top of the rise. He stopped and pointed to the mountains.

They had broken out of the earth three hundred miles away to the north, near the border with Thailand, and they stretched all the way to Johor in the south, forming a vertebration that divided Malaya in two. In the tender light of morning, the mountains had the softness of a scene on a silk painting.

"This always reminds me of the week I spent in China, in Fujian province," Magnus said. "I visited Mount Li Wu. There was a temple there, a thousand years old—so the monks said. They grew their own tea, those monks. They told me that the original tea tree had been planted there by a god, can you believe it? The temple was famous for the flavor of its tea, a flavor not found anywhere else in the world."

"What sort of flavor?"

"To preserve the innocence of the tea," he said, "only the monks who hadn't reached puberty could pick the leaves. And for a month before they started picking, these boys were not allowed to eat chilies or pickled cabbage, no garlic or onions. They couldn't touch even a drop of soy sauce, otherwise their breath might have polluted the leaves. The boys picked the tea at sunrise, just about now. They wore gloves so their sweat wouldn't taint the flavor of the tea. Once picked and packed it was sent as tribute to the emperor."

"My father thought you were mad to go into tea planting."

"He wasn't the only one who thought so." Magnus laughed, plucking a leaf from a bush and rolling it between his fingers under his nose.

Voices and singing floated from the tea pickers in the valley. Most of them were women, their heads shaded beneath tattered straw hats. Large wicker baskets were strapped to their backs and secured by bands across their foreheads. They collected close to fifty pounds of leaves a day, returning to the factory to unload their baskets before heading back to the slopes, going through the same routine again and again until the day ended. Looking at them, it struck me how deceptive the advertisements were that I had grown up seeing pasted on the walls of musty provision stores next to the faded posters for Tiger Beer and Chesterfield cigarettes; they had depicted voluptuous tea pickers in clean and brightly colored saris, their teeth gloriously white, their noses and ears glittering with gold rings and studs, golden bangles weighing down their wrists.

The workers I was looking at in the valley below were paid badly for doing one of the most mindless, exhausting labors ever devised. From my rambles around the estate, I knew that Magnus was a decent enough employer, providing houses for his workers and basic schooling for their children, but I realized that much of the women's laughter and singing rising from the slopes was bitter with the harshness of their lives. These women would return every evening to their dirt-floored shacks, their eight or nine or ten children and their toddy-pickled husbands.

"A sergeant in the army told me that the day after Gurney was shot, security forces moved in and evicted everyone living in Tras," Magnus said.

"Where's that?"

"A squatter village close to where Gurney was killed."

"They must have thought the villagers had been helping the CTs."

"At least the soldiers didn't burn their homes to the ground." Magnus's gaze seemed to be resting on another horizon drawn across a different, older world. "When I was on commando, I often rode past farmhouses torched by the *rooinek* soldiers. Sometimes the ruins still smoldered and smoke often plunged the whole veldt into a macabre twilight for days. There were dead sheep everywhere, thick with flies—the Khakis had tied them to horses and pulled them apart. Wherever we rode, the air always seemed to be vibrating with a low, constant humming. Flies made that sound." He stroked his chest in a distracted manner. "We were filled with such fury, such hatred for the English . . . it only made us more determined to fight them to the bitter end." His arm swept across the tea fields. "The first batch of seedlings came from the same estate in Ceylon where I had once worked as a prisoner of war. History is filled with ironies, don't you think?"

Clouds streamed past the mountain peaks, spirits fleeing the rising sun. I imagined I could feel a stirring deep beneath the earth as it sensed the approaching light.

"I'm going home tomorrow." I kicked a pebble and sent it skittering over the ledge. "Will you drive me to Tapah? I'll catch a train from there."

He glanced at me. "What will you do? Go back to your old job?"

"After the things I said about the government?"

"There are other gardeners you can get to design your garden, surely."

"Not in Malaya. There's nobody of Aritomo's reputation. And I don't want to go to Japan," I said. "I can't. I don't think I ever can." The gardener's refusal had felled a log over my path and I had no idea what to do. "Speak to him for me, Magnus. Ask him to reconsider," I said. "I've got money set aside. I'll pay him well."

"I've known him for ten years, Yun Ling. Once he's made up his mind, he never changes it."

On a ridge not far from us, a pair of storks, their wings edged with a singe of gray, sprang off from the treetops and flew over a hill, heading for valleys hidden from our sight. It was so quiet I could almost hear every downward sweep of their wings, fanning the thin mists into tidal patterns.

Magnus had more divisions to inspect before breakfast, and I told him I would return to Majuba House on my own. I was walking on a footpath between the tea fields and the margin of the jungle when I stopped abruptly. My eyes searched the columns of trees, but I did not know what I was looking for. Turning back to the path, I gave a start. Less than ten feet away, a figure was standing in the shadows. It started to move toward me. I took a step back, but it kept on coming. It entered a patch of sunlight, and I let out a breath of relief. It was a girl, about nine or ten years old, her face and clothes smeared with mud. She was an aboriginal, and she was crying.

"*Kakak saya,*" she said, her words shuddering out between her sobs. "*Tolong mereka.*"

"*Mana?*" I asked, kneeling to look into her face. I shook her shoulders gently. "Where?"

She pointed to the trees behind her. I felt the jungle press in closer. "We'll call the police," I said, still speaking Malay. "The *mata-mata* will help your sister."

I stood up and began walking back to the house, but the girl grabbed my hand and pulled me, trying to drag me to the trees. I resisted, suspecting a CT ambush. I shaded my eyes and squinted at the slopes, but the tea pickers had not yet reached this section of the estate and there was no sign of any Home Guard. Crying more loudly, the girl yanked at my arm again. I followed her but froze when we came to the jungle fringe.

For the first time since the war ended, I was about to reenter the rain forest. I feared that if I went in I would never come out again. Before I could turn around, the girl tightened her grip on my hand and pulled me into the ferns.

Insects ground out metallic clicking sounds. The cicadas wove a mesh of noise over everything. Birdcalls hammered sharp, shiny nails into the air. It was like walking into a busy ironmonger's workshop in the back alleys of Georgetown. Sunlight sifted down through the lattices of branches and leaves overhead, unable to sink far enough to dispel the soggy gloom at ground level. Vines hung from the branches in broad, sagging nooses. The girl took us along a narrow animal track, the stones greased with moss that threatened to send me sprawling at the slightest lapse in concentration. For fifteen, twenty minutes I followed her beneath tree ferns that spread their fronds over us, watering the light into a translucent green.

We emerged into a small clearing. The girl stopped and pointed to a bamboo shack beneath the trees, the roof covered in a balding thatch of *nipah* fronds. The door was half-open, but it was dark inside. We moved closer to the hut, making as little noise as possible. In the trees behind us, branches cracked and then something heavy dropped to the ground. I spun around on my heel and looked back. The trees were still. Perhaps it was only a ripened durian, its armor of thorns shredding the leaves as it fell. I became aware of another sound running beneath the noise of the jungle, a vibration pitched so low it was almost soothing. It was coming from inside the hut.

The door refused to move when I nudged it with my foot. I tried again, pushing harder this time. It swung open all the way. On the beaten-earth floor, three bodies lay in a moat of blood so dark and thick they seemed to be glued to it. Hundreds of flies crawled over their faces, distended bellies and loincloths. Their throats had been slit. The girl screamed and I clamped my palm over her mouth. She struggled, swinging her arms madly, but I held on to her tightly. The flies rose from the bodies and swarmed to the underside of the thatch roof, blackening it like an infestation of mold.

The smell of food assailed me as we approached the kitchen. Frederic and Emily were seated at the table. They stopped talking and looked up when I entered, the girl peering from behind me. Emily made us sit at the kitchen table, where a planter's breakfast had been laid out—plates of crispy bacon, sausages and eggs, fried bread and strawberry jam. Frederik poured us tea, sweetening it heavily with condensed milk. I drank a few mouthfuls. The heat spread through my body and stilled my shivering. I told them quickly what had happened.

"Where's Magnus?" Emily's eyes gouged into mine.

"Still out in the fields, I think. I don't know."

"Get Geoff!" she snapped at Frederik. "Tell him to find your uncle. And ring the police. And Toombs. Go!"

A maid brought out two blankets and Emily draped one over the girl's shoulders, giving the other one to me. Frederik returned with Magnus a short while later, the dogs pushing past them to sniff at the girl's legs. She screamed and shrank into her chair. Emily shouted at the dogs and they slunk off to a corner.

"Damn it, Yun Ling," Magnus said, "you should have come home straightaway!"

The girl started crying again. "Don't shout-*lah*, you're scaring the poor thing," Emily said, frowning at Magnus.

"She wanted me to follow her," I said.

"Going into the jungle was *blerrie* stupid," he said. "*Blerrie* stupid! Your father would cut off my balls if anything had happened to you."

"Nothing happened to me."

Glaring at me, he pulled out a chair and dropped into it heavily.

When Toombs arrived the girl climbed down from her seat and clung to his leg. The Protector of Aborigines got down on one knee and questioned her gently, his Malay much more fluent than mine. After a while he took her hand and brought her back to the table, telling her to finish her cup of tea. She drank a sip, then another, her eyes never leaving Toombs.

"She wouldn't tell us her name," Emily said.

"It's Rohana," Toombs said. He turned to me. "Those bodies you saw—they were her sister, brother and cousin."

"What were they doing in the shack?" I asked.

"Not a shack, really. A hide. They were waiting for wild boars to come out at night. They left their village to go hunting two days

73

ago. They took Rohana with them. She was playing not far from the hide yesterday evening when she heard shouting. She hid in the trees."

"She saw what happened?" Magnus asked.

"Four CTs, two of them women," Toombs replied, glancing at the girl. Her eyes, large and dark, stared at him over her cup. "They forced her siblings and cousin into the hide. She heard them shouting a moment later. Then screams. When the CTs came out again, they were carrying the boar her brother had shot. One of them saw her and they gave chase. Rohana ran into the jungle. She spent all night hiding."

The police arrived an hour later, led by Sub-Inspector Lee Chun Ming. Rohana and I were questioned separately, Toombs sitting in with the girl when it came to her turn. Sub-Inspector Lee asked me to show the police the hide where we had found the bodies. We went in two cars, driving as near as we could to the spot where I had found the girl, before continuing on foot into the jungle.

Later, on our way back to Majuba House, we passed groups of tea pickers squatting by the roadside, smoking *kretek* cigarettes and talking among themselves, their baskets by their feet. Their eyes followed us as we drove past. News of the killings had already spread swiftly through the estate.

It was evening when Sub-Inspector Lee and his men finished questioning the estate workers. I went to my room and packed my bag. When I had finished I lay down on my bed to rest, but my mind refused to settle. I went out to the terrace. A corner of the backyard was visible from where I stood. Emily emerged from the kitchen a moment later, three joss sticks pressed between her palms. Standing in front of the red metal altar of the God of Heaven hanging on a wall, she lifted her face to the sky, raised her hands to her forehead and closed her eyes, her lips moving soundlessly. When she finished praying, she stood on her toes and inserted the joss sticks into the incense holder between the two oranges and the three little cups of tea. Strands of smoke from the joss sticks climbed up to the sky. The smell of the sandalwood incense drifted to me, lulling me into a brief moment of peace before it too dispersed with the smoke. I realized then what I had to do before I returned to Kuala Lumpur.

"*Eh*, where are you going?" Emily complained when she saw me walking out past the kitchen. "We're eating dinner soon. I'm cooking *char-siew* tonight."

"I won't be long."

Once again I followed Ah Cheong through the house, and just like before, he did not speak a word to me. We passed the room where I had sat with Aritomo on the morning we had first met, nearly a week before. The housekeeper did not stop but led me along a walkway that ran beside a small courtyard with a rock garden. He paused outside a room with a half-open sliding door and knocked softly on the door frame. Aritomo was behind his desk, arranging a pile of documents in a wooden box. He looked up at me, surprised. "Come inside," he said.

Despite the bite in the air, the windows were open. In the distance, the mountains were receding into dusk. I looked around the room, searching for what I wanted. A bronze Buddha about a foot long reclined on the windowsill, the curve of his arm resting on his hip, gentle as the line of the mountains behind him. A black and white photograph of Emperor Hirohito in a military uniform hung on a wall; I looked away. The far end of the room was segmented by bookshelves lined with volumes of Malayan history and memoirs written by Stamford Raffles, Hugh Clifford, Frank A. Swettenham. A pair of bronze Chinese archers, about nine inches high, posed on the desk, pulling at bows that had no strings or arrows. A bamboo birdcage hung on the end of a thin rope from the ceiling, empty except for a stub of half-melted candle. The gardener appeared to be a collector of antique maps; there were framed charts of the Malay Archipelago and Southeast Asia, hand-drawn in detail by eighteenth-century Dutch, Portuguese and English explorers.

Hanging at the far end of the room was a painting of a mansion built in the Anglo-Indian style so popular in Penang. A broad verandah ran around three sides of the house, buckled into place by a portico in front. Stamped into the pediment in the center of the roof: ATHELSTANE, and below it 1899. Behind the house, the green waters of the channel separated Penang from the mainland. I remembered how proud my sister had been when she had finished the painting.

Aritomo scraped back his chair and came to stand beside me. I continued to stare at the painting. "The police questioned me about the Semai," he said. "It must have been a terrible shock for you, discovering them like that."

"It's not the first time I've seen dead bodies." I studied his reflection in the glass. "The smell . . . I thought I had forgotten the smell. But one never does."

He reached out a hand to adjust the tilt of the frame. "Your home?"

"My grandfather built it."

The house had stood at the eastern end of Northam Road, a long stretch shaded by angsana trees and lined with the mansions of high-ranking colonial officials and wealthy Chinese. "Old Mr. Ong was our neighbor," I said, no longer seeing the house in the painting but in my memory. "He had started out as a bicycle repairman before becoming one of the wealthiest men in Asia. And it all happened because he fell in love with a girl." I smiled, remembering what my mother had once told Yun Hong and me. "Old Mr. Ong wanted to marry the girl, but her father refused to allow it. His was an old, wealthy family, and he looked down on the illiterate bicycle repairman. He told him to leave his home and never bother them again."

Aritomo crossed his arms over his chest. "Did he?"

"It took only four years for Ong to become a very rich man. He built his house directly across the road from the girl's family home. It was the biggest house on Northam Road. And the ugliest as well, my mother always said." I looked at myself in the glass. My eyes were shadowed, sunken into my face. "Ong didn't let anyone know he owned it. The afternoon after he moved in, he had his chauffeur drive him across the road in his silver Daimler. He spoke to the girl's father again and asked for her hand in marriage once more. Her father, naturally, gave his permission. The wedding took place a month later. It was the most lavish the island had ever witnessed, so the old people used to say."

"One of the things I like about Malaya," Aritomo said, "it is full of stories like this."

"I often saw Old Mr. Ong in his garden, dressed like a coolie in a tatty white vest and loose blue cotton shorts, carrying his songbird in a cage. He always spoke to the bird with more tenderness than I had ever seen him show any of his wives."

Aritomo pointed to the pediment. "Athelstane. That was Swettenham's middle name."

I glanced at him in surprise, then remembered the first resident general's books on his shelf. "That's what my grandfather called it. A silly, pretentious name for a house," I said. "I'm sure the neighbors laughed at my grandfather, and us."

"I will look for it, next time I am in Penang."

"It was destroyed when Jap planes bombed the island." Aritomo's face showed no reaction. "We had moved out only a few days earlier. We left everything behind—all our photographs. All of Yun Hong's paintings too."

It unsettled me that I should see one of her paintings here; I felt she was still alive, about to appear at the door of my bedroom to tell me some gossip she had heard from her friends. I reached out my hand and touched the painting. The smudge of condensation I made on the glass disappeared a second later, as though it had found a way to enter the watercolor painting.

"I want to buy this from you."

Aritomo shook his head. "It was a gift."

"This painting means nothing to you." I turned to face him. "I'm asking you to sell it to me. You owe that to me, at the very least."

"Why? Because of what my country did to you?"

"Sell it to me."

He smoothed the air with his hands. "I have being thinking over your offer since your visit."

I tensed up, wondering what he was about to tell me. "You'll design and build my garden?"

He shook his head. "You can learn to do it yourself."

It took me a moment or two to grasp the nature of his proposal. "You're asking me to be . . . *apprenticed* . . . to you?" It was not what I had wanted from him at all. "That's ridiculous."

"I will teach you the skills to build your own garden," he said. "A simple, basic garden."

"A halfhearted Japanese garden isn't good enough for Yun Hong."

"That is all I can give you," he said. "I do not have the time—

or the desire—to create a garden for you. Or for anyone else. The last commission I undertook taught me never to accept another."

"Why would you want to do this? Why did you change your mind?"

"I need someone to help me."

The idea of being his apprentice, at his beck and call, did not appeal to me in the slightest. When I was recovering in the hospital after my imprisonment, I had vowed to myself that no one would ever control my life again.

"For how long will you teach me?" I asked.

"Until the monsoon."

The rainy season, I calculated, would return in six or seven months' time. I walked slowly around the room considering his proposal. I was unemployed, but I had saved enough money not to have to work for a while. And I had the time. Aritomo's offer was the only way I could give my sister a Japanese garden. It was only for six months, I told myself. I had endured worse. I stopped moving and looked at him. "Until the monsoon."

"Taking on an apprentice, especially a woman, is not a small matter." He raised a warning finger. "The obligations imposed on me are heavy."

"I'm aware that it won't be a weekend hobby."

Frowning, he went to a shelf and pulled out a book. "This will help you understand what I am doing."

The thin volume was bound in a gray cloth cover, its title printed in English beneath a line of Japanese calligraphy. "*Sakuteiki,*" I said.

"The oldest collection of writings on Japanese gardening. The original scrolls were written in the eleventh century."

"But garden designers didn't exist at that time," I said. Aritomo's eyebrows lifted. "Yun Hong told me," I added. "One of her gardening books mentioned it, I remember."

"She was right. Tachibana Toshitsuna, the man who compiled *Sakuteiki,* was a member of the court nobility. He was said to be highly skilled with trees and plants."

"My Japanese isn't good enough to read it."

"That copy in your hands is a version I translated into English and published years ago. It is yours. Now, to your lessons," he said, cutting me short as I started to thank him. "In your first month, you

will be working at the various sites of the garden still under reno-
vation. We will start at half past seven. The work will end at half
past four, five, even later if we have to. You will have an hour's rest
for lunch at one o'clock. We work Mondays to Fridays. You will
come in on weekends if I ask you to."

I had known that it would not be easy to convince him to design
and create a garden for me. But now I realized that the hardest part
was about to begin. All of a sudden I felt unsure of myself and of
what I had agreed to.

"The girl who had once walked in the gardens of Kyoto with her
sister," Aritomo said, peering into my eyes as though searching for
a pebble he had dropped into the bottom of a pond, "that girl, is
she still there?"

It was some time before I could speak. Even then my voice
sounded small and dry to me. "So much has happened to her."

His gaze did not shift away from my eyes. "She is there," he said,
answering his own question. "Deep inside, she is still there."

CHAPTER SEVEN

Sunrise was still an hour away, but I could feel it coming as I lay in my bed, feel the light curving around the earth. In the internment camp I had dreaded its arrival; it meant another day of unpredictable cruelties. As a prisoner, I had been afraid to open my eyes in the morning; now, when I was no longer in the camp, now when I was free, I was frightened of closing my eyes when I went to sleep at night, fearful of the dreams that were waiting for me.

Reading Aritomo's translation of *Sakuteiki* through the night, I remembered some of the fundamentals of Japanese gardening that Yun Hong had told me. Aritomo's commentary on the origins of gardening in Japan made me realize that my knowledge of it was only the thin rakings of the topsoil.

The practice of designing gardens had originated in the temples of China, where the work was done by monks. Gardens were created to approximate the idea of a paradise in the afterlife. Mount Sumeru, the center of the Buddhist universe, was referred to more than once in *Sakuteiki* and I began to appreciate why so many of the gardens I had seen in Japan had a distinctive rock formation as their central feature. Mountains loomed large in the geographical and emotional landscapes of Japan, and over the centuries, their presence had permeated into its poetry, folklore and literature.

Perhaps that was the reason Aritomo had come to the mountains here, I thought. Perhaps it was why he had made his home among the clouds.

The earliest reference to designing gardens in Japan had been recorded in the Heian period, about a thousand years ago, which had emphasized *mono no aware*, the sensitivity to the sublime, and was marked by an obsession with all aspects of Chinese culture. The gardens created in this period, none of which still existed, had been designed to replicate the extensive pleasure gardens of the Chinese aristocrats living across the Sea of Japan. They had been built around lakes to facilitate boating activities, literary parties and poetry competitions, occasions when songs were sung and words were floated on water.

In time, the influence of China was eroded by the aesthetics of the subsequent Muromachi, Momoyama and Edo eras, when Japanese gardeners established their own principles of composition and construction. The designs of gardens in Japan were no longer influenced by the fashions of the antique continent across the sea, but by the landscapes of Japan's own countryside. The growth of Zen Buddhism steered the move toward a stricter asceticism, the excesses of the previous eras raked away as monks reflected on their faith by creating less cluttered gardens, paring down their designs almost to the point of emptiness.

I put the book down and closed my eyes. Emptiness: it appealed to me, the possibility of ridding myself of everything I had seen and heard and lived through.

Earlier that evening before going to bed, I had informed Magnus that I would not be leaving Cameron Highlands. He was delighted, but his lips pressed together when I told him that I was looking to lease a bungalow in the area. "You can't live alone," he said.

"It's not safe, Yun Ling," Emily said from her armchair on the other side of the living room, looking up from the novel she was reading.

"The hills are crawling with CTs," Magnus said, his voice rising. "Look what they did to those young Semai!"

"I lived on my own in KL," I said. As a prisoner, I had been surrounded by hundreds of people; now, I protected my privacy. "And anyway," I pointed out, "Frederik has his own bungalow."

"He's a *man*, Yun Ling, and a soldier," Magnus said. "And he's living inside the estate. Look, I've already told you—you're welcome to stay with us for as long as you like."

"It's not fair to impose on you."

He glanced at Emily before turning to me again. His chest rose and fell as he took in a long breath and let it out. "We've got a few vacant bungalows in the estate. My assistant managers used to stay there. I'll speak to Harper, see which bungalow's suitable for you."

"I'm not fussy, but it has to be near to Yugiri. And I insist on paying you rent."

"In return," Emily said, "you must have dinner with us—once a week, at the very least. I don't want you to hide yourself away."

"She's right," Magnus said. "And another thing: I'll get a worker to escort you to Yugiri every morning. And he'll walk you home when you've finished in the evening."

"Pour me a glass of wine and we'll drink to that." I was glad of his offer of the guard. I *had* been worried about having to walk to Yugiri in the half-light of dawn.

While he uncorked a bottle of wine, I went around the living room, admiring the fever trees in the Pierneef lithographs. At the end of the row was a woodblock print of a leaf. Peering at it, I discovered Majuba House concealed in the lines of the leaf.

"That's Aritomo's," Magnus said.

Next to it was a box frame with a medal inside, the colors of its ribbon almost similar to those of the flag flying on the roof. "What does '*Oorlog*' mean?" I said, reading from the medal.

He corrected my pronunciation and said, "It means 'war.'"

I pointed to a sepia photograph of an old man wearing a top hat, his cheeks lathered in a thick white beard. "Your father?" I said.

Magnus handed me a glass of wine. "Him? *Ag, nee*, that's Paul Kruger, the president of the Transvaal Republic during the Second Boer War," he said. "Haven't you heard of the Kruger millions? No? Well, when the English occupied Pretoria they discovered that two million pounds' worth of gold and silver were missing from the Transvaal mint. A lot of money fifty years ago—think what it would be worth now!"

"Who had taken it?"

"There are people who believe that Oom Paul buried the gold and silver somewhere in the Lowveld, in the last days of the war."

"Like what the Japs are said to have done?"

He laughed, glancing at Emily. "Lao Puo, you've been complaining to this young lady about my weekend fun? Well, what the Japs in Tanah Rata buried is probably peanuts, compared to the Kruger millions."

"They can't be worth more than Yamashita's gold," I said. "Have you heard of it?"

"Who hasn't?"

"Strange, isn't it, there are always stories like this, whenever there's been a war," I said. "Has anyone found the gold Kruger buried?"

"They've been searching for fifty years," Magnus said, "but no one ever has." At the low rumble of thunder he glanced up to the ceiling.

There was another photograph further along the wall. "That's my brother, Piet—Frederik's pa. Taken shortly before he died," Magnus said, coming to stand beside me. "I asked Frederik to bring it with him when he came here. It's the only photograph I have of any of my family."

"Frederik looks a lot like his father."

Emily put down her novel to look at Magnus.

"We lost everything—my *oupa*'s diaries, my *ouma*'s recipe books, my stinkwood animal carvings," Magnus said. "Photographs of my parents and my sister. Everything."

"Do you still . . ." I stalled, then tried again. "Can you remember their faces?"

He looked at me for a long moment. In his eye I knew he understood my own fears. "I couldn't for a long time," he said. "But in the last few years . . . well, they've come back to me again. As you get older, you start remembering the old things."

"It's going to rain," Emily said.

She stood up and held out her hand to Magnus and together they went out to the verandah that looked onto the back garden. A gust of wind, moistened with rain from over the mountains, swirled into the sitting room, lifting the curtains. After a moment's hesitation I went out as well, standing apart from them.

"*Nou lê die aarde nagtelang en week in die donker stil genade van die reën*," Magnus said softly, putting his arm around Emily's waist and pulling her to him.

For some reason the sounds of those words shifted something in me. "What does it mean?" I asked.

"'Now lies the earth night-long and washed in the dark silent grace of the rain,'" Emily said. "It's from his favorite poem." She turned away from me and leaned closer against Magnus.

Lightning convulsed over the mountains. The rain rushed in a minute later, blurring the night.

Just before six o'clock I switched on the bedside lamp and got dressed in an old yellow blouse and a pair of shorts that came to my knees. I pulled on a pair of old cotton gloves I had obtained from Emily. The servants were lighting the stoves in the kitchen when I went in. I ate two slices of bread and drank a cup of milk. I heard Magnus coughing and clearing his throat in his bathroom as I opened the front door and left Majuba House. The estate's siren started up but was soon filtered by the distance and the trees.

Daylight was nibbling the margins of the sky when I arrived at Yugiri. I was a few minutes early so I went around to the back. Ah Cheong was leaning his bicycle against a wall. He nodded when I greeted him. Aritomo was at the archery range. I stood at the side and watched him. He finished his practice and told me to wait at the front of the house. When he came out again he had changed into a blue shirt and a pair of khaki trousers. He pointed to my writing pad. "I do not want you to make notes," he said, "not even when you go home at the end of the day."

"But I won't be able to remember everything."

"The garden will remember it for you."

I left the writing pad in the house and followed him into the garden, paying close attention as he listed out the work for the day.

The earliest gardeners in Japan had been monks, re-creating the dream of heaven on earth in the monastery grounds. From the introduction to *Sakuteiki*, I knew that Aritomo's family had been *niwashi*, gardeners, to the rulers of Japan since the sixteenth century, each eldest son carrying on from where his father had left off. There was a legend that the first Nakamura had been a Chinese monk in the Sung dynasty who had been banished from China. The monk had crossed the ocean to Japan, hoping to spread the teachings of the Buddha. But instead he had fallen in love with the daughter of a court official and had abandoned his vows, remaining in Japan for the rest of his life. Looking at Aritomo from the corner of my eye, I could almost believe that tale. There were aspects of a monk in his bearing, in the calm but single-minded focus of his approach, and in the slow and considered way he spoke.

"Pay attention." Aritomo snapped his fingers in my face. "What kind of garden am I making here?"

Thinking back to the parts of the garden I had seen, the winding walks and the different views, I made a swift guess. "A strolling garden. No, wait—a combination of a strolling and a viewing garden."

"From which era?"

This completely stumped me. "I can't pick out a particular one," I admitted. "It's not Muromachi; it's not entirely Momoyama or Edo."

"Quite so. When I designed Yugiri, I wanted to combine elements from the different periods."

I skirted a puddle of rainwater. "It must have made it more difficult to achieve an overall harmony in your garden."

"Not all my ideas were workable. It is one of the reasons why I am making these changes."

Walking in the garden I had heard about almost half a lifetime ago, I wished Yun Hong were here with me. She would have enjoyed it more than I. I wondered what I was doing here, living the life that should have been my sister's.

At each turn in the path, Aritomo drew my attention to an arrangement of rocks, an unusual sculpture, or a stone lantern. They looked as if they had been lying there on the beds of moss and ferns for centuries. "These objects signal to the traveler that he is entering another layer of his journey," he said. "They tell him to stop and gather his thoughts, to savor the view."

"Has any woman ever been taught to be a gardener?"

"None. That does not mean it is not permitted," he replied. "But physical strength is required to create a garden. A woman would not be able to last long as a gardener."

"What do you think the guards made us do?" I said in a burst of anger. "They forced us to dig tunnels, the men *and* women. The men broke rocks and we dumped them in a gorge miles away." I took in a deep breath and blew it out slowly. "Yun Hong told me once that what's required in creating a garden is mental, not physical, strength."

"You obviously have both in abundance," he said.

The anger roiled up in me again, but before I could reply the sound of voices and laughter came to us. "The workers are here," Aritomo said. "Late, as usual."

The men were barefoot, dressed in patched singlets and shorts, towels slung over their shoulders. Aritomo introduced them to me. Kannadasan, the one who could speak some English, was the leader. The other four knew only Tamil and Malay. White teeth flashed against dark skin when they heard that I would be joining them.

We followed Aritomo to the area behind the tool shed. Stones had been set down here, their dimensions varying from the size of coconuts to slabs that came up to my shoulders. "I found them around the caves near Ipoh during the Occupation," Aritomo said.

"You were already planning to make changes to the garden then?" I asked.

"I had to have a good reason to keep the workers here," he said. "So I traveled around, searching for materials I could use."

"Then you would have seen and heard what the Kempeitai were doing to people."

He looked at me, then turned and walked away, wedging a painful silence into the space between us. Sensing the palpable tension in the air, the workers averted their eyes from me. Looking at Aritomo's retreating figure, I realized that, however difficult it was for me, I had to put aside my prejudices if I wanted to learn from him.

I broke into a trot and caught up with him. "These rocks you found—all have unusual markings," I said.

For a long moment he did not reply. Finally, he said, "Garden designing is known as the Art of Setting Stones, which tells you how important they are."

I was filled with relief, although I did not let him see it. We walked back to the rocks and he examined them, rubbing them with his hands. The larger ones were five to six feet high, narrow and sharp-edged, their surfaces covered in striations. Weeds crawled up their sides, as if trying to pull them back into the cool, damp earth.

"Every stone has its own personality, its own needs." He selected five of them, touching them one after another. "Move these to the front."

My breathing constricted. His orders brought me back to the time when I had been a slave for the Japanese army. My resolve started fraying, even as I sensed his curious gaze on me. I looked around and remembered how, in the camp, I had forced myself to take the first steps in saving my life. That journey had not ended, I realized.

"And take off your gloves," Aritomo added.

"They're washable. I'll get a few more pairs."

"What kind of gardener will you be, if you do not feel the soil with your bare hands?"

We stared at each other for what felt like an endless moment. I held his gaze even as I pulled off my gloves and stuffed them into my pockets. His eyes dropped to my left hand. He did not flinch, but the workers muttered among themselves.

"What are you all waiting for? The grass to grow?" Aritomo clapped his hands. "Get to work!"

Two men lifted the first rock a few inches off the ground while Aritomo slid a jute-rope harness beneath it. The harness was connected to a windlass hanging from an eight-foot-high wooden tripod. Lashed together at the top with coils of rope, each of the tripod's legs could be adjusted to fit the contours of the terrain. Kannadasan cranked the windlass and the rock lifted heavily off the ground, a mountain shedding the moorings of gravity. When it was about three feet in the air Aritomo stopped him and handed me a brush with stiff bamboo bristles. I reached between the gaps of the harness and scraped the clumps of soil, roots and grubs from the rock. When I finished we trussed it with ropes, tying it to the center of a heavy pole. I lifted the front end of the pole onto my shoulder, but the weight crumpled me onto one knee. The workers scrambled around to help me, but I waved them away. Behind me I heard Kannadasan say, "Missee, too heavy for you-*lah*."

Aritomo stood to one side, watching me. I felt a stab of hatred for him. It's different now, I told myself as sweat rolled down the center of my back. I'm no longer a prisoner of the Japs, I'm free, free. And I'm alive.

The nausea subsided but left a sour coating at the back of my throat. I licked my lips and swallowed once, twice. "Wait, Kannadasan, *tunggu sekejap*." I adjusted the ropes and signaled to him.

"*Satu, dua, tiga!*" On the count of three we lifted the pole onto our shoulders again. The men whooped and shouted encouragement as, like a wounded animal, I staggered to my feet, fighting back the pain digging into my shoulder.

"*Jalan!*" I shouted, leading the way.

The morning was spent cleaning the rocks and carrying them to the area by the front verandah. When the last rock was set down, Kannadasan and the workers squatted on the grass and passed around a packet of cigarettes, drying their faces with their towels. I followed Aritomo into his house, into the sitting room. The paper-screen doors were closed, and I discovered there was a set of sliding glass doors behind them. Aritomo indicated a spot where he told me to sit. I pointed to my dirt-stained clothes. "I'm filthy."

"Sit down." Waiting until I complied, he pulled back first the glass doors and then the paper screens, opening up the garden. Above the trees, the line of the mountains serrated the sky.

Aritomo knelt next to me and directed Kannadasan and the other workers with his hands, indicating where he wanted the first stone placed. Once he was satisfied with its position, the men pestled it into the ground. He went through the same process with the remaining four stones, fixing each of them a slight distance away from the previous one, adjusting the harmonics of a music only he could hear.

"They look like a row of courtiers bowing and backing away from the emperor," I said.

He grunted in approval. "We are composing a picture within this frame." He pointed to the lines of the roof, the posts and the floor, his finger drawing a rectangle in the air. "When you look at the garden, you are looking at a work of art."

"But the composition isn't balanced," I pointed out. "The gap between the first and the second stones is too wide, and the last stone is set too close to the third one." I studied the scenery again. "They look like they're about to topple into the emptiness."

"Yet there is a dynamic feel to the arrangement, do you not agree?" he said. "Look at our paintings—they have large tracts of emptiness, their composition is asymmetrical . . . they have a sense of uncertainty, of tension and possibility. That is what I want here."

"How will I know where to place the stones?"

"What is the first piece of advice given in *Sakuteiki*?"

I thought for a second. "*Obey the request of the stone.*"

"The opening words of the book," he said, nodding. "This spot where you sit, this is the starting point. This is where the guest views the garden. Everything planted and created in Yugiri has its distance, scale and space calculated in relation to what you see from here. This is the place where the first pebble breaks the surface of the water. Place the first stone properly and the others will follow its request. The effect expands through the whole garden. If you follow the stones' wishes, they will be happy."

"You make it sound as though they have souls."

"Of course they do," he said.

We stepped down from the verandah and joined the workers. "Only a third of each stone should be seen above the ground," he said, handing me a spade. "So dig deep."

He left us to our work. The handle of the spade blistered my bare palms. The ground was not hard, but I was perspiring within minutes. It had been years since I last did any form of strenuous physical work and I had to stop and rest often. Aritomo returned two hours later when we had buried all five rocks up to the level he wanted. He knelt down and packed the soil tightly around the base of the rocks, telling me to do the same.

I dug my fingers into the loosened ground; the soil felt cool and moist on my skin, soothing the pain in my left hand. Such a simple, basic act, to touch the earth we walked on with our bare hands, but I could not remember the last time I had done it.

By evening, my body was stiff and aching. Before going home, I went past the section where we had planted the rocks earlier that day. Gunnysacks of gravel stood on one side, ready to be spread over the area. I touched the rounded peak of one of the rocks, giving it a push. It was solid, unmovable, as though it was a protrusion from the bedrock rising up from leagues beneath us and not something we had set there just that morning.

Aritomo came out from the house, a big chocolate Burmese cat padding behind him. He saw me looking at it.

"This is Kerneels," he announced. "Magnus gave him to me."

For a few moments we watched the shadows of the rocks pull

across the ground. "Where are the plans and drawings for the garden?" I asked. "I'd like to look at them."

He turned to me, touching the side of his head lightly. At that moment it struck me that he was similar to the boulders on which we had spent the entire morning working. Only a small portion was revealed to the world; the rest was buried deep within, hidden from view.

CHAPTER EIGHT

The bungalow I had leased from Magnus was ready for me to move into at the end of the first week of my apprenticeship with Aritomo. Frederik, who had been coming to Majuba House every evening, offered to help me move my things when we were having dinner on the Friday.

"Tomorrow morning suit you?" he said. "Say around nine?"

"Better say yes," Magnus said from the other side of the dining table. "The young man is leaving us soon."

"Nine o'clock is fine," I said. My body was sore from working in Yugiri all week long, and I welcomed the thought of having some-one to help me.

Before going to bed that night, I spent a few minutes by the ter-race balustrade, between the shadows cast by the marble statues. The imminent rain in the air smelled crisp and metallic, as though it had been seared by the lightning buried in the clouds. The scent reminded me of my time in the camp, when my mind had latched on to the smallest, most inconsequential thing to distract myself: a butterfly wafting from a patch of scrub; a spiderweb tethered to twigs by strands of silk, sieving the wind for insects.

The opening strains of "Und ob die wolke" stretched languidly out from the sitting room's open windows. Magnus was playing his Cecilia Wessels records again. Down in the valley, a bead of light appeared in the trees around Yugiri. I stared at it, wondering what Aritomo was doing in his house.

The aria ended. I waited, knowing what would follow. Tentative music from a piano started up a moment later, assembling into the shape of a Chopin nocturne. It was Magnus's habit to play the Bech-stein every night before he put out the lights. The first nocturne gave way to another, and soon I heard the opening sighs of the larghetto from Chopin's first piano concerto. Magnus had had it transcribed for a solo piano. He always played it as his last piece for the night. It was Emily's favorite, he had told me. She would be lying in her bed at this moment, falling asleep to the music he was playing for her.

I closed my eyes and yielded to the music as it floated into the darkness of the mountains. The last few notes, when they came, hovered in the air, vanishing into the stillness a moment later. I knew I would miss this nightly ritual of Magnus's when I moved into my own bungalow.

Just before going back inside, my eyes turned toward Yugiri again. I searched for the light among the trees but could not find it; it had been extinguished while I was looking elsewhere.

Magersfontein Cottage sat on four stubby concrete piles tacked into a hillside a quarter of a mile from Majuba House, built in the typical Anglo-Indian style. Rust patched the corrugated tin roof, and the chimney's plaster had fallen away, exposing the red bricks beneath. A broad verandah looked out to the tea-felted slopes. A rain tree bent toward a window on one side of the bungalow, eavesdropping on the conversations that had taken place inside over the years.

"The servants have cleaned it up as best as they could," Frederik said as he carried my bag inside from his Austin. "You've got running water and electricity but no telephone. And don't expect it to be the E & O"—he laughed—"or even the Coliseum Hotel."

The house smelled of damp and the rattan chairs and tables were rickety and mismatched. The sagging bookshelves contained some mildewed copies of *Punch* and *Malayan Planters' Weekly*. A fireplace with a crate of wood by the hearth took up one side of the small living room. It gave me a childlike pleasure that I could have a fire on cold evenings; some days I even forgot that I was in the tropics, with the line of the equator just missing the Malayan peninsula by a fraction of an inch on the map.

"It's good enough for me," I said.

"You should put something on that." Frederik pointed to the wound crusting my elbow. "Get some gentian violet from Emily."

"It's just a scrape." I pulled my sleeve down over it.

"I'm going to Tanah Rata," he said. "Come with me."

"I really should unpack."

92

"You need to stock up on food, don't you?"

He was right. I had to start cooking for myself from now on. "Come on," he said, sensing my resolve weakening. "I'll buy you breakfast at Ah Huat's *kopitiam*—people drive in from miles around for his *roti bakar*."

Set in a plateau from which it took its name, Tanah Rata was surrounded by low hills. Here and there a bungalow could be seen on the crests of wooded ridges; these houses were owned by the European rubber companies and made available as holiday homes to their senior and, more often than not, European staff.

"The first time I came here," Frederik said, slowing down the Austin as we entered the village, "I thought there was a law requiring the homes here to have these awful mock-Tudor facades. At least Magnus showed some originality when he built his house."

We parked in a vacant lot by the *pasar pagi*. The open-air morning market was already crowded, the air heavy with the smells of freshly spilled blood and innards from chickens slaughtered at the request of customers. Meat hung on thick hooks; fish, prawns and milky-white squid were piled on beds of melting ice chips, the water dripping onto the ground and forcing everyone to skirt around puddles. Old Malay women squatted beside earthenware pots of curry. We squeezed our way between the Chinese and Indian housewives who thought nothing of stopping in the middle of the thoroughfare to gossip, unconcerned that they were obstructing everyone behind them.

The shops along the main street were quieter, the crowd mostly Europeans—one of the more polite words we used to describe anyone who was white, regardless of where they came from. We gave the shopkeepers a list of things we wanted, showing them the permit from the district officer and instructing them to deliver our shopping to Majuba.

"There's Ah Huat's," Frederik said, pointing to the shop at the end of the row. "Come on. I hope we can get a table."

The *kopitiam* was of the type found in every town and village, a place where old men in singlets and flappy cotton shorts spent their mornings chatting and drinking coffee from saucers. Felicitations in red Chinese calligraphy streaked down a large and unframed mirror on one wall. The marble tabletops were yellowing, stained with tidal layers of old coffee spills. On the radio a woman was singing a Mandarin song. Behind the counter and just below the mirror sat a fat, middle-aged Chinese man, his surprisingly elegant fingers clacking away on an abacus as he shouted out orders to the kitchen. He dug the long nail of his little finger into his ear and then peered at what it had excavated. "Ah, Mister Fledlik! *Cho san!*" he shouted when he saw us. "*Wah*, your gur-fen?"

"Morning, Ah Huat. *Cho san.*" Frederik darted a half-apologetic, half-embarrassed glance at me. "And, no, she's not my girlfriend."

Our half-boiled eggs, coffee and *roti bakar* came a few minutes later. The slabs of crusty, toasted white bread covered in butter and coconut jam tasted as good as Frederik had promised. Following the example of the old men in the shop, Frederik poured his coffee into a saucer and blew on it.

"My mother used to scold us if we did that," I said. "Low-class, she called it."

"But it tastes so much better like this." He picked up the saucer and slurped noisily from it. "Try it."

I stirred my cup, churning up the sludge of condensed milk lying at the bottom. Glancing around quickly, I poured the coffee into my saucer and held it up to my mouth. But I put it down again immediately—it reminded me too much of the way I had eaten my meals as a prisoner.

"Did you grow up in the Cape too?" I said. "You don't sound like Magnus at all."

"My mother would have beamed with joy to hear that," Frederik said. "She looked down on the Boers. Oh, how she looked down on them."

"Why?"

"She was English, born in Rhodesia. God only knows why she married my father—he wasn't wealthy or a joy to be with. Even as a young boy I could see that they weren't happy together. After he died, we moved back to Bulawayo."

"How old were you?"

"Eight or nine. My father had always sided with the British, much to Magnus's disgust. It's why they didn't get along, I think."

He explained how he had always been fascinated by his uncle in Malaya, the uncle who owned a tea estate in the mountains. "When I was fifteen I took a P & O ship from Cape Town to spend Christmas here," he said. "It was so different from what I had read, all those Maugham stories my mother wouldn't let me touch."

"My parents wouldn't let me read them either," I said, smiling. "But my sister would borrow them from her friend and then pass them on to me."

"Magnus told me what happened to your sister. I'm sorry."

I looked away from him. More people were coming into the *kopitiam.* Frederik cracked his half-boiled eggs against his saucer and scraped out the insides of the shells with a teaspoon. He added a few shakes of white pepper and a generous amount of soy sauce to the watery eggs before bringing the bowl to his lips.

"You've certainly picked up our habits," I said. "How long did you stay, on your first visit here?"

"Just for a month," Frederik said, wiping his lips with his handkerchief. "I knew I wanted to come back again one day. There was no other place in the world I wanted to be." The memory of his happiness lit up his eyes; the light was dulled a few seconds later, perhaps by the awareness of his lost childhood. In that fleeting moment I saw the boy he had once been, and I was given a glimpse of the old man he would one day become.

"You came back, in the end," I said.

"My mother died four years ago. I wrote to Magnus. He asked me to move here, help him run the estate," Frederik said. "I couldn't take him up on his offer—I wanted to finish my studies. You're going to eat that?" He eyed the last piece of toast on my plate. I pushed it to him. "The Rhodesian African Rifles was disbanded after the war, but it was reestablished last year," he said. "When I heard my old regiment would be sent to Malaya to fight the Reds, I signed up again." He paused to look around the shop. "I thought it'd be an easy campaign—hunting communists. But it hasn't been like that at all."

"Where were you during the war?"

"Burma. Saw some real horrors there . . ." He hesitated. "So how do you do it? How do you face a Jap, day after day, after what they did to you?"

I took a few moments to consider my answer. "There's so much to do, so really there isn't time for me to think about anything else when we're working," I said. Frederik looked disbelieving, and I decided to be frank with him. "But now and then, something he says—a word or a phrase—spikes into a memory I thought I had buried away."

I recalled the incident that had occurred the previous evening. Aritomo had brought me to a stack of trees he had had felled a month earlier. They had been trimmed. "Get one of the men to saw these *maruta* into smaller pieces and take them away," he ordered. Instead of carrying out his instructions, I had turned around and hurried away. I heard him calling out to me, but I did not stop. I walked faster, heading deeper into the garden. I tripped, got up and continued walking, going up the slope until I came to the edge of a high drop, with only the mountains and the sky before me. I did not know how long I stood there. After a while I sensed Aritomo coming up to my side. "*Maruta*," I said, staring ahead. "That was how the officers in the camp referred to us: *logs*. We were just logs to them. To be cut up, incinerated." For a few moments the gardener was silent. Then I felt him take my arm. "You're bleeding." He gripped my elbow and pressed his handkerchief against my wound.

"*Tiew neh ah mah chau hai!*" Loud, friendly swearing in Cantonese brought me back to the *kopitiam*. Frederik was staring at me. I blinked a few times, drank my coffee and turned around in my seat. A group of gray-haired Chinese men were sitting a few tables from us. A scrawny man opened a Chinese newspaper. Someone called out, "*Diam, diam! Mo chou*," and conversation withered into an expectant silence. The man looked at each of his friends and in a slow, careful manner began to read aloud from his newspaper.

"I see this in every *kopitiam* I've been to," Frederik said. CTs were known to come to places like this to catch up on the news and to pass messages to their couriers. "I'm leaving tomorrow," Frederik said. "My men have been asked to help move squatters from their settlement to a new village."

During the Japanese Occupation thousands of Chinese had gone to live at the fringes of the jungles, doing their best to avoid any contact with the Kempeitai, hoping not to be rounded up and massacred. The war had been over for six years, but those people had remained in their settlements, living off the land as subsistence farmers. The communists used the squatters as a source of food and medicine, information and subscription money; the squatters were the Min Yuen, the People's Movement. Lieutenant-General Sir Harold Briggs, the director of operations, had recognized that they were the biggest problem of the Emergency. Across the country, half a million people—every child, every grandmother, every family, even their entire livestock—were in the process of being moved by the army into specially constructed "New Villages."

"Which settlement are you moving?" I said.

"You know better than to ask me that." He grinned, shaking a finger at me. "And you can't ask me where the Sun Chuen is sited either."

"Just checking how well you keep secrets." I was quiet for a moment, then said, "I had to go to one of those New Villages, when I was a prosecutor."

"Was that you—the Chan Liu Foong case?" He looked at me with heightened interest. "It was all over the news."

"It was the last case I prosecuted."

Chan Liu Foong, a thirty-year-old rubber tapper, had been caught supplying food to the terrorists and acting as their courier. I had visited her home in Salak South, some ten miles outside Kuala Lumpur, to give myself an idea of how she had smuggled out supplies and information. The New Village to which she had been resettled was home to six hundred squatters and their families. A double fence, seven feet high and topped with barbed wire, protected an open stretch of no-man's-land ten feet wide. Armed sentries in watch-towers guarded the perimeter. The villagers were searched and their faces matched against the photograph in their identity cards every morning when they went through the gates, and the procedure was repeated when they returned home in the evening.

"The police showed me Chan Liu Foong's home," I said. "It was empty. Special Branch had taken the husband into custody and their four-year-old daughter was placed in a welfare facility."

I remembered the sullen faces that had peered at me from the windows of the neighboring homes. To stop the other villagers from helping the communists, a curfew had been put in place. Most of the villagers worked as rubber tappers in an estate five miles away. They were only allowed outside the fences from eight in the morning until one in the afternoon. This had affected their means of earning a living; rubber trees have to be tapped at dawn, before the sap dries up.

"Didn't they deport her to China in the end?" Frederik said.

I nodded.

"Her husband and daughter? Were they allowed to go with her?"

"My job was to make sure the terrorists were punished."

Frederik broke off a piece of toast, wiped the last of the egg from his saucer and popped it into his mouth.

It was raining when we came out from the *kopitiam*. We sheltered in the five-foot walkway outside the row of shops, waiting for the skies to clear. A low, red-brick building stood on a rise, just before the road turned and went down the mountain.

"What is that?"

"It used to be a convent school, before the Japs turned it into a hospital for their troops. It's a hospital for the British army now," he said. "Someone told me that, shortly after the surrender, our soldiers found some young Chinese girls living there. The Japs tried to pass them off as TB patients."

"*Jugan ianfu*," I said.

"Sorry?"

"Military comfort women."

"Ah. We came across some of them in Burma when the Japs surrendered," he said. "They were going home. We gave them a lift."

"Those girls would never have been accepted back by their families." I flinched as lightning streaked the sky. "The shame of what they'd become would have been too great."

"It wasn't their fault," Frederik said.

"Nobody would want to marry them, knowing that they had serviced two, three hundred men all through the war."

He glanced at me and stuck a hand out beneath the awning. "It's letting up. Come on, let's run for it."

Arriving back at Magersfontein Cottage, he switched off the engine and reached for the seat behind, taking out a brown paper package from a shopping bag. "For you. A present."

I opened it, laughing when I pulled out the bottle of gentian violet. "So that's why you snuck off to the Chinese medicine shop."

"In case you get any more scrapes."

The bottle was heavy and dark. Stroking the label with my thumb, I looked at him. "I'll cook you a meal when you come back to Majuba."

"Anything but chicken feet please." He shuddered. "Can't understand how you Chinese can eat those things."

"Why not? They're nice and crunchy!"

He laughed, then fell silent when he realized that I was not smiling. He looked at me, his eyes searching my face. I gazed steadily back at him. He leaned over and kissed me. His hand stroked my shoulder, then slid down my back. After a few seconds I pulled away from him.

"Come inside," I whispered in his ear. "I'll need some help with the gentian violet."

Siva, the young Tamil assigned to be my guard, waited for me outside my bungalow every morning to escort me to Yugiri. In the evenings I walked home on my own, varying the time and using a different route every day.

The irritability that had been building up inside me subsided after I slept with Frederik. I had always been considered the more homely of my mother's two daughters and after the war it had come as a surprise to me to discover that men found me attractive. Once I had recovered from my injuries, and to convince myself that I was still physically attractive, I had slept with a number of men. The fact that I never took my gloves off when I made love only seemed to intrigue them more. Looking back on that period of time, I wondered if all I had been trying to do was to assert my influence over another person, after having been powerless for so long.

Despite my fears of a CT attack, I enjoyed living on my own again, in these mountains where the breath of trees turned to mists, where the mists entered the clouds and fell to earth again as rain, where the rain was absorbed by the roots deep in the earth and drawn out as vapor again by leaves a hundred feet above the ground. The days here opened from beyond one set of mountains and ended behind another, and I came to think of Yugiri as a place lodged somewhere in a crease between daybreak and sunset.

One morning, as the workers were laying down their tools to take their tea break, Aritomo took me to a section of the garden I had never been to before. He pointed to a neatly trimmed lawn in front of us. "Notice anything unusual about it?"

I squatted down for a closer look. "Something about it looks odd." I grazed my palm over the tips of the grass, half hoping I could extract the answer from them; they tickled but told me nothing. I stood up. "What's so unusual about it?"

He beckoned for me to follow him on a track going up a slope. The sound of rushing water came from behind the trees. Maple leaves lapped above our heads, their shadows silk-screened onto our arms, onto the track. The effort of keeping up with him left me breathless.

"This is the highest point of Yugiri," he said when we reached the crest.

The foothills began here, rising into mountains tonsured in clouds. Spread out below was the garden, his house placed somewhere in the center. A corner of its red terra-cotta-tiled roof was wedged among the branches, like a kite abandoned by the wind.

We resumed walking and came to a pool fed by a meager waterfall. Tall reedlike plants grew along the banks. "Calamus," he said, breaking off a few leaves. "My wife loved their fragrance." He crushed the leaves and offered them up to my nose, filling my head with their sweet perfume.

"Where is she now?"

"Asuka died years ago."

We sat down on a stone bench and I lifted my face to the sun for a moment. "That wheel looks old," I said.

The waterwheel, about fifteen feet in diameter, was perched on the far edge of the pool beneath the waterfall. It was turning slowly, frothing the water over a weir and down along a narrow stream fringed with ferns and rocks wrapped in moss.

"Soldiers looted it from a Buddhist temple in the mountains outside Kyoto two centuries ago. The abbot had angered one of the Tokugawa shoguns by supporting a group of rebels. It was a present from Emperor Hirohito."

The sharp intake of my own breath sounded loud to my ears. I sat very still. Aritomo had rested his right foot on a rock by the edge of the pool and appeared to be absorbed in adjusting his shoelace. Somewhere behind us a bird called out. Hearing the emperor's name always took me back to the camp: it had been run on Japanese time; each day at dawn we had had to bow in the direction of the emperor. At that time of the morning he would have been sitting down for his breakfast in his palace, the officers told us. Yun Hong had once remarked that we were fortunate that Tokyo was only an hour ahead of Malaya.

"I often sit here, listening to the wheel turn." Aritomo closed his eyes. "Even now, as it rotates slowly in the water, it seems to sing a mournful sutra," he murmured. "It reminds me of an old monk, the last one remaining in an abandoned temple, chanting till the day he dies."

"There are inscriptions on the undersides of the paddles," I said.

"Not many people would have noticed them." He opened his eyes. "Prayers carved by monks. With every turn of the wheel, the paddles press into the water, imprinting the holy words onto its surface," he said. "Just think—once, these prayers were carried from the temple in the mountains all the way to the sea, blessing all those they floated past."

In my mind I saw the stream winding down these mountains, leaving Yugiri, to be pulled into a river. I saw the prayers steam off the water in the morning sun as the river flowed through the rain forest, past a tiger and a mouse-deer drinking from it, past Malay kampongs and aboriginal longhouses and Chinese squatter settlements. I saw a farmer in his paddy field by the river's edge uncrook his back and gaze upward to the sky, feeling a cool breeze on his face and a long moment of unexplained contentment.

"These prayers," I said, "you believe they're effective?"

"My garden *was* left undamaged in the Occupation."

"That's probably more because of who you are, because the wheel was the emperor's gift," I said. "No looting or uncivilized behavior from the emperor's troops, not this time. It didn't help you at all, did it, when our soldiers returned."

He stood up in one abrupt movement and walked to the ledge overlooking the garden. He curled a palm at me to join him. "There is the lawn I showed you earlier," he said. "You could not tell me what was unusual about it."

From where I stood, the Taoist symbol of harmony was visible on the clearing between the trees, the two teardrops of its positive and negative elements forming a perfect circle. "You cut the grass to different levels," I said. It was so simple; I should have seen it immediately. "You played with light and shadow."

"Appearances," he said.

The clouds knitted close. The yin-yang symbols embossed on the lawn by shadow and light disappeared, and the grass was only grass once more.

In my free time on weekends I explored the tea estate. Vast areas of Majuba were still covered in jungle. The trees, hundreds, thousands of years old, merged into the rain forest draped over Malaya. The estate had its own provision store, a toddy shop, a mosque and an Indian temple. The workers were housed inside a fenced compound guarded by sentries Magnus had trained. On Saturdays the estate bus would take the workers into Tanah Rata for a day's outing. Sometimes I'd stop and watch the men playing *sepak takraw*, using every part of their body except their hands to keep the woven-rattan ball in the air for as long as they could.

To build up my physical endurance, I went on regular hikes. One Sunday morning, not long after I moved into Magersfontein Cottage, I climbed up the lower slopes behind it. The trail was well marked, curving around the hill toward Yugiri. I reached the top of the escarpment forty, fifty minutes later. The mountains hovered in the air, severed from the earth by a buffer of low fog. I could see all the way to Pangkor Island, dreaming in the Straits of Malacca. To the east, the mountains went on for as far as my eyes could see, and it was easy to convince myself that the thin, shining strip laminating the horizon was the gleam of the South China Sea.

Parts of Yugiri were visible through the tree cover, like glimpses of a landscape beneath a field of clouds. I searched for the landmarks in the garden, buoyed by a sense of discovery when I recognized them. From the waterwheel dialing away tirelessly on its high ridge, I followed the stream as it stitched its way downhill beneath the tree canopy. My eyes leaped over to Aritomo's house. A figure was standing outside the back door. Even across this distance I knew that it was not Aritomo. The wind thickened, numbing my face. Another man appeared a few minutes later, and I thought I recognized Aritomo.

He stopped and raised his face to the mountains. After a minute or two he turned back to the other man, and they walked to the path that would take them out of Yugiri and into the jungle. Through the breaks in the trees I caught glimpses of Aritomo. The other man was harder to spot, his khaki clothes blending into the surroundings. The canopy soon closed over the path, like the ocean sealing over the wake of a passing ship, and I lost sight of them both.

CHAPTER NINE

*Three days after the meeting with Tatsuji, I wake up with no knowl-*edge of who I am, no memory of who I have been. It frightens me, and yet at the same time I feel a sense of release. My doctors assured me that memory loss is not a symptom of my condition, but of late these episodes have been happening more and more frequently. The moment passes, but I continue to lie in bed. Reaching across the sheets I pick up the writing pad next to me, reading through it at random. *You make it sound as though they have souls.* It takes a few seconds before I remember that I wrote this. I scan through a few more pages, jarred by each word I think is not quite right. I stop at the mention of Chan Liu Foong, the woman I prosecuted just before being sacked; I wonder what happened to her and where her daughter is now.

It is more difficult than I have imagined, setting down things that happened so long ago. I question the accuracy of my memory. That afternoon at Magnus's *braai*, after Frederik drove me back from Yugiri—it stands out with such clarity in my mind that I wonder if it actually took place, if the people there actually said what I think I remember. But does it matter? Nearly all of them are dead.

But Frederik was right—I feel I *am* writing one of my judgments, experiencing the familiar sensations as the words snare me in their lines until I lose all awareness of time and the world beyond the page. It is a feeling in which I have always taken pleasure. It provides me with more than that now: it gives me some control over what is happening to me. But for how long this will last, I have no idea at all.

The reclining Buddha lies in a pool of sun on the windowsill. Tatsuji pokes around the study while I bring out the woodblock prints. They are kept in an airtight camphorwood chest. I lay them on the desk. Tatsuji is admiring a pewter tea caddy he found on one of the shelves, his fingers stroking the bamboo leaves carved on its surface. He puts it down carefully and hurries over to my side.

I lift the corners of the first sheet; dust and the smell of camphor the papers have absorbed over the years swirl up and taunt my nose. Tatsuji turns away and compresses a succession of sneezes into his handkerchief. Regaining his composure, he takes out a pair of white cotton gloves from an old but well-preserved leather satchel and puts them on. One by one he moves the sheets from the stack to another pile, counting as he goes along. The paper on which each *ukiyo-e* has been printed is approximately the size of a serving tray. Each print is contained inside a rectangular or circular border and every piece of the *ukiyo-e* appears to have a different design.

"Thirty-six pieces," he says.

He skims a large magnifying glass over the first print, distorting the shapes and the colors beneath like the lights of a city skyline seen through a rain-spattered window. "Remarkable," he murmurs. "As good as *The Fragrance of Mists and Tea*."

He is referring to a well-known *ukiyo-e* of Aritomo's: a vista of the tea fields of Majuba estate. Aritomo had donated that particular woodblock print to the Tokyo National Museum before I met him, and its iconic status has increased over the decades, surpassed only by Hokusai's *The Hollow of the Deep-Sea Wave*. I suspect the reference to *The Fragrance of Mists and Tea* is Tatsuji's unsubtle way of reminding me that I have allowed it to be reproduced in a number of art books. I have even seen the print on the T-shirts sold in the souvenir shops in Tanah Rata.

"They were all made before I knew him," I say.

"Creating an *ukiyo-e* print is a time-consuming and difficult process," Tatsuji says. "The artist has to draw an outline on a piece of paper before pasting it on a block of wood. An inverse copy of the drawing is then carved on it. A print like this, with such a variety of colors and depth of detail, would need seven, perhaps ten, different blocks." Bewilderment tugs at his face. "I do not see any duplicates here. Why go to all the trouble and then make only one copy of each work? Are you sure there are no other pieces lying around the house?"

"These are the only ones he left behind. He sold his prints to buyers in Japan," I say. "I've always suspected that was how he supported himself—he never took on any commissions to design gardens when he was living here."

"I have tracked down all of the prints he sold. None of those I have seen is a copy of these." Tatsuji's voice has the faintest tremor in it, and I notice the shine in his eyes. His already high standing in the academic world will be elevated further once his book on Aritomo—with the inclusion of these prints—is published.

"There's another print hanging in Majuba House," I remember.

"I would like to see that too."

"I doubt Frederik will object. I'll ask him."

Tatsuji puts down his magnifying glass. "The subject matters of the *ukiyo-e* are also unusual."

"Unusual? In what way?"

He pulls a print from the pile, holding it up in his hands like a piece of fabric offered by a merchant. "You have never noticed it?"

"They're scenes of mountains and nature. Common subjects for *ukiyo-e*, I would have thought."

"All of them are views of Malaya," he says, "every single one of them. There is nothing here that is related to his own homeland, none of the usual motifs beloved of our *ukiyo-e* artists: no winter landscapes, no scenes of Fujiyama or the Floating World."

I page through the sheets again. Each piece contains recognizable elements of Malaya: lush tropical jungles; lines of rubber trees in estates; coconut trees bowing toward the sea; flowers and birds and animals that are found only in the equatorial rain forests—a rafflesia, a pitcher plant, a mouse deer, a tapir.

"It has never occurred to me before," I say.

"I suppose it is not something you think about when you see it all around you." He strokes the *ukiyo-e*. "I would like to examine these in detail before I decide which ones I want to be included in my book."

"They are not to be photographed or taken out of Yugiri without my permission," I warn him.

"That goes without saying."

Keeping my voice light, I say, "I've heard that you collect human skin, that you buy and sell tattoos."

He shapes the knot of his tie with his thumb and forefinger. "I keep that aspect of my work circumspect."

"So you should."

"*Horimono* has never been accepted by the Japanese public, but there are wealthy collectors keen to own pieces of tattoos created by famous *horimono* masters," Tatsuji says. "Sometimes, a man might wish to sell his skin; on a few occasions I have acted as a broker for such transactions."

"So how much does a man's skin fetch?"

"The price varies," Tatsuji says. "It would depend on the identity of the artist, the scarcity of his works, the quality and size of the piece in question."

The memory of a museum in Tokyo I visited ten years ago comes back to me. The museum was famous for its collection of tattoos. They were of various sizes and age, sealed and preserved inside glass frames. I had walked among the hangings on the walls, looking at the faded ink on human skin, repelled and, at the same time, fascinated.

"What made you become interested in tattoos?"

"The worlds of *ukiyo-e* and *horimono* overlap," Tatsuji replies. "Quite a number of *horoshi* created woodblock prints too."

"Yes, yes, you've told me that already. 'They fill their buckets from the same well.' Now tell me the *real* reason."

He breathes in deeply and then exhales. "The first time I saw the *horimono* Aritomo-*sensei* put on my friend's back . . . at that time I knew nothing about tattoos, but even then I realized that it was magnificent, a work of art. I thought it was wonderful that an *ukiyo-e* artist could also create similar drawings on the human body. Seeing that *horimono* started me on a lifelong obsession with them."

"Your friend's tattoo wasn't preserved . . . after his death?"

Tatsuji shakes his head. "For years I have been searching for other *horimono* created by Aritomo-*sensei*, but I have never found any." He is silent for a moment. "Tattoos created by *horoshi*—by masters—are very much sought after," he continues, "but as an outsider it was difficult for me to enter their world." His gaze drops to the *ukiyo-e* on the table. "To earn their respect, their trust, I had myself tattooed."

It is an extraordinarily intimate revelation for him to make, having only met me twice. I sit down on the edge of the table and cross one leg over the other. They still look good, my legs, firm and unblemished by any liver spots, with no cobwebs of varicose veins anywhere. "You had a tattoo put on your whole body?"

"A *horimono*? Oh no. No, I asked for a tattoo to be put here." He runs his right hand over his left arm, from the shoulder to about two inches above the elbow. I stare at it but see nothing underneath his sleeve. "It was difficult to get a *horoshi* to work on me," he says. "I had to provide letters of recommendation and references. Even then they turned me down. But in the end one of them agreed to work on me. Word spread once I had the tattoo, and the other *horoshi* started recommending their clients to me, clients who wanted to sell their *horimono*."

"I'd like to see it," I say, aware that I am being ill-mannered.

Tatsuji's thumb probes the dimple in the knot of his tie. He comes to a decision and removes the silver cuff link on his left wrist. He proceeds to roll up his sleeve, his movements so precise that each fold seems to have the same width—about an inch and a half. Reaching his elbow, he pushes the rolled-up sleeve to his shoulder, exposing the tattoo wrapped around his upper arm. I get off the table and lean in to take a closer look. Inside a field of gray clouds, two white cranes pursue each other in a loop, almost catching one another.

"The artist captured the birds well," I say.

"It is not as good as the tattoo Aritomo-*sensei* put on my friend."

"Your wife was fine with it, when you came home with this?" I ask.

"I have never married." He strokes one of the cranes. "Like you."

I ignore the last bit and instead study the colors on his arm. "What you told me about Aritomo . . . that he was a tattoo artist," I say. "If it was disclosed to the world, it would ruin his reputation."

"His name would become immortal."

"The gardens he created have already made him immortal," I correct him.

Tatsuji rolls down his sleeve with the same careful movements he showed earlier. "Gardens change over time, Judge Teoh. Their original designs are lost, erased by wind and rain. The gardens Aritomo-

sensei made no longer exist in their original forms," he adds, buttoning his cuff. "But a tattoo? A tattoo can last forever."

"*The palest ink will outlast the memory of men.*" From out of nowhere the old Chinese proverb comes to me, and I wonder where I have heard it before.

"Only if it has been preserved properly."

"Years ago I went looking for the gardens Aritomo had designed. It was the one and only visit I ever made to Japan."

"Did you find them?" The look on his face tells me he already knows the answer.

"It *was* difficult locating them," I admit. "The old families whose gardens he had made had died since the war; the descendants had dispersed, their ancestral homes sold or subdivided. An apartment block or a road had been built over where his gardens had once been. I found only one of his gardens that still existed. It had been turned into a neighborhood park."

"Ah, that was in Kyoto, in the old Chushojima suburb. I have been there."

"As I walked in it, I could tell that it was not the original design he had created. It lacked his spirit."

"Yugiri is the only garden that still bears his imprint," Tatsuji says.

I pull out the last sheet of woodblock print from the pile. It is a triptych, three vertical rhomboid frames almost coming together, pyramids with their tops cut off. The objects inside the frames are misshapen. Feeling queasy all of a sudden, I press my palm on the table for support, terrified that my illness has taken another turn, removing my ability to recognize shapes and forms. The doctors have said nothing about this. I blink my eyes a few times, but the objects remain warped.

Tatsuji takes the *ukiyo-e* from me and holds it up high, tilting his head back to study it. The light through the rice paper molds his face with colors, transforming him into a performer in a Beijing opera I once attended. I want to ask him if the print looks normal to him, but I am afraid of what he will tell me.

An idea pushes its way out from my confusion. "Give it to me," I tell Tatsuji.

He looks puzzled at the urgency in my voice. I take the print from him, nearly snatching it, and spread it on the table, smoothing it out with my palm. I take a step back, and then another. He glides backward to stand next to me. Both of us look at the *ukiyo-e*.

The distortions in the print are gone. We are standing at the edge of three parallel lotus ponds narrowing into the distance. The trees, the sky and the clouds all have been brought into the water, into the drawing. Relief charges into me. My laughter sounds loud in the study, unnatural, but I don't care. I laugh again. Tatsuji looks at me, amused but not sure why.

"Cunning," he says, "the way he has done it, playing with perspective. I should have seen it immediately."

"*Shakkei*," I say.

"He taught you that?"

"It was in everything he taught me."

"The old palace gardeners I spoke to all mentioned Aritomo-*sensei*'s talent for Borrowed Scenery. It was his strongest skill, but it was never given the recognition it deserved."

"Perhaps it's because he did it so well that people weren't aware of it," I reply. "How often does one notice the clouds above us, the mountains over the fence?"

Tatsuji considers my words for a moment. He tidies the desk and packs his gloves and magnifying glass into his satchel.

"I'll have a room prepared for you to work in, probably in a day or two," I say. "You're not pressed for time?"

"Well . . . I would like to finish the book as quickly as possible." He buckles his satchel and looks up at me. "This will be the last book I will ever write. I am retiring after this."

"I can't see you spending your days on a golf course."

"I have a promise to keep, a promise I made many years ago."

Struck by the sorrow in his voice, I am about to ask him more about it, but he takes his satchel, bows to me, and leaves the room. At the door he turns to me and bows again.

Leaning on the windowsill, I stare at the mountains. *Shakkei*. Aritomo never could resist employing the principles of Borrowed Scenery in everything he did, and the thought comes to me that perhaps he may have even brought it into his life. And if he did so, had there come a time when he could no longer distinguish what was real and what were only reflections in his life? And will this also happen to me in the end?

Before strolling to Majuba that evening, I decide to sweep the fallen leaves from the *kore-sansui* garden below the front verandah. The five stones I helped set into the earth have been worn smoother now, and the lines on the bed of gravel have been rubbed away. I stand there at the edge, trying to remember the last time I saw it, the pattern Aritomo had raked into them. He had his favorites: the contour lines of a map, the memory rings of a tree, the ripples on a lake. After a moment or two I comb out a series of lines, the gravel crackling softly beneath my rake. By the time I have finished shadows are flooding the furrows between the lines, like water from a rising tide.

Branches and wild grass have narrowed the trail I so often used when I was apprenticed to Aritomo, obstructing the way in a few places. I spend some time clearing them, perspiring and growing ever more annoyed. The earliest stars are just appearing when I cross over into the tea estate. I had forgotten that night comes quickly to the mountains.

In the last year I have heard the odd story or two about Frederik from people who spent their holidays in Cameron Highlands. Frederik had made Majuba Tea Estate his home even before Magnus's death, and except for occasional visits to England and South Africa, he has lived in Cameron Highlands since he came here in the fifties. He occupied one of the bungalows in Majuba when he took over the running of the estate. On her seventieth birthday Emily persuaded him to move into Majuba House. Over the years, I heard about various women with whom he was involved, but he never married. Given his mania for indigenous gardening, I wonder if his quest to restore everything to what he considers to be endemic to the highlands has extended to the Cape Dutch house his uncle had built and of which he had been so proud. I hope not.

The aged eucalyptuses lining the driveway have not been taken out, and their bark peelings cover the ground. I bend to pick one up—it feels like old vellum, cracked and dried up. Coming to the end of the driveway, I stop to look at Majuba House. The lights from inside spray a golden nimbus around it, reflecting in the pond. I am glad to see Frederik has kept it the way it was when Magnus was still alive, even if the Transvaal flag is no longer flying. A green pennant with the Majuba Tea Estate logo, an outline of a Cape Dutch house, flaps gently from the flagpole.

The strelitzias along the walls have been replaced with red hibiscus. *So common*, I think as I walk up to the front door. A maid takes me along the corridors to the living room. The house has been kept the way it was, and I wonder if it is out of respect for Emily. The bronze sculpture of the leopard remains on the sideboard: the predator forever chasing its prey.

The furniture in the living room is the same yellow wood pieces Magnus brought over from the Cape, although the upholstery has been redone in blue and white stripes. The Bechstein piano stands in one corner. The Thomas Baines paintings and the Pierneef lithographs have not been replaced; I almost expect the roots of the fever trees to have cracked the frames and dug themselves into the walls. I remember reading in a magazine somewhere that the works of these two artists are now worth a fortune.

Moving past Magnus's Boer War medal, I stop before Aritomo's woodblock print of Majuba House, the same one that Frederik wanted my permission to use. I think of the other prints Tatsuji and I examined earlier today, and I think of his tattoo.

There are more books now than before, the additional shelves taking up an entire side of the room. I tilt my head and study some of the titles: *Adrift on the Open Veldt*; *The Voortrekkers*; *On Commando*; *De La Rey: The Lion of the Transvaal*. There are books on the Great Trek and the Boer War, and novels and poetry collections in Afrikaans by writers I know nothing about: C. Louis Leipoldt, C. J. Langenhoven, Eugene Marais, N. P. van Wyk Louw.

"Magnus never talked much about the Boer War, or his life in South Africa," Frederik says. I did not hear him enter. He is dressed in a gray blazer, a white shirt and a light blue Jim Thompson silk tie; it always pleases me to see someone who has made the effort to be properly dressed. "Those books helped me understand the world he had left behind," he adds.

"It was your world too."

"But it's no longer there. It's gone." For a moment he looks lost. "You once said something about old countries dying—to be replaced by new ones. Do you remember that?" His hand makes an awkward flutter in the air, as if he suddenly realizes that he has asked me to do something I might no longer be able to.

"It was the day we met for the first time," I say, relieved that I can recall it instantly. "At the *braai* –" I nudge my chin at the windows looking out onto the garden behind the house. The warm glow of shared memories; of the few people left, Frederik is the only one with whom I can truly feel this. "And I was right, wasn't I? Malaya became Malaysia. Singapore broke away from us. And there's Indonesia, India, Burma . . ." Moving further down the shelves, I pull out *The Red Jungle* and show it to him. "I still have the copy you signed for me."

"It continues to sell rather well, that and my book on the origins of tea. Unlike my novels—those are out of print now."

"Are you working on anything at the moment?" For a second I am tempted to tell him about what I have been writing.

"Can't run a tea estate and still have enough time to write. Perhaps when I retire, I'll start writing seriously again. Update *The Red Jungle*." He hands a tumbler of whisky and soda to me. "I hear that Chin Peng wants to come home. Is that true?"

The rumors about the secretary general of the Malayan Communist Party have been floating around in the last few months, but I have not given much thought to them. "He can try all he wants, but the government will never let him come back."

"Why not? He's an old man now. He's been in exile for almost forty years. I think all he wants is to go back to the village where he was born."

"Once you step out of your world, it doesn't wait for you. The world he used to know is gone forever." I lower myself into an armchair, the chill of its leather seeping through my slacks. "You look vexed. And I doubt it's caused by the plight of poor old Chin Peng."

"Just some problems with the workers."

"Ah, yes. The television sets."

"The servants have been gossiping to Ah Cheong again, I see."

"What do you expect your workers to do after a day's work, if you refuse to let them have TVs in their homes?"

"Electronic transmission signals have an adverse effect on insect life in gardens. Research done by universities has proven this," he says. "I can show it to you."

"You think that by prohibiting TVs in the estate, the signals will disappear and not come into your garden?" I give a derisive laugh. "Consider the rain when it falls on Majuba. Whether you put a bucket outside to catch some of it or not"—I rattle the ice cubes in my glass—"the rain still comes, still floods the earth."

"Laugh all you want, woman, but the butterflies *have* returned in greater numbers since I banned TV sets from the estate. So have the insects. And there *are* more birds in Majuba now. Oh yes." He grew excited. "In fact, I saw a bulbul. Only yesterday. And a pair of green magpies this morning. We're getting a lot of birdwatchers coming here."

"I thought Emily's joining us?"

"She's getting dressed," Frederik says. "She moved into the guest room a few years ago. Said she didn't need such a big bedroom anymore." He smiles, lines crowding into his face. "You might remember that room—it was the one you stayed in when you first came here."

We sit in silence for a while, nursing our drinks. He gives me a sheaf of papers when my glass is empty. "I wanted to take this to you, but the past few days have been mad."

"What is it?"

"Your consent for me to use Aritomo's drawing." The look in his eyes sharpens. "We spoke about it, remember?"

"Of course I remember. I'm not senile yet. Give me your pen?" I sign the papers and push them across the table, the momentum fanning them open like stepping stones across a pond.

"You should at least read them first," he chides me, gathering up the papers and knocking them into an orderly pile. The skin of his hands, I notice, is spotted with age. The joints of two of his fingers are clogged and swollen, like knobs on the branches of a bonsai tree.

"You wouldn't cheat an old woman."

"Don't be too sure." His smile balances on the rim of his tumbler for a moment. "How long are you staying in Yugiri?"

"I haven't really decided—until Tatsuji completes his work here, at the very least."

We both look to the door when Emily enters. Frederik puts down his glass and hurries over to her, guiding her by the elbow. I stand up. Emily's hair, pulled back in the way I remember, has whitened completely. Dressed in a gray *qipao* and a cardigan around her shoulders, her body is thin and bowed. Lines pleat her face and her eyes have a smudge of feebleness in them.

"*Wah* . . . if only Magnus could be here today," she says, a smile floating to her lips, her voice arid with age.

"Hello, Emily." The thought occurs to me that I am now much older than she was when I met her the first time. Time seems to overlap, like the shadows of leaves pressing down on other leaves, layer upon layer. "You're looking sprightly."

"*Choi!* That word always makes me think of old men with skinny legs walking their noisy lapdogs."

The smells of food leak from the kitchen; the scent of the coriander is familiar to me, even after nearly forty years, but the name eludes me and I have to hunt for it in my mind. I wonder if the decay is spreading faster than I have been warned it would, but I elbow that thought aside. I groan to cover my relief when I remember the name. "*Boerewors.*" It is a terrible feeling, being unable to tell if my forgetfulness is normal for my age, or if it's indicative of the steepening of the slide. *Boerewors.* I tell myself I must include the name in what I have been writing when I get back to it later tonight.

"I have them flown in from the Cape every six months," Frederik says. "Along with a box of Constantia red."

A wine for exiles. It was something Aritomo once said.

Coming to the end of our dinner, Emily begins to drift in and out of our conversation, confusing the present with the past. Frederik catches my eye once or twice when it happens and I give him a small nod of sympathy. Now and then he corrects her gently, but mostly he plays along, letting her take pleasure in her memories.

"A nightcap?" Frederik asks her when we get up from the dining table to move to the living room.

Emily pats her hand over her mouth. "It's past my bedtime already." She looks at me. "You'll have to forgive an old woman for all the nonsense I talked-*lah.*"

"I enjoyed it," I assure her.

"We'll have tea one of these mornings? Just the two of us."

I promise her, and Frederik takes her back to her room. "Not one of her better nights," he says when he returns to the living room a few minutes later. "She's usually sharper in the morning. But I know she's really pleased to see you." He hands me a glass of sherry and sits across from me. "Has that historian of yours looked at the prints yet?"

"He'll be coming to Yugiri to catalog them."

"What he said the other day, about Aritomo dabbling in tattoos? Magnus had a tattoo. Here." He touches the area above his heart with his palm, as though he is about to swear an oath. "I had forgotten all about it until he mentioned it."

Somewhere in the house a clock starts chiming. I wait until it has stopped and the house has settled into silence again. My chair creaks softly when I lean forward. "He showed it to you?"

"We were hiking in the mountains one day—this was when I was a boy, visiting him. On our way home we stopped to cool off under a waterfall. That's when I saw it." He nods in growing realization when I do not respond. "You've seen it too?"

"He never liked talking about it." I twist my body to look at the woodblock print on the wall behind me. "I'd like to borrow that to show it to Tatsuji."

"I'll get one of my boys to send it over to Yugiri." He hesitates. "I spoke to some friends in Singapore and London. And Cape Town," he says. "I'll have some names for you soon."

I stare at him, wondering what he is talking about.

"Specialists," he explains. "Neurosurgeons."

"You think I wouldn't have known how to do that myself?" My voice is loud in the stillness. "I don't need any more experts to tell me what I already know. So stop doing whatever you think you're doing for me. Just stop it."

His eyes cool into stone. "Anyone ever tell you what a hard-arsed bitch you are?"

"Many have thought it, I'm sure, but you're the first man who's had the balls to say it to my face," I reply. "I've seen all the experts I want to. Endured all their tests, their prodding. No more, Frederik. No more."

"You can't just ignore . . ." His hand rises and dies in the air.

"Primary progressive aphasia. Caused by a demyelinating disease of my nervous system," I say. I have never spoken the name aloud to anyone else, except to the doctors who diagnosed me. A superstitious fear numbs me, the fear that the illness will now hasten its spread over me, bring me to the stage where I will not be able to speak its name coherently. That will be its goal, its victory, when I can no longer even curse it by its name.

"I once read something about Borges," I say. "He was blind and very old, spending his last days in Geneva. He told someone, 'I don't want to die in a language I cannot understand.'" I laugh bitterly. "That is what will happen to me."

"See a few more doctors. Get more tests done."

"The last time I stayed in a hospital was when the war ended," I say, keeping my voice level. "I'll never put myself inside another one again. Never."

"You have anyone looking after you in KL? A live-in carer? A nurse?"

"No."

"You can't live alone," Frederik says.

"Magnus said that to me once, you know." The memory makes me smile, yet it also saddens me. "I've lived on my own for most of my life. It's too late for me to change my ways." I close my eyes for a moment. "While I'm here, I think I ought to restore the garden to the way it used to look, when Aritomo was alive." The idea came to me when I was looking at his print earlier in the evening.

"You can't do it by yourself. Especially now."

"That woman who's doing your garden—what's her name? She can help me."

"Vimalya?" He makes a sound that is somewhere between a snort and a laugh. "Restoring a garden like Yugiri would go against all her principles."

"Speak to her, Frederik."

"The garden's the last thing you should be worrying about, if you ask me."

"I have to do this now. Soon Yugiri will be the only thing that will still be able to speak to me."

"Oh, Yun Ling . . . ," he says softly.

The music drifts through the house, a whisper from an older

time. The melody is familiar but I cannot place it. I look at Frederik from the edge of my eye, wondering if I am the only one who is hearing it.

"She listens to it every night, before she sleeps," he says, as though he knows what I am thinking. "Built up an extensive record collection of the same piece of music too, with different pianists—Gulda, Argerich, Zimerman, Ashkenazy, Pollini. Whenever I'm overseas I look for another version for her. But she only listens to the larghetto. It's never changed in all these years. Only the larghetto."

The loose skin of his neck pulls tight as he offers his face to the lights in the ceiling. "It's the Yggdrasil Quartet in support again tonight," he says after a while. "I found it in Singapore some months ago. She's been playing it very often."

"Yggdrasil? What's that?"

"It's from the Norse myth."

"I've never heard of it."

"Yggdrasil is the Tree of Life," he says. "Its branches cover the world and stretch up to the sky. But it has only three roots. One is submerged in the waters of the Pool of Knowledge. Another in fire. The last root is being devoured by a terrible creature. When two of its roots have been consumed by fire and beast, the tree will fall, and eternal darkness will spread across the world."

"So the Tree of Life is already doomed from the moment it is planted."

Bringing his gaze to me, he says, quietly, "But it hasn't fallen yet."

I lean back into my chair, close my eyes and listen to the larghetto. The piano is accompanied only by the quartet and the music has the bleak purity of a set of stones lying on the bed of a stream, a stream that dried up a long time ago.

CHAPTER TEN

The Art of Setting Stones was different from what I had thought it would be. I had walked through the gardens in Kyoto with Yun Hong when I was fifteen, but I had had no inkling of the amount of work required to construct and maintain them. And neither had Yun Hong, I suspected, feeling disloyal the instant the thought entered my head.

Aritomo kept me running about, and at first I suspected it was because he wanted me to fail, to give up in frustration and leave Yugiri. But I never saw any sign of resentment in him once he had taken me on as his apprentice. The work was exhausting but I began to enjoy it. The tools he used were old and specialized. I had to memorize their names and learn to clean and care for them. I thumbed the beads of their names in an endless loop as I went about my work: *Kakezuchi. Nata. Kibasami. Shachi. Tebasami.* Mallet. Hatchet. Hedge-trimming shears. Windlass. Pruning shears. *Kakezuchi. Nata. Kibasami. Shachi. Tebasami.* The loop lengthened with each passing day, as more and more beads were added to it.

Some days if I was early, I would watch Aritomo at archery practice, making sure to stand outside his line of sight. A sense of calm filled me as I observed his slow, deliberate movements.

In addition to carrying out the tasks Aritomo assigned me, I was required to interpret his instructions to the workers. Except for Kannadasan, they were all disinterested gardeners. From my first day I sensed Romesh would be the one to cause trouble. He was in his thirties with small, hard lumps of muscle on his body. When he began to turn up later and later for work, reeking of toddy fumes, Aritomo asked me to inform him not to bother coming anymore.

Romesh showed up at Yugiri the day after I conveyed Aritomo's message to him. He stood outside the house and began shouting.

For once he was not drunk. The rest of us were working nearby and stopped to watch, edging closer to get a better view.

"Come out, you Jap sister-fucker!" Romesh screamed in Malay, shifting back and forth on his feet. "I want my money! Come out! Come out!"

Aritomo emerged at the front door a moment later, the magazine he had been reading still in his hand. "What is he so upset about?" he asked me.

"He wants you to pay him."

"Is that all he said? Well, he *has* been paid."

"Not in full," I said, interpreting Romesh's reply for Aritomo.

"It would not be fair to the others if I paid him in full, would it? He has not done as much work," Aritomo said, twisting his magazine into a tube.

Romesh snatched the *parang* from Kannadasan's hand before I had finished translating. Too shocked to move—to think—I watched as he swung the machete toward the side of Aritomo's neck. Instead of backing away, Aritomo slid *into* the attack in a smooth movement and jabbed the end of his rolled-up magazine into the worker's windpipe. Romesh choked, making gurgling sounds, his hand scrabbling at his throat. Tightening the magazine with a quick twist and holding it like a chisel, Aritomo stabbed at a point on Romesh's wrist. The man's fingers went dead, the *parang* dropping to the ground. Still struggling for air, Romesh swung a punch at Aritomo with his other hand. Aritomo deflected it, turning it into a wrist lock and forcing Romesh to his knees. Romesh screamed in pain.

"I will break this as easily as a twig," Aritomo said, his face close to Romesh's. There was no need for me to translate. Romesh's body sagged. Aritomo released his lock on the man's wrist and carefully backed away.

Time resumed. The wind moved again. The fight had lasted ten, perhaps fifteen seconds, but it felt much longer. The workers rushed forward to help Romesh up. He pushed them away, crawling off before staggering to his feet. He walked unsteadily out of the garden, rubbing his wrist. He did not look back.

I turned around to say something to Aritomo—although I had no idea what—only to discover that he had already returned inside. I picked up the *parang* in the grass and gave it back to Kannadasan.

Leaving Yugiri that evening, I waved to Ah Cheong as he waited outside the house for Aritomo to appear. The servant held the gardener's walking stick in his hand, his last duty for the day before he cycled home to Tanah Rata.

I chose a track that followed the hemline of the jungle before curving back to my bungalow. I was in no hurry to return home. In spite of my fatigue, I still had problems falling asleep, sometimes lying awake in my bed until the early hours of dawn. There were so many voices in the dark: the moans of the prisoners, the shouts of the guards, my sister's crying.

Watching Aritomo fight off Romesh—even if it was to protect himself—had shaken me worse than I had realized. There had been a cold, detached air to him when he was disarming Romesh, and I suspected he would have done more than break the man's arm if Romesh had not conceded defeat. There was so much about the Japanese gardener I did not know, could not even guess at.

The lights of the farmhouses and bungalows sprinkled themselves across the valleys. Tea pickers hurrying home waved to me. The tearful smell of wood smoke from cooking fires fanned across the twilight, carrying with it the faint barking of dogs. In the camp we had looked forward to this moment of the day, when we were finally allowed to return to our huts, each one of us glancing around to see who had not survived, too numb to feel anything when we missed a friend or a familiar face.

The track divided in two. Instead of going straight home I took the path to Majuba House and called to the Gurkha to let me through the gate. Going around to the back of the house, I passed Mnemosyne and her twin sister, then went down the steps to the lower terrace garden. Magnus had left most of the chengal trees untouched when he cleared the jungle. The formal lines of the gardens were breached by the beds of the plants he had transported over from South Africa—cycads with sharp-edged leaves pushing out of the ground like the tops of oversized, prehistoric carrots; strelitzias and blue agapanthus; aloes with their menorahs of red flowers struggling in the unfamiliar terrain.

Rising from the center of the lawn was a stone arch, plastered in white, a bell hanging from it. Magnus had told me it had once been rung to announce the end of the working day for the Javanese slaves on a vineyard in the Cape. Long after I had first seen it, this pale monolith still had the power to draw me toward it; I felt I had stumbled upon the last remnant of a forgotten civilization. Passing beneath the arch now, I reached up on my toes to knock the lip of the bell, calling up a faint echo from its rusted muteness.

Emily was standing by an ornamental pond, her eyes closed. I kept quiet as she breathed in and lifted her right foot away from her left. She moved with such slowness that I felt I was watching time being stretched out, the world around us sucked in by her energy as she went through a series of motions, one flowing seamlessly into another, water pouring into water, air merging with air. She executed the moves with such grace and controlled power that she seemed to be gliding inside spheres of reduced gravity.

She returned to her original position a few moments later, her arms coming to rest against her hips. I called out to her softly and she spun around to face me, her hands rising into a protective movement. "It's me," I said. "That was beautiful. It's *taijichuan*, isn't it?" I used to watch the old people doing it on the esplanade."

Wariness receded from her face, but its stain remained there for a moment longer.

The light of the stars chilled the air. A bronze sculpture of a young girl knelt on a block of granite among the reeds at the edge of the pool. Her eyes had a cold, innocent wonder as she peered eternally into the water. Emily noticed me looking at it. "We had her cast after we buried our daughter here."

"I didn't know you and Magnus had had a daughter."

"Petronella lived for only a few days after she was born." An old sorrow shaded Emily's eyes as she contemplated the sculpture. "I never met your mother. Am I a lot like her?"

At that moment I understood why my father had never liked Magnus, and why Emily had been so wary of me. I felt sure she was not inquiring about the physical similarities between her and my mother. "You're both very determined people," I said, picking my words with the same care I took when choosing the stones for Aritomo's garden.

Emily looked satisfied—even happy—with my reply. "Magnus wanted to marry her, you know, but as the only daughter of the great Khaw family, she couldn't see herself with a lowly *ang-moh* planter."

"But you could." Emily, I recalled, came from a well-off family too, although not as prominent as my mother's.

"Living here made things a lot easier, I suppose," Emily said. "Cameron is a world by itself. I'm sure you've already realized that by now. There were quite a lot of mixed-race couples here before the war. I used to think that we had all come here to get away from the disapproval of the world."

"How did you meet Magnus?"

"Beng Geok, my cousin. She invited me for a tiger hunt up at Penang Hill. Magnus was one of the guests," she said. "I couldn't stop looking at him when Beng Geok introduced us. That eye-patch! I felt it hid something deep inside him. I wanted to find out what it was. I just had to." She smiled. "You know how he lost his eye?"

"In the Boer War."

She looked at me. "I'm sorry about your mother."

I moved a few steps away, pretending to be interested in a bird alighting on the arch.

"I'm sure you haven't cooked dinner," Emily said. "Come and eat with me."

"Where's Magnus?"

"KL. He left early this morning. He goes once a month to get cash to pay our workers."

"He should have let me know. I wanted to get some books."

"Oh, we don't tell anyone when he's going or coming back. Safer-*lah*. Less chances of an ambush, you see. So," she said, "dinner?"

I nodded and followed her to the steps. At the top she paused and turned to me. "That night, when I first met Magnus . . . we stood on the balcony, watching the lights of Georgetown below us," she said. "It started drizzling, but he wouldn't let me go in. And then he said the lines of that poem to me: *Now lies the earth night-long, washed in the dark silent grace of the rain.*" Memory softened her face. "I asked him to write it down for me, but he refused. And you know what he said? 'I don't need to write it down for you, because you will always remember it.'"

123

For a while we stood there, twilight and the words of a poet whose name I did not know sinking into me.

Just before we went inside I said, "Was the tiger shot?"

"You think I cared, once I saw Magnus?" Her laughter sparkled in the dusk, and for just the briefest moment she appeared like a young girl again. "The trackers found some marks, but we never saw the tiger. It was probably the last one living there in the hills." Bending toward me, she whispered, "And I'll tell you a secret: I'm glad that it was never found and that we didn't kill it."

After a moment, I said, "I'm glad too."

"I like to think that it's still alive today," she said, looking out to the mountains, where night had already fallen, "still roaming the hills."

At the end of each day in Yugiri, I returned to my bungalow and put the kettle on to boil, switching on the radio while I waited. The news, if I happened to catch it, usually included a report of another planter and his family murdered by CTs. Dropping into my chair at the dining table, I drowned my hands in a basin of hot, steaming water, releasing the pain locked up in them. Some days it was so bad that I was surprised not to see blood in the water. The agony was always worse in my left hand, the scars redder than the skin around them. Looking at the stumps, I remembered the trick of the disappearing thumb my father had so loved to show me when I was a girl, how it had made me squeal with delighted terror.

Soaking my hands one evening, I heard a car coming up the steep driveway. It stopped in front of my bungalow. The engine switched off, doors slammed shut and then Magnus called out to me. Wrapping a hand towel around my left hand, I went outside. He had a Chinese man with him, dressed in a khaki bush jacket, his crisp cotton shorts almost touching the white socks below the knees.

"Ah, you're home. Good," Magnus said. "Inspector Woo wants to talk to you."

Gesturing them to the rattan chairs on the verandah, I went inside, dried my hands and put on my gloves. The radio was still on, and I turned down its volume. Inspector Woo had crossed one leg over the other and was shaking out a cigarette from a silver case when I joined them. He offered one to Magnus, who declined it. I was about to reach out for one but stopped: I was not in the camp anymore; I did not have to hoard any cigarettes to barter them later for something I needed.

"You're quite isolated here," Woo said, striking a match to light his cigarette.

"What does Special Branch want from me?"

He showed no surprise that I had guessed who he was. "We want you to leave Cameron Highlands. Go back to KL."

I glanced at Magnus, then looked to the inspector again.

"Nine days ago, a bandit surrendered herself to the police in Tapah," Woo said. "She was part of the Perak Third Regiment. They're based in this area. Her commander knows you're living here."

Beyond the driveway, the tea fields were lapsing into dusk. A moth, its wings as wide as my palm, staggered around the verandah's lightbulb, searching for a way into the heart of the sun. "You think they're planning to do something to me?"

"You've prosecuted quite a few CTs. Successfully too. Chan Liu Foong's case made you very unpopular." Smoke whistled out from between Woo's pursed lips. "You're an easy target. And your father's involved in the independence negotiations."

"I didn't know that," I said.

"He's been made an adviser in the committee for the *merdeka* talks."

"Advising the government?"

"No. The Chinese party."

"Teoh Boon Hau wants to free Malaya from colonial rule?" Magnus shook his head, grinning. "Hard to believe."

"They need people who can speak English to represent the interests of the Chinese—*our* interests—in the discussions," said Woo. "It's only a matter of time before the British leave Malaya. We Chinese must stand together, whatever our differences: the Hokkien and the Teochew, the Hakka and the Cantonese, and even you Straits Chinese. We can't let the Malays have all the say. We have as much at stake here as them."

In the last two years the calls for self-rule had grown more strident among the Malay nationalists. Concerned for their future, the

Malayan Chinese had formed their own political party to have their voice heard in the negotiations for *merdeka*.

"My father can't even speak Mandarin," I said. "How can he speak for the Chinese?"

"He's hired a tutor to teach him," said Woo. "Even gave a short speech the other day at the Chinese Chamber of Commerce. It was quite remarkable, really. He began by saying, in perfect Mandarin, 'I am no longer a banana.' I was told it brought the house down."

"Banana?" Magnus said.

"Yellow outside, white inside," Woo said. "Look, Miss Teoh—you're a marked woman. You *have* to leave."

"Even if you throw every single one of the Emergency Regulations at me, Inspector," I said, "I'm not going anywhere."

"Be sensible, Yun Ling," Magnus said. "It's not safe for you here."

"We can't spare anyone to protect you." The inspector raised a finger in warning. "As it is, we're shorthanded already."

"I didn't ask for any protection, and I'm not going to." The legs of my chair scraped the floorboards as I stood up. "But thank you for your concern."

Inspector Woo flicked his cigarette over the railing. He scribbled on a piece of paper and gave it to me. "My telephone number. Just in case."

"At least move back into Majuba House," said Magnus.

"I like being on my own."

Magnus shook his head and gave up. Once inside the car he stuck his head through the window and said, "It's the Mid-Autumn Festival tomorrow. We're having a little party. You'll come? Good. Bring Aritomo. It starts at six."

Before going to bed, I went around the house to make sure the doors and windows were properly shut and bolted. I left the verandah lights on. The cicadas in the trees sounded louder than usual that night, and the jungle felt denser and much closer.

Aritomo stopped by my bungalow the following evening. He was dressed in a gray dinner jacket and matching trousers. His faint cologne smelled of moss after rain. A large cardboard box was looped in one arm, but he refused to tell me what was inside it. Worried that he would end my apprenticeship with him, I did not mention Inspector Woo's visit.

As I gave him his whisky and soda, his eyes fixed on the thin jade bracelet I was wearing. He took my wrist. "Imperial Chinese jade," he murmured. "You should not be wearing it in a place like this."

"It was my mother's," I said. "One of the few pieces of her jewelry she managed to hide before the Japanese came." She had buried it in a box under the papaya trees behind our house; after the war I had gone back there and dug it out. She had not recognized it when I showed it to her.

"It goes well with your dress," said Aritomo. "Like two leaves from the same tree."

I looked at my *qipao*, the pale green silk giving off a muted shimmer with every slight movement I made. "We'd better be on our way," I said. "I don't want to be late."

Arriving at Majuba House, he pointed to the barbed wire strung around the fence. "A weed that is strangling the country. It seems to have sprouted everywhere."

"It's necessary," I said. "You should consider some security measures for Yugiri." In the last light of sunset, the drops of dew clinging to the barbs glinted like venom on the tips of a serpent's fangs.

"And ruin the garden?" He looked so appalled that I laughed. He turned to stare at me. "That is the first time I have heard you laughing."

"There hasn't been much I found funny in the last few years."

The moon was ripening in the sky. On the terrace garden behind the house, the guests and the estate workers huddled by the buffet table: the Indians and Chinese at one side, the Europeans at the other. News of my apprenticeship with Aritomo had spread, and a number of the guests looked at me with open curiosity. Two or three guests ribbed Aritomo, asking him if he was opening a gardening school, but he only shook his head, smiling. This was the first time I was seeing him outside his garden; I was struck by how comfortable he was with the guests. He had become part of the landscape here.

Toombs, the Protector of Aborigines, had brought a wild boar he had shot, the animal skinned for him by one of the Orang Asli. The smell of the meat on the spit sweetened the air, making me queasy and hungry at the same time. Magnus stepped out from behind his *braai* to introduce us to a middle-aged American. He was good–looking despite his stockiness and the thinning hair combed flat against his head. "Jim's here on holiday. He's works in Bangkok."

"What are you doing there?" Aritomo asked.

"Losing all my money—not to mention my hair—trying to revive the local silk-weaving industry," the American replied. "Magnus tells me you've built yourself a Japanese house. I'm putting together a traditional Siamese home myself, on the banks of the *khlongs*."

"The canals," Aritomo explained when I shot him a blank look.

"You've been to Bangkok?" the American said.

"Oh, years ago," Aritomo replied, "when I started traveling around these parts."

Emily, handing out paper lanterns to the children, called out to me.

"Give this to her," Aritomo said, passing me the box he was holding. The three men drifted over to the rattan chairs on the lawn. I walked over to Emily and handed her the box. She shook it lightly and put it down on the table.

"I'm so glad you brought him with you," she said. "We haven't seen much of him lately."

"They've known each other for a long time?" I asked, glancing at Aritomo. He finished his glass of wine and took another one from a maid.

"Magnus and Aritomo?" She thought for a moment. "Ten, fifteen years I suppose. They used to be such good friends, you know."

Magnus whispered something to Aritomo, who threw back his head and laughed. "They seem fine now," I said.

"He used to come over every weekend, and he'd always bring something with him. Used to drink a lot and get quite *mabuk* with Magnus and their friends. But he's visited us less often since the Occupation. Always got some reason—busy-*lah*, tired-*lah*."

"Did something happen between them?"

"What, you mean a quarrel? Nothing so dramatic-*lah*. It was the war, I think. It changed their friendship in some way." She opened another carton and took out a batch of paper lanterns, each one pressed flat. She gave one to me. It extended like an accordion when I pulled at both ends. "It always makes me feel like a little girl again, when I see these," she said. "Did you play with lanterns, when you were growing up?"

"My parents celebrated Chinese New Year, but not the other festivals."

"I'd be surprised if they did. Magnus told me they were very *ang-moh*."

Aritomo, still deep in conversation with the American from Bangkok, caught me watching him, but I did not look away. "Old Mr. Ong—he was our neighbor—used to hold moon-watching parties. We'd see his children playing with lanterns. His first wife always gave us mooncakes. I've always wondered if it's true—that secret messages were hidden inside mooncakes by some rebels plotting to overthrow the Chinese emperor."

"*Aiyo*, get your facts right . . . the *rebels* were Chinese," Emily said. "They wanted to end the Mongols' rule. The uprising was planned to take place on Chong Qiu. And the messages were not always hidden inside the cakes."

"Where were they hidden?"

"Sometimes they were *on* the cakes. The cake mold would have the message carved into it. The finished cake would be cut into quarters."

"The message could only be read when all the pieces were put together," I said.

"Clever, *hor*? Just imagine—hidden in plain sight!"

"So Chong Qiu is to celebrate this uprising."

"You modern-modern girls. All that university education and you don't even know something like this, your own traditions some more," Emily said. "Ask any of the children here and they know the story—even the Indians and Malays."

"That's because you tell it to them every year," Magnus said, bringing our drinks.

"They like to hear it," Emily said, giving the last lantern to a girl.

Magnus winked at me and turned to the children. "Come, *mari mari*, boys and girls, Auntie Emily is going to tell you a story. Come, come." Most of the children understood and spoke some simple English, but he repeated his words in Malay, ending with another exhortatory *mari mari* and curling his fingers at them.

The children gathered around us. Emily flung an annoyed look at Magnus, but it was obvious she was enjoying herself. Once the children had settled down on the grass, Emily asked, "Do you all know why today is also called the Moon Festival?"

"Because the moon is so big tonight?" a boy piped up.

"That's a good one!" Toombs said with a chuckle.

"Keep quiet-*lah*, you," Emily shot back.

Pulling her skirt over her knees, she knelt on the grass. "Once upon a time, the world had ten suns," she began. "Every day, each one of them would take turns to shine in the sky. But then one morning something strange happened, something that had never happened before: all ten suns decided to show up at the same time. The world became too hot. *Wah!* The trees caught fire, and *whoosh!*—entire jungles went up in flames. Soon all the rivers and seas were boiled away, the water turned into steam. Animals died and millions of people were suffering."

Some of the children's mouths were hanging open, their eyes wide and staring at Emily. One boy got to his knees, turning around to look for reassurance from his parents.

"The emperor of China was worried," Emily continued, "but all his cleverest advisers told him there was nothing they could do. 'It is the Will of Heaven,' they said.

"But a young court clerk asked for permission to speak. He said he had heard of an archer called Hou Yi, who could shoot down anything from the sky, anything at all, however high they flew— swallows, storks, eagles. His arrows, it was said, could even pierce the clouds. "Your Majesty," this young official said, "perhaps Hou Yi could be asked to shoot down the suns?'"

Emily's voice carried to the other guests, and one by one they broke off from their conversations to listen. Aritomo, I noticed, had sat up in his rattan chair, no longer talking to the American silk merchant beside him.

"The emperor thought the young clerk's idea was good. 'Send messengers to bring this Hou Yi to see me,' he commanded. 'Quickly!' When the archer arrived, the emperor told him what he had to do. Hou Yi listened and then asked to be taken to the highest tower in the palace. The emperor, carried on a sedan chair by his slaves, followed Hou Yi all the way up to the top of the tower.

130

Higher and higher they climbed, until they arrived at the very top. This was an open space where the emperor performed ceremonies to greet the sun on the first day of every New Year.

"The ten suns were so bright and hot that when Hou Yi looked down at the scorched land, he noticed that there were no shadows anywhere. It was so bright that even the blue sky had become completely white." Emily looked at the children. "Hou Yi took up his bow. Now, this Hou Yi was a very big man."

"How big?" A skinny boy broke in.

"How big, Sanjeevi? Oh, bigger than Mr. Magnus, but without his huge stomach of course. Big like that tree there, but a bit shorter." Emily's eyes brushed over the other children. "Ah, but if Hou Yi was big, then his bow was even bigger, twice his size." She wet her lips before continuing. "Hou Yi took out his first arrow. It was long and thick, like a spear. He pulled his bowstring." Hands pushing on her knees, Emily rose to her feet stiffly and took up a shooting stance, stretching her arms wide. The younger children laughed. I glanced at Aritomo; he was leaning back in his chair, his arms crossed over his chest, his face in the shadows.

"Hou Yi pulled the bowstring. He pulled and pulled and pulled until the emperor feared the string would snap. He closed one eye and aimed his arrow at the closest, fiercest sun." Emily paused, her arms still in the pose of the archer about to release his arrow. She let the silence stretch out. "He shot the arrow." Emily made a sharp whistling sound with her lips. "It flew up into the sky, toward the sun. It hit the sun right in the center. The sun burned brighter for a second, then a minute, then another minute. Moans and groans filled the air. Hou Yi had failed. But then the sun weakened, the flames died, and it disappeared from the sky. People cheered and shouted and clapped, even the emperor. Hou Yi wiped his sweating brow and shot his arrows, again and again. He never missed. The emperor and his courtiers and his slaves—everyone in the world—could feel the terrible heat disappearing, as one by one the suns died.

"Finally there was just one sun left in that empty sky. As Hou Yi was about to shoot down the last sun, the emperor leaped up from his chair and shouted, 'Stop! You must leave it to shine, or the world will be covered in darkness.'"

"But the moon-*leh*? What about the moon?" a girl in pigtails asked.

"*Aiyah*, Parames, wait-*lah*, I'm not finished yet." Emily stopped for a second and made a show of gathering her disrupted thoughts. The children groaned loudly. "Where was I *hah*? Oh, yes. So the last sun was saved. Years later, when the emperor was dying, he made Hou Yi the new ruler of China," she continued. "Hou Yi loved being an emperor so much that he asked the gods to make him immortal."

"What's that?" Parames asked.

"It means forever and ever he cannot die," Emily replied. "The gods decided to give him a magic pill to eat, so that he would live forever.

"Now, Hou Yi had a beautiful wife, Chang Er. He loved her so much he wanted to give half the pill to her, so he kept the pill in a box to surprise her. Chang Er saw he was hiding something and became curious. One day, when her husband was out hunting, she opened the box. She saw the pill and picked it up. And then . . ." Emily pinched the invisible tablet between her forefinger and thumb, looked around furtively, and then popped it into her mouth, forcing it down her gullet. The children shrieked.

"Immediately she felt her body become lighter and lighter," Emily said. "Her feet lifted off the floor, higher and higher. She floated out of the window, into the sky. She went up and up and up. But she did not want to leave Hou Yi, and so, as she flew past the moon, she decided to stay there. It was the closest she could be to her husband. When Hou Yi came home and realized what she had done, he was heartbroken. But he realized that, on one single night every year, when the moon was at its largest, he could see his wife, Chang Er, still living there on the moon."

She stopped and pointed to the full moon rising over us. "There she is, dressed in her robes, with long flowing sleeves, waiting for Hou Yi to join her."

Like the children, the grown-ups tilted their faces to the moon. For a while there was only silence in the garden. I looked as well, and it seemed to me that the shadows on the surface of the moon did appear like a woman in a robe.

Emily clapped her hands. "Time to light your lanterns, children."

The guests cheered Emily, raising their drinks to her. Laughing and shouting, the children ran off, their lanterns bobbing like fireflies in the dark. Emily opened the box Aritomo had given her. Lying inside were three rice paper lanterns, each one about a foot and a half high, their cylindrical frames constructed from thin bamboo sticks. Emily lit them and placed them on the buffet table, between the dishes of food. The lanterns spilled out shards of color onto the white tablecloth.

"They're all Aritomo's prints," I said, recognizing the style from the illustrations in the copy of *Sakuteiki* he had given me. He had transformed his woodblock prints into lantern shades.

"He used to give me these lanterns for Chong Qiu, before the war," she said. "They're pieces that aren't good enough, he told me, pieces he would have thrown out anyway."

"Nothing wrong with this one." I took the lantern and spun it slowly on my left palm. Melting wax from the candle holder spilled onto my glove. The mountain scenery on the print flickered. "Good enough or not, they must be worth something." An idea occurred to me. "Have you kept all of them? I'd like to see them."

"Cannot," Emily said. "Don't look so offended-*lah*. Wait until everyone goes home later, then you'll see why."

I set down the lantern on the table and closed my hand into a fist, cracking the skin of wax that had hardened on my palm.

Tea and mooncakes were served after dinner. The cakes came in square, octagonal and round shapes, each one about two inches thick and covered in a soft brown skin. Emily cut them into quarter slices and handed them around. Those who had come with children left shortly after; the other guests did not remain for much longer. Magnus had used his influence to obtain an exemption from curfew for his guests, arranging for them to be escorted home in groups by members of the Auxiliary Police. The servants were cleaning up when Emily caught my eye and nodded toward Aritomo. I watched him moving over to the buffet table. He carried two of his lanterns to the oil drum in which Magnus had cooked the *boerewors* and lamb chops. In the dark, with the pair of glowing lanterns in his hands, he looked like a monk leading a religious procession.

"Bring me the other one," he called out over his shoulder to me.

I did as he asked. The guttering candles in the lanterns made them look as though they were shivering. He dropped the first one onto the embers in the oil drum. It caught fire instantly, the flames tearing through the print, consuming the shade in seconds.

I touched his elbow. "Give them to me."

He looked at me, then dropped the other lanterns into the drum. The glow from the flames rippled across his face. We watched the lanterns burn to the end. The ashes flaked away into the night, edged in glowing red, soundless as moths.

He brushed his hands over the embers. "Let me walk you home."

"I'll get a flashlight from Magnus."

He shook his head and pointed to the cloudless sky. "I borrow moonlight for this journey of a million miles," he said.

CHAPTER ELEVEN

*One morning, I stood outside the archery hall and waited until Arit-*omo finished his practice. When he returned his bow to its stand, I said, "I'd like to try."

Perhaps I caught just the flicker of incredulity in his eyes; with Aritomo it was often difficult to gauge his reaction. "You cannot do it without the proper clothes," he managed to say at last.

"*Proper clothes?* Well, don't you have a spare set lying around? Emily will know someone who can alter it for me."

"Why would you want to learn *kyudo*?"

"Doesn't it say in *Sakuteiki* that to become a skilled gardener you ought to take up one of the other arts too?"

He reflected on my reply for a moment or two. "Perhaps I have an old set of clothes somewhere."

I returned to the archery range a few days later, carrying the *kyudo* kit in a bag. Before entering the practice hall, I removed my shoes and placed them on the lowest step. In a space sectioned off by a curtain at the back of the hall I changed into a thin white cotton robe and black *hakama*—loose pleated pantaloons. Emily had done the alterations for me herself, and the kit fitted me well.

Coming out from the cubicle, I held up the long, tangled straps of the *hakama* and gave Aritomo a perplexed look. He showed me how to tie them around my waist with a series of loops and knots. Then he gave me an odd-looking leather glove, similar to the one he wore during his practice. "The *yugake* has to be worn on the drawing hand." I struggled with its separate components—the three leather pieces, the various straps and padding—and in the end I had to let him put it on for me.

We knelt on the *tatami* mats and bowed to each other. I repeated his every movement. I resented these rituals. They were tainted with the memories of the acts of obeisance I once had to perform for my captors.

Aritomo selected a bow from the stand, offering it to me on his open palms. The bow, made from compressed bamboo and cypress wood, came up past my head when I rested one end on the floor. Pulling the bowstring all the way into the shooting position, I fought the bow's unwillingness to bend to my will.

"There is no need to use brute strength. The power comes not from your arms, but from the earth, rising through your legs, up along your hips, and into your chest, into your heart," Aritomo said. "Breathe properly. Use your *hara*, your abdomen. Pull every breath deep down into you. Feel your body expanding as you breathe: that is where we live, in the moments between each inhalation and exhalation."

I did as I was told, choking a few times before I could achieve some semblance of what he wanted from me. I felt I was drowning in air.

He nocked an arrow to the string of his own bow—there were two arrows to every round and the second was held between the fingers of the drawing hand as he pulled the bow. He drew the string with an ease I envied, now that I knew how hard it was to do it. The fletched end of the arrow was brought low to his ear, as though he was listening to the vibrations of the feathers. The world around us collected into an expectant stillness, a drop of dew poised on the tip of a leaf. He released the arrow and it struck the center of the target. He maintained his position for a second or two longer before lowering his arms, the bow coming down with the weightlessness of a crescent moon sinking into the mountains. Repeating the entire process, he shot the second arrow dead center again. I plucked at the string of my bow but failed to replicate the sound I had heard.

"*Tsurune*," he said, glancing at my hands. "The song of the bowstring."

"There's even a name for that?"

"Anything beautiful should be given a name, do you not agree?" he replied. "It is said that one can gauge the ability of a *kyudo-ka* just from hearing the quality of the sound of his bowstring when he shoots. The purer the *tsurune*, the greater the archer's skills."

By the end of the hour's practice my arms, shoulders and stomach muscles were trembling and sore, but I also noticed Aritomo squeeze his fingers and then grunt in pain.

"Arthritis?" I said. I had seen the slight swelling in the joints of his fingers.

"My acupuncturist blames it on the damp air."

"Then you shouldn't be living here."

"That is what my acupuncturist says too."

I followed him back to the house to change into my work clothes. We went all the way to the western side of the garden, where the ground began to swell into the foothills. Just before coming to the perimeter wall, Aritomo turned off the path and continued uphill. A short distance further, the track ended at an exposed rock face, about ten feet high and just as wide, ferns curling from its base.

"I found this when I was clearing the land," he said.

I wondered if we had stumbled upon a sacred stone left behind by a tribe of rain forest aborigines, a tribe that, centuries before, had trekked into extinction. The iron buried in the stone had bled up to the rock face. In the morning light, shorelines of rust overlapped and glowed. I stretched out my hand and traced the unknown continents and nameless islands the lichen had mapped on the pitted surface.

"The Stone Atlas," murmured Aritomo.

I glanced at him, this collector of ancient maps.

Just after midday I stopped working to return to my bungalow. I went past the empty pond. Aritomo was checking its clay bed.

"It should be hard enough for us to fill it soon," he said, looking up at me. I continued on my way, but he called out to me. "You waste time going back for lunch. Eat here with me." Noticing my hesitation, he added, "Ah Cheong is a good cook, I assure you."

"All right."

The pavilion's roof was taking shape. Mahmood, the carpenter, and his son Rizal were unrolling their rugs on the grass next to a stack of planks. Side by side, father and son knelt to perform their prayers, prostrating themselves toward the west.

"Sometimes I wonder if they will fly away on their magic carpets when the pavilion is completed," Aritomo said. He glanced at me. "Think of a name for it—the pavilion."

Taken by surprise, nothing came to me. I stared at the half-finished structure, thinking furiously. "The Pavilion of Heaven," I said finally.

Aritomo grimaced, as if I had waved a putrefying object beneath his nose. "That is the sort of phrase ignorant Europeans come up with when they think of . . . *the East*."

"Actually, it's from one of Shelley's poems. 'The Cloud.'"

"Really? I have not heard of it."

"It was one of Yun Hong's favorite poems." I closed my eyes and opened them again a moment later. "*I am the daughter of Earth and Water, / And the nursling of the Sky; / I pass through the pores of the ocean and shores; / I change, but I cannot die.*"

Remembering how Yun Hong had so often spoken these lines, I stopped; I felt I was stealing something from her, something that she had treasured.

"I have heard nothing about a pavilion," Aritomo said.

"*For after the rain, when with never a stain / The pavilion of Heaven is bare, / And the winds and sunbeams with their convex gleams / Build up the blue dome of air, / I silently laugh at my own cenotaph, / And out of the caverns of rain, / Like a child from the womb, like a ghost from the tomb, / I arise, and unbuild it again.*"

My voice wandered off into the trees. By the half-finished pavilion the carpenter and his son touched their heads to the ground one last time and then began rolling up their rugs.

"The Pavilion of Heaven . . . ." Aritomo looked even more doubtful about my choice of name than before. "Come," he said. "Lunch should be ready."

He gave me a full tour of his house before we ate. It was constructed in the style of a traditional Japanese dwelling, with a broad verandah—which he called an *engawa*—running around the front and sides. The room where he received his guests was located in the front of the house. The bedrooms were in the eastern wing, while his study lay in the western wing. In the center of the house was a courtyard with a rock garden. Walkways, covered but open at the sides, connected these different sections. The twists and turns made the house feel larger than it actually was. It was the same technique he had used when he designed his garden. All the rooms opened onto a verandah, and the only concessions he had made to the mountain climate were the glass sliding doors he had put in; one could sit warmly inside the house and view the garden on even the coldest of days. The stark decoration heightened the gleaming emptiness of its cedar-wood flooring. In the sitting room stood a folding screen decorated with a field of tulips, the flowers covered in gold leaf gleaming in the shadows. A seventh-century pale limestone torso of the Buddha, its arms and head broken off, glowed in one corner.

We finished our meal with a pot of green tea on the verandah. It was the end of the week and I could tell that he was feeling lazy, in no hurry to get back to the garden. Thunder rumbled from far off. Kerneels came and rubbed against Aritomo. Stroking him, he started telling me about the temple gardens his ancestors had worked on and how, by helping to maintain them, he had upheld the traditions his family had begun.

"You must go and see them," he said.

"The temple gardens? I'd like to."

His gaze became distant, and for a moment I almost thought he was losing his sight. "Todaiji. Tofukuji. And the pond garden at Joju-inji," he said. "And of course Tenryuji, Temple of the Sky Dragon, the first garden to ever use the techniques of *shakkei*."

"*Shakkei?*"

"Borrowed Scenery."

"Borrowed? I don't understand."

There were four ways of doing it, he explained: *enshaku*—distant borrowing—took in the mountains and the hills; *rinshaku* used the features from a neighbor's property; *fushaku* took from the terrain; and *gyoshaku* brought in the clouds, the wind and the rain.

I turned his words over in my head. "It's nothing more than a form of deception."

"Every aspect of gardening is a form of deception," he replied, the hollowness in his voice echoed in his eyes.

We were quiet for a minute or two. Then he picked up the pewter tea caddy and spooned some more leaves into the pot. "That's beautiful," I said, pointing to the caddy. It was the size of a mug, with a long elegant neck. Bamboo leaves were engraved all along its sides.

"A gift from Magnus." He replaced the cap and it slid back into place without a sound, pressing out all the air inside the caddy. "What do you think of the tea?"

"It's bitter," I replied. "But I like the way it clenches my tongue."

"The Fragrance of the Lonely Tree. Grown in a small plantation outside Tokyo, high in the mountains. Cameron Highlands reminds me of it." His eyes gazed inward. "When I was young we would go there in the summer, when it got too hot and humid for my mother. My father was friends with the owner."

I cut a slice from Emily's mooncake and gave it to him. "That night at Majuba, just as we were going home," I said, "you mentioned something about borrowing the moonlight . . ."

He looked blank for a second. "Ah! *Hai*, it was something a poet wrote before he passed away. His death poem."

It began to rain. Ah Cheong appeared and set two bowls of bird's-nest soup on the table. Aritomo had a fondness for swiftlets' nests, eating them once a week. They were either cooked in a broth or, more to my tastes, served chilled in bowls of rock-sugar syrup and herbs. He believed, like many Chinese, that the nests were good for his health, cooling his internal body temperature and alleviating his arthritis. Formed from strands of the swiftlets' saliva that had hardened in the air, these nests were found only in the high reaches of limestone caves. They were a delicacy few people could afford to consume frequently.

He shook out a pill from a bottle and swallowed it with a spoonful of soup.

"What's that for?"

"Blood pressure. The bird's nest is supposed to help too."

I did not think there would be much to stress him, living here, but I said nothing and finished the soup. "How long does it take to become a skilled garden designer in Japan?"

"Fifteen years. At least." He smiled. "You look shocked. That was in the old days. Apprenticeship is usually only four to five years these days." He shook his head. "Standards have dropped, like for everything else."

"Still . . . it's a long time, five years."

A memory wisped across his face, like rain drifting over a mountain. "My father began teaching me when I was five," he said. "On my eighteenth birthday he gave me a satchel filled with sketchbooks and just enough money to walk for six months across Honshu. 'The best way to learn is to look at nature. Draw what you see, what moves you. Return only when the winter snows begin to fall,' he told me."

"That was harsh of him."

"Oh, I thought so too, at first," Aritomo said. "But those six months became the happiest time of my life. I had no duties to anyone, no obligations. I was free."

He stayed with rice farmers and woodcutters at night. He took shelter in grass huts when it rained, and begged at temples for a bed to sleep in, for a bowl of rice, a cup of tea. Day by day he saw the countryside with changing eyes. "The smallest things made me stop to look, to draw, to feel: the light coming through the furry flowers of wild grass in a meadow; a cricket springing off a stone; the heart-shaped flower of a banana tree nestling among the leaves," he said. "Even the silence of the road would halt me. But how does one capture stillness on paper?"

On some parts of his journey he was on the same path the poet Bashō had taken two hundred years before, when he had walked alone on his narrow road to the interior. "I felt I was seeing the same views he had recorded in his journals. There were days when I would not meet another person on the road. I took long, arduous detours just to see a famous valley, or to visit a monastery on a mountain peak. I lived in the seasons and, like the grass and the trees, I changed with them—summer to autumn. When the year came to its end, I made my way home, following the clouds that were carrying the first of the winter snows. Matsu, our gatekeeper, did not recognize me at first. I had run out of money weeks earlier. I looked like a beggar, but I went immediately to my father's study. I took out my sketchbooks from my travel-worn satchel and placed them on his desk. He glanced at the first few pages, closed the sketchbook and looked at me for a long moment. I felt I had disappointed him. 'I do not need to see the rest,' he said, looking straight into my eyes. 'When spring comes, you will start as a junior gardener in the palace gardens.'"

Aritomo gazed at me for a while. "It was the longest winter I had ever endured. I could not wait for it to end. I was nineteen when I became one of the emperor's gardeners," he said. "I used to see his son Crown Prince Hirohito in the palace gardens. I was just a year older than him."

"Did you ever talk to him?"

"He was very keen on marine biology. He asked me once if I knew anything about it. I told him I was just a gardener."

I looked at my hands, and I thought of how Aritomo had spoken to the man who had caused me so much pain, who had brought me so much loss.

"Hirohito was twenty-five when he became emperor," Aritomo continued. "By then my views on gardening had become fixed. I knew what I wanted, what was right for a garden. Some of the older gardeners did not like me, but they could not do anything to me. I was very talented. I am not boasting—I *was* talented. And the emperor liked me, liked my designs. I rose through the ranks of the palace gardeners quickly. I married Asuka." He pointed to my cup. "That tea comes from her father's plantation."

"You've told me that she died. Was it from an illness?"

"In the Year of the Tiger, in 1938, when I myself was thirty-eight, my life changed. Asuka became pregnant." He stopped, his eyes blurred by memory. "It would have been our first child."

Our faces, I saw, were glazed into the surface of the table. "What happened?"

"She was too frail. She died in childbirth; she and the baby. My son." He rubbed at an old water stain on the table with his thumb. I knew I ought to tell him how sorry I was to hear about that, but I had never liked people using that word with me.

"Why did you come to Malaya?" I asked. "Why did you choose this place?"

Kerneels climbed on Aritomo's knee and settled down on his lap. "We could accept commissions from clients outside the palace, subject to the approval of the Imperial Bureau of Gardens. Our clients were from the aristocracy. Empress Nagako had a cousin who wanted me to design a garden for him. So, not long after Asuka died, I returned to work—it was the only way I could go on," Aritomo said. "What a disaster! From the very first day he and I fought over my designs. He thought he was an expert gardener. He imposed his own ideas. A month into the project, he demanded I make changes to my designs. Extensive changes."

"And did you?"

"The emperor spoke to me. He asked me to apologize and make the changes. I refused. No one was going to change my designs just so they could put in a tennis court." Aritomo winced. "A tennis court! So I resigned. For a year I did not know what to do. I did not accept any more commissions. I visited the Floating World, drank too much and made a fool of myself with the women there. One day I remembered the tea planter from Malaya I had met a few years before. I had never taken up his offer to visit. Yes, I said to myself. I will write to him. I will go to Malaya. Do some traveling."

"Have you ever gone home since then?"

"It is not my home anymore. My parents are dead. What I know, what I remember, all the friends I once had, all have been swept away in the storm." He gaze lowered to his palms, lying on the table. "All I hold now are memories."

I looked at him, this man who had made his home in these highlands, who watched over his garden as one vague season replaced another, as years passed and he grew older.

"A garden borrows from the earth, the sky and everything around it, but you borrow from time," I said slowly. "Your memories are a form of *shakkei* too. You bring them in to make your life here feel less empty. Like the mountains and the clouds over your garden, you can see them, but they will always be out of reach."

His eyes turned bleak. I had overstepped the bounds between us. "It is the same with you," he said a moment later. "Your old life, too, is gone. You are here, borrowing from your sister's dreams, searching for what you have lost."

We sat there on the verandah, each of us adrift in our own memories, our tea slowly relinquishing its heat into the mountain air.

The rain stopped, and I got up to leave. In the main corridor leading to his front door, I paused to look at a horizontal scroll about two feet long. Painted in black ink and water on a plain white background, the scroll showed a frail old man leading a craggy-backed water buffalo by a rope tied to a ring in the beast's nostrils. The man was about to pass through a moon-shaped gateway set into a high wall but was halted by a guard's raised hand. Beyond the entrance lay a gray wash, sinking into the grainy emptiness of the rice paper.

"*The Passage to the West*," Aritomo said. "My father painted it. He gave it to me before he died."

"Who's the man with the buffalo?"

"Lao Tzu. He was a philosopher in the Chinese court, two and a half thousand years ago. Disillusioned by its excesses, he wanted to have nothing more to do with that life. You see him at the Hanku Pass, about to leave the borders of the kingdom, to ride out into the unknown lands in the west."

My hand hovered over the two figures. "He's being stopped by the guard."

"The gatekeeper of the pass. He recognizes the sage, and he begs him to stop for the night, to reconsider." Aritomo's face was in shadow and I saw only the glint of an eye, the plane of a cheek, a line curved around one end of his lips. "Lao Tzu agrees. That night he sets down on paper the principles and beliefs that had guided him all his life, the *Tao Te Ching*." Aritomo paused for a second. "*Heaven's way is like the pulling of a bow, bringing down the high and raising up the low. It takes from what is excessive, and gives to what is lacking. The way of Man is the opposite.*"

"After he had finished writing it," I said, "did he turn around and head back home?"

"At daybreak, the old sage gave everything he had written to the young man. Pulling his buffalo by its rope, he went through the gate and out into the wilderness. No one ever saw him again." He stopped. "Some people think he never existed, that he was just a myth."

"But here he is, fixed in water and paper for eternity."

"'The palest ink will endure beyond the memories of men,' my father once said to me."

Studying the drawing again, it seemed to me that the gatekeeper no longer appeared to be stopping the old man from going through the gate, but was, instead, bidding him a sad farewell.

Chapter Twelve

The murder of the high commissioner continued to weigh on our thoughts as the year came to its end. Morale among the planters and miners across the country had plummeted further, and an increasing number of European families were packing up and leaving Malaya for good. Christmas at Majuba was a subdued affair. I turned down most of the invitations to the parties I was invited to. People continued to drop in at Majuba House for Magnus's weekend *braais*. The visitors were varied: retired barristers from KL who tried to talk law with me, engineers from the Public Works Department, doctors, Indian Anglican priests, senior police officers, Malay civil servants. In my first few weeks at Majuba I had felt obligated to show up at these events, but I soon stopped going. Ever since I had come out from the camp, I could not tolerate being in crowds for long.

Magnus had allowed the security forces to bivouac on his property. Sometimes I'd walk past a meadow and see tents being put up by men from the First Gordon Highlanders or the King's Own Yorkshire Light Infantry, who patrolled the jungle and the hills. Most were around my age, many of them younger.

Five months after Gurney's death, General Gerald Templer flew into Kuala Lumpur to take up the post of high commissioner. Magnus kept me informed whenever I dined at Majuba House, but the bits of news were like a caravanserai on a desert horizon, spirits in the mirage, irrelevant to me. All my energies were directed toward my lessons in Yugiri.

I enjoyed my archery practice with Aritomo. There was more to the Way of the Bow than hitting the target. The central purpose of *kyudo* was to train the mind, Aritomo said, to strengthen our focus through every ritualized movement we made in the *shajo*. "From the moment you walk to the shooting line, your breathing must be regular," he said. "Your breaths must match every move you make, until the arrow has left not just your hands, but also your mind."

Each session began with us sitting quietly for a few minutes, purging our thoughts of all distractions. I discovered how much clutter bounced around in my head. It was difficult for me to sit there and not think of anything at all. Even with my eyes closed, I was conscious of everything around me: the rustle of the wind, a bird picking its way across the roof tiles, the itching on my leg.

"Your mind is just like a strip of flypaper hanging from the ceiling," Aritomo complained. "Every thought, however fleeting and inconsequential, sticks to it."

Every detail of the eight formal steps in the process of shooting was prescribed, even down to the sequence of breathing, and I felt a satisfaction in conforming to the precise and ritualized movements. I practiced the pattern of regulated breathing on my own, and I felt my mind and body slide gradually closer into harmony. In time I came to understand that, in decreeing the way I had to breathe, *kyudo* was showing me how to live. In the space between releasing the bowstring and the arrow hitting the target, I discovered a quiet place I could escape into, a slit in time in which I could hide.

The two of us would stand at the shooting line; I imagined us looking like the pair of bronze archers on his desk. I enjoyed seeing the arrows fly from my bow. It had been difficult at first, when they too often veered to the sides or fell short of the *matto*.

"You let go of your connection with the arrow too early," Aritomo said. "Hold it with your mind, tell it where you want it to go, and guide it all the way to the *matto*. And when it strikes, hold on to it for a moment longer."

"It's not alive," I said. "It obeys no one."

Motioning for me to step aside, he raised his *kyu* and nocked an arrow into the bowstring. He drew the bow to its limit, the stiff bindings releasing little clouds of fine dust into the air as the bow flexed. He aimed the arrow at the *matto* and closed his eyes. I heard his breaths come out in longer, quieter segments, softer and softer, until it seemed as though he had stopped breathing altogether.

Let it go, in my mind I urged him. *Let it go.*

A smile hovered around his lips. *Not yet.*

I was certain that I had not seen his lips move, and yet the voice in my head was unmistakable.

Keeping his eyes shut, Aritomo released the bowstring. Almost immediately I heard the arrow hit the *matto*. Aritomo opened his eyes and we both turned to look at the target sixty feet away. The fletched end of the arrow stuck out of it, drawing a line of shadow across its surface and transforming it into a sundial. Even from where I was standing, I could see that he had sent the arrow right into the dead center of the target.

On the days when it rained too heavily for work in the garden, Aritomo would conduct the lessons in his study. He would bow to the emperor's portrait as he entered the room, ignoring me as I looked away in my resentment. He described in detail the history of gardening, matching his lessons to what we had been working on before the weather drove us inside. He taught me the finer points, explaining the concepts and techniques passed on to him by his father. He would pin a large sheet of paper on a corkboard, crowding it with pencil sketches to illustrate his teaching. He never allowed me to keep those drawings, tearing them up when he had finished.

Coming to the end of one of these lessons, I noticed a sheet of paper trapped beneath a stone on his desk. I pulled it out and held it up to the light. It was a print of irises, the paper flecked with mold, like the rusty spores on a fern. "Yours?" I asked, remembering the lanterns we had burnt on the night of the Mid-Autumn Festival a few months ago.

"Something I made a while back. A collector in Tokyo wants to buy it."

"Do you have any other pieces? I'd like to look at them."

He took out a few prints from a box. These were not of flowers, as I had expected, but demons, warriors and enraged gods brandishing swords and halberds over their heads. I returned them after a cursory look, not concealing my distaste.

"Characters from our myths and folktales," he said. "The warriors and thieves are from *Suikoden*—the Japanese translation of the Chinese novel *Sui Hu Chuan*."

The name was an arrow fired from my youth. "*The Legend of*

the Water Margin," I said. The book, a classic of Chinese literature, was known to most Chinese, even those who, like me, were mute in our own language. "I read it when I was fifteen. Waley's translation. I didn't finish it, but I don't think it had drawings like these."

"Older *ukiyo-e* prints often depicted characters from the novel," Aritomo said. He thought for a moment, then took out a small sandalwood box from a cupboard and placed it on his desk. I was wearing my leather gloves, which I did when I was not working in the garden. Now I watched him pulling a pair of cotton gloves over his hands; I searched his expression for any hint of mockery, but there was none.

He unlocked the box and carefully lifted out a book. "This is a copy of *Suikoden*. It is two centuries old," he said. "The illustrations were hand-printed by Hokusai himself." Seeing that I had no idea who he was talking about, he sighed. "You must have seen the picture of a big wave, frozen into stillness as it is about to crash back into the sea," he said. "There is a small boat caught in the hollow of the wave, and in the distance, Mount Fuji."

"Of course I've seen it. It's famous."

"Well, that was made by Hokusai." He wagged a cotton-white finger at me. "Most people think they know him, if only because of *The Hollow of the Deep-Sea Wave*. But he was much more than that."

He slid the book toward me. A vertical line of Japanese writing in red ink climbed down one side of the ash-gray cover. The book opened from right to left, and the first *ukiyo-e* print was of a view of a narrow mountain, with a minuscule temple clinging to its side. The room became completely still as I paged through the book.

"They're very detailed," I said.

"Depending on the colors he wanted to have and the effects he wanted to achieve, he would have had to carve more than one wooden block."

"They look like Japanese tattoos," I said. "*Irezumi*, aren't they called?"

"That"—he glanced at me—"is an unrefined word. Do not use it. Ever. Tattoo artists refer to them as *horimono*—things that are incised."

"*Horimono*." I repeated the word. It was so foreign, my tongue so unused to its shape, like how his name had once sounded to me. "During the war crimes trials in KL," I said, "I had to record the interrogation of a Japanese prisoner of war. The guards had removed his shirt and his chest, arms, and back were tattooed with birds and flowers, and even a demon with bared teeth. One of the guards later told me that the man's tattoos covered his entire body—his thighs, buttocks, legs."

"That is unusual for someone in the army," Aritomo said. "Full-body tattoos are seen only on criminals and the outcasts of society."

"The tattoos seemed . . . alive."

"He must have had a good *horoshi*—a tattoo master."

"Magnus has a tattoo," I said. "Did you know that?"

"You have seen it?" Aritomo looked at me.

"He came to Penang for a weekend. I was sixteen or seventeen then," I said. "He invited us to tea at the E & O."

The gardener crossed his arms over his chest, waiting for me to explain.

The ceiling fans in the hotel lobby fought a permanent losing battle with the humid air, the brass tips of their wooden blades volleying shards of light onto the walls and the marble floor. Dressed in a linen jacket over a white cotton shirt, a maroon tie and sharply creased gray trousers, Magnus was quite unlike the image of a planter I had in my head. The black silk eye-patch over his right eye gave him a roguish charm, and I could not help but notice how it drew glances from the other hotel guests, particularly the women.

"Only the four of you?" he said to my mother. "Where's Kian Hock?"

"Up in Batu Ferringhi," she replied. "Camping on the beach with the scouts."

A waiter showed us to a table on the terrace by the sea, among the Europeans and wealthy Chinese and Malay families. Magnus hung his jacket over the back of his chair. My parents nodded at a number of people who recognized them. A pair of Chinese boys, about five or six years old, chased each other around the tables, much to the obvious disapproval of the European *mems*. In the narrow stretch of water between Penang and mainland Malaya, liners and steamers and tramps sailed past the hotel, some coming in from the Indian Ocean, others from the Andaman Sea, all of their passengers, I was certain, rejoicing at entering the Straits of Malacca after weeks and months out in the open water.

"How's your estate?" my father asked. My parents seemed uncomfortable with Magnus, and this made me even more sensitive to the tension in the air.

"Doing rather well, Boon Hau," Magnus replied. "You should come and see."

"We should," my mother said. I recognized the tone in her voice, which she used with my father when she was making promises she had no intention of keeping.

"What happened to your eye?" The question had been troubling me from the moment I had first seen him.

"Don't be rude, Yun Ling," said my mother.

Magnus waved away her reprimand. "I lost it fighting in the Boer War."

"That was in Africa," my sister said.

"Ja," Magnus said. "The Brits tried to take our land. We fought back, but they burned our farms and put our women and children in concentration camps."

"Look here," my father interrupted before I could ask Magnus what a concentration camp was. "I don't want you talking any of that rubbish to my girls. You Boers were a bunch of thugs. You lost the war. Naming your tea estate 'Majuba' isn't going to change history."

"It's my small way of honoring the battle where the Brits were soundly thrashed," Magnus said in a silky voice. "And it gives me great pleasure to know that in Malaya and all over the East they're taking in a bit of Majuba every time they have their tea."

"Somebody at the Penang Club mentioned that you're flying the Transvaal flag," my father said.

"It's the flag of my home, the country I fought for," Magnus said. "You don't begrudge me that, surely."

"What about the garden, Mr. Pretorius?" Yun Hong asked in the silence that had hardened over our table. "Has the Japanese man started building it?"

"How on earth did you know about that?" Magnus asked.

"The girls read the feature on your estate in the *Straits Times*," my mother said. "You mentioned the Japanese gardener and the garden he was making. Hong has been fascinated by Japanese gardens ever since we visited Kyoto."

"It's coming along nicely, Yun Hong," Magnus said. He was sitting next to me and he turned his body to include me in the conversation. "Aritomo says it's not quite finished yet. He's clearing the trees at this moment. Perhaps in another year or so. You're most welcome to visit. He won't mind, I'm sure."

"Will it have a pond and a bridge over it?" Yun Hong asked Magnus. "And a rock garden?"

Before Magnus could reply, a waiter walking past our table collided into one of the Chinese boys running between the tables. The waiter stumbled, tipping over the tray he was carrying. Spoons and china cups and saucers clattered onto our table, some crashing onto the tiled floor. Yun Hong shrieked a warning at me as hot liquid drenched my shoulders and arms, soaking my blouse. My mother pushed back her chair and rushed to my side, grabbing a table napkin and wiping me with it. "Are you all right? Yun Ling? Yun Ling!"

I did not hear her, nor was I paying attention to the burning on my skin. I was staring at Magnus: he had also been splashed with hot water. His shirt and tie were soaked, and I watched as a patch of blue slowly bloomed on the left side of his chest, just above his heart. Other colors were soon appearing as his shirt remained plastered to his chest: orange and red and green.

He saw me looking at it. "It's just a tattoo, Yun Ling," he said.

"That was the first time I had ever seen a tattoo close up," I said, gazing down at Hokusai's woodblock prints but not seeing them. "My parents were horrified that he had marked his body like that, like . . . a gang member."

Aritomo closed the book and returned it to its box, pressing down the lid firmly and snapping the clasps shut. Outside, the rain had stopped falling, but water continued to taper off the eaves.

Stepping out onto my verandah early one morning I was startled by a man standing in the driveway. Even in the murky light I knew that he was not Siva; he had taken ill a few days before, and knowing how shorthanded Magnus was, I had not seen the need to trouble him for another escort.

"Miss Teoh?" the man said. It took me a second or two before I recognized Ah Cheong's voice. We had hardly ever talked to each other in all the time I had been in Yugiri. He approached the verandah steps.

"What's wrong? Has something happened to Mr. Nakamura?" I asked.

"My elder brother . . . ," he said in halting English, "my elder brother is with the People Inside . . . but now he wants to come out from the jungle."

I went down the steps and broke into a brisk walk. Aritomo would be angry if I kept him waiting. "You've been in contact with him?"

"Ever since he went into the jungle, when the Emergency began," Ah Cheong replied, keeping up with me. "I'd hear from him once a month, sometimes two months."

"You've been giving him food? Money?" I slowed down, glancing at him. The housekeeper shook his head. He was not being truthful but I did not press him. I remembered that morning when I had gone for a hike and had seen the figure in khaki by the pond. He had probably been a CT. I was not sure now if the other person who had joined him had been Aritomo or his housekeeper. "What is it that you want me to do?"

"He wants to know if he can trust this . . ." Ah Cheong gave me a piece of brown paper. Unfolding it, I saw that it was one of the thousands of safe-conduct passes the government had air-dropped into the jungle.

"As far as I'm aware the government has always honored its promises to . . . communists who've surrendered voluntarily," I said. "What's your brother's name?"

"Kwai Hoon. How much will the government pay him if he surrenders?" We had arrived at the heart of the matter: the pragmatism of the Chinese; even in the midst of danger, one should determine how much one is able to profit from it.

"Well . . . it all depends on your brother's rank and importance, the usefulness of the information he brings with him. The reward for Chin Peng is set at two hundred and fifty thousand dollars." Chin Peng was secretary general of the MCP. I was quite certain that the communists were aware of the hierarchy of rewards already. "That's not the reason you're here, is it?"

"Kwai Hoon knows about you," the housekeeper said. "He knows you are here. He wants to surrender."

"He can walk into any police station. There's one in Tanah Rata. I'm sure he knows where it is—he's probably attacked it a few times already."

"He says the government won't cheat him if you bring him in."

"What does Aritomo say?"

The housekeeper's eyes evaded mine. "Mr. Nakamura will be very angry if I bring trouble to his house."

"There are proper channels for your brother to follow if he wants to surrender," I said, returning the safe-conduct pass to him. "There's really nothing I can do. And Special Branch will have a file on him. They'll know he's your brother. They'll want to question you. Whether you intended to or not, you've already brought trouble to Mr. Nakamura's house."

"Kwai Hoon's mother was my father's number one wife. My mother was number three. He never registered his marriages. We have not lived in the same town since we were boys. No one knows we are half brothers." The housekeeper continued to look at me, lacing and unlacing his fingers. I did not want to involve myself in his troubles, and I wanted to turn him away. Sensing my reluctance, he said, "He is waiting in the jungle behind your house. He has some friends with him. Help him. *Tolong-lah*, Miss Teoh."

The CTs pulled the curtains over the windows as soon as they entered through the back door. All four were Chinese, one of them a woman in her twenties. A chill ran through me at the thought that they had been hiding behind my bungalow, watching my every move since who knew when. I was about to switch on the lights, but a voice stopped me. We sat around the dining table in the kitchen, their pale complexions giving off a faint glow in the shadows. Ah Cheong's brother spoke to me in Mandarin, but realizing that I was struggling to keep up with his words, he switched to Malay. "We're with the Third Regiment, Southern Division," he said. "We want to surrender."

"Why?" I felt vulnerable speaking to a bandit outside a prison cell and unprotected by guards. It was hard to believe that I was sitting here sharing a pot of tea with terrorists when, a few months before, I would have been doing my best to ensure that they were hanged.

"Our superiors eat three full meals a day, while the rest of us starve. They get money to spend. Medicines when they fall sick. Their women are allowed to live with them." Kwai Hoon's fist thumped his chest. "I complained about these things at the Central Committee meeting. I criticized the leaders." His chair rocked as he became more worked up. "Three days ago the commander ordered me to meet up with another regiment in Tanjong Malim. It was just an excuse to get us away from the camp—take us to some spot in the jungle to kill us."

One of the other CTs spoke up. "It won't be long before they realize we're gone. We have to move."

Kwai Hoon turned to me again. It was getting brighter outside and I could see his face more clearly. "I want to bring the *mata-mata* to our camp before it's abandoned. The more officers we catch, the more money we'll get. And I know where Chin Peng is. I want you to talk to someone with authority, someone who can give us the best deal. You would know who to speak to."

Nearly all of the shops in Tanah Rata had already closed up for the Chinese New Year. I turned off the main road and drove down a leafy road to the Smokehouse Hotel, purple bougainvillea growing in front of its mock-Tudor facade. With its low wooden ceiling beams, thick brown carpets, heavy furniture and walls decorated with oils of fox-hunting scenes in dusty gold-painted frames, the hotel reminded me of the country inns around Cambridge. The clerk at the reception desk pointed me to the telephone in an alcove behind the lobby. Inspector Woo answered just as I was about to hang up, and I told him about Kwai Hoon's intention to surrender. His low whistle scraped up a storm of static over the line.

"He's a member of the South Perak Regional Committee," he said. "Very high up. He'll know the names of all the unit leaders and committee members."

"Well, right now he's at my bungalow with three of his comrades. He'll lead you to their camp, but you have to come immediately."

154

"Why is *your* ladle in this pot?" Woo asked.

A porter pushed a trolley of luggage past me, followed by a European couple. I lowered my voice. "As you've warned me before, Inspector, I'm well-known to the CTs."

At a few minutes before eleven, Inspector Woo and his men drove up to my bungalow in unmarked cars. The tea fields around my bungalow were deserted, but the police placed blankets over the CTs' heads before leading them into the back of a windowless van.

"So the buggers just showed up here, out of the blue, asking for your help?" Inspector Woo asked when his men slammed the van doors shut and locked it.

"Shocking ignorance of social etiquette, isn't it?" I replied. "They could at least have left a message asking when would be a good time to call on me. How much money do you think they'll get?"

He took a long draw on his cigarette. "Twenty thousand dollars, maybe. Might even be more if the raid bags us some high-ranking communists. You might get a share of it too. A small share." He looked at me, and I knew he was expecting me to turn it down.

"Doesn't it make you angry, knowing that they're going to get the reward, while you policemen are the ones risking your lives?"

"The scheme has provided us with quite a lot of useful intelligence." Woo threw his cigarette away and got into his car. "If I were you, Miss Teoh," he said, "I'd be very careful for the next few months. If the CTs hear about your role in this, they'll want to make an example of you. And they have a very long memory." He slammed his door shut and wound down the window. "You're visiting your family for Chinese New Year? In case we need to get in touch with you."

My father had asked me the same question a week ago. "I'll be here, Inspector Woo."

"Well, happy New Year anyway, Miss Teoh." Woo gave the order to his driver to start the engine. "*Kung Hey Fatt Choy!*" he wished me again as he drove away.

Tidying up the kitchen, I thought about what Kwai Hoon had told me earlier, when we had been waiting for Inspector Woo. "I was trained by the British, you know," he had said. "Force 136. There were about a hundred of us. They sent us for training in Singapore when the Japs landed. And now we're enemies." He went to the windows above the sink and parted the curtains. "He's not far from here."

"Who?"

"Chin Peng. There's his base." He pointed through the window to a mountain peak. "Gunung Plata."

I glanced at the rifle he had set down on the table—the wooden butt had been chewed away by termites. "You'll be a very rich man, if you can lead them to him."

He looked around the kitchen. His comrades were in the sitting room. He lowered his voice and said, "You were a prisoner of the Japs, yes?" I did not reply, and he went on. "We had a few Japs with us."

"What were they doing?"

"Those bastards refused to surrender when they lost the war. They wanted to keep fighting. They came to see us, begged us to give them shelter. And in return they showed us where the army had hidden their store of guns."

"They're still with you, these Japs?"

"Most of them have deserted in the last few months. They left the jungle, surrendered themselves," he said. "Three months ago the Central Committee decided that the Japs who were still with us couldn't be trusted any longer. I was ordered to kill them." He sucked in his lower lip. "We left our camp one morning—me, my men, and the four Japs. I told them we were to meet a senior official and escort him back to camp. Those Japs had been with us since 1945; they'd become my friends." He pulled in his lips again, the sound wet and obscene. "When we got to a swamp, we shot them."

"If you ask nicely," I said, "I'm sure Templer will give you a medal for that."

"Eh, no need to be so insulting-*lah*." He glowered at me for a moment. "The Jap I was closest to . . . I decided to shoot him last, you know, for the sake of our friendship. Just before I shot him, you know what he tells me? He says he's heard rumors of a huge pile of war loot the Jap army had stashed away in the jungle—gold bars and gemstones, stolen from us Chinese. If I let him live, he'd help me find it."

"A man about to be shot will say anything."

"Yes, we both know that's true, don't we?" he said. "Well, any-way, the rumors of the loot have been floating around for years. Central Committee even organized a team to find it."

"What did you do to that Japanese, your friend?"

"What I've always done," he said. "I obeyed my orders."

Aritomo did not inquire about my lateness in coming to Yugiri, and I did not make any excuse for it. Planting a bed of ground cover later that afternoon, I stood up abruptly and turned to look at him. He was standing completely still, staring at the mountains around Gunung Plata. On the wind, the faintest cracklings of gunfire came to us, followed a few seconds later by the thumps of mortar shelling. We looked at each other and, after a minute or two, returned to our work.

All children are expected to travel from the farthest corners of the world for a reunion dinner with their parents on the eve of Chinese New Year. To ignore it is to be deemed unfilial, the worst crime a person can be accused of. One can be an embezzler or a murderer, but if one were judged to be filial to one's parents, society—at least the society I was brought up in—will find it easier to forgive you. Emily made disapproving noises when I told her that I would be staying in the highlands for the entire fourteen-day duration of the lunar New Year. "Then you must eat with us that night. And bring Aritomo," she added. "Frederik's coming as well."

Majuba House was decked out in red: red banners, red paper lanterns and red squares of paper with the Chinese character *fook* in black calligraphy to entice more wealth into the home. Branches of furry-budded cherry blossom in porcelain vases decorated the hallway. Emily's parents had passed away years ago, and since she was an only child herself, there were just the five of us for the din-ner. The servants had returned to their villages and the house was quiet. Emily had spent the past month preparing the food—a typ-ical mixture of Chinese, Malay and Indian dishes: roast pork in a thick soy sauce glaze, beef *rendang*, fish-head curry, crabs caught off Pangkor Island simmered in a coconut curry sauce, chicken curry fragrant with crushed stalks of lemongrass taken from her vegetable garden. Magnus served us wines from his cellar. "From the Groot Constantia vineyards," he said, holding up a bottle. "They supplied Napoleon with these when he was banished to St. Helena."

Aritomo took a sip, held it on his tongue and then swallowed. "A wine made for exiles."

"Like it? I'll give you a bottle to take home," said Magnus.

"Lao Tzu should have taken some with him," I whispered to Aritomo. He smiled, and I was aware of Frederik studying us from the other side of the table.

There was just too much to eat, but we finished all of it anyway, Aritomo helping himself again and again to the fish-head curry. I preferred the beef *rendang*, its coconut curry sauce simmered until it was almost dry. At the end of the meal Emily pushed her plate aside and announced, "We've arranged some *yen-hua*."

"What's that?" Frederik asked.

"Smoke flowers," she said, looking at the clock. "Come—let's go outside."

The estate workers and their families were already gathering on the lawn behind the house. The fireworks started a few minutes later. Yellow and red and white dandelions lit up the sky, pinned there for a few seconds before dribbling away, only to be followed by a blue agapanthus blooming here, a red starfish flaring there. I thought of "the People Inside," sitting in their camps and looking through the net of leaves at the smoke flowers illuminating the night sky. I wondered if my father was eating his dinner at that moment with my mother and brother. I wondered if my mother was well enough to come out from the bedroom where she had been spending her days since the war ended. My family's last reunion dinner had been ten years before. My sister had still been alive then.

"Can I come and see you later?" Frederik whispered to me. I gave him a nod.

"That should scare away the evil spirits for another year," Emily said, as the last spittle of fire died away from the night sky.

CHAPTER THIRTEEN

Ah Cheong closed up three of the six rooms in the house after his wife's death and had the furniture taken to the storeroom. Only the study, the sitting room and the bedroom are cleaned and aired weekly. The housekeeper follows me around as I open up the rooms, searching for a suitable work space for Tatsuji. The rice paper screens and the sliding doors have been ravaged by moths and sickened with mold. Cobwebs muffle the rafters, the husks of consumed insects hanging in them like tiny, primitive bells. My bare feet awaken the dust from the disintegrating *tatami* mats. In the largest of the three empty rooms, a leak has rotted the roof, staining the walls and the floor. Aritomo's will had provided for sufficient money to maintain his house and the garden, but for the last eleven, twelve years I have had to make up for the ever-increasing shortfall, paying Ah Cheong's and the garden workers' salaries and for any repairs that had to be done. Not once have I ever considered selling the property.

In the end, I decide there is only one room that is still in an acceptable state for Tatsuji. It is situated next to the study at the end of a short corridor, its doors opening out to the courtyard garden.

"Get someone in to clean up the room. I don't want you doing it yourself," I instruct Ah Cheong. "And while we're at it, we might as well have the other rooms spruced up."

He leaves to make the arrangements. I gaze at the rock garden in the courtyard. The rocks are completely smothered by moss. Birds nesting in the eaves have streaked the whitewashed walls with their droppings.

Later that day, two of Ah Cheong's female cousins arrive from Tanah Rata to dust and scrub and wipe. In the storeroom I come across a rosewood table and a pair of matching chairs tangled among a puzzle of furniture. I have Frederik's workers carry them to the workroom, and a shop in Tanah Rata delivers a desk lamp I ordered. By late afternoon the room is cleaned and readied for Tatsuji, and I instruct one of the workers to leave a message for him at the Smokehouse Hotel.

I walk around outside the house, making a note of what needs to be repaired or replaced. The long stretch of gravel separating the archery hall from the target bank is covered in weeds and lallang. I am about to take the three steps up into the hall when I remember to take off my shoes. I pull the blinds all the way up. The cedar wood floors, like those in the unused rooms, are also covered in a layer of dust. I stand there, my thoughts disarrayed like arrows scattered from a fallen quiver. Then I see Aritomo's bow, still resting on the stand, its string broken. I wipe the dust off with my palm. Next to it is my own bow. I take it up. The string is slack, and I unknot it. The bow is unyielding, releasing spores of dust into the air when I force it into a curve to restring it. It takes a few attempts to remember the method of knotting the string to both ends of the weapon. Eventually it is done, although Aritomo would have laughed if he'd seen it. The string is no longer as taut as it ought to be. I rummage in the cupboard at the back of the hall for a paper target, but find none. Returning to the front of the hall, I stand in the shooting position and make an effort to remove all thoughts from my mind. The most fundamental thing Aritomo taught me returns. I begin to regulate my breathing, pulling each breath deep into my body to center myself. It is a struggle, as though my lungs have shriveled like aged wineskins and no longer have the capacity to fill out the way they once could.

When I feel I am ready, I aim the arrow and draw back the bowstring. My shoulders resist, protesting at the strain. I release the arrow before my mind is still. It falls on the weed-covered gravel, halfway between the *shajo* and the target bank.

Birdsong sparkles the air; mists topple over the mountains and slide down their flanks, slow and soundless as an avalanche witnessed from miles away. Instinctively I turn to look behind me, expecting Aritomo to chide me with a look or a scathing word. I see only my own footprints on the dusty floorboards as the bamboo blinds creak softly in the wind.

The gardener who works for Frederik has agreed to see me in Yugiri. I wait for her outside the house at half past seven the next morning. "You're late," I say when Ah Cheong brings her to me.

"Only fifteen minutes-*lah*." Vimalya Chin is a Chinese-Indian in her early thirties, dressed in a short-sleeved checked shirt and a pair of khaki shorts that expose her hard brown calves.

I remind myself I am no longer in my courtroom, but I find some comfort in old habits. "I don't want dogs in my garden." I point to her mongrel sniffing at the irises. Giving me an annoyed look, Vimalya calls the dog to her with kissing sounds and leashes it to a tree. I look away when she lets the dog lick her mouth. Disgusting.

"So, what is it that you want me to do?" She looks around as we start our walk through the garden. "With all these exotics, it'll take a lot of work to turn the place into an indigenous garden."

"I have no intention of doing that! Frederik didn't tell you why I wanted to see you?"

The gardener shakes her head.

"Have you been here before?" I ask.

"Once, when Mister Frederik wanted me to work in his gardens. He brought me in here, just for a look."

"He probably wanted you to see what his gardens should *not* look like."

"What is it that you want me to do here?" she asks again, her hand jiggling the keys in her pocket.

"Will you stop that?" She pulls her hand out of her pocket. "I want you to restore it to what it used to be," I say.

She glances at me. "I'm not an expert in Japanese gardens."

"I am."

"Then you don't need me."

"I require someone to carry out my instructions, to supervise the workers."

"Do you have the original plans for this place?"

"They're all inside here." I touch my temple. "All here." Seeing that she is uncertain, I say, "Come along, I'll give you an idea of what needs to be done. You can decide if you want the job or not." I will have to uproot my memories from the soil I have buried them in. But isn't that what I have been doing for the past week? "Those hedges on the shore on the other side . . . you see them?" I ask when we come to the pond. "They have to be trimmed, every layer defined clearly—they have to look like waves surging onto a beach. And thin the lotus pads. Let the water breathe."

The air grows colder as we go deeper into the garden and I point out to Vimalya the things I want done. We stop for a while at the stone basin; its sides are completely furred with moss. I remember the morning I bent over it and peered through the gap in the bushes at the mountain. The view is obstructed by branches growing over the hole. The mountain is no longer visible, and for a moment I wonder if it is still there.

"Cut these branches away." I show her how large the gap has to be. "And scrub the basin."

"Japanese gardens are supposed to have a theme, aren't they?" Vimalya asks.

I nod. "A gardener will evoke memories of a famous view, or create certain feelings: solitude, tranquility or a mood of reflection."

"Well, I don't see a single, unifying theme here. It feels odd to me. Yet it's somehow also familiar," she says. "It's as if I *know* the various scenes that are being re-created but I can't identify them."

Only a handful of visitors have ever remarked upon this aspect of Aritomo's garden. "So," I say, "are you interested in helping an old woman fix up her garden?"

"My grandfather used to work here—Kannadasan."

"We worked together."

"He used to talk about you when I was a little girl. I had forgotten all about it until Mister Frederik mentioned you." She grinned. "It made me curious to see you."

"Bring him along the next time you come."

"He died a few years ago," she said. "He often mentioned the Japanese gardener—how he had saved him from being taken to work on the Burma Railway." Her shoulders lifted and dropped as she let out a sigh. "All right. Look, I'll help you fix up the garden. It'll be something to tell my children one day. But I can't be here all the time."

"You only have to make sure your men follow my instructions," I say. "I'll make a list of the things to be done. Can you start as soon as possible?"

"How long are you staying here?"

"I don't know. Not very long."

When we return to the pond half an hour later she stops and looks around her. "From what you've been telling me, it's just about aesthetics, isn't it? The garden I mean?"

"Of course not. The garden has to reach inside you. It should change your heart, sadden it, uplift it. It has to make you appreciate the impermanence of everything in life," I say. "That point in time just as the last leaf is about to drop, as the remaining petal is about to fall; that moment captures everything beautiful and sorrowful about life. '*Mono no aware*,' the Japanese call it."

"That's a morbid way of looking at life."

"We're all dying," I say. "Day by day; second by second. Every breath that we take drains the limited reserves we are all born with." I can see that she is not interested in the subject of death, believing, like so many young people, that it has no relevance to her.

"I can start tomorrow," she says. "I have to go—I have another garden to look at."

"I'm sure you can find your way out. And don't forget your dog."

I stand at the edge of the pond and gaze at it after she has left. In my head I hear Aritomo's voice again. *Do everything correctly and the garden will remember it for you.* Over the years I have sometimes wondered why he never wanted his instructions set down on paper, why he was so fearful that his ideas would be stolen and replicated. After staying away from Yugiri for so long, I am now starting to understand, to truly understand, what he meant. The lessons are embedded in every tree and shrub, in every view I look at. He was right—I have committed everything he taught me to my memory. But the reservoir has begun to crack. Unless I write them all down, who will be able to decipher his instructions when I am no longer capable of making anyone understand them, when I myself can no longer understand what I'm saying?

Tatsuji comes to work on the *ukiyo-e* at nine in the mornings, staying on until an hour or two after lunch. I instruct Ah Cheong to give him tea and snacks at midmorning. Occasionally I catch a glimpse of the historian strolling in the sections of the garden near the house—he knows better than to stray any further without my permission. There is always an attentive look on his face, even when he is merely sitting on a bench. From the window in the study I often see him reading from a slim and old hardback book, his legs stretched out and crossed at the ankles, sitting so still that he seems to have become another stone in the garden.

I spend the mornings writing down the instructions for Vimalya, making them as detailed as possible. News of my return to Yugiri has gone out, and I have been receiving notes and letters from people I have never heard of, requesting permission to visit the garden. Invitations to talk about Aritomo and his garden arrive from the Cameron Highlands Tourism Office, the Rotary Club, the Highlands Hikers' Association, the Expats' Club, the Tanah Rata Gardening Society. I spend the morning sorting them and throwing them away. That is when it happens. As before, there is no warning.

Unfolding a letter from an envelope, I gradually become aware that the paper in my hand is filled with unrecognizable scribbles. The world becomes so quiet that I seem to be able to hear the flow of my bloodstream. After a while—perhaps no longer than a minute or two—I pick up another sheet of paper. My hands are trembling. The writing on it is also illegible. Lifting my gaze to a pile of books on the desk, I find the titles on their spines to be indecipherable. I reach for a writing pad and write something on it, but my hand is shaking too much. I breathe in and out a few times until I feel I am ready, and then I print out my name slowly. Even though my hand's memory tells me I am writing it correctly, what appears on the paper is a line of hieroglyphs.

A surge of panic sends me out of the study. The passageways confuse me; I feel I am trapped in a maze. Tatsuji calls out to me as I rush past him. Hearing the faint sound of knocking, I follow it to the back of the house. Ah Cheong is cutting vegetables in the kitchen, his cleaver beating out a rhythm on the thick chopping board. He looks up, startled by my appearance. He puts down his cleaver, wipes his hands on a towel and brings me a glass of water. Tatsuji has followed me into the kitchen and is staring at me. I take the glass from Ah Cheong, relieved to see that the trembling in my hand is less obvious now. I drink the water slowly, and when I finish I realize I am still holding something in my hand. I open my fingers to find a wrinkled piece of paper. Smoothing it out, I see my name, looking just a bit wobbly and uncertain, but recognizable.

I fold up the paper and instruct Ah Cheong to put up a sign at the entrance to discourage those who show up hoping to be allowed in. But I know that they will still come.

The Smokehouse Hotel appears not to have changed much in the last forty years. The purple bougainvillea is still there, larger now, flowering up the mock-Tudor walls all the way to the roof. The prints of foxhunting scenes still hang inside. The lobby is busy with tourists. As is my habit, I am early. A waiter shows me to a table on the rose garden terrace. Elderly Europeans sit in the sun, enjoying their tea and scones. The air is powdered with the fragrance of roses.

The tranquility of my surroundings fails to calm me. I am still unsettled, *frightened* if I am to be honest—and I must be, I have to be—by what happened this morning. The neurosurgeons have warned me that these episodes will start occurring more and more frequently, their durations lengthening every time. They could not find the reason for this rapid degeneration of my brain. I do not have a brain tumor; I am not suffering from dementia nor have I been afflicted by a stroke. "You're one of the luckier ones," the last of the many neurosurgeons I consulted had said to me. "There are cases where the aphasia is immediate and total."

Emily arrives a few minutes later, helped into her chair by her driver, who looks almost as old as she is. I offered to pick her up from Majuba House when she invited me for tea, but she prefers to have her own man drive her. After what happened this morning, I am glad that she refused my offer. Driving here from Yugiri, I was fearful that the road signs would suddenly become incomprehensible to me.

"You're still doing *taiji*," I say. "I can tell—you walk like someone ten years younger."

She dismisses her driver and smiles. "I try to do a short session every morning-*lah*. I used to teach once a week, but I'm too old to do it now."

Our tea arrives a few minutes later. Emily bites into a scone and I look away as strawberry jam bloodies the corner of her lips. She wipes her mouth, chews slowly and swallows. "How's your family?"

She already asked me this at our dinner in Majuba House a few nights ago. "My father died a year after *merdeka*. Hock—my elder brother—moved to Australia with his family. He was killed in a car accident a few years ago. I'm not close to his wife and sons."

An old Chinese couple being shown to their table waves to Emily. "They were in my *taiji* class," she says, leaning closer to the table. "You should go to the class. There's a new teacher. She's very good—I taught her myself."

"It's a bit too late for me."

She looks into my eyes. "You're sick, aren't you?"

I put down my knife on the plate, silently cursing Frederik's loose lips.

"I'm not blind-*lah*," Emily goes on. "Coming back here so suddenly, and after all these years, when you've never visited us." She leans forward, her neck stretching out. "So, what is it? Cancer? Don't look so angry-*lah*—old people are allowed to be tactless. Otherwise where's the fun in growing old?"

I point to my head with a finger. I am in no mood to give her the details of my condition; it seems easier to let her think what she wants.

She touches my wrist lightly. "We might be suffering from different illnesses, but it means the same thing in the end, doesn't it? Our memories are dying." We do not speak for a few moments. Then she says, "At my age, you know what I wish for? That I should die while I can still remember who I am, who I used to be."

"Most people would just ask for a peaceful, painless death. Preferably going to sleep and never waking up again."

"We're not *most people*," she retorts. "At least I hope *I'm* not." She takes a small bite of her scone. "Does Frederik know?"

"I've told him." I make a mental apology to Frederik for questioning his discretion earlier.

"If there's anything we can do, you must let us know." She waits for me to agree, and then says, "Did you ever find out where your sister was buried?"

"I put up a soul tablet for her in the Kuan Yin temple in Penang."

"That's good enough."

"The tablet is nothing more than a piece of wood."

"You never made that garden for her?"

"I tried. But I was never happy with the results. I wasn't good enough to do it on my own."

Emily takes another scone from the dish. "You could have hired somebody from Japan."

"Building a garden for Yun Hong was not going to ease my pain, nor would anything that I did. I realized that."

"Remember when you came to stay with us, all those years ago?" She smiles. "There was so much anger in you. Of course you had good reasons. But I still see it in you, that anger. Oh, you've hidden it well. And maybe it's not the same as it used to be. Not as strong. But it's there."

Later, as we are leaving the Smokehouse, she stops me. "*Aiyah*, I almost forgot—one of my friends is the head nun in a temple. She wants to see you."

"See me, or see the garden?" I say.

"She wants to talk to you about Aritomo."

"In relation to?"

"How should I know? Ask her yourself-*lah*."

I consider it for a moment. "Fine. Tell her to come."

Returning to Yugiri an hour later, I find Tatsuji at the *katsunigi-ishi*, the stone where guests are required to remove their shoes before entering the house. He is tying his shoelaces, and he looks up when he senses my presence. "I was just going back to my hotel. I need to talk to you about the *ukiyo-e*."

"What is that book you're always reading?"

Straightening up, he hesitates, then removes the book from the pocket of his linen jacket and gives it to me. I look at an anthology of Yeats's poems, surprised.

"You were expecting something else?" he asks.

I shrug and return the book to him.

"A friend read me one of Yeats's poems when I was a young man," he says. The sense of loss in his voice is old, as though it has been a part of him for most of his life, and for some reason I am struck by its similarity to my own.

"Come with me," I say.

His face brightens when he realizes I am taking him into the garden. The leaves on the maple by the house are rusting, the branches pushing out from behind the thinning foliage. I lead him deeper into the trees, following the path to the waterwheel. Red bromeliads straining to bloom spike the slope. Since coming back to Yugiri I have not gone to look at the waterwheel. I am relieved to see it is still there. But it no longer turns, no longer grinds the water with the patience of a monk. Lichen daubs the sides of the wheel and two of its paddles are missing. The waterfall is now a trickle, and the pool is choked with algae and drowned leaves and broken-off branches.

If Tatsuji is appalled by the state of neglect, he does not show it. "The emperor's gift," he announces. From the rigid way he holds himself I suspect he would have bowed to it if I were not present. "How many turns has this wheel made since it was built, I wonder?"

"As many as the earth has made around the sun," I say, humoring him.

"Emperors and gardeners." Tatsuji shakes his head. "Do you know what happened to the Chinese emperor after the communists took over? They rehabilitated him. He ended his days as a gardener."

The inscriptions beneath the remaining paddles are grouted with moss; the writing is fragmented, the prayers garbled and weakened, and I realize that a day will come when they will be silenced completely.

"*Shobu,*" Tatsuji says, pointing to the plants along the banks. He breaks off a leaf and holds it up. "They are a symbol of courage for us because they are shaped like swords." He crushes it and the burst of scent flings me back to the first time Aritomo brought me here. I take the broken leaf from Tatsuji and inhale deeply. I can see it all so clearly in my mind, that morning. I must remember to add it to what I have written down.

"I was chatting to some hikers in the hotel lobby this morning," Tatsuji says. "They were waiting for their guide to show them the trail Aritomo had taken on that last day."

"You'll see a lot more of them in the coming days," I say. "In a month's time it'll be thirty-four years to the day Aritomo got lost in the jungle. And there'll be tourists hoping to see the garden."

The search for Aritomo was only reported as a minor item in the newspapers, but it soon generated sufficient interest for journalists from Singapore, Australia and Japan to flock to the highlands. The reporters were followed closely by Buddhist and Taoist monks, Chinese and Indian mediums and travelers of the spirit world, all of them trying to convince me they knew where Aritomo had gone, into which ravine he had fallen, or who had abducted him. They had come from all over: Ipoh, Penang, Singapore—even from Bangkok and Sumatra—and all claimed to have knowledge of where Aritomo was or of what happened to him. Some were well-meaning but most were charlatans, hoping to collect the reward of ten thousand Straits dollars I had posted. The police followed up on the more plausible leads, but with no success.

For years after his death, I continued to receive interview requests for me to talk about Aritomo. Then came the inquiries asking for permission to visit Yugiri. I turned away every one of them. Interest in Aritomo did not die off completely, but I was relieved when it waned over time. The periodic flashes of curiosity over the decades usually occurred during the reissues of his translation of *Sakuteiki*, or when one of his early *ukiyo-e* prints went on sale in an auction in Tokyo. Over the decades the story of his disappearance had obscured him, like mists blurring the outlines of a mountain range, transforming it into whatever shapes people wanted to see.

"Since coming here I've discovered an entire cottage industry centered just on Aritomo-*sensei*," Tatsuji says, shaking his head, half in admiration, half in disbelief. "Walking tours and talks, beer mugs and books and postcards and maps."

"I wouldn't waste any money on those books if I were you. They're rubbish, every one of them. Written by people who never knew him."

"Some of the theories *are* quite credible," Tatsuji says.

"Which?" I throw a few of them at him: "The one that says he was kidnapped by the communists? Or that a tiger mauled and ate him? Some even think that he was a spy and had been recalled home to Japan."

"If he did return to Japan, no one ever saw him."

"You know which theory is my favorite?" I ask. "The story a *bomoh*—that's a Malay witch doctor—told me: that an aboriginal sorceress had fallen in love with Aritomo and had bewitched him to live with her in the jungle."

"I remember the morning when I read about Aritomo-*sensei*'s disappearance in the news," Tatsuji says. "That was the moment he became a real person to me, and not just a name. Strange, is it not, that a man should become real only when he vanishes?"

Elephant-ear ferns between the rocks flap gently, and I fancy for a moment that they are straining to eavesdrop on our conversation.

"What do you think really happened to him?" Tatsuji asks.

"Look around you." My hand draws a circle in the air, throwing a lasso over the mountains. "Do you know how easy it is to lose your way in the jungle? Just one wrong turn and suddenly you wouldn't know where you were." I point to a ridge behind us, a crack running up its side. "See that viewing tower jutting out there, among the trees? His favorite walk goes past that. You think you would be able to find your way out from the jungle if you went off the path there?"

"Probably not."

"People get lost in the jungles up here. It happens quite often, although the papers don't report it. And forty years ago the highlands weren't as developed as they are today. This place was wilder then."

Tatsuji's eyes take in the hills in a long, slow sweep. Going to the edge of the slope, I tell him about the Taoist symbols Aritomo had etched with light and shadows on the lawn below. He shades his eyes with his hand and peers down. "I do not see them."

"Too much cloud-shadow," I reply.

But when we walk past the area later I realize it is not the clouds that have rubbed away the symbols but the grass growing wild. The boundary between positive and negative, male and female, darkness and light, has been lost. Like so many other features in Yugiri, the positive and negative elements created by Aritomo are based on illusion, visible only when the right conditions are present.

"Why did you come here to see him?" Tatsuji asks.

"I asked him to design a garden for my sister," I reply, "but he turned down my commission."

"Yet he accepted you as his apprentice."

"He said he would teach me to make the garden myself. He needed an extra pair of hands to work the garden, and to interpret his instructions to his workers. That's what he told me."

"You do not sound convinced."

"I've always had the feeling that . . ." I hesitate, afraid of sounding foolish. "I've always felt he had other reasons for wanting to teach me. But he never told me," I add. "And I never asked him." I stopped wondering about it years ago, but since coming back to Yugiri the question has been floating just beneath the surface of my mind, its shape refracted by the water of time.

"You met him in the first week of October of 1951," Tatsuji says.

Again, the depth of his knowledge both impresses and disturbs me. "It was the day after the communists killed the high commissioner."

"I am reading Mr. Pretorius's book about the Emergency: *The Red Jungle*. Fascinating—I never knew that there were Japanese soldiers fighting with the communists."

We resume our walk. Tatsuji stops at every view, examining every stone lantern and statue, and it is nearly an hour later when our walk brings us back to the pavilion. Vimalya's workers have swept the leaves and cleaned the area around it. The lotus pads they hauled out from the pond are piled to one side. A shoal of carp swims out to us, a tattered orange and white banner pulling through the murky water. In my head I hear the echo of my voice from a long time ago, reciting the lines from a poem. *I am the daughter of Earth and Water . . .*

Tatsuji is looking at me, and I realize I was mumbling to myself. "How is the work on the *ukiyo-e* coming along?" I ask.

"I've almost finished examining them and writing up my notes," Tatsuji says. "Do you speak or read Japanese?"

"*Nihon-go?* I used to. I learned it when I was in the camp." The memory comes to me of an abandoned squatter village a few miles outside Kuala Lumpur I once visited to take photographs for a war crimes hearing. The villagers had been taken away by the Japanese to a nearby field and made to dig their own graves before they were shot. Through the broken doors and windows of the houses I glimpsed tables and chairs, a rocking horse lying on its side, a doll on the floor. Pasted on a wall in front of a ransacked provision shop was a poster in English, exhorting the villagers to use the Japanese language. Someone had crossed out the word "*Nihon-go*" in red and scrawled "British Come!" beneath it.

Tatsuji is speaking, and I bring my mind back to the present. "The first piece of the *ukiyo-e* was made in early 1940, according to Aritomo's notes on the back," he says.

"That was the year he came to Malaya."

"To put his disgrace behind him, perhaps?"

"Disgrace?" I look at him sharply.

"There are not many people still alive who would have known about it," Tatsuji says. "Aritomo-*sensei* had been commissioned to build a garden for a member of the imperial family—"

"But he resigned. He told me so. He wasn't willing to sacrifice his vision to accommodate the client's needs."

"Is that what he told you?"

"What happened exactly, Tatsuji?"

"There were arguments. They turned vicious. He lost the commission before the work was even a third of the way completed. To make things worse, the emperor sacked him. Everyone heard about it. It was a tremendous loss of face for him. From that moment on, he could no longer call himself the emperor's gardener."

"He never told me that," I say quietly.

"In the last few years I have spoken to the few people still living who knew him . . ." He looks out over the water, to the lotus flowers nodding in the breeze.

"What is it that you're trying to say?" He reminds me of some of the lawyers who cannot get straight to the point.

"I think," he says, scratching at the peeling wood of the railing, "Aritomo-*sensei* played a small but important role in the war."

A breeze disturbs the wind chime hanging beneath the eaves. It sounds brittle and out of tune. The rods, I notice, are cancerous with rust.

"He protected a lot of people from the Kempeitai," I say. "He kept a lot of men and boys from being taken to the Burma Railway."

"I believe he was working for the emperor when the imperial army attacked Malaya."

"You've just told me that the emperor had sacked him." I realize that I must sound like I'm back in the courtroom, picking up on some inconsistency in a witness statement.

"I have often wondered if this was his chance to redeem himself, to repair the damage to his reputation. It certainly gave him a strong reason to leave Japan."

"To do what? You think he was a spy?" I give the historian a skeptical look. "I'll admit that the possibility had occurred to me shortly after Aritomo went missing, but I dismissed it."

"People think he went missing only once in his life, but I disagree," Tatsuji says. "He did it twice. The first time was when he left Japan before the Pacific War started. No one knew where he went or what he did from that moment onward, until he showed up in these mountains."

"Look, everyone knows now that there were Japanese spies everywhere in Malaya years before the war, working as tailors and photographers and running little businesses. But they were living in *towns*, Tatsuji," I say, "in places that had some strategic importance to your army. Aritomo was here. *Here*." I rap my knuckles on the wooden railing. "He had hidden himself away in his garden. And, anyway," I add, "if he was still working for your country, why did he remain in Malaya, long after the war ended? Why did he never return home?"

Tatsuji is silent, the intent look in his eyes telling me he is studying my words from various angles.

"What did you do in the war, Tatsuji?"

There is a moment's hesitation. "I was in Southeast Asia."

"Where in Southeast Asia?"

He turns his gaze to the heron picking its way between the lotus pads. "Malaya."

"In the army?" My voice hardens. "Or the Kempeitai?"

"I was in the imperial navy's air wing. I was a pilot." He leans slightly away from me, and I notice how rigidly he contains himself. "When the air raids over Tokyo began, my father moved to his villa in the countryside," he says. "I was still in the pilots' training academy. I was an only child. My mother had died when I was a boy. I visited my father whenever I could get a few days' leave."

He closes his eyes and opens them again a moment later. "There was a labor camp a few miles away from our villa. Prisoners of war had been shipped from Southeast Asia to work in the coal mines outside the town. Every time some of them escaped, the men in the village would form search parties. One weekend when I was visiting my father, I saw them with their hunting dogs and their sticks and farming tools. They made wagers as to who would be the first to find the escaped prisoners. 'Rabbit hunting,' they called it. When they were recaptured, the prisoners were taken to the square outside the village hall and beaten." He stops, then says, "Once I saw a group of boys club a prisoner to death."

For a long time neither of us speaks. He turns to me and gives me a bow so deep I think he is going to topple over. Straightening up again, he says, "I am sorry, for what we did to you. I am deeply sorry."

"Your apology is meaningless," I say, taking a step back from him. "It's worth nothing to me."

His shoulders stiffen. I expect him to walk away from the pavilion. But he stands there, not moving.

"We had no idea what my country did," he says. "We did not know about the massacres or the death camps, the medical experiments carried out on living prisoners, the women forced to serve in army brothels. When I returned home after the war, I found out everything I could about what we had done. That's when I became interested in our crimes. I wanted to fill in the silence that was stifling every family of my generation."

The chill in my bones leaches into my bloodstream; I restrain myself from rubbing my arms. Something he mentioned earlier is troubling me. "Those boys in the village," I say, plumbing the depths of his eyes, "you were with them when they punished the prisoners, weren't you? You took part in the beatings."

Tatsuji turns his back to me. His voice comes faintly over his shoulder a moment later. "Rabbit hunting."

It begins to rain softly, raising goose pimples on the pond's skin. In the branches above the pavilion, a bird keeps repeating an ascending three-note cry. I want to be angry with Tatsuji. I want to ask him to leave Yugiri and never come back here again. To my surprise, I feel only sorrow for him.

CHAPTER FOURTEEN

Rain had prevented the clay on the pond's bed from drying out properly, but then one morning, Aritomo announced that it was time to fill it.

We spread a final layer of pebbles and sand over the clay, the bed dipping toward the six standing stones we had set down in the center. A week before we had diverted the stream into a catchment area beside the pond. Using a shovel I broke open the wall of the low dyke. Water flooded into the pond, gathering up the puddles already waiting there. As the swirls and ripples died away, a fragment of the sky was slowly re-created on earth, the clouds captured in water.

"The level of the water must be just right," Aritomo said. "Too low or too high, and it will affect how the pavilion looks. It will not be in harmony with the height of the shrubs planted around the pond, or the trees behind the shrubs, or even the mountains."

"I'm not sure I understand."

Aritomo's gaze swept over the pond. "Close your eyes," he said. "I want you to listen to the garden. Breathe it in. Cut your mind from its constant noise."

I obeyed him. Beneath my eyelids the captured light throbbed and gradually faded away. The sounds of the water filling the pond quieted. I listened to the wind and imagined it passing from tree to tree, from leaf to leaf. In my mind I saw the wings of a bird stirring the air. I watched leaves spiraling from the highest branches to the mossy ground. I smelled the scents of the garden: a lily, newly opened; ferns heavy with dew; the bark of a tree crumbling beneath the voracious assault of termites, the smell powdery with an undertone of dampness and rot. Time did not exist; I had no idea of how many minutes had passed. And what was time but merely a wind that never stopped?

"When you open your eyes again"—Aritomo's voice seemed to come from far away—"look at the world around you."

My eyes skimmed over the water to the camellia hedges; to the trees rising to the mountains, the mountains entering the folds of clouds. I never allowed my gaze to rest too long on any particular object, but I let it see all things. In that one instant I understood what he wanted from me, what I would need to comprehend to be the gardener he had spent his lifetime becoming. For the first time I felt I was inside a living, three-dimensional painting. My thoughts took shape with difficulty, expressing only the thinnest layers of what my instincts had grasped and then let slip. A sigh, both of contentment and of sorrow, drained out from deep within me.

I checked the water level daily. When it was deep enough, we put in lotuses and planted reeds along the edge. Aritomo also stocked it with koi from a breeder in Ipoh. About a week after we started filling the pond, he ordered me to bring out the coil of copper wire from the tool shed. I carted it in a wheelbarrow and set it down by the pond. Using a pair of wire-cutters, he snipped the copper into short lengths and showed me how to form them into fist-sized balls, before leaving me to it.

"What are they for?" I asked when he returned and I had about forty of them in a pile. They looked like the rattan *sepak takraw* balls kicked about by children in every kampong and schoolyard.

He picked one up and flung it far out into the water. It sank immediately, frightening the fish. "The copper stops the growth of algae."

We circled the pond, throwing in the copper balls. We had almost finished when he stopped and lifted his face to the cloudless sky. He silenced me with a finger just as I was about to speak. I followed his gaze, but saw nothing at first. Then, far off in the sky, a bird peeled itself from the sheet of bright sunlight and descended rapidly, spiraling down closer and closer to earth until I could make out a heron, its plumage a smoky gray-blue. Drawing a halo over the pond, it dropped to skim across the water, racing with its own image, flying so low that I thought its reflection would break free of the surface.

Sweeping up its wings, it landed in the shallows, sending ripples radiating across the pond.

"*Aosagi*," Aritomo said, a note of wonder in his voice. "I have never seen it here before."

"Where do you think it's come from?"

He shrugged. "Perhaps from as far away as the steppes of Mongolia."

"Perhaps even Japan?"

He nodded slowly, almost to himself. "Yes, perhaps."

Before going home that evening, I stopped at his house, entering through the back door. Ah Cheong was on his way out to his bicycle, and he smiled. He had been friendlier toward me ever since I helped his brother to surrender, occasionally even bringing me a flask of water when I was working on my own in the garden.

"Kwai Hoon sent me this," he said, giving me a cutting from the *Straits Times*. It was over a fortnight old. "What does it say?"

A photograph accompanying the news article showed the bodies of the CTs the police had shot, laid out in a row in a jungle clearing in front of a helicopter. Kwai Hoon had refused to reveal the sum of the reward he had received when the journalist interviewed him, but the former political commissar of the Malayan Communist Party said that he would use the money to open a restaurant.

"You tell your brother I expect to eat for free at his restaurant for the rest of my life," I added when I had read it to him. "And I only eat abalone and lobster and shark's fin."

The housekeeper grinned. "Mr. Nakamura is waiting for you."

The *kore-sansui* garden in front of the house had been completed a month before. I felt a sense of accomplishment whenever I saw it. I knew I would find Aritomo there, raking out parallel corrugations in the fine white gravel. He did that every few days, changing the patterns every time and asking me to guess what he was trying to create. Today he was drawing lines around the rocks with the sharpened end of a stick, walking backward to obliterate his footprints. The gap between each line was not uniform, narrowing here, bulging out there. When he finished he came to stand next to me.

"Waves surrounding a chain of islands." I knew it was the wrong answer the instant I spoke.

"Nothing so poetic today," he said, smiling. "Just the contour lines of hills on a map."

"The heron is still at the pond. It seems to have made its home there."

"It will continue its journey sooner or later."

"What did you want to see me about?"

He put down the stick and asked me to follow him to his study. He bowed to his emperor's portrait before going to the wall of paintings. He stood there, looking at each of them, his head turning slowly from left to right. Finally, he lifted my sister's watercolor from its hook and held it out to me.

I looked at it and then swung my eyes back to him. "You said it was a gift."

"You have been stealing little glances at it every time you come in here."

Etiquette required that I decline his offering a few more times, in case he had changed his mind, but he was right—I had been coveting it ever since I failed to buy it. Extending both my hands, I took the painting from him. Then, surprising even myself, I bowed to him, pleating my body almost in half. When I raised my head again we were both aware that it had been made in complete sincerity.

Magnus was standing on the verandah when I got home, a photograph album clamped in his armpit. A tiffin carrier stood on the table. He noticed the painting in my hand before I could hide it from him. "He gave it to me," I said.

"I'm glad it's back with you." His smile had just the faintest tinge of regret in it. "You haven't been coming for dinner for a while now. I thought I'd better check on you." He indicated the tiffin carrier. "Emily made chicken curry. And there's rice."

"Thank her for me. Gin *pahit*?"

"That sounds *lekker*." He sat down in a rattan chair. I went inside and returned with our drinks. "Templer and his wife heard about Aritomo's garden," he said. "They'd like to see it."

"He's not keen on having visitors to his garden."

"That's why I'd like you to speak to him. And these aren't just any visitors," Magnus said. "Templer's the most powerful man in Malaya."

"You're turning soft, Magnus, letting a British civil servant walk all over you. Are you taking down your flag too?" I taunted him with a grin.

"The flag stays."

"Templer will have no qualms ordering you to remove it."

Stories of the new high commissioner had circulated across the country from the first day of his appointment, brought up here to the highlands by government officials who recounted them in the NAAFI or at the Tanah Rata Golf Club. In the weeks after he took up his post in Kuala Lumpur, Templer had spared no one from a tongue-lashing if he found them to be inefficient, sacking those he deemed incompetent.

Magnus tapped his chest with his fist. "He's never met anyone like me."

"When is he coming?"

"We won't know his itinerary until the very last minute," Magnus said. "It's part of his tour to 'win the hearts and minds of the people,' as he calls it. We haven't told anyone else, of course. Not even the servants."

"They'll know some VIP is coming the moment Emily tells them to polish the silver."

"*Gats*, you're right." He chuckled. "I'd better warn her." He pushed the leather-bound photo album across the table to me. "I thought you might like to look at this."

The photographs documented the stages of work in Yugiri, from its beginnings as a jungle to what it looked like before the Occupation. I turned a few more pages and then stopped. "When did you meet Aritomo?"

Magnus rubbed his eye-patch with a knuckle. "Summer of 1930—no, 1931. That's right—it was the week after Japan invaded China. I was in Tokyo, trying to get the Japs to buy my tea. People were celebrating in the streets. There were banners and public demonstrations everywhere." He took a long swallow from his glass. "I told the tea broker how much I had enjoyed the city's temple gardens. I asked so many questions that the poor man was embarrassed when he couldn't answer me. The next day he introduced me to Aritomo. The emperor's gardener himself—I could hardly believe it! He gave me a private tour of the imperial gardens. They were magnificent." He stopped and thought for a moment. "They're efficient people, those Japs. It's no surprise they almost won the war."

"You admire them," I said.

"And so do you, in your own way," he replied. "Why else would you be here?"

"I'm only doing this for Yun Hong."

Magnus gazed steadily at me. I resumed looking through the photographs. A few pages later I stopped and pointed to a photograph of Aritomo giving instructions to four shaven-headed young Japanese men. They were shirtless, their short, muscular bodies struggling with the burden of the waterwheel. The photographer had caught them in stark contrasts, as if casting them into statues commemorating some workers' revolution.

"He brought his own people?" I asked.

"Five . . . maybe six of them. They stayed for a year to clear the land and train the local workers."

"Strange, isn't it, that he chose to come to Malaya . . . chose to make it his home."

"Actually, I'm to blame for that," Magnus said.

"What do you mean?"

"Well . . . I invited him to visit. I didn't know he would fall in love with Camerons after staying here less than a week." His eye roved around the verandah, looking for a suitable place to rest. "He stayed here—in this bungalow—when he first came to Majuba."

"He never told me." It was odd how Aritomo's life seemed to glance off mine; we were like two leaves falling from a tree, touching each other now and again as they spiraled to the forest floor.

"Like you, he didn't want to stay with us either. I'm beginning to wonder if Emily and I smell bad." He scratched his chest distractedly, but stopped when he realized I was staring at him.

"Your tattoo," I said, closing the album. "Did he do it for you?"

He rubbed his glass with his fingers, rupturing the beads of condensation on it. "You've never forgotten it?"

"How could I?" I said. "It was Aritomo, wasn't it?" The suspicion had been growing in me ever since Aritomo showed me his copy of the *Suikoden*. Looking at the expression on Magnus's face, I realized it was true. "Let me see it."

He appeared not to have heard me. I was about to ask him again when he began unbuttoning his shirt. His movements were deliberate, as though he was prying out tacks in a corkboard. He stopped when his shirt was open a third of the way down his chest. The delta around his neck was tanned and crinkled; further below, the skin was pale and smooth and soft. Pinned above his heart was the tattoo, smaller than I had remembered it to be. It was a beautifully rendered eye, the blue of the iris nearly matching Magnus's own. It was set against a rectangle of colors that I realized represented the Transvaal flag.

"It's very detailed," I said.

Magnus looked down at his chest, his voice congealing in his throat. "I told him I didn't want something too Japanesey."

The colors had remained vivid, glistening. "It looks as though he's done it just a short while ago."

"He mixes the inks himself." Magnus stroked the tattoo with his fingers and then looked at their tips, as though expecting them to be stained with pigments.

"Was it painful?"

"Oh *ja*." He winced at the memory. "He warned me, but it was worse than I had expected."

"Why did you get it?"

"Vanity," he replied. "It was like a medal, setting me apart from other people. I'd always felt incomplete, because of this." He touched his eye-patch. "I was taken to a bathhouse in downtown Tokyo. *Jislaik*, what an experience! The men walking around completely *kaalgat*, tattoos on their entire bodies . . . dragons and flowers . . . warriors and beautiful women with long black hair. They were disturbing, those tattoos. But I found them beautiful too."

"When was your tattoo done?"

"When he was visiting us, I told him about the tattoos I had seen in that bathhouse. He offered to do one on me, a small one, if I sold him the piece of land he wanted." Magnus buttoned his shirt and smoothed the wrinkles. "He gave me a good price, even invested some money in my estate. It certainly made things easier for me— money was tight at that stage."

In the trees, a nightjar called out. It was the first time I had heard one since moving into the bungalow. The locals called it the *burung tok-tok*; some of them would gamble on the number of times it made its distinctive knocking sound. The bird called again and out of habit I began to count off its cries against the number I had in my head; it was something I had done in the camp, when I lay in my bed, trying to distract myself from the mosquitoes and fleas feeding on me.

I became aware of Magnus's eye on me. "Did you win?" he asked, smiling.

"I've never won a bet on the *tok-toks*."

He stood up to leave. "Keep the album. Give it back to me when you're done with it."

I walked him down the verandah steps to his Land Rover. "That feeling of incompleteness—did it go away after you were tattooed?"

He stopped to look at me. An old sadness dimmed his eye. "It'll never go away," he said.

The *tok-tok* bird began calling out again after Magnus drove off and the noise from his car faded away. I stood there on the driveway, counting its cries. Once again I lost the wager with myself.

The past week had been more strenuous than usual and so, the next morning, I was happy to be lazing in my bed until I heard someone calling for me. The spill of the sun across the bedroom walls told me it was about half past seven. I put on a dressing robe and looked at Yun Hong's painting for a moment before going outside. Aritomo was on the verandah, a rucksack held loosely in his hand.

"There you are," he said. "I have run out of birds' nests."

"The herbalist in Tanah Rata doesn't stock them," I reminded him. "And he won't be open at this time, not on a Saturday."

"Get dressed. Go on." He clapped his hands. "And wear hiking shoes. We're going up into the mountains."

We set out on foot, heading for the hills north of Majuba estate. Far to the east, clouds ringed Mount Berembun. The tea fields soon gave way to uncultivated slopes. At the edge of the jungle Aritomo turned and looked back for a moment, his eyes scanning the way we had come. Satisfied, he pushed into the ferns. After a second's hesitation, I followed him.

It is hard to describe what entering a rain forest is like. Conditioned to the recognizable lines and shapes one sees every day in towns and villages, the eye is overwhelmed by the limitless varieties of saplings, shrubs, trees, ferns and grass, all exploding into life without any apparent sense of order or restraint. The world appears uniform in color, almost monochromatic. Then, gradually, one begins to take in the gradations of green: emerald, khaki, celadon, lime, chartreuse, avocado, olive. As the eye recalibrates itself, other colors begin to emerge, pushing out to claim their place: tree trunks streaked with white; yellow liverworts and red sundew in shafts of sunlight; the pink flowers of a twisting climber garlanded around a tree trunk.

At times the animal track we took disappeared completely into the undergrowth, but Aritomo never hesitated, plunging into the vegetation to emerge onto another trail seconds later. The noise of insects sizzled in the air, like fat in a smoking wok. Birds cawed and whistled, disturbing the branches high above us, showering us with dew. Monkeys ululated, fell into a petulant silence and then picked up their cries again. Broad waxy leaves sealed off the way behind us. To my surprise I found that I had no trouble keeping up with Aritomo—my stamina had improved since I started working in Yugiri.

"Where are we going to get the nests?"

"The Semai," he replied, his eyes fixed on the track ahead, not slowing down his pace. "Much cheaper than buying it from those cutthroat Chinese."

I had seen the nests in Chinese medicine shops, displayed inside finely crafted wooden boxes, next to jars of dried tigers' penises and ginseng roots resting on red velvet. "Why would the Semai sell to you?"

"They had some trouble with the authorities during the Occupation," he said. "Magnus asked me to help them. Since then they have always given me a good price for the nests."

Trees leaned in at odd angles, as if they were being pulled to the ground by the vines manacled around their branches. An emerald sunbird flitted past, a barb of light still glowing from the sun it had absorbed before it flew into the jungle. Aritomo drew my attention to the plants in the undergrowth as we climbed. Once he stopped to stroke the pale trunk of a tree. "The *tualang*," he said. "They grow to two hundred feet. And this"—he stooped over a low, unremarkable-looking shrub and tapped it with his stick, giving me a mischievous look—"is what the Malays call *tongkat ali*. Its roots, they tell me, can revive a man's wilting libido."

If he was hoping to fluster me, then he failed; before the war, such direct references to sex would have embarrassed me, but not anymore. "We should harvest and sell it," I said. "Think of the fortune we'll make."

The sun was high up when we emerged from the trees onto a rocky slope, the ground bare except for a few scraggly clumps of lallang. All along I had assumed that we were going to an aboriginal village so I pulled up short when I saw the cave ahead, gouged into the side of a sheer limestone cliff, its mouth guarded by stalactites.

Aritomo took a pair of flashlights from his rucksack and offered one to me, but I shook my head. "I'll wait here for you," I said.

"There is nothing to be frightened of," he said, switching his flashlight on and off a few times. "I will be right in front of you, all the time."

The moist, ripe stench of bird droppings hit us the moment we entered the cave. I switched on my flashlight immediately, even though there was enough sunlight from outside to illuminate our way for the first six, seven paces. My breathing sounded loud to me, jagged. We rounded a bend and entered the second chamber. Aritomo offered his hand to me. After a moment's hesitation, I took it. We were on a raised walkway hammered together from cast-off plywood planks, the boards flexing beneath our weight. Darting wings and clicking sounds crisscrossed the darkness of the cavern.

"What's that?" I whispered.

"Echolocation," Aritomo replied, just as softly. "The birds use it to find their way in the dark."

Sweeping the flashlight around my feet, I let out a cry of disgust. Mounds of guano lay beneath the planks, rippling with thousands of cockroaches. Sweeping my flashlight up, the outer edge of the fan of light picked up what seemed to be a network of cracks in the walls; pointing the light higher, I saw that they were centipedes, each one about ten inches long, their legs sticking out from thin, tubular bodies. They reminded me of the skeletons of a shoal of prehistoric fish, pressed into rock by time. Disturbed by the light, they came alive, scuttling off into the gloom.

The passage widened the deeper we went into the mountain, the ceiling rising higher. The ground dropped and rose, occasionally leveling out. My anxieties fell away, but I continued to hold on to Aritomo's hand. The air improved when we came to another cavern, larger than the two we had already passed through. Sunlight broke in through the roof a hundred, two hundred feet above, illuminating the rocky floor. Swiftlets darted through poles of light, and the echoes of dripping water corroded into the mineral silence.

Voices came from the back of the cave. Lit by the weak glow of a hurricane lamp, a pair of Orang Asli men stood below a bamboo scaffolding, staring upward into the gloom. Both were in their thirties, thin and dressed only in loose-fitting shorts. They seemed unaware of us until Aritomo whistled to them, dislodging a flock of swiftlets into flight.

The two men looked unhappy when they saw me. "You no bring people," one of them said to Aritomo.

"She will not tell anyone, Perang," Aritomo said.

"I won't even know how to find my way back here," I told Perang in Malay.

He turned to the man beside him, his chest and arms covered in watery black tattoos that had lost their shape, spilling across his skin. The tattooed man shrugged. "One time only," Perang warned me. "You no come again, *faham*?"

"*Faham*," I said, nodding.

They returned their attention to the darkness above us. I followed their gaze, feeling the ground drop away from me. At first I could see nothing. Gradually I made out movement along the wall of the cave. A boy of about eleven was shimmying up a bamboo pole, like an ant on a reed. He was about seventy, eighty feet up, unsecured to any rope. Now and again he stopped and hung from a ledge with one arm; with his other hand he cut the nests from the rock, dropping them into a bag tied around his waist.

"What about the eggs?" I asked, staring at the boy, my voice cowed by the immensity of the cavern.

"They steal the nests before the birds lay them," Aritomo said. "When the female discovers her nest is gone, she will make another.

They will leave that nest for her to lay her eggs. They do not take any nest if there is a chick in it."

My neck grew stiff from craning my head upward, and I had already forgotten my own fears of the cave when the boy climbed down the scaffolding. Perang took the bag from him and squatted by a low, flat rock beneath a fall of sunlight. He shook the bag's contents out onto the rock. Specks of dust swirled and eddied in the light. The nests, a number of them covered in feathers, varied from reddish brown to a faint yellow-white. Their shape reminded me of human ears.

Aritomo picked only the whiter ones. The dark-colored nests, he whispered to me, had absorbed the iron and magnesium in the cave walls. He paid for them, and as we left the swiftlets' cave I heard Perang shouting from behind us, "You no come again!"

We rested on a broad ledge looking into a deep ravine. I was relieved to be out of the cave. I breathed in deeply, letting the cold, damp air scour all residue of the cave's sticky stench from my lungs. Opposite us, a cataract poured off an outcrop, the water broadening into a white feather as it fell, to be swept away by the wind before it could reach the earth.

Aritomo filled two cups with tea from a thermos flask and gave one to me. I remembered what Magnus had asked me on the previous evening. "The high commissioner and his wife want to visit Yugiri," I said.

"The work is not finished."

"You can let them see the sections that have been completed."

He considered my suggestion. "You have worked very hard in the last five months. Why don't you show them around?"

It was the first bit of praise I had received from him since I became his apprentice. I was surprised at how good it made me feel. "Will I ever become a competent garden designer?"

"If you continue to work at it," he said. "You do not have a natural talent for it, but you have shown me you are determined enough."

Uncertain as to how I should respond to that, I kept quiet. We were like two moths around a candle, I thought, circling closer and closer to the flame, waiting to see whose wings would catch fire first.

"That first day when you came to see me," he said, a moment later, "you mentioned that you had become friends with Tominaga Noburu." He was looking toward the mountains, his back straight, his body still. "What was he doing in your camp?"

"Working us to death," I replied. "He worked all of us to death."

He looked at me. "Yet you are here, Yun Ling. The only one who survived."

"I was lucky." I met his stare for a second, then turned away.

From his rucksack he took a pair of nests and placed them in my palm. They had the brittle lightness of biscuits. It felt strange holding them so soon after they had been torn from a crease in a rock high up in a cave. I thought of the swiftlets, hurrying back to the cave after their hunt, relying on the echoes they made, those sparks of sound to light their way in the dark, only to be met with a returning, shapeless silence where their nests had once been. I thought of the swiftlets, and sadness clogged my chest, hardening like the strands of the birds' saliva.

Aritomo pointed to the sky in the east. A wall of clouds was pushing up behind Mount Berembun. "Tomorrow's rain lies on the horizon."

My eyes wandered from one end of the mountains to the other. "Do you think they go on forever?"

"The mountains?" Aritomo said, as though he had been asked that question before. "They fade away. Like all things."

CHAPTER FIFTEEN

At a few minutes before ten on a Friday morning, two weeks after Aritomo and I climbed to the swiftlets' cave, a black Rolls-Royce pressed between two Land Rovers stopped in front of Majuba House. Magnus and Emily were waiting on the driveway to welcome the high commissioner and I went to join them, closing the door before the dogs could get out. The Gurkha was standing at attention. Eight Malay policemen got out from the Land Rovers and formed up by the entrance to the house. Sir Gerald Templer emerged from the Rolls and then helped his wife out. The high commissioner was a thin man of medium height in his fifties, dressed in a khaki bush jacket and sharply creased trousers of the same shade. His eyes pounced on the flag draped around the pole on the roof before darting to Magnus, his trim mustache flexing down the corners of his mouth. I caught the gleam in Magnus's eye; he was enjoying the irony of Templer's presence in Majuba. "We really should have more British officials coming to pay their respects," he whispered to me as we stepped forward to greet the Templers. Emily jabbed her elbow into his side.

"Welcome to Majuba," he said, shaking Templer's hand.

The high commissioner turned to the woman standing next to him. "My wife, Peggy."

"We heard that your estate was worth a visit," Lady Templer said.

Magnus started the tour immediately; Templer's lack of patience was already legendary. We followed him to the Twelfth Division, a section chosen because the slope was not too steep but it would nonetheless give us the best views of the tea-covered valleys. A tall, middle-aged police officer fell back from the group to walk beside me. "Thomas Aldrich—chief inspector," he introduced himself.

188

"You're Teoh Boon Hau's daughter, aren't you? I was told you're showing us the Jap's garden. You're here on holiday?"

"I live here," I said, quite certain that Special Branch had opened dossiers for every one of us in Majuba before the high commissioner's visit.

The skies were cloudless, the clear air polishing the light to a high sheen. A breeze rose intermittently from the valley floor, skimming over the treetops. The high commissioner and his wife walked easily on the rutted lane to the workers' homes. A ten-foot-high fence, topped with barbed wire, surrounded the compound. Two members of the Malay Home Guard, trained by Magnus, stood to attention and saluted Templer. Faded washing flapped on clotheslines. Hens trailing lines of yolky chicks scuttled away at our approach. An old woman squatting outside her home waved at us, the rolls of fat squeezing out between the layers of her sari. Unseen hands kneaded her doughy face as she chewed her *sirih* in a slow, unthinking rhythm. Now and again she spat out a jet of blood-red betel-nut juice onto the ground in front of her.

"Your father's been extremely helpful in the *merdeka* talks," said Aldrich. "I think there's a good chance Malaya will be independent within a few years."

"You sound enthusiastic," I said. "Independence could mean the end of your job."

"You Chinese are more terrified of *merdeka* than we whites," he said with a lopsided grin.

What he said was true, especially among the English-educated Straits Chinese—the King's Chinese, as we called ourselves. We had seen how the movements for independence had turned violent in India and Burma and the Dutch East Indies, and there were fears that a similar kind of communal violence would also tear Malaya apart. Uncertain of how we would fare under the rule of the Malays, we preferred the British to run the country until Malaya was ready for independence. When that would be, no one was willing to say.

"The CTs say they're fighting for independence too," I said. "Ironic, isn't it? If you gave *merdeka* to Malaya, they'd have their legs kicked out from under them in no time."

Aldrich nodded toward Templer. "That's why he's keen for Malaya to be independent as soon as possible. It'll be a fatal blow to the communists. Anyway, after the way we abandoned you all to the Japs, do we really still have any right to rule?"

Magnus gave the Templers a quick history of the highlands as they walked, telling them how William Cameron had surveyed the mountains by riding on elephants. "Like Hannibal crossing the Alps," he said, and Emily's eyeballs rolled over like a pair of fish sunning their bellies.

"People thought I was mad when I started the estate." Magnus threw a quick smile at me. "And they were right. I fell under the spell of this magnificent plant from the very beginning." He plucked a bright green shoot from a bush, rolled it between his fingers under his nose and gave it to the high commissioner's wife. "These evolved from plants first discovered in the eastern Himalayas. An age before Christ was born, a Chinese emperor already knew about them. He called it the froth of the liquid jade."

"The emperor who discovered tea after some leaves dropped into a pot of water he was boiling?" Aldrich said. "That's just a myth."

"Well, *I* believe it," Magnus retorted. "What other beverage has been drunk in so many different forms, by so many various races, over two thousand years? Tibetans, Mongolians and the tribes of the Central Asian steppes; the Siamese and the Burmese; the Chinese and the Japanese; the Indians and, finally, us Europeans." He paused, lost in his dream of tea. "It's been drunk by everyone, from thieves and beggars to writers and poets; from farmers, soldiers and painters to generals and emperors. And if you enter any temple and look at the offerings on the altars, you'll see that even the gods drink tea."

He looked at each of us in turn. "When the English took their first cup of tea, they were really drinking to the eventual fall of the Chinese Empire."

Templer's face reddened, and his wife touched him lightly on his arm. Aldrich said, "Well, you can't deny that China made immense profits selling tea to the world." For some reason the thin, sharp smile that barbed his words gave me the feeling that he was goading Magnus intentionally.

"True, at first," Magnus replied. "But the flow of silver into

China in exchange for tea became a cause for concern. So the English found a way to reverse the flow. You know how they did it?"

"Lao Kung . . . ," Emily warned her husband. She shot a beseeching look at me to silence him, but I shrugged helplessly.

"Opium." Magnus answered his own question. "Opium from the East India Company's fields in Patna and Benares. Sold to China to counter the loss of silver from England's treasury. And so the Celestial Kingdom became a nation of opium addicts, all because of our desire for tea."

"You're talking rot," Aldrich said.

"Oh? You English went to war with China twice—twice—to defend your right to sell opium. Look in the history books—they're called the Opium Wars, in case you miss them."

"Shall we continue our tour?" Emily said, pushing past Magnus to stand in front of him. "You must see our workers' nursery."

With Emily interpreting, the Templers stopped at the nursery to chat with the elderly women who looked after the infants while the mothers were out picking tea. The babies slept in saris hanging on ropes from the roof beams. Every now and again one of the women would give these cocoons a gentle push.

The high commissioner left the women and walked around the compound, peering through the windows of the workers' shacks and checking the conditions of the buildings. Magnus did not appear unduly worried—he was not an exceptionally caring employer, but he made sure his workers were well treated. He was strict with them, disciplining them and docking their pay for any misbehavior that disrupted the efficiency of production. And, unlike some rubber estates I had been to, there were no suspiciously pale-skinned children running around.

We waited patiently when the high commissioner spoke to the tea pickers as they worked the slopes, feeding fistfuls of leaves into their baskets. Templer insisted on shaking the hand of every one of the workers he saw in the estate, and he wanted to hear the troubles they were experiencing in the Emergency.

"Your brother's doing well, Miss Teoh," Aldrich said, when the others had gone a short distance ahead of us toward the factory. "It's been difficult for him in the force."

"Difficult?" A derisive laugh gurgled up from the back of my throat. Kian Hock was one of a small number of Chinese inspectors in the Malayan Police Force and my father had been using his influence to advance Hock's career. He had done the same for me until I got myself sacked.

"After the Japs surrendered, the men who had been in the bag in Changi refused to have anything to do with those who had escaped instead of remaining at their posts. Your brother's often seen as one of them, someone who's had an easy, comfortable war."

"You seem more forgiving," I said, "despite your own experiences."

His eyes grew hazy. "Strange, isn't it, how people like us can always seem to recognize one another. I was in Changi for a year before the Japs sent me to the railway."

"You're lucky to have survived," I said.

"Where it comes to luck, you certainly beat everyone I know. The sole survivor of a slave-labor camp? Location of said camp unknown." His eyes did not absorb any of the warmth from his smile. "I must tell you I found your RAAPWI report . . . intriguing, if rather brief."

For a second I didn't know what he was talking about. Then I remembered the report I had given to the military agency for the Recovery of All Allied Prisoners of War and Internees when I was in the hospital. "There wasn't much for me to tell," I said.

From far in front I saw Magnus glancing at us. Aldrich waved at him to continue ahead to the factory without us. "Fantastic work you did with Kwai Hoon, by the way," he said. "He assured us he wouldn't have surrendered if it hadn't been for you."

"He said he'd show you where Chin Peng was hiding."

"Unfortunately the camp was abandoned by the time our men got there. But we think he's still somewhere in these parts," he said. "Their top brass—people like Chin Peng—are using Cameron Highlands as their HQ, our informant tells us."

"Go and catch them, if you know they're here."

Aldrich squinted into the valleys. "Have you any idea how many vacant bungalows, chalets, huts, and shacks are out there? We can't search or watch every one of them. When we *do* get wind of a meeting, they always manage to flee into the jungles before we arrive."

I wondered why he was telling me all this. From the corner of my eye I saw that Magnus and the Templers had already gone inside the factory. The visit to Yugiri would be next.

"This man—our informer," Aldrich continued, "he mentioned something he had heard, that somebody in Majuba estate is helping the CTs—supplying food and money. Perhaps even information."

"Who is it?"

"Our man doesn't know."

"Any of the workers here could be helping them," I said. "The guards can't watch over them all the time. Magnus has been asking for more constables. No one's responded to his requests."

"Magnus Johannes Pretorius has a reputation for turning the most unfavorable of circumstances to his advantage."

"What are you talking about?"

"He wasn't interned during the Occupation. And he kept Majuba out of the Japs' hands."

"Aritomo interceded on his behalf."

"Nakamura Aritomo." The thin smile flashed again. "Ah, of course. I'm surprised the War Crimes Tribunal didn't investigate *him*."

"You think Magnus is helping the CTs?"

"Well, he's not exactly fond of the British, is he?"

"He has his reasons."

"And the CTs never attacked Majuba." Aldrich raised a forefinger. "Not once."

"Many of the farms here have not been attacked either," I pointed out. "If the senior communists *are* using Camerons as their base, as you said, it wouldn't make sense for them to attack us, would it? They wouldn't want the attention."

"Some of the planters have been paying the CTs protection money to keep them off their land," Aldrich said.

"Those rumors have been floating around since the early days of the Emergency," I said. "Why are you so interested in Magnus? Do you have evidence that he's paying off the CTs?"

"We'd like you to keep your eyes open for any unusual activity in the estate, tell us if you see or hear anything we should know about," Aldrich said. "Keep us informed about what Magnus is up to."

"You want me to spy on him?"

The smile on the chief inspector's face remained unchanged. "You're in a perfect position to help us, Miss Teoh. You've been living there for what, five months? Six? You're part of the scenery now. Coming here to study under the Jap was so unusual, so eccentric, if I may say so. No one would suspect you of working for us."

I started to walk away from him, but he stopped me. "Special Branch is also interested in your Jap gardener. We're quite curious as to what he's doing up here. We don't want to be forced to deport him, do we?"

"On what grounds?" Despite telling myself not to be intimidated, I had to fight off the fear rising up inside me. The reams of laws under the Emergency Regulations gave the security forces nearly unlimited powers in matters relating to the insurgency.

"Oh, don't you worry. I'm sure we'll manage to come up with something."

"Then I'll wait for you to do just that." I turned and strode toward the tea factory, leaving him to follow behind me.

In the time I had spent in Yugiri, I had come to feel that the garden had in some way become mine. To show it to others who had not worked there seemed like a violation of something private I shared only with Aritomo. I was the last one to get out from the car when we arrived at the entrance to Yugiri. I had not expected to feel this reluctance to take them into the garden, and I almost hoped I would see Aritomo there, waiting to turn us back.

"Well, let's get a move on, shall we?" said Templer.

I touched the wooden plaque on the wall, then pushed the door open. Everyone fell silent as they followed me into Yugiri.

The light in here seemed softer, older, the air sharp with the tang of the yellowing bamboo leaves. The turns in the track disoriented not only our sense of direction, but also our memories, and within minutes I could almost imagine that we had forgotten the world from which we had just come.

Lady Templer and Emily let out murmurs of amazement when we emerged from the path at the edge of the pond. Seeing the garden anew through the eyes of these people, I was reminded of Aritomo's skill. The six narrow rocks rising from the water reminded me of fingers, reaching out to catch a magical sword

flung far out into the water. For a moment I wondered why Aritomo had not followed the advice in *Sakuteiki* and limited the number of rocks to five, as he had done for the rock garden at the front
of his house.

"The pond is called Usugumo," I said. "Wisps of Clouds."

"Odd name for a pond," said the high commissioner.

"Look at the water," his wife said. The wind had died down, and
the clouds on the water's edge were like the reflections of faces peering into a well.

"Clever," said Templer.

"I've been meaning to ask you—what does 'Yugiri' mean?" said
Lady Templer.

"Evening Mists."

"A name even more obvious than Wisps of Clouds. I must say I
expected something more obscure."

"Yugiri is a character from *The Tale of Genji*." From the polite
expression on her face I knew that she had no inkling of what I was
talking about. "He was the firstborn son of Prince Genji."

"How interesting. And the pavilion? Does it have a name?"

"Aritomo hasn't decided on one."

The high commissioner pulled out a Leica from a bag carried by
one of his assistants. "I'm afraid Mr. Nakamura has prohibited all
photography in his garden," I said. Shooting me a peeved look, Templer thrust the camera into the bag.

Aritomo was waiting for us outside his house, dressed in a dark
blue cotton robe and a pair of gray *hakama*. Except during the
times when we were practicing archery, I had never seen him in traditional Japanese clothes.

"So kind of you to let us see your garden, Aritomo," Emily said,
following closely behind me.

He smiled at her. "You are always welcome here, Emily."

"You've made a lot of changes to the place," Magnus said, coming up to us a moment later.

Aritomo gave him and the Templers a bow. "Yun Ling has been
a satisfactory guide, I hope."

"She's been wonderful," Lady Templer said, "so knowledgeable
and enthusiastic."

"I have a demanding teacher," I said, glancing at Aritomo.

Lady Templer touched my arm. "The pavilion was charming. You really should give it a name, something special."

"The Pavilion of Heaven," Aritomo said. I looked at him, surprised. He nodded to me once.

"How . . . *oriental*. But your house!" Lady Templer said, her eyes sweeping past Aritomo. "If I didn't know better I would have sworn we were somewhere in Japan."

"So you're Hirohito's gardener?" said Templer.

"That was a long time ago," Aritomo replied.

Aldrich introduced himself to Aritomo and added, "Some Japanese civilians are driving around the country on a pilgrimage, visiting places where their troops had fought our chaps."

Light seemed to hone Aritomo's eyes. "Who are they?"

"They call themselves the Association for the Recovery of Our Fallen Heroes, or something ridiculously grandiose like that," Aldrich said. "They've requested police protection for their travels, but we're too shorthanded to bother with them. Have they contacted you?"

"I have not seen nor spoken to anyone from home since the war ended," replied Aritomo.

"You've never gone home?"

"No."

The high commissioner had other farms in the highlands to visit and Lady Templer drew Aritomo and me to one side when they were leaving Yugiri. "Why don't you design a garden for us, Mr. Nakamura?" She looked hopefully at him. "After what we saw this morning, the grounds at King's House look terribly dull."

"At this point in my life, I am only interested in working on my own garden," Aritomo replied, his angular and precise words fitting into the space between us, leaving no room for anyone to change his mind.

"That's disheartening to hear." She frowned, then aimed a smile at me. "But there's nothing to stop you from designing one for us, is there?"

"When Aritomo feels I'm ready," I replied, "your garden will be among the first I'll work on."

"I'll hold you to that promise, my dear girl," she said. She turned to Aritomo. "You really should open your garden to the public. It's a great shame, keeping something so beautiful to yourself."

I was watching Aritomo carefully. Sadness eclipsed his eyes. "Yugiri will always be a private garden."

Resting on the verandah of my bungalow, I wondered why Aldrich's news about the Japanese traveling around the country had troubled Aritomo. I picked up my notebook and turned the pages, looking through the newspaper cuttings again, skimming over the masses of information I had scribbled down. The pale blue envelope fell out from between the pages onto the floor; I picked it up and looked at it.

I had never told anyone my real reason for working in the War Crimes Tribunal, not even my father or my brother, Hock. I had been looking for information that would help me find my camp, and I had hoped that being a research assistant would give me an opportunity to speak to the Japanese war criminals being tried in Malaya. I had also found a Japanese woman to teach me more of the language.

The normal rules of court procedure had not been strictly applied in the war crimes hearings. The tribunal gave weight to uncorroborated information, accepted circumstantial and hearsay evidence from the victims of the Japanese. I interviewed the Japanese officers and recorded their statements, but I also slipped my own questions in, asking them if they knew anything about my camp. I made sure that the cases I worked on were so well constructed that the war criminals would never get a reprieve. My tenacity impressed the prosecutors but my health deteriorated as I followed up on every piece of evidence I found and sat in on every interrogation session I could. I convinced, cajoled and threatened the reluctant victims to testify against the Japanese criminals. It was not possible to remain detached from my work, naturally. There were times I could not go on reading the documents when I remembered the fear and pain I had gone through. During those occasions, I had to push myself to continue, to sift through the information for that one thing I was looking for. But there was never a mention of the camp where Yun Hong and I had been imprisoned. When I left the tribunal to pursue my studies, I kept my notebook. A part of me still hoped that I might find the answer there.

I visited Captain Hideyoshi Mamoru on the day he was to be hanged. He had been sentenced to death for the massacre of two hundred Chinese villagers at Teluk Intan, a fishing village on the west coast of Malaya. Surviving witnesses testified that he had ordered his men to march the villagers into the sea. When the water had come up to their waists, the soldiers had opened fire on them. The sea was so bloodied, a villager told me, that it took seven tides to wash the stains from the beaches.

A Sikh guard brought me to Hideyoshi's cell. The Japanese was curled up on a wooden pallet. He sat up when saw me come nearer to the metal bars. I waved the Sikh away.

"You seem calm, unlike some of the others," I said to Hideyoshi.

"Do not be fooled, Miss Teoh," he replied in fluent English—I recalled from his file that he had spent part of his military training in England. He was a slender man in his forties, made thinner by the deprivations of the war, like every one of us. "I am frightened, oh yes, very much. But I have had enough time to prepare myself. You want to know why?"

"Why?"

"From the first day I saw you walking into the courtroom, I knew you would do your duty thoroughly. I knew I would be hung."

"Hanged," I said. "Not hung."

"No difference to me," he said. "You were in one of our camps, *neh*?"

"I *was* in a Japanese camp." They were the exact words I had used on the other men I had helped deliver to the hangman. By now I knew what Hideyoshi's next question would be. Every one of the prisoners I had spoken to had invariably asked the same question when they discovered that I had been interned. Hideyoshi did not disappoint me.

"So where were you sent?" he asked. "Changi? Java?"

"It was in Malaya, somewhere in the jungle."

Hideyoshi got up from his pallet and shuffled to the bars. "The camp was hidden?" Though he reeked of stale perspiration I still took a step closer to him. "All the other prisoners were killed, yes?" he said. "How could it be that you are the only one who lived?"

"You've heard of that camp?" I whispered.

"Only rumors—how do the Malays describe them?"

"*Khabar angin.*"

"News scribbled on the wind." He nodded. "I *did* hear of those camps, yes."

"Tell me more about them." It was difficult to keep my voice steady.

"What can you do for me in return?"

"I can speak to someone higher up, perhaps get your case reviewed."

"And what reasons will you give?" Hideyoshi asked. "The evidence against me was brilliantly presented to the court. Brilliantly."

He was correct: it would appear highly suspicious if I were to intercede on his behalf. I looked around the passageway; I had to find out more about what he knew. I had to. It was the only scrap of information I had come across after all this time.

"If I write a letter to my son," he said, "will you post it to him for me? Intact. Not censored?"

"If I'm satisfied that what you tell me is true."

"They were only rumors," he repeated, as though worried that he had promised too much. I stared at him. "Kin No Yuri," he said, and then translated it for me even though I understood what it meant. "Golden Lily."

"That tells me nothing," I said, raising my voice. From the other end of the corridor the Sikh guard looked at me. I signaled that everything was fine.

"It is the name given to the kind of place you were sent to," Hideyoshi said. "You would know more about it than me if you had been taken there."

It was all he knew, I realized, all he could tell me. The sense of hope that had fired me up a short while before, the hope that some-one else knew of the camp I had been sent to, disappeared. I backed away from the bars.

"You are not going to keep to our agreement," he said, "are you?"

I spun around and walked away from him. I returned to his cell half an hour later. He opened his eyes and looked up when I called his name. I passed him some writing materials between the bars and went to lean against a wall, watching him write. A short while later he came to the bars and handed me a letter sealed inside a light blue envelope. He looked at my hand, the hand with the missing fingers. "You should forget all that's happened to you," he said.

The address on the envelope was written in English and Japanese. "How old is your son?"

"Eleven. Eiji was three, almost four when I last saw him. He will not remember me."

I weighed the envelope on my palm. "I thought it would be heavier."

"How much paper do you need to tell your son you love him?" he replied.

Staring at him, this man who had ordered an entire village to be killed, I felt a profound sadness for him, for us.

When the guards came to take Hideyoshi, he asked me to walk with him. I hesitated, then I nodded. Walking along the passageway, we passed the other prisoners in their cells. A few of them stood to attention, saluting him from behind the bars. Hideyoshi kept his eyes straight ahead, his lips moving soundlessly.

The sky was streaked with the carnage of sunset when we came out to the yard at the back of the prison. Hideyoshi stopped and turned his face upward, breathing in the light from the first stars of the evening. The guards pushed him up a flight of steps to the hanging platform and positioned him beneath the noose. They looped the rope around his neck and tightened it. He stumbled but regained his balance. One of the guards held up a blindfold. Hideyoshi shook his head.

A Buddhist monk, appointed to conduct the rites for these executions, began to pray, thumbing the string of beads twined around his fingers as line after line of prayers unreeled from his throat. The droning washed over me. Hideyoshi and I looked at one another until the trapdoor cracked open and he dropped into an abyss only he could see.

The siren announcing the end of the working day whined through the air, pulling me from the thicket of my memories. Returning the notebook to my room, I spent a few minutes looking at Yun Hong's watercolor. I recognized the restlessness taking hold of me, a forewarning of the periods of despair that used to swamp me before I came to the highlands. I knew when these moods were imminent, when they would loom over the horizon of my mind.

I put on a cardigan, wound a scarf around my neck and walked to Yugiri. Banks of clouds were trapped in the hollows between the ridges. At Usugumo Pond I stopped and lingered. The garden felt larger, now that the pond was filled, and I realized that this liquid mirror was another form of *shakkei*, borrowing from emptiness to create more emptiness. The stones and pebbles with which we had lined the pond were now submerged in water. It gave me a deep feeling of satisfaction to know that we had done everything properly, even if the results of our efforts were not visible. The drowned stones imparted a different character to the water, made it seem older, denser, its secrets hidden away.

In the shallows, the gray heron stood on one leg, grooming itself. It stopped and eyed me, then returned to contemplating itself in the water. For some reason it had remained here, always returning to the pond after it had been absent for a day or two.

The rusty screeching of crickets filled the air. On the opposite bank, movement in the tree ferns caught my attention. I tensed up, preparing to run if I had to. Aritomo slipped out from behind the ferns a second later. I sighed, relief loosening my limbs. Like the heron, Aritomo paused, staring at me from across the water. Then he walked toward me.

Twilight dampened the air with a watery haze, weighing down every leaf in the garden with the sadness of another day ended. Aritomo stopped beside me and leaned on his walking stick, gazing at the heron. For the first time since I knew him, it struck me that he was no longer young.

"*A pond guarded over by waterfowl will bring peace to the house,*" I murmured, recalling a line of advice from *Sakuteiki*.

Creases flared out from the corners of his smile. For a timeless moment I looked straight into his eyes, and he stared at me with the same concentration he had shown when he was studying the target, just before he released his arrow.

Above the highest mountains, the last of the day evaporated from the sky. "The Pavilion of Heaven . . . Yun Hong would have been delighted."

"I am glad."

The heron flapped its wings once, twice, beating the stiffness out of them, the sounds echoing away into the trees. Droplets of water fell from the bird's legs as it flew off, blooming into overlapping bracelets on the pond's surface.

Movement high above us, higher than the heron, caught our attention. We both raised our faces to the sky at the same time. Aritomo pointed with the handle of his walking stick, looking like a prophet in an ancient land. In the furthest reaches of the eastern sky, where it had already turned to night, streaks of light were fanning out. I did not know what they were at first, but when I realized what I was looking at, a sigh misted from between my lips.

It was a storm of meteors, arrows of light shot by archers from the far side of the universe, igniting and burning up as they pierced the atmospheric shield. Hundreds of them burned out halfway, flaring their brightest just before they died.

Standing there with our heads tilted back to the sky, our faces lit by ancient starlight and the dying fires of those fragments of a planet broken up long ago, I forgot where I was, what I had gone through, what I had lost.

"My grandfather taught me the names of the planets and stars," Aritomo said. "We often sat in his garden at night, studying the scatterings of light in the sky through his telescope. He was very proud of it, that telescope of his."

"Tell me their names," I said. "Point them out to me."

"The stars are different here." His eyes swept across the sky again, and I wondered whether the loss I caught in his voice would accompany him for the rest of his life.

"In one of the gardens he made, my grandfather used only white stones. Completely white, almost luminous," Aritomo said, still looking up into the sky. "He set them in patterns that mirrored the positions of the constellations he loved most: the Winnowing Basket; the Sculptor's Tool; the Purple Forbidden Enclosure." The names from his lips sounded like offerings to the dome above us. "He wanted the people visiting that garden to feel as though they were walking amongst the night sky."

The torrent of falling stars dried up, but the sky continued to exhale a luminance, as though it had retained the light from the meteors. Perhaps the illumination was trapped not in the sky but in our eyes, in our memory.

"My *amah* used to warn me that they're bad omens, these meteors," I said. "*Soh pa sing*, she called them—broomstick stars, sweeping away all of one's good luck. I've always disagreed with her—how can something so beautiful be unlucky?"

"They remind me of our *kamikaze* pilots," Aritomo said. "My brother was one of them."

A few seconds floated past before I spoke. "Did he survive the war?"

"He was among the first batch of pilots to volunteer."

"What made him do that?"

"Family honor," Aritomo replied. That justification, so often uttered by the Japanese prisoners I had met, had always repelled me. He continued. "It is not what you think. Our father passed away shortly before I left Japan. Shizuo blamed his death on the troubles I had caused our family."

He scratched at the pebbles on the bank with the tip of his walking stick. "Before I met you, before you came here, I never knew anyone personally who had lost friends or family in the Occupation. Oh, I knew of those here who had been brutalized by my people—the men and women in the villages, the workers here, even Magnus and Emily. But I kept myself above all of that. I kept out everything that was unpleasant. I attended only to my garden."

The first stars of the evening were just appearing, faint and timid, as though overwhelmed by the deluge of light a few minutes before. Staring into the void, I felt I could stand there until dawn came, turning with the earth, watching the stars stencil their cryptic patterns across the sky.

Aritomo reached out his hand and touched my cheek once, lightly. I caught his fingers, pulled him to me and kissed him. He broke away first. He stepped back and slipped past me, merging into the shadows spilling out from the trees. I turned to watch him as he headed back to his house. He slowed down, then stopped walking.

For a few moments I did nothing, keeping just as still. Then I went toward him, and together, in silence, we walked back to his house, our breaths nothing more than clouds burned away by the light of the stars.

CHAPTER SIXTEEN

Two hours after midnight, I stop writing. I do not want to face what I have remembered, among all those pages and pages of words. But they are there, crouching behind a stone in my mind, waiting to come out again. Putting down my pen on the desk and pushing back my chair, I slide open the door and walk along the darkened verandah to the front of the house.

The world is frosted in moonlight. A nightjar calls out, then stops. I wait for it to resume, but it disappoints me. Rubbing the circulation into my wrists, I remember how, after that evening with Aritomo by the pond, I would often look up if I happened to be outside at night. But I never saw anything like that again, that monsoon of falling stars teeming across the sky.

I had forgotten about Captain Hideyoshi Mamoru. The memory of my conversation with him had come back to me as I was writing. I wanted to stop, but instead allowed it to unfold from my pen. Thinking about my own words again, I am appalled. Had I been so unfeeling as to correct a man's grammar a short while before he was to be hanged? Hung, hanged—what did it matter?

As a judge I have presided in civil and criminal cases. I have sentenced people to death for murder, drug trafficking and armed robbery. I have always taken pride in my detachment, my objectivity, but now I wonder if these are merely the attributes of a deadened heart.

Before going back inside, I look to the sky again. The stars are still, unmoving. Not a single marker has been dislodged from its position on the eternal map.

For the past few days, Professor Tatsuji has been spending more time in the garden. We have not spoken much since our conversation in the Pavilion of Heaven a week ago. I have given him permission to explore Yugiri, but he doesn't seem to wander far from the house. Some days I see him by the pavilion, just standing there, hands behind his back. I want him to examine the prints as quickly as he can, but for some reason, the sight of him gazing out to the water fills me with a reluctance to rush him. More than once I have caught him staring at the sky, as though searching for something behind the clouds.

I wonder if there is any truth in Tatsuji's suspicion that Aritomo had been sent to Malaya by the emperor. The answer is elusive, like ink in water.

This morning, I intercept Ah Cheong when he comes out from the kitchen with a tray of tea and scones. "I'll take it to him," I say.

Tatsuji's attention is fixed on the prints spread out on the desk when I enter his workroom. The bamboo blinds are rolled up, the sun on the cedarwood floor hot when I walk barefoot across it. His copy of Yeats's poems lies on the desk. He continues to stare at a woodblock print, only glancing up when he becomes aware of me. In the second before he looks away, I see his eyes are filled with grief.

Hesitating for a moment, I set the tray down next to a print of a Malay fishing village. The village seems to be located somewhere on the east coast. I wonder what it is about the print that has so affected him.

He clears his throat a few times. "They are all untitled. I have arranged them in chronological sequence." He turns the sheet over and points to a vertical line of Japanese script behind it. "This one is dated the fifth month of the twentieth year of the Showa *jidai*— the Era of Enlightened Peace."

I knew that each era in the Japanese calendar corresponds to an emperor's reign. "When did Hirohito become emperor?"

"Christmas Day, 1926. That would make it 1945 when Aritomo wrote this. May 1945."

"Three months before Japan surrendered." In my mind I picture Aritomo sitting here in Yugiri, making this print while I was still a prisoner: each of us unaware of the other; unaware that our paths would converge one day.

I reach over and hold up the print. On a beach, rows of cuttlefish are drying on wooden racks. Behind them, coconut trees bow to each other, their leaves so finely etched that I can almost hear them rustling in the salted wind. Aritomo has set the entire scene inside the outline of a large cuttlefish, covering the outer edges with overlapping prints of smaller cuttlefish in translucent dark blue ink, shadows on shadows.

"The ancient Chinese called the cuttlefish the Scribe of the Ocean God, because it carries ink in its body," I murmur. "Something Aritomo once told me. Is the quality of the prints acceptable for your book?"

Tatsuji clears his throat again. "Most of them. Not as good as Kanaoka's works, of course. But then, no one's is, I suppose." I look at him, and he explains, "Kanaoka lived in the seventh century. He is remembered for the realism of his work. A horse he painted on a wall in a palace was said to come alive at night and gallop in the grasslands outside, beneath the autumn moon."

"Some of the pieces have been damaged by moisture," I point out.

"Even if they are in tatters, I want people to see them. They will go into my book—with your permission, of course." He studies the fishing village again and, in a softer voice, says, "This is the first time I have been back since the war."

"Only the older people like me—like us—remember it now," I say.

He lifts his gaze from the *ukiyo-e* and looks at me. "You are not well, are you?"

I am silent for a moment. "You told me you were a navy pilot." He nods.

"Where were you based? Butterworth? Singapore?" I wonder if he was part of the first wave of planes that bombed the streets of Singapore and Penang. Perhaps he was in the squadron that sank the *Prince of Wales* and the *Repulse* off the east coast.

Tatsuji squints through the windows, as though he has seen something on the horizon. "My base was outside a fishing village."

"Where was it?" I reach behind me and pull up the other rosewood chair, sitting close to him.

For a long while he does not say anything. Finally he begins to speak in a slow, steady voice.

"It was raining on the morning I was scheduled to die. I had not slept. All night the rain had blown in from the South China Sea, the water lashing the thatched roofs of our billets. The monsoon should have already ended, yet the rains still came, day after day.

"Colonel Teruzen, my flight instructor, was already on the verandah, looking out to the beach. Lightning flashed between the low-lying clouds and the sea. 'No flying today,' he said when I went to join him. His relief was evident. He was forty years old that year, and I knew he would survive the war. And for that I was glad.

"The small airfield was outside Kampong Penyu, on the southeastern coast of Malaya. The runway was parallel to the beach. The billets were now empty of pilots except for Colonel Teruzen and me.

"'No flying today,' I repeated. I would live another day. A sense of relief made me light-headed and ashamed. But stirred into that were also the increasing frustrations and uncertainties of waiting.

"I'd been assigned my duty over two months before, together with the other pilots in my squadron. Six of us had flown from the naval air base in Kyushu all the way to Luzon. We spent a night at the Luzon air base, leaving early at dawn the next day to avoid being detected by the Americans. An hour after taking off from Luzon, my plane developed engine problems, shuddering as it struggled to carry the five-hundred-pound bomb attached beneath. These planes had not been constructed to carry such a load. They were shoddily built by that time. There was nothing I could do. Our airplanes were so basic at this stage of the war that we did not even have radio to communicate with one another. I could only watch my fellow pilots speed away, flying south, toward Malaya. And then they were gone.

"I examined my charts for the nearest landing strip, praying that the faltering engine would not stall. Forty minutes later I made a rough landing on the Bacolod air base. It was just a collection of wooden huts surrounded by low mountain ranges, their peaks clipped off by the storm clouds. The only sign of life was a windsock, fluttering madly as though a bird was trapped in it.

"The ground crew consisted of a middle-aged limping mechanic and his assistant. I described the fault in the engine to them. 'How long will it take to fix it?'

"'We'll have to wait for the engine to cool, but from what you described . . .' The mechanic sucked his teeth. He understood my desperation: I had to die together with my squadron comrades. We had gone through our aviation training and graduated together from the Imperial Naval Academy. I did not want to be left behind. 'There's an old Mitsubishi engine in our workshop,' he said. 'Maybe we can salvage some parts from it. We'll be as quick as we can.'

"He stood to attention as I sensed someone coming up behind me. I turned around, and for the first time in a year I saw Colonel Teruzen again. He narrowed his eyes in slight amusement and I raised a belated salute.

"'Lieutenant Yoshikawa,' he said. 'Kind of you to drop in for a visit.'

"'Trouble with my airplane, sir,' I replied, flustered by his unexpected appearance.

"He glanced at the aircraft behind me, his eyes clouding over. 'You've been assigned to the *tokko* unit?'

"'I—all of us in my class—volunteered,' I said. 'What are you doing here? I heard you were in Tokyo.'

"'I am touring our air bases in the South China Sea,' he said, 'reporting to Admiral Onishi on the efficacy of sending all you young pilots to your deaths.' The anger in his voice was clear—he had trained so many of us. '*A million hearts beating as one*,' he said, quoting the suicide pilots' slogan, by now repeated throughout all of Japan. 'A waste. A terrible, terrible waste.'

"I was tired, and my uniform was already wet and sour from the humidity. 'Where is everyone?' I asked.

"'The last pilots left yesterday. A convoy of American warships were spotted in the Sulu Sea,' Colonel Teruzen said. 'We are awaiting the next batch. Perhaps they will be sending children soon. Come,' he said. 'We will get you some breakfast. You can report to the CO later. He is usually drunk by this time.'

"I followed him to a room in a low building two hundred yards from the hangar, bare except for a desk and a faded map of the Philippines pinned on a wall. I bowed to a photograph of the emperor. Colonel Teruzen leaned against the door frame and watched, his arms folded across his chest. 'Where are you headed?' he asked.

"'The southeast coast of Malaya,' I said.

"'Kampong Penyu?' He frowned. 'I thought we had abandoned that base.'

"'I do not know, Teruzen-*san*. I merely follow orders.'

"He came closer to me, and I remembered our last day together in Tokyo. I had made the decision to fulfill my duty, to put aside my own needs. I did not wish to be reminded of those days, gone the way of all *tokko* pilots now. "How is Noriko?"

"'There was an air raid,' he said, his face rigid. 'She was in the house preparing our dinner. The whole neighborhood was destroyed. The fires burned for days.'

"For a long moment we stood apart, and then I stepped forward and embraced him."

The mechanic took five days to repair my engine, and another three days to fine-tune it. I was torn between the need to rush him and the urge to prolong my stay. Teruzen took me hiking in the nearby hills. There was no need to talk much now—we understood each other's shades of silences. A new intensity came into everything we did. And for the first time since we met, so many years ago, I was rid of all futile guilt. At night I would lie awake and feel his presence next to me. He slept fitfully. His hair had turned a light ash, and there were more lines around his eyes.

"We had met at my father's house in Tokyo. Teruzen had been the naval adviser sent to oversee the manufacture of the airplanes being built by my father. Japan had just taken Singapore and the war across Asia was going extremely well. There was an immediate understanding between us that night when I looked into his eyes after I bowed to him. I lingered around as my father introduced him to the other industrialists.

"He came regularly to discuss the production and engineering details of the airplanes with my father, often staying the night. I was eighteen years old. All around me were exhortations to join the forces to protect our homeland. It was easy to get caught up in the hysteria, to be willingly seduced by the newspapers' stories of the heroic fighter pilots. Every high school student in Japan wanted to be a navy pilot.

"I completed my preparatory aviation training and applied to the Imperial Naval Academy, where he taught. Sometimes he would invite a few of us from class back to his home. It was there that he first showed me some of Aritomo's *ukiyo-e*. He had a large collection of them. 'They were made by the emperor's *niwashi*,' he told me once when I was visiting him by myself.

"'The same man who gave you the tattoo?' I said. I had already seen the pair of herons chasing each other in a circle on the upper left corner of his back. Repelled by it at first, I changed my mind the more often I saw it. It had struck me as odd that a man of Teruzen's class would have himself tattooed. I took the opportunity to ask him about it now, and Teruzen replied, 'We were close friends.'

"Something in his voice made me ask, 'What happened?'

"'The emperor sacked him. Aritomo left the country a few years ago. No one knows where he went.'

"On a few occasions, Teruzen took me to the gardens Aritomo had designed and he told me stories about the gardener. Now when I look back on them, those were the happiest days of my life. But that was also the period when I met his wife, Noriko. She was then in her thirties, her soft beauty in stark contrast to her robust-looking husband. I knew that I would have to end our relationship.

"Japan was losing the war by then. We began to hear of Vice Admiral Onishi's plans to defend our country. Pilots were being asked to launch suicide attacks on American warships. These pilots were called 'Cherry Blossoms,' blooming for just a brief moment of time before they fell.

"I received my assignment after my graduation. I did not tell Teruzen when he brought me to Yasukuni to worship the spirits of our fallen warriors. There, in the holy silence of the shrine's court-yard, I told him that I would not see him again.

"Even now I can still see it so clearly in my mind—the sorrow in his face. He closed his eyes, as though saying a prayer to the dead all around us. When he opened his eyes again, he said, 'Promise me we will meet again here after the war.' I agreed, but I knew it would not happen. The war had brought us together, but once it ended, everything would change again. He would have Noriko to return to. I bowed to him and walked out of the shrine.

"Ten days after I made the emergency landing on Bacolod, my plane was once again ready for me to fly onward to Malaya. When I thanked the mechanic, he looked at me, and then at Teruzen walking toward us from the other side of the runway. 'If I had had the courage, I would have damaged the engine beyond repair,' he said. 'There have been too many wasteful deaths.'

"'If I had had the courage, Naga-*san*,' I said, 'I would have asked you to do it.' We bowed to each other. Then, as he was leaving, he stopped and turned back to me. 'I'll say a prayer for you at Yasukuni Shrine when this war is over.'

"Teruzen came up to me and knocked on the plane's fuselage. The metal sounded thin and hollow. 'Your father consulted me on their construction,' he said. 'But these are not what we wanted to build. They dishonor your family's name. They shame our nation.'

"'My father built some of the best airplanes before the war,' I said. 'But we ran out of materials. We ran out of spirit.'

"Teruzen gripped my shoulders. 'We never ran out of spirit.'

"I pulled out a sheet of paper from my battered flying suit and said, 'You gave this to me, not long after we met.'

"He glanced at it and pushed my hand away. 'I don't need it. I know it by heart.'

"'I would like to hear it in your voice again,' I said. 'Please . . .'

"'*I know that I shall meet my fate, somewhere among the clouds above . . .* ,' he said, speaking in English. It was the first line from Yeats's poem 'An Irish Airman Foresees His Death.' I closed my eyes and listened to him, hearing the resigned anger in his voice as he came to the last line. I knew then that, unlike our last parting, I would not try to forget him again. I opened my eyes slowly. 'I was a fool, wasn't I, that day at Yasukuni?' I said. 'All this wasted time.'

"'But so was I, to agree to your request.'

"'And yet we did the right thing, of that I am certain,' I said.

"The morning was overcast, the windsock limp. A pair of herons rose from the trees on the edge of the jungle. We watched them fly higher and higher, disappearing into a screen of soft rain between the valleys, heading for a haven that would never be revealed to me. In Teruzen's eyes I saw the same yearning I had felt when I watched those birds. I knew what he wanted of me but would never voice out loud. I shook my head. 'I can't.'

"He lowered his eyes. 'I understand.'

"I climbed into the cockpit and strapped myself in.

"'I'll let your father know I met you here,' he said.

"'He'll be happy to hear that,' I said. I closed the canopy before he could say anything else.

"The engine misfired a few times before catching, its uneven rumbling throwing out black smoke into the wind. Opening the throttle, I murmured a prayer that the plane would take me over the South China Sea and all the way to the shores of Malaya. The plane began to move, held back by the bomb hanging underneath, a bird carrying a cancerous growth. I was nearly out of runway when it grudgingly tipped up its nose and rose off the asphalt. I circled the airfield once, watching Teruzen standing on the runway. As I lifted higher and higher into the sky, the heat from the tears I had been holding back fogged up my goggles.

"I was ninety miles off the coastline of Malaya when the monsoon clouds met me, stacked high and dark. Raindrops, hard as bullets, splattered onto my windscreen. I had an uncomfortable sensation that I was being followed. I twisted around in my seat to search the skies behind, wondering if an American fighter had seen me and was toying with me. The skies were empty, but the feeling refused to leave. Visibility dropped to zero a moment later; if I could not see anything, then neither could I be seen.

"The plane rocked from the cross-currents of wind and water. I did not have enough fuel to climb above the storm. I could only keep to my present course and hope I would not fly into a mountain. I checked the charts every few minutes, and the demands on my concentration kept me from thinking about Teruzen and my father.

"Soon I glimpsed faint lights below me. Examining my charts again, I shouted with relief. I had reached Kampong Penyu. I dropped from the sky toward the runway, but the configuration of lights below signaled to me that the conditions for landing were impossible. I had no other option but to land there, but first I had to make sure I survived the landing. I flew on and found a clearing about a mile away. I skimmed low over it and released the unarmed bomb, hoping that in the darkness and rain it would land on something soft. Freed of that awful weight, the plane reared up into the air. I swung around back to the airfield, trying not to lose sight of it in the storm. I landed, the wheels jarring on the runway, kicking up a rush of water. A moment later I hit a series of potholes. I spun across the runway. I heard the undercarriage snap. My head slammed into the glass, and I lost consciousness.

"I woke up in a sparsely furnished room. A man was looking out through the windows to the beach, his back turned to me. I recognized him, and for a moment I thought I was dreaming. The sound of waves came to me. The man turned around. I tried to sit up but recoiled from the pain. 'You have fractured two of your ribs,' Colonel Teruzen said, moving to my bedside. 'The medical officer has done whatever he could, which is not much at all. They are desperately short of supplies.'

"'My airplane?' I asked.

"'The ground crew is trying to see if they can salvage it.'

"'You were behind me, all the way from Bacolod,' I said, recalling the sensation I had had of being followed. He brought a glass of tepid water to my lips. I finished it and he wiped my mouth with his handkerchief. 'You managed to land in one piece, unlike me,' I said. A renewed sense of failure came over me.

"'Ah, but that is to be expected. I *was* your teacher, after all.'

"'Is there anyone from my group still here?'

"A fond smile buoyed to his face. 'Lieutenant Kenji. His engine developed a fault on the morning he was supposed to fly—three days ago. He was quite speechless when he saw me.' The smile disappeared. 'The fault has been fixed and he has received his orders. He will fly tomorrow.'

"'He is younger than I am,' I said. 'He is a child. *I* should go first.'

"'You are in no shape to pilot a plane, Tatsuji!' he snapped.

"'You should not have followed me here, Teruzen-*san*," I said. 'You have disobeyed your orders.'

"'What happened to your father?' His question caught me before I could evade it. But what was the point of avoiding his question now? It was, as the Irish poet had written, a waste of breath, the years that had gone past, the years to come. There was only this present moment to live and die in. So then, slowly, I began to tell Teruzen about the last time I had seen my father.

"Once my assignment to the *tokko* units had been approved, I traveled to our family's country retreat near the foothills of Gunma-ken. My father had moved back there when the air raids began. Tokyo had been badly bombed by the Americans, and I was glad to see the old maple-lined avenues of my youth untouched. The leaves were preparing to surrender themselves to winter; they were redder than I remembered ever seeing them—perhaps they were stained by the sadness of war. I pulled the cord hanging by the gate. I imagined I could hear the bell tinkling deep inside the house. A few minutes later the bolt was drawn back. I hid my shock when my father appeared. He had never been a strong person, but now he looked angular and bony, his eyes haunted. He was dressed in his old gray *yukata*; it was too large for him now.

" 'You did not tell me you were coming,' he said.

"For a long moment we merely looked at one another, feeling like strangers. Then, I did something I had never done before: I embraced him. He stroked my head, whispering my name over and over again. Finally he pulled away, smiling at me. Despite the undisguised joy in our meeting, I sensed a tension in the air.

"We had tea on the *engawa*. It was something we used to do often, and I was soothed but also saddened by the memories. I did not know how to broach the subject of my assignment. For a while we spoke only of those days before the war but then, to my surprise, he himself raised the subject of Vice Admiral Onishi's *tokko* program.

" 'I have been instructed to build more airplanes for the war,' he said. 'It will not matter if they are of inferior quality, as long as they fly. They want them as fast as we can produce them.' He shook his head in disgust.

" 'It is the emperor's wish,' I said. 'The planes will help us defend ourselves against the Americans.' These words, which I had heard so often on the radio, now sounded hollow to me.

"My father had raised me since my mother's death; he could tell the reason for my visit simply by looking into my eyes. He started crying, soundlessly, his eyes wide open. He was the head of one of the largest *zaibatsu* in the country, and to see him like this shocked me. I knew then we would lose the war.

"I stayed for five days. We never mentioned the war again. On my last morning I sensed an unusual stillness in the air when I woke. I went through the house and found my father in the garden. He was gazing at the koi pond, now empty of fish. He was dressed completely in white. 'Where are the servants?' I asked, and he said, 'I have sent them away.' His tone, more than his words, frightened me. I understood then why he was dressed in white and what he was about to do.

"'No, *oto-san*,' I said.

"He held out his hand to me. I took it, feeling the remembered sensation of solidity in him. He squeezed my hand and let it go. Then he walked to the back of the house. I hurried after him, calling out to him, but he did not stop, did not look back. We came to the *kore-sansui* garden. He had designed it himself. The gravel had been raked and a reed mat placed on the edge of a rectangle of white sand. I recognized our ancestral swords on the mat: the long *katana* and the shorter *wakizashi* next to it. On a tray stood a cup and a small *saké* pot.

"My father stared at the lines in the gravel, soundless ripples expanding outward from a point in the center. Or were the ripples returning to silence? It was his habit to create new patterns every evening when he returned from work. It relaxed him. Now he said, 'The Buddha has pressed his thumbprint into the earth.'

"'Do not do this.' My voice was shaking, but he was calm and purposeful as a ship entering a safe harbor after sailing through a storm out at sea. He knelt on the mat and poured a cup of *saké*. I felt as though I was training in my fighter plane again, the oxygen sucked from my lungs, about to black out from going against the invisible forces that bound the sky to the earth.

"'Life is fair, is it not?' he said. 'I built the airplanes that sent other people's sons to their deaths. So it has to be balanced out—my son must die too.' He looked steadily at me. 'Understand that I am not compelling you to disobey your orders. I accept that you must carry out your duty. In turn, you must accept what I have to do.'

"He sat for a while, so still that I hoped, I prayed, he would never move again. I would rather that he had turned to stone than to go through with this. He picked up the *wakizashi* and unsheathed it. The morning sun trapped in the blade made me glance away. 'So this is how it will end, the great Yoshikawa family,' my father said.

"I restrained him by his arm and he said, so softly, the way he always did when I was a child and he wanted to wake me from sleep, 'Tatsu-*chan* . . .' The pain in his voice wounded me more than if he had shouted at me. 'It will be good to sleep peacefully again. I am so tired, my son. So tired.'

"'*Oto-san* . . .'

"He took my hand and stroked it. 'I had hoped to see you one last time, and now I have. What more can I ask for? Do not stay. Go.'

"I shook my head. 'I am your son.'

"*Oto-san* nodded. He held the blade in his right hand and opened his robe. He breathed slowly, deeply, savoring each breath. The garden was silent, the birds were gone. I picked up the *katana*, ready to sweep down in case his pain became too great to bear, in case he hesitated.

"But he never wavered."

"Teruzen and I were the first people on the runway. Lieutenant Kenji and the commanding officer joined us a few minutes later. Porcelain cups and a bottle of *saké* lay on a table in front of us. I thought of the many ceremonies I had attended during the early days of the *tokko* program. Each time we had drunk a cup of *saké* with every one of the pilots and bowed to them, before they climbed into their planes. Looking back, I suppose many of us already knew the war was lost, but the battle still had to be fought. There was no other way.

"The white *hachimaki* wrapped around Kenji's head was painted with the rising sun, as though he had been shot in the middle of his forehead. I poured the *saké* and we bowed in the direction of the emperor in his palace. Teruzen drank his cup of *saké*, but he did not bow. In a boyish yet determined voice Kenji read out his death poem, bowed to us and climbed into his plane. 'Have a good flight,' I said to the last member of my squadron. 'You won't have long to wait,' he shouted back. 'See you in Yasukuni!'

"He took off, and I waved to him until he was lost from sight and was never seen again. No one would ever know if he had succeeded in striking a blow against the Americans. I was the last pilot left now. Teruzen lifted his arm, wound back his body and flung his cup into the sky. He threw it so high and so far that I did not hear it shatter when it fell back to earth. When I turned to look at him again he was already walking back to our billets.

"We spent our days on a beach not far from the base, under a makeshift shelter of coconut palms. On clear days the faint outline of Tioman to the south could be seen on the horizon. The local fishermen said a princess from China sailing the seas in times long forgotten had transformed herself into that island. Teruzen and I talked about visiting it, but the seas were too rough.

"'Hard to believe,' he said, pointing to the sea, 'but just about fifty miles north of here our planes sank two British warships.'

"My injuries were healing faster than Teruzen would have liked. A week after Lieutenant Kenji's departure, I was informed that the mechanic was unable to salvage my plane. I saw hope blazing in Teruzen's eyes when he told me the news. It was late in the morning and the skies had cleared. We had gone past the fishing village with the racks of salted fish drying in the sun.

"'I will have to find another plane,' I said.

"'You fool!' It was the first time I had ever heard him raise his voice. 'You and I—we have been given a second chance at what we once threw away. We are no longer bound by duty to anyone.'

"'You want me to be a coward!' I said. 'You want me to abandon my oath and my honor.'

"'There is nothing you can do now,' he said. 'We have lost the war; we simply refuse to accept it.'

"'I cannot put my own needs before my duty,' I replied.

"'I am asking . . .' He faltered. 'I am asking that you put *my* needs first.'

"I stared at him. 'Where would we go?'

"He looked out to the emptied sea. 'We do not have to go anywhere,' he replied finally. 'This place would be good enough, wouldn't it? To live out our days here, far from the rest of the world. A house on this beach, and time eternal.'

"For a long moment I let myself be seduced by his dream. I allowed myself a brief moment of all the possibilities that were now opened to me, the life that I could now have. I remembered the herons we had once seen, flying off to some unreachable sanctuary. But I knew it was impossible. It was impossible. 'If I do not carry out my orders, then my father's death was in vain,' I said, trying to find a way to explain my decision to him. 'He accepted that I had to fly, and if I failed in doing that, then what was the point of his death?' I stopped and hardened my resolve. 'That is why I am asking you to let me have your airplane. The bomb carriage from mine can be attached to it.'

"Teruzen's face aged, looking so similar to my father's before he died that I felt as though the war had ruptured the structure of time itself. For the first time since I had known him, he broke down. 'I should not have followed you here,' he said. 'I was selfish. I wanted to see you, just for the time you had left.'

"'You knew my fate from the first day you taught me to fly,' I said softly. I touched his shoulder. 'Nothing can change it.'

"Teruzen's plane was a two-seater Yoshikawa K41, one of my father's earlier models. Painted on the fuselage was Teruzen's family crest: a pair of herons, flying in a circle in eternal pursuit of one another. He spent a morning instructing me while it was modified to carry the bomb. He had not spoken much to me after that day on the beach, except to discuss the workings of his plane. Late one evening he said, 'I want to take you up there and fly with you one more time. Let you get a feel for it.'

"In the cockpit, I handled the controls while he sat behind me. For the first time I truly understood why my father had been ashamed of the substandard aircraft he had been forced to build later in the war. Compared to mine, Teruzen's airplane was smooth and powerful, an eagle to my sparrow. I remembered our first flight together in the training plane at the academy, and a great sadness overtook me.

"'Go higher,' Teruzen said. 'As high as you can.'

"We climbed above the clouds, where the last rays of the sun still reddened the sky. We flew on and on as beneath us the earth rotated into night. Soon the stars appeared over our canopy. 'Once, when I was on night patrol,' I said, 'I did not want to land. I had this urge to keep flying, I felt I would always remain safe in the darkness.'

"'That would be wonderful, to remain forever in flight,' he said, his voice soft but clear in our glass capsule. I felt his hand grip my shoulder and I reached out to cover it with mine. There may have been a million hearts beating together for a suicide pilot like me, but up here, on this night, all I could hear and feel were his and mine.

"Three times my orders came, and three times they had to be canceled due to bad weather. On the afternoon of August 5, 1945, I

219

received my fourth set of orders. An American aircraft carrier had been sighted off the coast of Borneo, heading north. I would leave at eight the next morning. The weather was predicted to be fine and sunny.

"After the farewell dinner given by the remaining personnel of the base, Teruzen and I took a walk on the beach. The moon had come up over the sea. The waves were quiet. Teruzen was calm and resigned, offering tips and suggestions on how to get the best out of his plane.

"'No more talk of the war,' I said.

"He looked at me and nodded.

"'Tell me what you will do after this is all over.' I wanted to look into a part of his life that I would never be able to share.

"'I will probably be classified as a war criminal and tried.'

"I shook my head. 'Tell me what you will do,' I said again.

"He looked out to the sea, understanding what I wanted from him. 'I will come back here, to this island, and build a house . . . there.' He pointed to a spot beneath a row of coconut trees. 'Live out the remainder of my life here. I will take a boat out every morning, catch fish and watch the sun rise over the ocean.'

"'It will be a good life,' I assured him.

"'I will think of you every day,' he said, looking at me.

"'I have written my death poem. Would you like to hear it?'

"'Tell me tomorrow.'

"We resumed walking. I did not want to waste any time with sleep, but eventually he said, 'You must get some rest. You will need your reactions sharp when you fly tomorrow.'

"'I want to be here tonight, on this beach,' I said.

"'Go to sleep,' he said. 'I will wake you.'

"I lay down on the cool, damp sand. The stars above seemed close enough to grasp. All I had to do was reach out for them. Instead I took his hand and held it, not letting it go even when I drifted off to sleep.

"He was gone when I woke up. It was almost ten to eight, the sun already high. I ran all the way back to the base, cursing myself. The Yoshikawa K41 was standing on the runway, its engine pumping smoke into the air. My watch showed twelve minutes past eight. I stopped to catch my breath and then sped off toward it. There was no time now, the aircraft carrier would be out of range soon.

"The K41 began to move. I could not believe it. The throttle opened up and the plane began to taxi to the start of the runway. Through the canopy glass I saw Teruzen's face. The K41 rolled to a stop. For an eternal moment he stared into my eyes. He blinked once and smiled. His hand came up, his palm open as though he could touch me from across the distance. I knew I was shouting at him, shouting till I was hoarse, even though at that moment I could hear nothing at all.

"He dropped his hand. The plane lurched forward, then gathered speed. I pushed every ounce of strength into my legs to catch up with him. I changed my direction, hoping to intercept it halfway down the runway, even as I knew it was impossible. The K41 rose from the ground. I fell and picked myself up, my eyes never leaving Teruzen as he made a low circuit over the airfield. I have no doubt that our eyes met one last time. He closed the circle and banked off into the direction of the sun.

"And it was at that moment that the sky changed color. It turned completely white, before breaking up into streaks of red and magenta and purple. I closed my eyes tight, but still the light came through, blinding me. It was only weeks later that I found out that the Americans had dropped their first atomic bomb on Japan. At that instant, as Teruzen flew off in my place to meet the ship, the war was effectively over.

"And so it came to be that I was the cherry blossom that never fell to earth, saved by the order of a silent emperor given voice by defeat. I was twenty-two years old when the war ended and Emperor Hirohito gave the first electronic broadcast ever made by a Divine Being to his people, exhorting us to accept defeat and to 'endure the unendurable.'

"How correct he was. I endured."

For a long while after Tatsuji stops talking, we sit there in silence. He has not touched his tea, and neither have I. His gaze returns to the *ukiyo-e* of the fishing village.

"I am an old man now, older than Teruzen was when he flew off that morning," he says. "Once this book on Aritomo is finished, I am going back to Kampong Penyu. I have bought a piece of land there, the exact spot Teruzen talked about. And there I will build the house Teruzen had wanted for us. And this time," he vows, "this time I am never going to leave again."

"Were you interned when the war ended?"

"In Singapore. I was put to work with hundreds of others. We cleaned up the rubble in the streets, cleared the drains, fixed the fallen power lines. After I was shipped home, I left the navy." He rises stiffly to his feet. "I never visited the Yasukuni Shrine again. I never went to the Kagoshima war museum, where it is possible to see and touch some of the planes used by the *tokko* pilots, planes they had salvaged from the sea. I never wanted to see them again," he says. "To me, that beach, half an earth's turn from Japan, is the only place Teruzen's spirit can ever find a sense of peace."

"What will you do there?" I ask, as he once asked the man he loved, and still loves.

"Every morning, at dawn," he replies, his eyes looking faraway, "I will row out to sea in a little boat. I will turn toward the spot where I last saw Teruzen's plane, and I will wait for the sun to rise."

Chapter Seventeen

Aritomo did not change the way he treated me when we were in the presence of other people. There was a part of him that I knew I would never be allowed to enter. Occasionally, when we worked in the garden, I would find him staring at me, a contemplative look on his face. He never glanced away when I met his eyes, but continued to look at me.

Following a period of relative quiet, the CTs intensified their activities, killing over three hundred civilians in one month. And they seemed to be targeting women and children now. A two-year-old girl on a rubber estate was shot while playing with the family cook. A planter and his wife were ambushed on a trunk road; the terrorists killed the woman, but left her husband alone. Just a week before that, five CTs had entered the brownstone church in Tanah Rata during morning mass and killed the French priest leading the service. The wives of the planters and miners who had vowed to stay on in Malaya with their husbands were advised to pack up and leave with their children, and some European families in Cameron Highlands had already done so.

Templer had classified regions infested with CTs as "Black Areas," tightening food rationing and imposing onerous curfews over them, intending to make life for the inhabitants so miserable they would withdraw their support for the communists. Despite these measures, the list of Black Areas increased sharply, outnumbering the White Areas that were completely free from infiltration by the CTs. It reminded me of the game of *go* with its black and white stones that Aritomo sometimes played with me, encircling my pieces to change them to his color.

Lying in my bed at night, I listened to the army shelling a CT camp in a valley nearby. Some nights I would go out and stand on the verandah. The sky throbbed from the detonations, lit up by these unnatural northern lights. "Aurora equatorialis," Magnus called them.

Returning from Yugiri one night, I went around to the back of the bungalow. I had started to use the back door so as not to be silhouetted against the front doorway when I switched on the lights. I was about to go in when a figure emerged from behind the trees, pointing a pistol at me. "Inside!" he said. "Hurry up!"

The kitchen light was switched on. I blinked. The blinds had been pulled across the windows. There were three people already sitting at the small dining table. One of them was a woman a few years younger than me, with a hard thinness to her frame, her short hair badly cut. The men were in their twenties or early thirties. Their khaki uniforms were grimy, the three faded red stars marking their caps looking like drops of dried blood. The man with the pistol shoved me into a chair, my momentum nearly toppling me onto the floor.

"Take all the food you want," I said. "There's money in my purse."

The woman stood up and came to me. "Deputy Public Prosecutor Teoh Yun Ling," she said in English, each word coming out slowly.

"Not anymore," I said. "You should keep up with the news." She slapped me. *It's nothing*, I told myself over the pain. *You've suffered beatings before.* The ringing in my ears died away after a minute and I could hear a moth flapping around the kitchen light. My eyes darted around the room, searching for a weapon, anything that would give me an advantage. A *Planter's Weekly* lay on the table, but unlike Aritomo, I would not know how to make use of it.

The woman went to the countertop and switched on the wireless, turning the dial to a local Chinese station. A song filled the kitchen, a well-known ballad my mother had liked, although she could not understand the words: "Yue Lai Xiang."

"Whenever I hear this, I think of my sister," the woman said. "She used to sing it all the time. Her name is Liu Foong. Thanks to you, she was deported to China."

"Don't they do things just how you like them in China?"

One of the men moved toward me. I told myself to keep my body loose so the pain would be lessened. It was an old trick I had learned in the camp. But it still hurt anyway. He beat me until I was nearly unconscious as the song wailed to its end. Blood ran into my eyes and dripped down my chin. Dimly I heard them ransacking the kitchen cupboards, stuffing their bags with whatever they could find.

The woman returned and kicked my chair over. My left shoulder hit the floorboards. I cried out. She squatted down by my side. Through my swelling eyes I saw a knife in her hand. I tried to roll away but she caught me by the ankle and dragged me back to her. I kicked out frantically and connected with her chin. She grunted, raised her knife and stabbed me in my thigh. I screamed, even as I heard another voice from far away, a voice I recognized as also mine, screaming from a lifetime ago.

Thin, white curtains lapped at the windowsill. Everything was white, the walls, the ceiling, even the floorboards. I thought I was back in my old room in Majuba House. My vision was blurry, and my eyelids felt gummy. A woman in a bed at the other side of the room moaned softly to herself. Voices murmured in the corridor outside. The wheels of a passing trolley squeaked. Noticing that I was awake, the nurse went outside the room and returned with a doctor a few minutes later.

"You're in the Tanah Rata Hospital," the doctor told me. I knew him from one of Magnus's *braais* or dinner parties. Teoh—no, that was my name. Yeoh. Dr. Yeoh. "You've lost a lot of blood," he went on. "The Jap gardener went looking for you when you didn't show up for work. If he hadn't . . ."

"How long have I been in here?" My voice sounded strange.

"Two days," the nurse said, helping me sit up in my bed.

My face was mummified in bandages. I could tell it was swollen when I touched it. A dressing was wrapped around my thigh where the terrorist had stabbed me.

Sub-Inspector Lee from the Tanah Rata police station came later that morning, arriving the same time as Magnus and Emily. My hands were bare, and I looked frantically around for my gloves. Magnus reached into his pocket and handed them to me.

"The woman who stabbed you sounds like Wong Mei Hwa,"

Sub-Inspector Lee said after I had described everything that had happened. "We heard she's in the area. She's in the MCP's Lau Tong Tui."

"What's that?" I asked.

"Special Service Corps." He glanced at Magnus and Emily. "Assassination squads. You're lucky to escape with just your injuries."

"She said her sister was a woman I prosecuted—Chan Liu Foong. She was deported."

"Ah . . ." Lee studied his notes. "You helped some high-ranking CT surrender a few months ago—it's possible that the MCP was taking revenge. Did Wong Mei Hwa mention anything about that?"

I shook my head.

"What the devil is he talking about?" Magnus broke in. "You helped some CTs surrender?"

I told them what had happened.

"I remember that!" Emily said. "It was in the *Straits Times*, I remember now. The man got a big reward. He said he was going to open a restaurant."

"I didn't want to say anything—you would have been worried," I said.

"*Blerrie* right!" Magnus exploded. "You put all of us at great risk!"

"Not so loud-*lah*!" Emily said. Magnus pushed back his chair noisily and stalked off to the far end of the ward.

After the sub-inspector left, Emily opened the thermos flask she had brought and filled a bowl with chicken-essence soup. "Drink this. Can *poh* your body. I boiled it myself. There's ginseng in it."

It tasted vile, but I knew it would be easier to swallow it than refuse her. "We called your father," she said, watching me to make sure I finished every oily drop in the bowl. "He wants you back in KL."

I wiped my lips. "I'm not leaving."

"Well, you can't continue staying on your own!" Magnus said, returning to stand over the foot of my bed. A nurse silenced him from across the ward and Emily gave her an apologetic smile.

"I'm not a child, Magnus," I said.

"You heard Lee—that woman could have killed you. Go home

to KL. You can always come back again once the Emergency is over."

"And when will *that* be?" I said. "Perhaps you can tell me?"

Emily touched Magnus's hand, and he swallowed his temper with visible effort. He sighed. "Come on, Lao Puo," he said, pulling Emily to her feet. "Stop tiring her out with all your chatter—let the stupid girl get some rest."

With the nurse's reluctant assistance, I hobbled to Dr. Yeoh's office to telephone my father. The office was a large, sunny room at the end of a long corridor and my brow was damp with perspiration when I got there. Dr. Yeoh was out and the nurse, after some fretting and some sharp words from me, left to do her rounds.

"Thank God you're safe, Ling! I've been worried sick about you," my father said. "I have to be in Singapore tomorrow. I don't know how long I'll be there, but I'll send my driver to Majuba for you. Just let me know when you'll be discharged."

"I'm all right. It's nothing serious."

"Nothing serious? You were assaulted! And stabbed! I hold Magnus responsible for this."

"I insisted Magnus let me have my own place, Father. I hope you didn't tell Mother what happened."

"I didn't. But there's no point anyway—she doesn't recognize me or Hock anymore." *And you should be here, looking after her.* He did not say it aloud, but I could hear his thoughts.

"Magnus offered us a safe place to hide out during the war," I said. "You never told me that."

"Under the protection of his Japanese friend? It was unacceptable," my father said. "And *you* . . . to work for a *Japanese*! After what they did to us . . ."

"Yun Hong would still be alive if you had taken Magnus up on his offer," I said. "We would all have been safe. And Mother wouldn't be . . . She would still be fine."

"You think I didn't look for you? That I didn't do everything I could to find out what happened to you and Hong? I've lost count of how many Japs I begged to let me know what had happened to you. I paid them whatever they wanted. But they toyed with me! Told me they knew nothing. Said you were not on any of their records."

"Don't bother sending your driver, Father," I said. "I have no intention of leaving."

All I could hear was silence. Then he hung up.

When I woke up that evening, Aritomo was in the same chair Magnus had sat in earlier. He put down his book—Somerset Maugham's *The Trembling of a Leaf*—and went over to a side table on which stood a tiffin carrier.

It was already dark outside. "What time is it?" I asked, sitting up against my pillows.

"Just after six." He opened the lid of the tiffin carrier, lifted out the top container and gave it to me. I looked inside and smiled, shaking my head. The movement set off spasms of pain over my face. "Bird's-nest soup," I said, once the pain had subsided. "I'll be back at work again in no time."

"So you are staying?"

"The monsoon hasn't started."

He went to the window. Pressing his face close to the glass, he peered out at the sky. "I think it will be delayed this year," he said.

He visited me every day while I was recovering in the hospital. He always brought a tiffin carrier of bird's-nest soup with him, watching me to make sure I ate it. Then he would push me out to the hospital garden in my wheelchair. The garden was nothing more than a broad, sloping lawn with some hydrangea bushes planted around its borders; we redesigned it again and again during those occasions when he wheeled me along the paths.

"Ah Cheong's getting married tomorrow," he told me when he arrived one evening. "Some girl in Tanah Rata. His mother arranged it. He invited us, but in your condition I thought it best to decline."

"You must give him money," I said. "Put it in a red envelope."

"I have already done so," he said, opening the tiffin carrier.

I was getting tired of bird's-nest soup by now but I kept silent, not wanting to hurt his feelings. "What's this?" I said when I looked into the first tray and caught the smells steaming from it.

"From Ah Cheong. Abalone. There is shark's-fin soup as well. And some grilled lobster. It seems his half brother is providing the food for the wedding banquet. Owns a restaurant in KL, apparently. I never knew he had a half brother." Aritomo's smile was so brief and quick that I almost missed it. "Did you?"

On my last afternoon in the hospital a nurse brought Magnus out to the garden. He had a bunch of lilies and he smiled broadly when he saw Aritomo there, helping me move about with a pair of crutches. He gave the lilies to me.

"A bit late to be giving me flowers, isn't it?" I said, smiling as they helped me to a bench. "I'll be discharged tomorrow."

"They're from Frederik. He only heard what happened two days ago. He's been in the jungle."

For a while we talked only of inconsequential things. More than once I noticed Magnus fidgeting. Finally he turned to me and said, "Your father rang me yesterday."

"Oh, for god's sake. I've already told him not to send his driver."

"That's not why he called. He wants me to stop letting you stay by yourself in Majuba." Magnus rubbed the strap of his eye-patch. "And after what's happened, Yun Ling, I have to agree with him."

"You're asking me to move out of Magersfontein Cottage?" I said sharply.

"Emily's packed your things and moved them back to our house."

I understood the quandary he had been placed in, but I was furious with him nevertheless. "I'll look for another place to stay. Outside Majuba."

Magnus turned helplessly to Aritomo. "Will you talk some sense into her?"

Aritomo did not speak for a few moments. Finally he said, "You can stay with me."

I resumed working in Yugiri after a month. Aritomo gave me only the easier chores, keeping back the heavier tasks until I had built up my strength. Magnus and Emily tried to change my mind about staying in Yugiri. I ignored them. People would talk and I knew gossip would reach my father within days, but from the moment I moved into Yugiri I felt insulated from the world beyond its borders. Despite the killings going on all across the country, it was the first time in years that I felt at peace. But the world outside soon intruded; I had been foolish to think that it would not.

Coming to the end of our *kyudo* practice one morning, I noticed Ah Cheong from the corner of my eye. He was standing outside the archery hall, not saying a word until Aritomo had shot his second arrow and lowered his bow.

"There are some people at the gate who wish to see you, sir."

Aritomo's attention remained fixed on the *matto*; his arrows were slightly off-center. "I am not expecting anyone. Tell them to go away."

"They said to tell you that they've come from Tokyo. They're from—" He glanced at the scrap of paper in his palm and tried to read it. Sensing Aritomo's impatience, he gave it to me.

I could just about make out the Japanese characters. "*The Association to Bring Home the Emperor's Fallen Warriors*," I read slowly.

The sun slipped out from a seam in the clouds. In the distance, birds erupted soundlessly from a tree, like leaves stripped by strong wind. Aritomo looked around the archery hall as though seeing something about it he had not noticed before. The joss stick he lit to mark our practice hour was burning down to the end. A final line of smoke, now untethered, curled away into the air.

"Let them wait on the front *engawa*," he said. The housekeeper nodded and left. Aritomo looked at me. "Come with me."

I hung up my bow at the back of the hall, then turned back to look at him. "I don't want to meet these people."

I strode past him, but he caught my wrist, gripping it for a second before letting go. He went to the urn and blew gently at the stem of ash. It disintegrated, flouring the rim of the urn and the air around it, and then a passing breeze dissipated it into the light.

A woman stood apart from the three men, all of them studying the rocks in the *kore-sansui* garden and commenting in low voices. They turned around when Aritomo called out to them; I received only a cursory glance. The men wore black suits and ties in muted colors, except for one who was completely bald and in a gray traditional robe. The woman was in her fifties, dressed in a well-tailored emerald blouse and beige skirt. The pearls around her neck were as delicate as morning dew beaded on a spiderweb.

The first man put down his briefcase, took half a step forward and bowed. "I am Sekigawa Hisato," he said in Japanese. "We should have informed you of our visit in advance, but we are grateful that you have agreed to see us." He was in his fifties, a narrow-shouldered man made larger by the confidence of acting as the leader of the group. It was a position he was accustomed to, I suspected. The others bowed as Sekigawa introduced them in turn. The man with the shaven head was Matsumoto Ken. The woman, Mrs. Maruki Yoko, smiled at me. The last man, Ishiro Juro, merely nodded indifferently.

"The Association to Bring Home the Emperor's Fallen Warriors was formed four years ago," Sekigawa explained, as they sat on the *tatami* mats around the low table. I felt his gaze linger on me as I folded my legs into the *seiza* position. "We have been traveling to all the places where our soldiers fought and died."

Ah Cheong came out to the verandah with a tray of tea. Once Aritomo had poured for everyone, Sekigawa sniffed his cup and lifted his eyebrows. "Fragrance of the Lonely Tree?"

"Yes," said Aritomo.

"How wonderful! Exquisite!" He took a sip, holding it inside his mouth for a moment before swallowing. "I have not had this since before the war. Where did you get it?"

"I brought a few boxes of it with me when I moved here, but it is almost finished. I will have to order more soon."

"You cannot obtain it anymore," said Sekigawa.

"Why not?"

"The plantation—the tea fields, the storehouse—all were destroyed in the war."

"I . . . I had not heard . . ." All of a sudden Aritomo appeared lost.

"*Hai*, it is very sad." Sekigawa shook his head. "The owner and everyone in his family were killed. Very sad."

Mrs. Maruki shifted her position and said, "We are here to find—" She paused and gave me an uncertain look.

Aritomo gathered his thoughts together. "Yun Ling speaks *Nihon-go* well enough."

Mrs. Maruki nodded. "We are here to find the bones of our soldiers, to take them home for a proper burial."

"They will reside in Yasukuni with the souls of all our soldiers who died in the Pacific War," added Matsumoto.

"The beaches of Kota Bahru, and the area around Slim River," Aritomo replied after thinking for a moment. "The heaviest fighting between the British and Japanese forces occurred there."

"We have already been there," Mrs. Maruki replied. "My brother was killed at Slim River." She waited expectantly. Aritomo said nothing, and neither did I. Something about this group of people made me uneasy. I gave Aritomo a sidelong glance but his face was unreadable.

"How do you differentiate the bones of the British troops from the Japanese ones?" I asked. "I doubt if the families of British soldiers would appreciate their bones being taken back to a heathen shrine."

Mrs. Maruki's head jerked back, as if I had spat in her face. Her cheeks reddened.

Sekigawa slipped in with the conciliatory voice of a seasoned peacemaker. "The act is symbolic," he said. "We take only pieces of bone from each site we visit." He pinched a bit of air with his thumb and forefinger. "Very small pieces."

"The families are always grateful that some remains of a son, a brother or a father can be brought home," Mrs. Maruki said.

"There are no dead soldiers in Yugiri," Aritomo said.

"Of course, of course. We know that," replied Sekigawa. "We hoped that you might be able to tell us of any other places you may have heard of, places that we have been unable to find any information about."

"We have been to all of the well-known battlefields," Mrs. Maruki said. "We want to visit the unknown ones, the forgotten ones. Civilian holding centers as well."

"Civilian holding centers?" I said. "You mean slave-labor camps. I'm sure you'll find those in your army's records."

Ishiro Juro, who had been silent all this time, spoke up. "The army destroyed all of its . . . unnecessary documents when it became clear that we would not win the war."

"Well, maybe I can help you," I said. "I'll show you where the Kempeitai tortured their prisoners. The buildings around the government rest-house in Tanah Rata are still unoccupied today. The locals say that on some nights they can hear the screams of the victims." I pressed on, relentless as a jungle guide hacking through the undergrowth with my *parang*. "The villagers speak about a mass grave somewhere in the Blue Valley, a few miles from here. Hundreds of Chinese squatters were taken there in trucks and bayoneted by your soldiers. I'd be happy to make inquiries about it for you. In fact, I could probably find fifty, a hundred, probably even two hundred, of these places for you, all across Malaya and Singapore."

"Such . . . *regrettable* incidents are not within the scope of our organization's purpose," Mrs. Maruki said.

I turned toward Matsumoto, pointing at his robes. "You're a Shinto priest, aren't you?"

He tipped his head. "I took my vows a year after the surrender. I have no reservations about conducting a blessing ceremony for these places. Sometimes that is all we can do—help the souls of the dead find some peace, be they Japanese or British, Chinese or Malay or Indian."

"They're dead, Matsumoto-*san*," I said. "It's the living you should be helping—those who were brutalized by your countrymen, those who were denied compensation from your government."

"This does not concern you," Ishiro said.

"Yun Ling is my apprentice," Aritomo said before I could reply. "Treat her with courtesy."

"Your apprentice?" Ishiro said. "A woman? A *Chinese* woman? Is that permitted by the Bureau of Imperial Gardens?"

"The bureau ceased to have any hold over me years ago, Ishiro-*san*," Aritomo replied.

"Ah, the bureau . . . ," Sekigawa interceded. "That brings us to another reason we came to see you, Nakamura-*sensei*." He took a cream-colored envelope from his briefcase. "We were asked to deliver this to you." He held it in both hands, treating it with the reverence shown to an ancestral tablet. Embossed in gold in the center of the envelope was an emblem of a chrysanthemum flower. Aritomo received the envelope with both hands and placed it on the table. Sekigawa glanced at it, then looked to Aritomo again. "We are to wait for your answer."

Aritomo sat there, completely still. All of us were looking at him. No one said anything, no one moved. Finally he picked up the envelope again and broke the seal with his thumbnail. He removed a piece of paper that he unfolded and began reading. The paper was so thin that the black brushstrokes written on it appeared like the veins of a leaf held up to the sun. At length he refolded the document, his thumb pressing hard into each crease. He sheathed the letter into the envelope and carefully set it down on the table.

"We understand that you are to be reappointed with immediate effect to your former position in the palace," Sekigawa said. "Please accept our congratulations."

"My work at Yugiri is not finished."

"But surely the letter makes it clear that the bureau has forgiven you for what happened between you and Tominaga Noburu," Sekigawa said.

The sound of that name jolted me. I was grateful that the Japanese were looking at Aritomo and not me.

"You have heard what happened to Tominaga-*san*?" Ishiro said in the silence.

"I have not kept up with events in Japan," Aritomo replied.

"He served in the war. He returned to his grandfather's home after the emperor announced the surrender," Ishiro said. "The servants reported that a few days later he went out to the tennis court in his garden and committed *seppuku*."

Learning of Tominaga's death stunned me; he had been the last link to my camp, the only other person I knew who had been there, who I had suspected was still alive. And now he too was gone.

"Did he leave a note?" Aritomo finally spoke again, the hollowness in his voice the only indication that Ishiro's words had affected him.

"None was found," said Ishiro. "The servants said that, the day before he killed himself, Tominaga-*san* burned all his papers—his documents, his notebooks, his diaries. Everything."

"Perhaps he was afraid that the Americans would put him on trial," Aritomo said.

"His name was never mentioned in any of the hearings," Sekigawa said, "not by any of the witnesses or any of our people who were charged. I am sure that Tominaga-*san*, like so many of us, simply could not bear to see our country occupied by foreigners."

A familiar, half-forgotten fear seeped slowly through me as I studied the priest, Matsumoto; I should have been able to recognize a former Kempeitai officer from the first moment I saw him, but he had learned to camouflage himself well. "And how about you, Matsumoto-*san*? Was your name ever mentioned in any of the war crimes hearings?"

The Shinto priest did not look away, but his companions leaned back into a wary, watchful silence. "I should have realized earlier that we were speaking to a former Guest of the Emperor," he said.

"*Former?* We will *always* be guests of your emperor."

Sekigawa attempted to lighten the heaviness in the air. "Ah! In a month's time the American occupation will end. We will be free again. Seven years under the Americans. It feels so much longer!"

"If you like, we will extend our stay here for a few more days, to give you more time to reconsider your reply," said Ishiro.

"That is not necessary." Aritomo stood up in a fluid movement that allowed no argument. The other three looked at Sekigawa. He nodded and all of them got up at the same time, Matsumoto helping Mrs. Maruki to her feet.

"We have heard so much about your garden," said Sekigawa. "May we see it?"

"Oh, and the waterwheel too," Mrs. Maruki added. "It was a great honor, I am sure, to be presented with such a gift by the emperor."

"I am making some renovations in that section," Aritomo said, with just sufficient regret for the lie to almost convince me too. "Another time, perhaps, when all the work here has been completed."

"You must inform us when it is possible to visit," Sekigawa said.

"Come back when the Emergency is over. It will be safer to resume your search then," Aritomo said. "The countryside is not a safe place to be at this moment."

"We *have* had problems from the authorities," Ishiro said. "They refused to let us visit quite a lot of places."

"How long will the Emergency last?" Mrs. Maruki asked. She

was, I recognized, the type of woman who was unwilling to leave until she obtained something, however insignificant.

"Years, I would think," Aritomo replied. "Years and years."

The envelope was still lying on the table, the chrysanthemum crest gleaming like the sun's distorted reflection on the surface of Usugumo Pond. Aritomo poured himself a cup of tea and held out the teapot to me. I shook my head.

"Is it true, that you've been asked to go home?" I was worried by the possibility that he might.

He set the teapot on the brazier. "Apparently there is a shortage of us now—the younger gardeners have been killed or wounded in the war and the older ones can no longer keep up with the work." He swirled the tea in his cup a few times, squinting into it. I wondered if he was thinking of the tea plantation his wife had grown up in. "I have been away from Japan for so many years," he said. "So many years."

"Why haven't you gone home? Even for a visit?"

"Not while it was occupied by the Americans. I cannot bear the idea of it, all those foreign soldiers in our cities."

"It wasn't too unbearable for you living here when Malaya was occupied by foreign soldiers!"

"Go back to your old life in Kuala Lumpur," he snapped. "You will never become a well-regarded gardener if you carry such anger with you."

For a while we said nothing to each other. "You were friends with Tominaga, weren't you?" I asked. "What happened between the two of you?"

"There is a temple up in the mountains. I want to ask the nuns to say prayers for Tominaga. Will you come with me? Tell the workers they can have the day off tomorrow."

Thunder grumbled in the clouds. My thoughts kept circling around the conversation with the Japanese visitors. There was another reason for their presence in Malaya, I thought, something of which I suspected Aritomo was aware, but would not reveal to me.

Drawing back his right sleeve with his left hand, Aritomo picked up the teapot and filled his cup almost to the brim. He put the teapot down in the exact spot from where he had lifted it and pivoted on his knees to face the mountains in the east. He remained in that position for what seemed like a long time. Then, like a flower drooping to touch the earth, he brought his head low to the floor. Straightening his body a moment later, he held the cup in his hands and touched it to his forehead.

I left him there, giving one last farewell to the man he had once known, a man who had already traveled past the mountains and journeyed beyond the mists and the clouds.

Chapter Eighteen

The road going higher into the mountains was muffled in a thick mist. It was cold inside Aritomo's Land Rover, our breaths coating the windscreen in a milky cataract. Now and then he would wipe it clean to see ahead. In the terraced fields of the vegetable small-holdings, roosters bugled for the sun. Just before reaching the village of Brinchang, Aritomo swung into a narrow dirt road, following it uphill until it ended in a small clearing. We parked and got out of the car.

"There are two trails to the top," Aritomo said, hitching a ruck-sack onto his back. "We'll take this one here, the more difficult one."

He forced his way into the ant ferns and lallang grass. I kept close to him. A narrow track lay behind the foliage. I walked carefully, trying not to slip on the patches of moss. To my right, the ground sheared away into a river about twenty feet below, the water shredded white by half-submerged boulders. The jungle was a monochromatic wash. The vague shapes of trees solidified when we passed them, only to disappear behind us. Birds called out, impossible to spot in the dense foliage. Thick, half-exposed tree roots terraced the path into loamy steps that sank beneath my weight. At an escarpment we stopped to watch the sun come up. Aritomo pointed to a scattering of low buildings on the far end of the valley as a rip opened in the mist cover. "Majuba." It was the only word he had uttered since we entered the jungle. I recalled the previous occasion when we had hiked to the swiftlets' cave, how talkative he had been, revealing the secrets of plants and trees to me.

"There's the house," I said, catching a glimpse of the flickering flame of the Transvaal flag. Remembering Templer's displeasure when he had seen it, I told Aritomo about it. I had hoped to make him laugh; instead a thoughtful look descended over his face.

"Do you remember me telling you of my walk across Honshu, when I was eighteen?" he said. "I spent a night in a temple. It was falling to pieces, and there was only a solitary monk still living there. He was old, very old. And he was blind. The next morning, before I left, I chopped some firewood for him. As I was leaving he stood in the center of the courtyard and pointed above us. On the edge of the roof a faded and tattered prayer flag was flapping away. 'Young man,' the old monk said, 'tell me: is it the wind that is in motion, or is it only the flag that is moving?'"

"What did you say?" I asked.

"I said, 'Both are moving, holy one.'"

"The monk shook his head, clearly disappointed by my ignorance. 'One day you will realize that there is no wind, and the flag does not move,' he said. 'It is only the hearts and minds of men that are restless.'"

For a while we did not speak, but stood there, looking into the valleys. "Come on," he said eventually. "There is still a long way to go."

A shower had soaked the jungle, and we had to leap over puddles of water on the track. Aritomo pulled himself lightly over the roots, moving with a determined ease, responding to a call only he could hear. Branches, riven down by previous storms, obstructed the track, smearing our hands and thighs with lichen and shreds of sodden bark when we clambered over them.

"How much further, this Temple of Clouds?" I asked after we had been climbing for an hour.

"Three-quarters of the way up the mountain," Aritomo replied over his shoulder. "Only the very devoted ever go there."

"I'm not surprised." We had not met anyone else on the path. Gazing around us, I imagined that we had moved back millions of years to a time when the jungle was still young.

"There it is."

The temple was a collection of low, drab buildings barnacled to the side of the mountain; I was disappointed, having expected more after the arduous climb. A stream ran past the temple, draining into a narrow gorge. In the sprays steaming over the drop, a small rainbow formed and wavered. Aritomo pointed to the rocks on the opposite bank. They seemed to be trembling. A second later I realized that

239

they were covered with thousands of butterflies. I watched them for a moment but was impatient to move on.

"Wait," Aritomo said, glancing up to the sky.

The sun hatched out from behind the clouds, transforming the surface of the rocks into a shimmer of turquoise and yellow and red and purple and green, as though the light had been passed through a prism. The wings of the butterflies twitched and then beat faster. In small clusters they lifted off from the rocks, hanging in the light for a few moments before dispersing into the jungle, like postage stamps scattered by the wind. A handful of the butterflies flew through the rainbow above the gorge, and it seemed to me that they came out looking more vibrant, their wings revived by the colors in that arc formed by light and water.

We walked up to the temple's entrance. A pair of cloth lanterns, once white, hung from the eaves, like cocoons discarded by silkworms. Blackened by decades of soot and incense smoke, the red calligraphy painted on them had ruptured and bled into the tattered cloth, words turned to wounds.

No one was there to greet us when we entered and went up a flight of broken stone steps. The noise of the river quieted. In the main prayer hall a nun in gray robes shuffled past us, the bouquet of joss sticks in her hands fumigating the air. Huge coils of sandalwood incense hung from the rafters, turning in languid, infinite spirals. Gods stood on altars, fierce-eyed and scowling, some carrying tridents and broadswords pierced with metal rings, all covered in a sparse fur of dust and ash.

I recognized the red-faced figure of Kwan Kung, the god of war, from the few times my *amah* had taken me along to a temple in a Georgetown alley, when she would beg the gods for her weekly lottery numbers. She never once won any money but it never stopped her from going back, week after week. The god of war was clad in black armor, his yellowed beard gathered in one gloved hand. "He's also the god of commerce," I told Aritomo. "Business is war, I've heard it said."

"And war," Aritomo replied, "is a business."

Kneeling on a padded wooden stool before another deity was a woman in her seventies, her hands shaking a wooden container filled with flat bamboo sticks. She rattled the container until a single shoot edged out and clattered onto the floor. She put down the container, bowed before the god and picked up the stick. She hobbled to the temple medium, a man with a tuft of beard on his chin. He turned to a chest of matchbox-sized drawers behind him and selected a piece of paper corresponding to the number on the woman's bamboo stick. The old woman leaned closer to the medium to hear the answer from the god.

"Do you want to try it?" whispered Aritomo.

"It can't tell me what I want to know," I said.

A nun came up to us, her placid features and shaven head making it difficult to guess her age. Aritomo wrote down Tominaga's name in Chinese characters and gave it to her. Then he took a bunch of joss sticks from her and dipped them into the flame of an oil lamp. He went to stand before the statue of the goddess of mercy, in a square of sunlight falling in through a hole in the roof. He closed his eyes, opened them again and inserted the joss sticks into a fat-bellied brass urn on the altar. White threads of smoke rose into the sunlight.

"Once, when I was being disobedient, my mother told me a story about a murderer," Aritomo said, his voice dry as the scent of sandalwood perfuming the air. "He had been sent to hell after he died. One day, as the Buddha was walking in a garden in paradise, he happened to glance into a lotus pond. And deep in the pond he saw this murderer, suffering the agonies of hell.

"The Buddha was about to resume his walk when he saw a spider spinning its web, and he remembered how the murderer had once refrained from killing a spider crawling up his leg. With the spider's permission, the Buddha took a strand from the web and dangled it into the lotus pond.

"Down in the depths of hell, the murderer saw something gleaming in the blood-red sky, dropping closer and closer to him. When it was just above his head, he reached out and pulled it. To his surprise, it bore his weight. He began to climb out of hell, to climb up to paradise. But the distance from hell to paradise is thousands and thousands of miles. The other sinners soon saw what he was doing, and they too began to climb up the web. He was higher now, almost out of hell. Stopping for a rest, he looked down and saw the thousands of people, men and women, old and young, all trying to follow him, all clinging on to the thread. 'Let it go! This thread is mine!' he screamed at them. 'Let it go!'

"But no one listened to him. He was terrified that the strand would break. A few of the others had almost caught up with him. He kicked at them, kicked them until they released their grip and dropped away. But his frantic movements broke the strand above him, and then he too plummeted back into hell, screaming all the way."

Swallows flew between the rafters, stirring the incense smoke in their wake.

"I couldn't sleep for weeks after hearing that tale," Aritomo said.

We left the prayer hall and went up another set of steps. Aritomo greeted some of the nuns we passed. At the top of the steps a path opened up into a small garden bordered by a low wall. In the Kinta Valley far below I could make out the town of Ipoh, the shophouses and tin magnates' mansions like grains of rice at the bottom of a bowl. Up in the mountains, above the tree line, the jungle thinned out, losing the strength to climb any higher.

"How would you improve this little garden?" Aritomo asked, sitting down on a wobbly stone bench.

My mind was still on the murderer, given his chance to escape hell only to lose it, and a few seconds passed before I replied. "I'd get rid of that hibiscus hedge—this space is too crowded for it. Then I'd fill in that halfhearted ornamental pond, and cut away most of that guava tree blocking the view," I said. "Simplify everything. Open up the garden to the sky."

He gave an approving nod. Unscrewing the cap of his thermos flask, he filled two cups of tea and handed one to me. From somewhere in the temple buildings below, the nuns had started their chanting, their voices rising to us.

"The nuns seem to know you well," I remarked.

"There aren't many of them left in this place; most of them are quite old," he said. "Once the last one is gone, the temple will be abandoned, I fear. People will forget that it ever existed."

For a while we sat there, sipping our tea. "I want to know what happened to you, in the camp," he said finally.

The heat from the cup passed through my gloves and warmed my palm. "No one wants to hear about us prisoners, Aritomo. We're a painful reminder of the Occupation."

He looked at me and then touched my brow, gently. I felt as though a bell deep inside me had been sounded.

"I want to know," he said again.

The first stone in my life had been set down years ago, when I had heard of Aritomo's garden. Everything that had happened since then had brought me to this place in the mountains, this moment in time. Instead of consoling me, this knowledge left me fearful of where my life would lead.

I began to speak.

CHAPTER NINETEEN

For an anglophile like my father, Teoh Boon Hau, there was only one Chinese saying that he believed in: *A family's wealth will not last beyond three generations.* Being the only child—and a son, no less—of a wealthy man, my father's main purpose in life was cultivating and enlarging the fortune made and left to him by his own father, and ensuring that his three children would not grow up to fritter it away. I suppose he had good reason to be worried: Penang was full of tales of millionaires' children who were addicted to opium and horse racing, or who had ended up as paupers, sweeping the narrow streets of Georgetown and begging for money at the morning market. He never failed to point them out to us.

We grew up in the house my grandfather had built on Northam Road: my brother, Kian Hock; Yun Hong; and I. My brother was twelve years older than I. I was the youngest, but Yun Hong and I had always been close, even with the three years' difference between us. She took after our mother and so was considered beautiful by many people, including our parents. Kian Hock and I had inherited our father's plumpness, and my mother scolded me whenever I asked for seconds at mealtimes. "Don't eat so much, Ling, no man wants a fat wife" became a familiar refrain at the table, a refrain I always ignored, although it did not make it hurt less. Yun Hong always defended me.

We spoke English at home, garnished with Hokkien, the dialect of the Chinese in Penang. My father had studied in an English missionary school when he was a boy and had not been taught to speak or read Mandarin, deficiencies he would pass on to his children: my brother went to St. Xavier's, while Yun Hong and I studied at the Convent Girls' School. The Chinese in Malaya who could not speak English looked down on us for not knowing our own ancestral tongue—"Eaters of the Europeans' shit," they called us.

In turn we Straits Chinese laughed at them for their uncouth ways and pitied them their inability to get good jobs in the civil service or to rise in our colonial society. There was no need for us to know any language other than English, my father had often told us when we were growing up, because the British would rule Malaya forever.

Our neighbor was Old Mr. Ong, the former bicycle repairman. He had kept his ties to his motherland. When the Japanese invaded China, he started the Aid China Fund to collect money for the Nationalists. For his reward Old Mr. Ong was made a colonel in the Kuomintang Army. It was just an honorary rank given to him by Chiang Kai-Shek, who in all probability scattered these around freely to the overseas Chinese as rewards for their generous donations, but Old Mr. Ong was very proud of it. He sent us a copy of the local Chinese newspaper with the photograph of him receiving the honor.

We had been neighbors with Old Mr. Ong for twenty years, but my father only became friends with him after the Japanese massacred hundreds of thousands of Chinese in Nanking. We found it hard to accept the news when we heard it—the slaughter, the rape of old and young women, of children; the mind-numbing savagery of it all. What enraged my father more was the fact that the British had done nothing to stop it, nothing at all. For the first time in his life he questioned the high standing in which he had placed the British, the admiration he had always felt toward them. When he heard that Old Mr. Ong had opened his home to the Kuomintang agents who were traveling the world to raise money and support, my father began attending the meetings. Together with Old Mr. Ong and a group of well-known Chinese businessmen, he visited the towns and villages in Malaya and Singapore, making speeches and urging the people to contribute to the Aid China Fund. Kuomintang agents accompanied them to describe to the audiences how hard the KMT soldiers in China were fighting the Japanese. Sometimes I was allowed to attend these campaigns. "You can always tell which side a man supports, just by looking at whose photograph he puts up in his home," I remember my father saying to me once as we drove home after a rally. "It's either a portrait of Sun Yat Sen, or that fellow Mao hanging next to the family altar." Our servants did the same thing in their quarters at the back of our house. A few days later my father ordered them to take down Mao's portrait.

In 1938, when I turned fifteen, the Japanese government wanted to buy rubber from my father. He refused to entertain them, but later changed his mind and agreed to meet the trade officials in Tokyo. He took us all with him—it was on that trip that my sister fell in love with the gardens of Japan.

The negotiations with the Japanese failed. My father refused to sell any rubber to them. The officials' wives were chilly to us after that: no longer smiling, no longer keen to show us around. Later Yun Hong told me that the KMT had instructed my father to accept the Japanese government's invitation and to report back on what he could discover. Unfortunately, the KMT failed to warn him of the long memories of the Japanese government.

Two years later, in the last weeks of 1941, Japanese troops landed on the northeast coast of Malaya, fifteen minutes after midnight and an hour before Pearl Harbor was attacked. People think that Japan entered the war through Pearl Harbor, but Malaya was the first door they smashed open. Japanese soldiers crawled up the beach at Pantai Chinta Berahi, taking the places of the leatherback turtles that emerged from the sea every year around that time to lay their smooth round eggs. From the Beach of Passionate Love, they cycled and fought their way down Malaya, riding their bicycles along the back roads past Malay kampongs and paddy fields and through jungles the authorities had assured us were impenetrable.

My father was confident that the British soldiers would stop them. But three weeks later the Japanese reached Penang. The British evacuated their own people to Singapore, leaving us natives to face the Japanese. The Europeans who had been coming to our parties for years—the Faradays, the Browns, the Scott brothers, all of whom my parents considered their friends—left on the ships, disappearing without a word to us. But there were also many who refused to run away, who refused to abandon their friends and their servants to the Japanese—the Hutton family, the Codringtons, the Wrights.

Kian Hock, my brother, was in the police force. He had been sent to Ceylon for training two months before the Japanese came. My father ordered him to remain there. Old Mr. Ong asked us to go with his family to his durian orchard in Balik Pulau, on the western side of Penang. "We'll be safe from the *Jipunakui* there," he told us.

We left home on the morning the Japanese planes started bombing Georgetown: Old Mr. Ong and his two wives and their sons and families packed into three cars; my parents, Yun Hong, and I in my father's Chevrolet. The roads leading out of Georgetown were crowded; hundreds of people were fleeing to the hills of Ayer Itam. All of us had heard what the Japanese troops did to the locals in every town they swept through.

The road became deserted as we neared Balik Pulau. We had passed only the odd Malay kampong. I had never been to this part of the island before. Old Mr. Ong's durian orchard was on a high, steep slope. As we drove in, Yun Hong pointed through the gaps in the trees to the sea below. "I should have brought my paints and brushes," she said.

From the front seat my mother said, without turning around, "We won't be here long enough for you to paint anything, darling."

The orchard's overseer was Old Mr. Ong's cousin, and he greeted us with all the ceremony due Old Mr. Ong's wealth and status. The overseer moved his own wife and daughters out of their home to accommodate the old man and his family. My mother looked as if she were about to cry when we saw the dilapidated one-story wooden shack that was to be our new home; she was even more horrified when she discovered that we had to use an outhouse. She wanted to go back to our home on Northam Road immediately, but my father stood firm.

Yun Hong and I soon got used to living in the shack. We spent our days exploring the orchard. The durian season had just started and the air was heavy with the smell of the spiky, ripening King of Fruits. Ah Poon, the overseer, warned us to be careful. "Can kill you-*lah*, if fall on your head." Nets were stretched out between the trees to catch the durian. Walking beneath them, I felt I was inside a circus tent, gazing up at the acrobats' safety net. Every time we heard the fruit dropping through the branches, we'd look up quickly, just to be on the safe side. Yun Hong could not tolerate the fruit, but I loved its pungent, creamy flesh. "Your breath stinks," she would complain after I had eaten my fill. "No man's going to want to kiss you."

We often went down to the beach, thrilled to have it all to our-selves. It was one of the few times in my life I could go swimming without having to worry about people staring at me and laughing and making snide remarks. This part of Penang looked out to the Andaman Sea, and once I even saw a pod of whales, their breaths erupting out of the water. They swam so close to shore that I could count the barnacles on their skin and hear their breathing, moist and hollow as though they were grunting through a rubber hose. The sound was familiar, yet also otherworldly. I would climb out onto the rocks and sit there for hours, watching them until evening fell and their presence was detectable only by their vaporous sighs. The whales stayed in the bay for a week and then one morning they were gone.

It was easy to forget that we were in the middle of a war, but once a week, Ah Poon, returning with supplies from a village a few miles away, would give us the news. KL had fallen, and then Singapore. Thousands of *ang-moh* had been sent to internment camps. The Asian Co-Prosperity Sphere was now in place—with Japan enjoy-ing the lion's share of the prosperity.

Then the Kempeitai began sweeping through Penang, rounding up people and taking them away in lorries. Old Mr. Ong warned Ah Poon to stay away from the village for a while. One afternoon my father made us go to Ah Poon's house. All the women, includ-ing Old Mr. Ong's wives, were queuing up to have their hair cut by Ah Poon's wife. They had decided it was prudent to make us look as unappealing as possible. That was the first moment I felt real fear.

We had been living in the durian orchard for nearly five months when the Kempeitai came for Old Mr. Ong. The secret police had been looking for him. They had also been looking for my father. Arriving in two lorries, they rounded us up in front of Ah Poon's house. We knelt beneath the noon sun, our hands behind our heads. Some of the orchard hands managed to slip away into the jungle when they heard the Kempeitai coming, but there had not been the opportunity for us. And anyway, where could we have run to?

The Kempeitai officers knew all our details. They compared our faces to the photographs in their dossiers. They ordered Old Mr. Ong and my father into Ah Poon's house. We could hear everything from where we knelt outside: the shouting, the beatings, the cries of pain rising into inhuman screams. The younger of Old Mr. Ong's wives fainted. I listened until I couldn't recognize my father's voice anymore. Then the house fell silent.

The officers emerged without my father or Old Mr. Ong. They gave an order and their men moved among us, pulling one after the other to their feet and dragging them to one of the lorries: all of Old Mr. Ong's sons and their wives, Ah Poon's teenage daughters, the workers' wives and children.

And then Yun Hong and I were selected too.

Weeping filled the air, our families begging the Japanese to let us go. My legs seemed boneless when I tried to stand up. I couldn't breathe. The guards shoved us into the back of the lorry. My mother was screaming. I had never heard her sound like that. A soldier punched her and then, when she fell, kicked her, again and again. He kicked her face, her head, her stomach. I broke away from the other prisoners and ran toward her. A guard jabbed me in the stomach with his rifle butt. I doubled over and collapsed to my knees. I had never felt such pain before. I forced down the fetid vomit rising up my throat.

"Get up, Ling!" Dimly I heard my sister shouting from behind. "Get up or he'll kill you!"

Swaying, I managed to get to my feet. I saw my mother lying on the ground. She was not moving. I could not even tell if she was still breathing. No one dared to tend to her. I looked back to the house where my father had been tortured. The guard shoved me and shouted. I limped back to the lorry. Yun Hong reached out and pulled me up.

The Kempeitai stopped at three or four other villages to collect more prisoners, packing them into the back until there was no space left to even sit on the floor. The air inside the tarpaulin canopy baked in the heat. The seats by the open tailgate were taken by the two guards. Some of us suffered from carsickness, vomiting down the front of our clothes. The smell made me nauseous. I tried to hold down my gorge, but it was impossible. Yun Hong helped me clean myself, but there was not much she could do.

The lorry stopped and we were ordered out to relieve ourselves. The women squatted on one side of the road while the men urinated against the trees on the other side. The guards smoked their cigarettes. Then we were on the move again. We crossed the channel to the mainland by ferry. At the Butterworth train station we were transferred to a goods train waiting by a siding. There were already prisoners packed into the cattle cars. I was thirsty—we had not had anything to eat or drink all day.

"You think they're taking us to Changi?" I asked Yun Hong, when the train began to move.

"I don't know," she replied. "I don't know."

We traveled for hours. The guards gave us a bucket of water to be fought over between the fifty, sixty of us packed into the carriage. Someone said we were heading south. Yun Hong was hopeful that we were being transported to Singapore. "Father will find us there," she said. "He'll get us out of this." She tried to keep our spirits up. "If they wanted to kill us," she whispered to me, "they wouldn't have gone to so much trouble."

The train stopped once. The doors opened and we climbed down stiffly. It was hot, the sun setting behind the mountains in the distance. We were relieving ourselves beside the tracks when I heard a train coming. Yun Hong pulled me to my feet and brushed down my skirt, doing the same for herself. Many of the other women were too exhausted to care.

The sound of the train grew louder. It rounded a bend in the tracks and slowed to a stop next to ours. Japanese soldiers unlocked the doors to the cattle cars. Grimy, exhausted-looking British soldiers, some dressed in filthy uniforms, others in loincloths, stumbled onto the tracks.

"They're being taken to the railway in Burma," a Eurasian woman next to me whispered. "Fucking Japs. Bastards."

The guards huddled together, smoking and chatting. One of the British POWs looked around. His eyes met mine just for a second. Then he sprinted across the tracks, heading for the trees. The guards shouted and fired at him. The man's body jerked and he collapsed into the wild grass. He tried to get up but couldn't. He started crawling toward the jungle. One of the guards strolled up to him and, pressing his boot on the man's neck, shot him in the head.

It was late in the evening when our train halted for the last time and the doors were pulled open. Thick jungle lay on both sides of the railway tracks. We were marched through the trees to a clearing where lorries were waiting. The drivers started up their engines and switched on their headlights. A guard threw blindfolds at our feet and gestured at us to put them on. Yun Hong gripped my hand. She was shaking. We had heard stories of how the Kempeitai would take their prisoners to a deserted spot in the jungle and shoot them.

The journey was unending. We seemed to be going uphill all the time. The roads worsened. Finally the lorry stopped. No one dared to move. In the sudden silence I heard shouting in Japanese. Then someone ordered us to remove our blindfolds. I blinked, dizzy and disoriented. Climbing down unsteadily from the lorry, I looked around us, shielding my eyes against the spotlights. Night had fallen. Through the trees I glimpsed a section of a high metal fence topped with barbed wire. Beyond the fence was only darkness. From platforms in the trees, armed men watched the fence and watched us.

I glanced at my sister. Our eyes met for a moment. We were worlds away from anything we had ever known.

The guards separated the women prisoners from the men and marched us to one of the attap huts beneath the trees. Inside, twenty to thirty women were standing at attention, their faces sallow in the light of the paraffin lamps hanging from the low rafters. A thin, bald officer inspected the new arrivals. He stopped in front of me. I shivered when his eyes stared into mine. He moved on to Yun Hong. When he finished he spoke to a guard, who bowed and pulled out half a dozen of the women from the lineup. Yun Hong was one of the chosen. Two of the women started to weep. The guard slapped them. The six women, including Yun Hong, were led away.

It was still dark when I left the hut with the other prisoners the next morning. I had not slept all night. My arms and face were swollen and itching from mosquito bites. We assembled on a parade ground. Yun Hong was standing on the far side with a group of young women. In the gray light I saw that her face was swollen and bruised.

A small, thin man introduced himself as Captain Fumio. "I am in charge here," he said through Father Jacobus Kampfer, the camp's interpreter. "It is dawn in Tokyo. The emperor is about to

have breakfast in his palace. You will show your respect to him."
He made us bow in the direction of Japan. We sang the "Kimi-
gayo"—those of us newcomers who did not know the words had
to move our lips, or risk being slapped. We were dismissed after the
singing. I watched as Yun Hong and her group were taken away.

"What are they doing to them?" I whispered to the Chinese
woman ahead of me, but she did not answer or pretended not to
have heard me.

We queued for breakfast in an open-sided shelter that functioned
as a kitchen and eating area. Each of us was given a bowl of thin
soup and a small slice of coarse bread. We had ten minutes to gulp
it down. Then the guards ordered us into single file and marched
us through the jungle to a cave in a mountainside that formed the
entrance to a mine. Supervised by Japanese engineers, the male
prisoners tunneled deep into the mountain, shoring up the passageways with wooden beams and concrete pillars. The women carried away the broken stones in bamboo baskets, dumping the
rubble into a ravine on the other side of the hill. Limping back to
the cave after I had emptied my basket, I noticed a number of
Japanese civilians walking about, consulting plans and plotting the
angle of the sun.

There were four levels in the mine, linked by a system of tunnels
and airshafts. There must have been a river running close by,
because a month into my internment, after it had been raining
heavily for days, the walls in the lowest level collapsed. Water
flooded the chamber, drowning the prisoners working down there.
We had to go in and pump out the water. The chief engineer told
us to leave the bodies there to be buried into the foundations.

Three hundred prisoners lived in the camp. There were seventy
or eighty Europeans: civilians and captured Allied soldiers. The
rest were Chinese and a handful of Eurasians. The British men kept
to their own, as did the Australians and the Dutch. But there were
no such divisions among us women. All forty-four of us slept in one
hot, crowded hut: Europeans and Chinese and Eurasians. The huts
were constructed from bamboo and thatched with attap and all
were sited under the trees.

None of the other prisoners knew where our camp was located;
they too had been blindfolded when they were transported here.

From my conversations with the Chinese women prisoners, I discovered we shared a common background: we all had fathers or relatives who had been active in stirring up anti-Japanese sentiments.

I asked about Yun Hong around the camp, but no one had seen her. Finally Geok Yin, one of the older female prisoners, said, "There's a hut behind the officers' kitchen. That's where they're keeping them. That's where they've taken your sister. If she's lucky she might only have to serve the officers."

For a few seconds I could not speak or move. Then I turned away from her. She was only telling me what I had known but refused to accept from the moment Yun Hong had been taken away from me.

I asked Father Kampfer to teach me Japanese. The Dutch missionary was in his sixties, and he had previously lived in Yokohama. Once they realized I could speak simple Nihon-go, the guards started treating me better than the other prisoners. I asked them to help me improve my Japanese, and occasionally they would even slip me extra rations or cigarettes. I used the latter to barter for food—there was never enough to eat, and I was always starving. Food was the one thing that obsessed all of us. I convinced the camp administrator to assign me to work in the officers' mess, preparing meals. I had never had to cook a meal in my life, but working in the kitchen would give me the best chance for survival, and I learned quickly. From the kitchen window I could look out to the hut where Yun Hong was held. Five times a day a line of Japanese men could be seen outside, waiting their turn.

One afternoon when I was working in the kitchen, a mine shaft collapsed. The officers rushed off from their half-eaten meals to assess the damage. Making sure that no one was watching, I slipped out of the kitchen and walked casually to the hut. The door was padlocked. I went around to the back and peered into a barred window. Through the dimness I could make out beds, partitioned by flimsy bamboo screens. A few girls were sitting on their beds chatting, some of whom I guessed were only fourteen or fifteen years old. I called out Yun Hong's name. The girls whispered among themselves before passing on my message. Yun Hong appeared at the window a moment later, her face covered with fading bruises. From the shock in her eyes I knew I too had changed.

"You're so thin," she said. "Think how pleased Mother would be, if she could see you now." Tears slid down her cheeks and over her lips. I reached between the metal bars and gripped her hands. I would have done everything I could to trade places with her. And I should have.

Each day was unchanging, differentiated only from the one before by who had been injured, who had fallen ill, who had died. At night we slept on wooden pallets, driven mad by fleas and mosquitoes, counting the calls of the *tok-tok* birds. We worked eighteen hours a day in the mine, surviving on a daily diet of a piece of bread and soup with bits of rotting vegetables floating in it. All of us suffered from a variety of illnesses: dysentery, beriberi, malaria, pellagra; very often a combination of them. I was fortunate to work in the kitchen, but I suffered my share of disease and beatings too. The lack of food and medicine, the heavy labor and the punishments slowly culled our numbers. We gave the worst of the guards nicknames: Mad Dog, Butcher, Pus-Face, Shit-Brains, the Black Death. It made us feel, if only for the briefest instant, that we had some control over our lives.

On two or three occasions I caught glimpses of lithe, brown figures beyond the fence, sliding soundlessly between the trees. "Orang Asli," a prisoner told me. "The Japs leave them alone. Some Jap was killed by their poisoned darts."

Every three weeks lorries with Red Cross markings would arrive at the camp, unloading steel boxes and barrels that the prisoners had to carry into the mine. Thinking that none of the guards was paying attention to him, an Australian private peeked inside one of the boxes. Fumio had him tied to a bamboo frame on the parade ground and whipped. He was then locked inside a low, tin-roofed cage for two days, where he was unable to sit or stand upright. He went insane, and in the end they had to shoot him.

The rainy season came, but still we had to trudge to the mine every morning in the unending downpour. The Japanese guards seemed to know only one English word, and everything had to be done "*Speedo! Speedo!*" Prisoners weakened and died, but there was always a new batch of men and women transported in to replace the dead.

Bribing the kitchen sentry with cigarettes to turn a blind eye, I sneaked away to see Yun Hong whenever an opportunity arose. I stole what little food I could for her: a piece of moldy bread, a banana, a handful of rice. We never spoke about what the Japanese were making her do. She would distract herself—and me—by talking about the gardens in Kyoto we had visited, describing them in detail in a dreamy voice.

"This is how we'll survive," she said once. "This is how we'll walk out of here alive."

"You still admire their gardens after all this?"

"Their gardens are beautiful," she replied.

She tried, once or twice, to talk about our parents, wondering aloud what had happened to them since we last saw them. I cut her off. I did not want to think about them; it would have driven me mad. Better to pretend that they were well and safe.

One of the girls in Yun Hong's hut hanged herself from the rafters. I saw them bring out the body. She was fifteen years old. Captain Fumio chose a Dutch girl from my hut to replace her. It gave me an idea.

"I'll tell Fumio that I want to take your place," I said to Yun Hong, when I saw her later that evening before another batch of men came to her hut.

"Don't you dare," she answered, her face pressing closer to the window bars. "Do you hear me, Ling?" She crushed my hand in hers. "Don't you ever dare do that!"

Looking at her, I realized it was the only thing that had kept her going all these months, the fact that I had not been made to service the Japanese in the camp. Later I found out from one of the friendlier guards that Yun Hong had tried to hang herself early on, but the officer waiting outside her cubicle, waiting for his turn with her, had stopped her before she could succeed. Fumio had warned her, "Kill yourself, and your sister will take your place."

Life in the camp became easier to endure, or perhaps I just grew used to it. The guards still slapped me for the slightest offenses: not bowing deeply or quickly enough, or taking too much time over my work. And I could not fail to see the men lined up outside Yun Hong's quarters. At least those women were given better rations than the other prisoners. A medical officer inspected them every fortnight to ensure that they were clean. Dr. Kanazawa would come to the officers' mess after every examination and sit there by himself, not saying a word to anyone.

"Those girls are the fortunate ones," he said to me one day, after turning around to make sure that we were the only people in the mess hall. "*Jugan ianfu* in the big towns serve fifty, sixty soldiers a day. *Hai, hai,* our girls are the lucky ones." I thought he said it more to convince himself than anyone else. I found out later that one of his duties included carrying out abortions.

Our Japanese masters ate well, so it was easy to pilfer scraps from the kitchen, sharing them with Yun Ling and the women in my hut. I had become such a familiar sight around the camp that no one bothered to stop and search me. I became careless.

As I was leaving the kitchen one night, Captain Fumio stepped out from the shadows and stopped me. He slid his hands under my clothes and ran his fingers over my body, his badly cut nails scraping my nipples. I flinched, as he would have wanted me to.

"*Soh, soh, soh,*" he whispered when his fingers grazed the pair of chicken feet I had tied with a string around my waist and concealed between my thighs.

In the interrogation hut, a guard held me down, forcing me to watch as Fumio placed the chicken feet on the table in front of me. He unsheathed his knife from his belt and, in one swift movement, cut off its claws, severing skin, flesh and bone. Another guard pinned my left hand on the tabletop and splayed my fingers. I was sobbing, begging Fumio to let me go. He brought his knife up again. I was struggling madly now. I kicked the guards, I stamped on their feet, but their grip never loosened.

"Fucking Chinese cunt," Fumio said in English, before switching back to Japanese, "Think you're so clever, stealing our food? Let me teach you one of our sayings: *Even monkeys fall from trees.*"

I screamed and screamed as he brought the blade down and chopped the two last fingers off my hand. The screaming seemed to go on and on. In the seconds before I blacked out, I found myself walking in a garden in Kyoto. And then I lost consciousness, and the pain was gone.

My injuries took a long time to heal. I was delirious and in constant agony, but Fumio sent me back to work in the kitchen before the week was out. The other prisoners did their best to look after me. Dr. Kanazawa had stitched up the stumps of my two fingers. He slipped me vials of morphine from the camp's dwindling supply, strictly reserved for the Japanese. I withdrew from the other prisoners, preferring to lose myself in my own thoughts. To distract myself I created a garden in my mind, calling it up from nothing more than memory. I did not see Yun Hong for weeks, although I asked Dr. Kanazawa to tell her I was suffering from malaria. But she found out what happened anyway. Fumio told her.

"I'll kill him," she said, when I had recovered sufficiently to steal away to see her. She reached between the bars for my hands, but I kept them at my sides. "Let me see," she demanded. I lifted my maimed hand, wrapped in a bandage. "Oh, Ling . . . ," she whispered. "The bastard . . ."

"It's healing." I told her about the garden I had found myself in, just before Fumio severed my fingers.

"We'll create our own garden," she said. "It'll be a place no one can take us away from."

Later that night, lying on my pallet, I thought again of what she had said to me before I left her. "If you ever get a chance to escape, Ling, I want you to take it. No, don't argue. Promise me you'll run. Don't think. Don't look back. Just run."

I had promised her. What other choice did I have?

Malaria took Father Kampfer, and Fumio appointed me as the prisoners' interpreter. One day, about two and a half years after I had arrived at the camp, the prisoners were ordered to build a hut. When it was completed Fumio ordered me to present myself there. He had another man with him, someone I had never seen before. From the deference Fumio showed him, I knew that he was somebody important. He was in his early forties, his hair cropped short, his face lean and narrow. He was dressed in white trousers and a white tunic with a mandarin collar. I wondered how he kept his clothes so spotless in the jungle. His name, he told me, was Tominaga Noburu, and he needed someone to translate documents in English into Japanese for him. "Father Kampfer used to do it for me," he complained.

"He'd still be alive if your men had given him the medicine he needed," I replied.

Fumio's hand pulled back in a movement that had become familiar to us all. Tominaga stopped him with a look. "Please leave us, Captain Fumio."

The captain's palm closed into a fist and then dropped back to his side. He bowed low to Tominaga and walked out of the hut. Tominaga indicated a pair of chairs to me and went to a portable stove to prepare a pot of tea. Diagrams and documents and maps covered his desk in the corner, and a portrait of Hirohito in military uniform gazed down from one wall. Pinned to another wall was a framed charcoal sketch.

"A *kore-sansui* garden," I said, recalling what Yun Hong had once told me, another lifetime ago.

"A dry rock garden, yes," Tominaga said, looking at me, the teapot in his hand forgotten for the moment.

"Where is it?"

He glanced at my hand, still wrapped in a stained dressing, although the injuries were healing. "You know something about our gardens?"

"There was a Japanese gardener living in Malaya, in Cameron Highlands," I said. "I don't know if he's still here." I thought for a few seconds. "Nakamura . . . something or other. That was his name."

"You mean Nakamura Aritomo? He was one of the emperor's gardeners."

"You've met him?" I grasped this thread from the life I had once known.

"Nakamura-*sensei* is a highly respected gardener," Tominaga replied, sitting down in the rattan chair across from me. "How is it that you know of him?"

I hesitated for just a fraction of a second. "The Art of Setting Stones has always fascinated me."

"What happened?" He pointed to the stumps on my hand. A weight pressed into his face when I did not reply. "Fumio," he said.

I lifted the cup to my nose. I had not tasted any tea since entering the camp. I had forgotten what it smelled like. Closing my eyes, I lost myself in its fragrance.

Tominaga realized very quickly that the standard of my Japanese was not as good as Father Kampfer's, but he did not dismiss me as I had feared he would. "But you are a subject of Japan now," he said, "and you should have a Japanese name." He insisted that I should be called Kumomori. I thought it wiser not to object to it, and in fact I think it was good for me in some ways: it was easier to pretend that the things I did were being carried out by a different person, a woman who did not have my name.

He loved to talk about gardening with me and I discovered that, in his spare time, he designed gardens for his friends. He studied his maps constantly, making copious notes. He inspected the mine five, six times a day. I had to follow him down the tunnels, interpreting his instructions to the prisoners. The guards sounded a warning to the prisoners whenever he was approaching. Everyone—even the guards—had to bow and look at the ground. I had not been inside the mine since I started working in the officers' mess. I was astonished by the extent to which it had been enlarged, how deep it now spread beneath the earth. Metal shelves had been riveted into the cave walls and packed full of steel boxes.

The months passed. The monsoons came and left. I envied their freedom. Each time I spoke to Yun Hong, I would ask her to tell me more about Japanese gardens so I could use the knowledge whenever I talked to Tominaga. I asked Tominaga to release Yun Hong, but he refused. "I cannot free one and leave the others. It is not right."

"But it's quite all right to let her be raped again and again? I don't care what's right or wrong, Tominaga-*san*," I pressed on when he said nothing. "All I want is for my sister not to suffer." I wondered if he had also forced himself on her. Even though I knew my sister would never forgive me, I said, "I'll take her place. Just get her out of that hut."

"You are too useful to me, Kumomori," Tominaga said.

Rumors that Japan was losing the war began to spread through the camp. The guards, sensing the change in the prisoners' attitudes, beat them with increased savagery. No, not "them," but "us." Us. There were times when I forgot that, however kindly Tominaga treated me, however much I was exempted from the guards' cruelty because of my friendship with him, I was still a prisoner, a slave of the Japanese. When I told Yun Hong about the impending defeat of the Japanese, she fell silent.

"They'll have to release us very soon," I said, wondering why she did not share my jubilation. "We'll be free to go home."

"And what will people say about me?"

"No one will know what happened here. I promise you."

"It'll come out eventually. Someone will talk." She looked away from me. "And you know."

"We'll never talk about this again when we get out of this place. No one will ever know," I repeated.

"Even if we never talk about it, it'll be there in your eyes, every time I look at you." Coarse laughter and men's voices came from the front. "You better go." She stepped away from the window, the gloom closing behind her.

At this stage, boxes were now being brought in every week. By now the number of prisoners in the camp had fallen below a hundred. The last batch of POWs had been transported to the camp four months before, and since then no other prisoners had arrived. Every two weeks Tominaga would leave the camp, driving away in a Red Cross van. On his return a few days later he would be morose and distracted.

I never asked where he had gone or even what he was doing in the war. He seemed to be happiest when he was discussing his theories of garden design with me. Sometimes he would draw on the sandy ground with a stick to illustrate an idea or a concept I had difficulty grasping. I never failed to question him about the smallest details. I was interested in what he said, but I also did it to prolong the time I spent with him, to delay my inevitable return to the realities of the camp.

"When the war is over, you must go to see Nakamura Aritomo's garden," he said to me one day.

"Will the war be over soon?"

He glanced at me, then turned away to look at the two waterfalls high up in the mountains above the camp. He had lost so much weight that his eyes appeared elongated and misshapen, as though they were melting down his face.

Tominaga had been absent from the camp for three weeks, the longest he had been away since I met him, and I thought I would not see him again. One afternoon, a guard whispered to me that he had returned. I waited for Tominaga to summon me as he had always done, but when night fell and I still had heard nothing from him, I sneaked out from my hut and went to his quarters. The hut was in darkness when I got there. I saw him a short distance away, walking between the trees, a paraffin lamp lighting his path. Silently I followed him toward the *jugan ianfu*'s hut. I hid behind a tree and watched him. The men waiting outside the hut stood to attention, bowing to him as he walked past them and went inside.

I was furious with him, but more so with myself. What had I expected from him? He was just like all of them.

He summoned me the next morning after we had sung the "Kimi-gayo" and bowed to the emperor in Japan. The guards seemed nervous and tense as they moved about the camp. Fumio was barking orders to some of them; I hurried away to avoid him. Tominaga was pacing back and forth outside his hut. He stopped when he saw me. "Come with me," he said. I refused to look at him. He grabbed my hand and pulled me behind his hut to where his Red Cross van was parked. He removed a strip of black cotton from his pocket, stretching it out between his hands. "Put this on!"

I stared at him, still wondering which of the women he had used the previous night. Despite our friendship, I was terrified that he was going to shoot me after he had blindfolded me. Perhaps it was *because* of our friendship that he was granting me this courtesy, this mercy.

"I had your sister reserved for me last night," he said. "I told her that I would get you out. My English is not good but she understood what I was telling her." Digging his hand into his pocket again, he removed a piece of paper, folded into a small square. "She asked me to give this to you." He pushed the note into my palm. "We do not have much time, Kumomori."

I recognized Yun Hong's neat, elegant handwriting when I

unfolded the paper. "*Remember your promise: Don't think. Don't look back. Run.*"

I glanced up from the paper at Tominaga, then looked behind me to the row of huts hidden among the trees. In the darkness of early dawn it was difficult to make them out.

He stepped toward me and I let him blindfold me. I felt him tying my wrists together with a length of twine. Gripping my elbow, he helped me into the back of the van. "Do not make a sound," he said before closing the doors. I heard him climb into the driver's seat and a second later the engine rumbled to life. The van lurched and began to move. At the gates he stopped to speak to the guards. I held my breath, straining to hear his words. And then we were on the move again. It was the first time I had left the camp since Yun Hong and I were brought here, almost three years before. *I'll come back to get you*, I vowed to her silently. *I'll find the camp again. I'll come back for you.*

The road—if there was a road at all—was bad. Now and again a sharp turn slammed me against the sides of the van. Branches clawed the roof. About forty-five minutes to an hour passed before the van swerved to a sudden stop. I heard him get out, walk around to the back and unlock the doors. He helped me out from the van, pulled off my blindfold and untied my hands.

We were in a small clearing. The moon was just sinking behind the mountains. I breathed in long and hard. He handed me a satchel with a bottle of water and pieces of steamed tapioca wrapped in pandanus leaves. Pointing to a track going downhill and into the trees, he said, "You will come to a river at the bottom. Follow it out of the jungle. Go. Forget everything you saw."

"Where are we? Tell me where the camp is."

He bowed low to me. "The war is over. In a few days the emperor will announce our surrender."

Joy and relief made me light-headed. "That means we'll be freed."

"None of the prisoners will be released, Yun Ling."

Hearing my own name uttered from his lips confused me. For a brief moment I did not know who he was addressing. Then I understood what he had said.

"Take me back to the camp!" I turned toward the van. "Take me back!"

He spun me around and slapped me, twice. He shoved me, and I fell facedown to the ground. I heard him climbing back into his van. The engine started, the van reversed, and then he drove off.

Silence returned to the jungle. I got to my feet, picked up the satchel and ran in the direction in which he had driven off. I slipped on patches of moss, I tripped over stones and roots. I had to stop frequently to catch my breath. Eventually I slowed to a walk. I got lost twice and wasted precious time trying to get back to my trail. In the end I had no idea if I was still going in the right direction. I wanted to give up, but I kept walking. I had to get back to the camp.

The sun was high when I came to the edge of a ravine. The sky was clear to the east but, behind me, storm clouds were moving in over the mountains. I drank the last mouthful of water from the flask and then threw it away. My eyes swept the valleys for the two waterfalls I had often seen from the camp. Using them as a marker, I searched for the mine, finding it a minute later below the shoulder of a limestone cliff. Hope revived me.

I clambered up a rock face to get a better view. The prisoners were gathered outside the mine's entrance, hemmed in by the guards. I tried to pick out Yun Hong from the crowd, but I was too high up. A man in a gray robe and an oddly shaped hat paced outside the mine, waving something in his hand that gave off smoke. Incense, I realized a second later.

From inside the mine a figure appeared, growing taller as he came up the sloping tunnel. He was dressed in white, and I knew it was Tominaga, even though I could not make him out clearly. He stopped in front of the prisoners and did something no one had ever done to them—to us—before: keeping his arms to his sides, he folded his body into a deep bow.

Straightening up again, he gave a signal to the guards. They began herding the prisoners into the jungle, away from the direction of our camp. Finally Tominaga was the only person left standing outside the mine. I had to move quickly, I had to get down to the mine and find out where the prisoners were being taken before I lost their trail. But something compelled me to see what Tominaga was up to.

He backed away from the entrance, moving until he was almost at the edge of the jungle. Then he stopped. On the wind came a series of faint detonations. And then, silence. Dust and smoke stormed out from the mine a moment later, but Tominaga continued to stand there, letting the cloud from deep below the earth engulf him completely. When the wind thinned the dust a moment later, he remained, stock still in the same position. Then he turned away from the mine and entered the jungle without a backward glance.

Then the hill above the mine sheared away, pulling everything down with it—trees, rocks, earth.

Rain was falling when I finally descended into the valley. I had no idea how much time had passed—perhaps two hours, perhaps four. I could not find the camp, then I realized that I was already inside it. The fence had been taken down. Every single one of the huts was gone, and the prisoners' vegetable patch had been covered with earth. Even the rubble had been removed. There was no trace of the camp left.

I ran to the mine, recognizing it only from the fresh landslide burying its entrance, saplings and trees sticking out of the churned soil. I looked at the jungle around me, searching for the path the prisoners had taken.

Thunder rolled from somewhere over the mountains. It sounded again, the ground trembling lightly, and I knew it was not thunder. A third explosion came, echoing in the mountains. I tried to pinpoint where it came from. It was impossible. I caught sight of a well-trodden path leading into the jungle and ran toward it. The rain fell harder, blinding me and turning the trail into a river of mud. I did not know how long I kept going, but eventually I had to stop and take shelter beneath some low-hanging branches.

It was late morning when I opened my eyes again. The storm was over, but water still dripped from the branches and leaves. Shivering, I stood up and went to the edge of an escarpment. The thin morning mists were lifting off from the treetops. The jungle seemed to go on forever, and I knew I would only get lost if I went further into it. I made my way back to the mine. The rain had washed down more debris from the mountain during the night. My knees gave out and I collapsed to the ground. My weeping was the only sound in the silence.

Eventually I got up. It was time for me to leave. Turning to the jungle where the guards had taken the prisoners, I fixed the shapes and colors of the mountains and the limestone ridges into my memory, and I vowed to Yun Hong that I would come back for her, to free her spirit from where she had been immured.

I limped back to the camp and continued into the jungle, retracing the path I had used on the previous day, hoping I would be able to find my way out. Branches and thorns drew blood from my face and arms. All the time I had the feeling that I was being pursued by a wild animal. Perhaps a tiger was tracking me. Or maybe a demon of the jungle was stalking me, making me walk in confused circles. I was feverish. My bones ached. The moment came when I knew I could go on no further. In a hollow formed by the buttresses of a fig tree I lay down and shut my eyes. I sensed the creature that had been hunting me closing the gap between us. The undergrowth rustled, then shook harder. I opened my eyes. I heard the creature coming nearer, and then the ferns in front of me parted.

An aboriginal boy of fifteen or sixteen stood before me. He wore only a loincloth, and he had a blowpipe held near to his lips. Keeping his eyes on me all the while, he reached into a small bamboo tube hanging by his waist and took out a dart about four inches long. He inserted it into his blowpipe, tamping a small piece of cloth down into the mouthpiece. Then he brought the mouthpiece to his lips. At the back of my mind lay the knowledge that those darts were tipped with poison, but I was too exhausted to care anymore.

The boy aimed the blowpipe at me, puffed up his cheeks and blew the dart into my chest.

The shouts and laughter of children came from a distance, waking me. My vision was watery, but I could see that the wounds on my arms had been dressed; they smelled of an earthy concoction. I was lying under a coarse blanket in the corner of a long room. I heard voices; it sounded as though there were many other people around me. Underneath the floorboards, pigs grunted and chickens scratched in the dirt.

Despite my repeated questioning, the Orang Asli refused to tell me what tribe they were. Twenty to thirty families lived together in the longhouse, each with its own space, completely open. They let me stay with them for a week. Maybe it was longer; I do not remember much of that period. I drifted in and out of consciousness. During the brief moments when I was lucid, I wondered if they had drugged me. A constant flow of people came to squat and gawk at me, but they kept silent. The Malay I spoke was not much different from theirs, but I suspected they felt it was safer to pretend not to understand me. Only once did the headman speak to me, to tell me that the boy had not been trying to kill me with his dart, but only to make me unconscious so he could go for help.

When I recovered my strength, the headman got the same boy to lead me back into the jungle. He took me to Ipoh, the nearest town. I sensed that he had been instructed to take a long and confusing route, to prevent me from finding my way back to them again. They did not want me to return and bring trouble to their village, I supposed.

It took us four, five days to emerge from the jungle onto a tarred road. He pointed me in the direction and said, "Ipoh." I asked for his name, but he only waved, turned around and slipped back into the jungle.

A lorry driver transporting a load of tapioca into town stopped and gave me a lift. He told me that Japan had surrendered twenty days before. The war was over.

CHAPTER TWENTY

The nuns in the temple were still chanting when I stopped speak-
ing. "The war was over," I said again. It should have made me feel
better, allowing what I had kept bottled up inside me to bleed away,
but it did not.

"Let me see your hand," Aritomo said. "Take off your glove."

He had seen it uncovered so many times already. I made no
movement. He nodded to me, and I removed my left glove, exposing the two stumps. He took my hand, his fingers stroking the
scars. "You are left-handed," he said.

"Fumio was aware of that too. I had to learn to do some of the
simplest things all over again."

"The sketch of the *kore-sansui* garden you saw in Tominaga
Noburu's hut," said Aritomo. "What did it look like?"

I thought for a moment. "Three stones in one corner, and two
low, flat gray rocks diagonally opposite them, and behind them a
miniature pine tree shaped like a dented temple bell."

"The dry mountain-water garden at his grandfather's summer
home at Lake Biwa," said Aritomo. "Three centuries old and
famous all over Japan." He paused. "Tominaga-*san* was a knowledgeable man where the Art of Setting Stones is concerned."

"But he's not as skilled as you."

"He considered himself to be. Tominaga-*san* was a cousin of the
empress," he said, so softly that I thought he was talking to himself. "We have known each other since we were boys of five or
six."

"It was him you quarreled with over the garden designs." I
should have realized it sooner. "Tominaga was the reason the
emperor had to sack you." When Aritomo did not reply, I said, "It
was absurd to fight over a garden."

"It was not merely about a garden. It was about what each one

267

of us believed. He was always unyielding in his views, his principles. I once told him he would make a good soldier."

"He couldn't have been that rigid," I said. "He disobeyed his orders. He helped me escape."

"Now that *was* uncharacteristic of him. He was always our government's strongest supporter, always loyal to the emperor, to our leaders."

"He never said anything bad about you. In fact he often praised the gardens you had designed."

Aritomo's face seemed to age. "But what he did to the prisoners . . . what *we* did to all of you . . ." He became quiet, then said, "You have never told this to anyone?"

"I tried talking to my father about it, once. He didn't want to hear about it. It was the same with my brother."

"What about your friends?"

"I was severed from the world I had known. There was no shadow beneath my feet. I felt I was moving through a landscape that was familiar but, at the same time, unrecognizable to me," I said. "Sometimes I'm so frightened . . . I'm frightened that this is how I will feel for the rest of my life."

"You are still there, in the camp," said Aritomo. "You have not made it out."

"There *is* some part of me still trapped there, buried alive with Yun Hong and all the other prisoners," I said, the words coming out slowly. "A part of me that I had to leave behind." I stopped. Aritomo did not hurry me. "Perhaps, if I could go back to the camp and release that part of me, it might make me feel complete once more."

"For all you know," he said, staring into the distance, "the camp—and the mine—could be just over those mountains."

"It wasn't this high up. And it was humid there, and hot." I breathed in deeply. "The air had none of this . . . this purity."

"Did you try looking for your camp?"

"After I recovered, it was all I did. I wanted to find where they had killed Yun Hong. I wanted to free her—her and everyone who had died there. Give all of them a proper burial. But no one knew anything about that camp—not the Japanese, not any of the prisoners of war or soldiers I spoke to." Scratching the stumps on my hand, I realized that I had not put on my gloves again. I was surprised that I was not embarrassed or awkward about it. "I visited a number of Orang Asli kampongs, and each time I would describe the village where I had been rescued, but no one knew anything about the aborigines who had saved me."

"What do you think were inside those boxes hidden in the mine?"

"We thought it was weapons and ammunition," I said. "But later, when we began to hear rumors that Japan was losing the war, I thought it was strange that they wouldn't make use of the weapons."

"A few months before our soldiers landed," Aritomo said, "Tominaga came to see me."

I sat forward and stared at him. "He came here? What did he want?"

"He presented the waterwheel to me, on behalf of the emperor." Aritomo studied the creases on his palms. "If it can console you in some way, however small, I can assure you that Tominaga did not rape your sister. He preferred men. Always had. I think he went to see your sister because he thought you would not have left without her."

"But I did leave without her. I abandoned her."

"That was what she wanted you to do. You kept your promise to her."

We sat there on the bench, listening to the voices of the aging nuns, left behind in this soon-to-be-forgotten temple. Perhaps they were summoning the clouds to come, to carry them away when the time came for them to leave this world.

For days after we returned from our hike to the Temple of Clouds, I felt restless, unable to concentrate on my work in Yugiri. By telling Aritomo about my sister's experiences, I felt I had betrayed the promise I made to her, to keep her suffering a secret.

There was a heightened awareness in Aritomo; I saw it in the way he lifted his face slightly every morning when we began our *kyudo* practice, as though he was testing the air or listening for a noise in the trees. It began to rain more heavily and for longer periods every day, sometimes for hours, but Aritomo would push us harder in the garden whenever the rain let up, scolding us if we took too long to complete the tasks he gave us.

He asked us to pollard the pine trees at the perimeter of his garden. Being the lightest, I was strapped into a rope harness and then hoisted thirty feet above the ground. Pine needles scratched my cheeks and arms and I had difficulty catching Aritomo's voice in the rising wind as he shouted his instructions to me. I had been up there for ten minutes when I saw him wave to the workers to lower me to the ground. Twisting in the harness to look behind me, I saw that the sky had turned black.

We ran back to his house, reaching it just in time. Standing side by side on the *engawa*, we watched the world dissolve into water. The mountains, the jungle, the garden, all disappeared into the rain.

An unnatural twilight shrouded the house. Lightning flickered through the rooms, illuminating the rice paper screens like spirits passing through worlds. He went into his study and switched on the desk lamp. It struck me that he had not bowed to the portrait of his emperor. In fact, the photograph, I saw, was no longer hanging on the wall.

"The monsoon has started," he said. "There will not be much work for the next few months."

"It won't rain all the time," I said lightly, hiding my concern that he was going to tell me that my apprenticeship with him had come to an end. I knew I was not yet ready to create my own garden.

"Listen to that." Above our heads, the rain thrashed in the winds, savaging the roof tiles. The garden, the house, the space between the two of us, all became a song hidden in the static.

"You want me to leave Yugiri?" I said.

"No," he said. "I want to create a tattoo for you."

Had I heard him properly over the tumult of the rain? "A tattoo? Like the one you made for Magnus?"

"You do not understand." He closed and opened his fingers a few times. "It will be a true *horimono*, covering the top half of your body."

"You're mad, Aritomo." I stared at him. "Have you even thought what my life would be like, if anyone knew I had something like that on me?"

"If you cared about what other people thought, you would never have come to see me."

"You said you had given up tattooing."

"Lately it has been calling to me again." He curled his fingers. Their joints seemed more swollen than I had realized. "The pain is getting worse. I want to make a *horimono*, Yun Ling. I never had the opportunity. Or found the right person."

He went behind the empty bamboo birdcage and peered between its bars. I saw his face, divided into long, narrow strips. He set the cage spinning with a flick of his wrist. His face became distorted. "I have no interest in making a single, small tattoo. But a *horimono* . . ."

The spinning of the cage slowed down, but its bars continued to ripple their shadows across the walls. I had the sensation of being inside a magic lantern, watching the world reel around me on a rice paper screen.

"Obtaining a *horimono* is a great honor," Aritomo said. "In Japan you would be asked for letters of introduction and you would be interviewed extensively by the *horoshi* before he decided if he wanted to work on you."

There was a soft crack of bamboo as he stopped the spinning birdcage. The walls seemed to continue revolving for a few seconds longer. He stepped away from behind the cage.

"What sort of designs do you have in mind?"

"The *horoshi* and his client discuss the matter before a decision is made."

"How do they decide?"

"Some *horoshi* keep drawings or photographs of the tattoos they have already created."

"Let me see them."

"I never kept them—they were not something I wanted to have lying around. And, anyway, I have never made a *horimono*." He thought for a second or two. Then he went to kneel before a chest of drawers in a corner of the study. He took out the box of wood-block prints he had shown me before and spread them out on his table.

"Most tattoo masters are expert woodblock artists—the skills are essentially the same," he said. "*Horoshi* often create pieces inspired by *Suikoden*."

"What are the procedures?"

He placed an *ukiyo-e* print on his desk. The process of tattooing would begin with *suji*, drawing the outline with a brush, he explained, his fingers moving around the print light as a dragonfly skimming over a pond. The outline would then be tattooed before the next stage, *bokashi*—filling in the drawings with colors.

"There are two ways to execute *bokashi*. More needles will be used where I want to put in darker colors. The ink is entered into your skin at a uniform level, the needles held like this." His fingers tapered to a point, as though he was trying to cast a shadow of a bird's head. He pecked my wrist in a vertical motion. "The effect of shading, like what you see here"—he indicated the camellia petals in the corner of the *ukiyo-e*—"is more difficult to create. The ink has to be inserted at different depths into your skin. I will require fewer needles, working them in at an oblique angle."

His slow, matter-of-fact explanation lulled me. "The *horimono* will be contained within a frame," he continued. "Or it can fade away into the surrounding skin, into *akebono mikiri*, a 'daybreak' design."

"Daybreak," I whispered. It called to mind a border with no visible boundary, a sky fenced in only by a barrier of light. "Any adverse side effects?"

"Well . . . in the old days, when cadmium was used in red ink, clients would experience fevers and pain. Some people have complained that their tattooed skin stopped perspiring, that they felt cool even on the warmest days."

"Like a reptile. How long would it take to complete the tattoos?"

"Most people can only endure an hour's session a week." He paused to do some mental calculations. "A *horimono* like what I have in mind will require about—oh, twenty to thirty weeks. Half a year. Perhaps less."

"I'll consider it," I said, laying out my words carefully between us, "if the tattoos—the *horimono*," I corrected myself, preferring the Japanese word as it did not have the same connotations, "if the *horimono* covers only my back."

He deliberated for a few seconds. "Let me see your body."

"Close the shutters."

"Only a fool would be out in this storm."

I continued to stare at him, and after a moment he obeyed me. Now and again the noise of the rain on the roof shifted as the wind changed, only to pick up a few seconds later, the erratic rhythm seeming to match my breathing.

Aritomo unbuttoned my blouse slowly and then turned me around, slipping it off my shoulders. I scrubbed some heat into my arms as he unclasped my brassiere. We had been naked in each other's presence so often, but now I felt awkward as I stood there in his study. He draped my clothes over the back of a chair and switched on another lamp, angling its shade at me. I shielded my eyes, the heat feeling good on my bare skin.

He circled me and I turned with him, a satellite moon pulled around a planet's orbit. "Keep still," he said. "And stand up straight."

I pulled back my shoulders, lifting my breasts and my chin. His touch was gentle at first, and then his thumbs began to press into my back. He stopped when I flinched, but I signaled to him to continue. His hands lingered over the scars from the beatings I had suffered in the camp. I felt the tips of his fingers stroking the marks.

"I will paint you from here"—he traced a curve along my shoulders and stopped at my back where it hollowed before rising into my buttocks—"to here. The *horimono* will not be visible under your clothes."

"The pain, is it bearable?"

"You have endured much worse."

I turned away from him and got dressed quickly. I adjusted the collar of my blouse and brushed my hair into place. "You've never done something like this on anyone else? Not even your wife?"

"You will be the only one, Yun Ling."

The sheets of *ukiyo-e* crackled when I picked them up, as though the demons pressed into the paper were struggling to escape their infernal prison. I put them down again quickly. "I don't want these on me."

"They mean nothing to you," he conceded.

"What do you suggest then?"

He was silent for a minute or two. "The *horimono* can be an extension of *Sakuteiki*. I will put in the ideas I have accumulated over the years, the things you should remember when designing a garden."

The possibilities were taking shape in my mind, like an unkempt bush being clipped into recognizable topiary. "Things I will never discover in any book or from any other gardener."

"Yes."

"All right." It seemed so easy, agreeing to let him tattoo me. I wondered which of my dresses I could never wear again.

"It is not uncommon for people to change their mind, to give up before the *horimono* has been completed," Aritomo said. "I want to be certain that I *will* get to finish it."

I went to the window and opened the shutters. Cold, moist air hit my face. The storm had weakened for the moment; the clouds over the mountains were swirls of silver and gray. I felt like a pearl diver on the ocean floor, looking at the soundless waves pounding the rocky shoreline far above me.

CHAPTER TWENTY-ONE

A line of cars were parked along the road outside the Smokehouse Hotel when Aritomo and I got there just after noon. The light on the terrace was painful after the dimness of the lobby. I shaded my eyes and looked around. Marquees had been set up in case it rained, but the skies were clear. Errol Monteiro's four-piece Eurasian band from Penang was playing on a low platform decorated with white bunting. I recognized most of the guests. A few of them glanced at us and then looked away quickly. The whole of Cameron Highlands had probably heard I was living with Aritomo by now. Magnus broke away from a cluster of people and strode over to us.

"My old friend," Aritomo said, smiling and giving him a bow.

"*Ja*, seventy-three years old today." Magnus grimaced. "Can you believe I was not even sixty when I first met you?"

The two men looked at each other, perhaps thinking of that moment when they had become acquainted, in a garden some-where in Kyoto. They were, I thought, the most unlikely people to have become friends, even if, as Emily had mentioned at the Mid-Autumn Festival, their relationship had been weakened by the war.

"Happy birthday, Magnus," I said, giving him a box wrapped in brown paper and tied with a ribbon. "From both of us."

"Ah, *baie dankie*." He shook the box lightly. "In the early years of our marriage Emily always scolded me if I opened any gift before the guests had all gone home. Said it was the sort of bad manners only *ang-mohs* have."

Behind him, I noticed a table piled with presents, all of them still wrapped in gift paper. "It's a good Chinese custom," I said. "Saves you from having to pretend you like the gift when you open it."

"So what is it?" he asked, lifting the box to his ear and shaking it.

"We bought a donkey for you." I laughed. "I'll let you two talk."

The band was playing a jaunty "Tuxedo Junction." Making my way through the crowd, I lifted a flute of champagne from a passing waiter, greeting the people I knew. The noise and laughter rose above the music; the mood was carefree, optimistic. Templer's measures seemed to be taking effect; the number of CT attacks had more or less halved. There were now more areas designated "White" than "Black" and the curfew had been lifted in most places.

"Did you hear?" Toombs stopped me, raising his voice above the music. "They killed another CT! Manap the Jap!"

"I've heard," I said. The son of a Malay mother and a Japanese father, the commander of the Tenth Regiment had been shot dead by a Gurkha patrol a few days before. Manap's head had carried a price of seventy-five thousand dollars.

By a flowering rambutan tree a short way off from the crowd I found a quiet, shady spot to enjoy my drink. Aritomo had been subdued on our drive here. It was more than a week since I agreed to let him tattoo me. He had not mentioned the *horimono* since and I did not raise the matter with him. Looking at the people on the other side of the lawn, laughing and chatting, I wondered how appalled they would be if they knew I would soon have a tattoo draped over my back. I tried to imagine what Yun Hong would have said, but I found I could not remember her face or even the sound of her voice. I thought back to the camp, to the last time I saw her, and slowly her face formed in my mind's eye. I had gone to see her at the window, bringing her a whole ripe mango. I had not had the chance to visit her in more than three weeks and her pale face in the dusky shadows shocked me. She refused to tell me what was wrong, but I pressed her until finally she admitted that she had become pregnant. Dr. Kanazawa had aborted the fetus two days earlier. That was the last time I saw her or spoke to her. Shortly after that Tominaga had smuggled me out of the camp.

Wiping away my tears, I saw Frederik coming toward me. "There you are," he called out.

"Magnus didn't tell me you'd be here." I forced a lightness into my voice.

"I just arrived a second ago."

I had not seen him in almost a year. He looked darker, and the air of toughness in him was stronger than I remembered. I pointed to the cuts on his cheeks. "What happened?"

"I got caught in an ambush."

My eyes examined him in a quick sweep. "No serious injuries, I hope?"

"A few scratches. Nothing as bad as yours." His eyes studied my face, slid down the length of my body, paused at my thigh, then floated up to my face again. "I heard about the attack. I couldn't get leave to see you. It's been a mad time. Did you get my card?"

"Yes. And the lilies. They were beautiful." I wanted to show my gratitude for his concern, and an idea came to me. "How long will you be staying?"

"I'm here for two days."

"We've nearly finished the work in Yugiri. If you're free early tomorrow, I'll take you through the garden."

"I've already seen it. That morning—when I went there to drive you back to Majuba. The first time we met." He was clearly annoyed that I seemed to have forgotten.

"Oh yes. But the garden wasn't ready then."

"I don't know how ready it was, but everything looked controlled, artificial."

"Then you've failed to understand what the garden is about."

"Gardens like his are designed to manipulate your emotions. I find that dishonest."

"Is it?" I fired back. "The same can be said of any work of art, any piece of literature or music." I had worked extremely hard in the garden, and to hear someone denigrating it angered me. "If you weren't so stupid you'd see that your emotions are *not* being manipulated—they're being awakened to something higher, something timeless. Every step you take inside Yugiri is meant to open your mind, to lead you to the heart of a contemplative state."

"I heard you're living with the Jap now."

The reason for his prickly mood had become obvious. "I'm sleeping with him, if that's what you're trying to ask me."

"It is."

I moved a few steps away from him, turning toward the guests on the lawn. "I first heard his name when I was seventeen. Almost half a lifetime ago," I said, my anger dissipating, replaced by a sadness for all that I had lost.

"It's only a name," he said.

"It was more than that."

To cheers and applause Emily and Magnus strode onto the platform. The band broke off from the song they were in the middle of and began to play the opening strains of "Happy Birthday." The cheering grew louder. Frederik looked at me, then walked off into the crowd.

Just above my head, a tattered, abandoned spiderweb hung from a twig. I thought of the story Aritomo had told me about the murderer climbing out of hell on the filament of web.

I reached up to brush the web from the twig, but stopped just before I touched it.

I was quiet during dinner, and Aritomo did not talk much. Most of the food remained untouched when we left the dining room.

Once alone in the bedroom, I took off my blouse and brassiere, then stepped out of my skirt. I put on a silk dressing gown and stepped, barefoot, out into the corridor.

The house was in darkness; the weak illumination from the room at the far end of the passageway pulled me toward it. In the spill of light outside the opened door, I stopped to look around. Water dripped from the eaves, the stones in the courtyard glowed faintly and I was reminded of the journey through the swiftlets' cave. The end of the passageway I had just come from seemed far away. I tightened the sash around my robe, then stepped into the room.

Aritomo was sitting in the *seiza* position. A charcoal brazier radiated warmth across the room. Spread out on the *tatami* mats was a cotton sheet, smooth and white. In a brass censer a stick of sandalwood incense unraveled a line of smoke. I faced Aritomo and sat in the same manner, having becoming used to it by now, my ankles and shins no longer feeling as if they were being slowly pulled apart. We placed our hands on the mat, looked at each other, and then bowed.

He poured a cup of heated *saké* and offered it to me. I shook my head, but he insisted. "The American occupation of Japan ended two days ago." He raised his cup to me and, reluctantly, I did the same, swallowing it in one gulp. The wine seared my throat and pressed tears from my eyes.

I stood up. I untied the robe slowly and let it fall. The chill touched my skin, but the *saké* was warming me. He watched me for a moment. Then he took a large white towel to wrap around my waist. Telling me to lie on my stomach on the sheet of cotton, he folded my clothes neatly and placed them on the mat. Then he came to kneel beside me, one hand balancing a wooden tray lined with his tools. His movements were purposeful and assured, the way he appeared when he was working in his garden. He dribbled some water from his fingers into a stone inkwell and ground an ink stick in it. Inhaling the sooty smell of the fresh, new ink, I could almost pretend to myself that I was in a scholar's study, observing him as he practiced calligraphy.

He wiped my back with a hand towel, then dipped a writing brush into the inkwell and shaped it against the side, pressing out the excess ink. He drew on the skin around my left shoulder with light, quick strokes. When he was finished he asked me to sit up. He passed a large mirror over that area for me to see.

The black outlines of flowers filigreed my skin—camellias and lotuses and chrysanthemums. I took the mirror from him. As I examined my back, he lit a candle and set it down between us. Opening a small wooden box, he lifted away the upper tray to reveal a compartment beneath. A row of needles was arranged on it, glinting in the light. He selected four or five and, biting off a length of thread from a spool, tied them to a thin wooden stick. Gesturing to me to lie down on the sheet again, he passed the needles through the flame of the candle a few times. The shadows on the rice paper walls wavered and, for a moment, I felt I had been inserted into a *wayang kulit*, becoming a character in the shadow play the Malays performed with leather puppets by the light of a paraffin lamp.

He blackened the needles by rubbing them against the ink-soaked calligraphy brush gripped between the last two fingers of his left hand. Then he stretched the skin on my shoulder and pushed the needles into me.

He had warned me, but still I could not help myself. I cried out at the first of a million cuts, my fingers clawing the sheet beneath me.

"Keep still," he said. I attempted to get up, but he pressed me down with his palm, repeating the incisions. I fought back the grunts of pain. I clamped my eyelids against the tears, but still they leaked through. My body flinched each time his needles bit into me; I felt my skin was being taken apart, line by line, stitch by stitch.

"Stop fidgeting." He wiped my back again and I turned my body to look. The white towel was covered in moist, red blotches.

"There was a Japanese engineer in the camp—Morokuma. He collected tattoos." My voice sounded hoarse, and I cleared my throat. "Prisoners who were tattooed would show them to him in exchange for cigarettes." Aritomo pressed the needles into my skin again, and I forced back a cry. "He'd photograph them. Later, when he ran out of film, he'd draw them in a sketchbook. He once asked me to translate the words in a man's tattoo. I made the mistake of doing it correctly."

Aritomo's hands ceased moving over my back. "What happened?"

"The man was a rubber planter. Tim Osborne. He had 'God Save the King' tattooed above a bayonet on his arm. Morokuma copied it into his book. Then he informed the camp commander. Tim was fifty-seven years old, but they gave him a beating anyway." I paused for a moment. "They cut the tattooed portion of his skin from his arm and burned it in front of all of us. He died two days later."

Outside, a passing breeze nudged the brass rods of the wind chime hanging under the eaves. The candle flame shivered, tilting the walls around us. For an instant I smelled burning skin again.

Aritomo worked for about an hour without speaking. The agony did not settle into a dull sensation, as I had hoped it would. Every subsequent prick of his needles hurt as much as the first. Finally he sat back on his heels and let out a long breath. He put his tools down on the tray and began to clean my back, dabbing the towel here and there. His touch was gentle, but the cloth was abrasive. "That is enough for tonight," he said.

Getting up unsteadily, I walked around the room, shaking out the stiffness in my arms and legs. Aritomo's fingers, palms and wrists were smeared with black ink. His fingers were rigid, and I realized they were causing him pain.

"Are you all right?" I asked.

"It will go away in a few minutes," he said.

I picked up the mirror and angled it above my back, letting out a cry when I saw the reflection. "It looks awful," I said. He had cleaned away the mess of smudged ink and bloodstains, but my skin was raw and bruised, already beginning to swell. A meshwork of lines overlaid my back, and even as I looked, a cluster of blood droplets beaded up from beneath my wounds, collecting on the skin before sliding down the curve of my back in a viscous crimson trail. It looked nothing like any tattoos I had seen, nor did it resemble anything from his woodblock prints, and I wondered if he had lied to me about his tattooing abilities.

"Until it is finished, this is how it will appear." He pulled my hand away. "Stop scratching it. Let it heal."

He helped me into a light cotton robe; the cloth stuck to my back, stinging me. "I thought there would be more blood," I said.

"Only unskilled *horoshi* inflict excessive pain or draw an unnecessary amount of blood." He looked at me for a moment, but I knew he was thinking of something else.

"What's wrong?"

"I forgot how addictive it can be, not only for the person being tattooed, but also for the artist."

"I wouldn't describe it as addictive."

"You will feel differently after a few more sessions."

The corridor was in darkness when I stepped outside. I felt disoriented as I followed Aritomo to the bathroom at the back of the house. The water in the upright cedar soaking tub had been heated, filling the bathroom with steam and a clean fragrance. Aritomo tested the water and, taking my hand, helped me into the tub.

"Stay in there until the water cools," he said. "Your skin will heal faster. Sit straight—do not lean back."

I pulled his arm as he was about to leave. "Get in with me."

He held up his hands. "Let me clean up first."

Sinking lower into the tub, the stiffness in my body slowly dissolved away into the water, mingling with the ink and blood eddying from my skin.

CHAPTER TWENTY-TWO

*With the monsoon's arrival, Aritomo dismissed the workers, instruct-*ing them to return only when the rainy season was over. There remained only the two of us to look after the garden. In the breaks between the rains I pruned and cleaned up the damage left behind by the storms. Working side by side with Aritomo, I found our iso-lation from the world outside comforting.

He would tattoo me at night, with the rain beating on the roof. After completing the outline of the chrysanthemum flower on my shoulder, he worked his way down my back. I had a full-length mirror put in the room. The thin, black outlines of his tattoos soon covered my body like contour lines. In the same manner he con-structed his garden, he engraved his designs on my skin without first putting them down on paper. He had to wait for the scabs to form and drop off before he proceeded with the tattooing. My back was constantly raw. More than once he warned me not to scratch the tattoos, fearing that I would damage them before the skin could heal.

After each session I would soak myself in the wooden tub, rest-ing my chin on the water's surface, steam drawing perspiration from my face. Standing in the bathroom after the end of a particu-larly long session, I studied my back in the mirror. He had begun to shade the tattoos in gray and light blue hues, and they appeared like clouds of smoke blown against my skin.

Once he saw that I could withstand the pain, he worked on the *horimono* for much longer, going on deep into the night until I thought the lamp in the room was the only light left burning in the mountains.

The temperature in the highlands frequently dropped to below ten degrees after sunset, and although the monsoon rains had made the

nights colder, I often sat with Aritomo on the verandah after dinner, the bamboo blinds rolled up into the eaves. We never put the
lights on, preferring to feel the garden.

As the *tok-tok* birds hammered out their calls, the kettle on the
brazier by the table began to steam. Aritomo spooned some tea
leaves into a clay teapot. He held the caddy in his hand, staring into
it. "There is just enough for one last brew."

"The Fragrance of the Lonely Tree? Don't you have more in the
kitchen?"

"No." He closed the caddy, put it aside and filled the teapot with
boiling water from the kettle. He swirled the water inside the teapot
and threw it out over the edge of the verandah onto the grass, leaving a smudge of steam in the air. He filled the pot again and poured
a cup for me.

"Why do you always do that?" I asked. It had always seemed
such a waste to me, especially now.

"To remove dirt from the leaves, of course," he replied. "We have
a saying: *The first brewing is fit only for your enemies.*"

"You did that on my first visit here too," I said, smiling.

"I did not know what you were," he said. He did not smile.

"But you do now?"

"Your tea is getting cold."

With each sip I felt I was also absorbing something melancholy
that had been infused into the tea leaves. When the teapot was
empty, I said, "I want to add another day to our sessions. We can
make it three, maybe four times a week."

"You have become addicted to it. No need to be embarrassed. It
always happens."

It was true what he said—I had begun to anticipate what he
would put on my body, and I had even started to enjoy the pain,
because for those hours when his needles tracked across my skin,
the clamor in my mind was deadened. I worried about what would
happen once the final cut was made, when the last open pore was
tamped and sealed with ink.

"The *horimono* is progressing faster than I had planned," Aritomo said. "I can start filling it with colors in a day or two. Hopefully we can finish before the monsoon is over."

"You seem in a rush to finish it too."

"The Emergency is coming to an end. Another White Area was declared today."

"You almost sound disappointed."

"Life has been suspended, somehow, during the Emergency," Aritomo said. "I often feel I am on a ship, heading for a destination on the other side of the world. I imagine myself in that blank space, between the two points of a mapmaker's calipers."

"That empty space exists only on maps, Aritomo."

"Maps, and also in memories." He breathed into his cupped hands. "One of the odd things about tattooing: the *hari* draw out not only blood, but also the thoughts hidden inside that person." He lifted his gaze to me. "What did you actually do in the camp?"

"I did whatever was required for me to live."

"Did that include working for the Japanese?"

The night had become colder. A long moment of silence slid by before I felt I could speak. "I gave information to Fumio. I told him who was planning to escape. I told him who was constructing a radio, where it was hidden. I still received my share of beatings, but I got better rations. I got medicines. Yun Hong found out. She begged me to stop. I refused."

An owl glided past the verandah, like a fragment of lost memory. "I left her," I said. "I left Yun Hong there."

Aritomo reached over to the brazier and opened its little door. He rested on his elbows and blew into it, sending sparks billowing out into the night.

At first I thought that the sounds of gunfire were memories trying to break into my dreams, but they continued when I opened my eyes, bursts of tiny detonations spaced unevenly apart. I sat up in bed. The milky light in the room told me it was about seven in the morning. Through the half-opened sliding doors I saw Aritomo below the *engawa*, looking toward Majuba estate. I got dressed and went out to join him. The clouds were ripe with rain and a strong wind was riling the leaves in the trees. Before I could speak four men in khaki uniforms appeared around the corner. The one in front pointed his rifle at us.

Aritomo moved past me to stand in front, obstructing me. The man drove the butt of his rifle into Aritomo's cheek, whipping his head to one side.

They tore the house apart, pushing the cupboards over and breaking the crockery in the kitchen. I hoped they had not harmed Ah Cheong, then remembered that it was Sunday. Once they were satisfied that they had found all the food and money in the house, the CTs marched us over to Majuba, taking the path I had so often used. The jungle seethed with insect calls. Soon I saw the familiar tea-covered slopes between the trees. We emerged from the jungle a moment later and continued to the estate. The metal gates at the workers' compound were open, the men and their families kneeling on the grass, watched over by armed CTs. The Malay Home Guard lay face down on the ground, not moving. Further down the dirt road, CTs were carrying out sacks of rice and boxes of tinned food from the co-op store. Passing the clinic, we saw more of them stuffing medicines and bandages into gunnysacks.

The security gate at Majuba House had been forced open. The walls and the front door of the house were pocked with bullet holes, the shutters splintered. Strelitzias were shredded over the lawn. Inside the house, glass and plaster and pieces of wood were strewn on the yellow wood floor, crunching beneath our feet. Light skewered in through the broken shutters and torn wire netting. The smell of gunpowder corroded the air, mixed with another stench; Brolloks and Bittergal were sprawled close together on the floor in the hallway, blood from their stomach wounds pooling around them, soaking into their feces. In the dining room we found Magnus and Emily kneeling on the floor. They looked up when we came in; blood ran down from a wound on Magnus's face. Hands shoved us down to kneel next to them. From the kitchen at the end of the corridor I could hear the servants sobbing.

"I am Commander Yap," a man with a gentle, studious face said. I wondered if he had been a teacher before he had taken up arms against the government.

"What the hell do you want?" Magnus said. A CT rammed the butt of his rifle into the side of Magnus's head. Magnus swayed on his knees, but remained upright. The CT was about to hit him again when Emily shouted, "Stop it! Stop it!"

"You two *chau-chibai*," Yap said, his eyes moving from Emily and back to me. "One married to an *ang-moh*, another one fucking a Jap devil."

He snapped his fingers. A female CT dragged a man to the front by his hair and kicked him onto his knees; his face was swollen and smeared with blood and dirt.

Yap turned to Aritomo. "One of your people. Inoki here has been fighting with us ever since his country lost the war. But now he wants to surrender, he wants to go home." He squatted down and brought his face close to Aritomo's. "In the jungle you hear many strange things. Many strange things. Inoki told us about the gold stolen by you Japs. It's hidden in the hills here, he says. So we're giving him a chance to find out where it is."

"Things must be getting bad for you, if you have started believing in fairy tales," said Aritomo.

Inoki shuffled on his knees toward Aritomo and spoke to him in Japanese. "The rumors, Nakamura-*san*, you must have heard them." His words gushed out in a torrent of fear and hysteria. "If you know anything about the rumors, tell these people. Please."

Aritomo looked away from him and lifted his head at Yap. "I am a gardener, not a soldier."

"Yamashita gold." Panic, and perhaps a desire to let the CTs know he was trying his best, made Inoki switch to English. "This we hear. Many time. The gold, Nakamura-*san*, the gold General Yamashita steal. Yamashita gold. Yes? Yes?"

"All nonsense," Aritomo said. "Just rumors."

Yap pointed his pistol at Inoki; the Japanese started keening, pulling at Aritomo's shirtfront. Aritomo made no movement, but continued to hold Yap's gaze. My eyes jumped from Aritomo to Yap, to Inoki, and back to Yap again. The CT commander's expression was gentle. He shot Inoki in the head. Emily screamed. Blood and flesh and bits of bone splattered the chairs and the floorboards of the dining room. I felt something warm and wet sticking to my face, but I fought the urge to wipe it away. In the kitchen, the wailing of the servants became hysterical. Through the ringing in my ears, I heard a man shouting at them, followed by the sounds of hard slapping. The crying weakened to low moans.

Yap turned his pistol on me.

"I know the area where Japs hid the gold. I'll take you there."
All of us stared at Magnus. Emily cried out softly, gripping his arm.

"Do not be stupid, Magnus," Aritomo said.

"Where is it?" Yap asked.

"In the Blue Valley. A few miles north of the river."

"How do you know this?"

"I heard it from Colonel Hayashi. I used to go hunting with him. He told me about the gold. Even pointed out the hill to me. They buried a stash of guns there too. I don't know if it's Yamashita's gold or not."

"You never looked for the gold yourself?" Yap asked.

"For god's sake, the man was piss-drunk! He was always talking rubbish anyway."

"Magnus . . . ," said Aritomo.

A man ran into the kitchen and whispered into Yap's ear. Yap listened, frowned and then said, "You . . ." He waved his pistol at Magnus. "Get up, old man!"

Moving with difficulty, Magnus pushed himself to his feet. Emily clung to him, moaning and shaking her head wildly. I grabbed her arm but she shook free of me, her elbow hitting my face as she flailed about. Magnus embraced her, murmuring to her, and she went limp in his arms. He kissed her, then pushed her away gently. He looked at Aritomo, then me. Emily stood there, her arms hanging down at her sides as the terrorists left the house, taking Magnus with them.

Emily ran out through the front door, Aritomo and I following behind her. The sickly whine of sirens came up the driveway about fifteen minutes after the CTs had gone. "They've taken Magnus," she cried even before the police got out from their vans. "The Blue Valley, they've taken him there."

A muscle in my leg erupted into spasms. A moment later I was shivering. Aritomo brought me back into the house and made me sit down in a chair in the hallway. "Breathe," he said, rubbing my back with long, hard strokes. After a few minutes I stopped shaking. He dug out his handkerchief and wiped my face with it.

"Was Magnus—was he telling the truth about the gold?" I asked.

"Hayashi was a drunkard—that much is true. And he did go hunting with Magnus once or twice. But if the gold *is* there, hidden in the Blue Valley, it would be the last thing Hayashi would have revealed to Magnus, drunk or not. Magnus and his friends have been searching that area for years."

The police came into the house and I recognized Sub-Inspector Lee. One of the workers had seen a group of terrorists entering Majuba, Lee told me. The man had run out to the main road and got a lift from a lorry into Tanah Rata. The police questioned every one of us who had been in the house during the attack. Two of the assistant managers and a tea picker had been hacked to death by the CTs. Harper's bungalow had been ransacked, but he was spending the night with the wife of a tin miner in Tanah Rata. The Gurkha sentry was found tied to a tree with barbed wire, his *kukri* buried in his chest.

Emily's fears and panic increased as the hours passed. "Why are you all still here?" she shouted at Lee. "What are you doing to find my husband?"

"KOYLI jungle patrols are already sweeping the hills around Majuba and the Blue Valley," Lee replied, referring to the King's Own Yorkshire Light Infantry. "We're doing everything we can, Mrs. Pretorius."

The moment the police left, Emily shut the door and turned to face Aritomo and me. "Magnus told me you've been paying the CTs to stay away from Yugiri," she said. "No, don't you dare pretend you don't know what I'm talking about! You hear me? Don't you dare!"

"Majuba was included in the deal," Aritomo said. "They've changed the rules, Emily. The agreement is broken."

She took a step closer to Aritomo. "I want . . ." Fissures spread into her voice. She gripped the back of a chair, lifting her chin to Aritomo. "I want my husband back," she said carefully. "I'll pay them whatever they want. Just tell them to bring Magnus back to me."

At the western boundary of Yugiri, I watched Aritomo climb up the fern-covered slope and fade into the dappled shadows of the jungle. I wanted to follow, but he refused. I sat down on a tree root to wait.

He returned about two hours later, his shirt dark with patches of perspiration, his arms and face bleeding from scratches. I stood and waited for him to speak, to tell me that Magnus was safe and was on his way home.

"They have gone," he said. "The camp was abandoned."

Despair hollowed me. "You'll have to tell Emily you couldn't find him."

On our way back to Majuba we walked past his house. Pieces of broken furniture and vases and torn-up books were beached on the lawn outside. Was it only this morning that the CTs had come into Yugiri, into the house? Something half-buried among the litter caught my eye. I picked it up. The ink painting of Lao Tzu had been ripped from its frame and torn in half. Aritomo took it from me and gazed at it.

"When Yap pointed his gun at me, what would you have said if Magnus had not spoken up?" I said, keeping my eyes on the damaged painting.

There was what felt to me like a long silence before Aritomo spoke again. "I would have told him the same thing I had already said—Yamashita's gold is only a rumor." His attention, I saw, was also fixed on the painting. Perhaps we were even staring at the same spot on it.

His reply disappointed me, but I accepted that it was the only thing he could have said. We were in the middle of a war, and logic and reason had no place in it.

"Special Branch told me that Magnus had been paying the CTs to stay away from Majuba."

He screwed shut his eyes, rubbing them with his thumb and forefinger. "Magnus is an honorable man, Yun Ling. He always has been. He refused to even consider the idea of it when I raised it with him."

"But you paid those bastards—"

"I could not let anyone disrupt my work in the garden," he said. "I could not."

"No garden is worth that."

"It also meant you were protected," he said. "They could have killed you when they came for you that night. Stay here. Clean up the house. I have to see Emily." He handed the torn painting back to me. "And leave that on my desk."

The KOYLI patrols found no signs of Magnus or the terrorists. More troops were dispatched into the jungle, guided by Iban trackers from Sarawak. Planters and friends of Magnus formed search parties, but their efforts were hampered by the rains. Whenever the weather cleared momentarily, Dakota airplanes circled the mountains and skimmed over the treetops, the speakers mounted on their wings hailing out offers of amnesty and rewards in Mandarin and Malay for the safe return of Magnus. I tracked down Frederik and told him the news over the telephone.

"I'll try and get leave and come," he said.

I hung up the telephone, then picked it up again and called my father. "Are you all right?" he asked. "I've been trying to ring you."

"You heard what happened?"

"Your brother was told about it this morning."

"Can Hock do anything to find Magnus? I'm sure he has informers and contacts among the CTs."

"I'll ask him. Templer's throwing everything he has at them." He paused for a moment. "By the way, I'm going to London with the *merdeka* delegation. We're leaving tomorrow."

"How long will you be gone?"

"A month. Maybe longer. Depends on how the meetings go. They look promising. Don't tell anyone yet, but we might be looking at independence within five years."

"Who's taking care of Mother?"

"The servants. And Hock, of course."

"Is there any improvement?"

"No. She's still the same. You've moved back to Majuba House?" He sounded hopeful.

"I'm keeping Emily company."

"I see. Tell her we're all praying for Magnus's safe return."

After we hung up, I realized he had not asked me to leave Cameron Highlands. For some reason his omission disappointed me.

The ridgebacks were removed from the house and placed outside wrapped in a rubber sheet but Emily refused to allow them to be buried. The smell was awful, and Ah Yan, the oldest and most superstitious servant, begged me to do something.

"Magnus will want to do it when he comes home," Emily said when I spoke to her.

I looked at her. "Of course, Emily."

The stench worsened. When Frederik drove up from Kuala Lumpur I got him to help me move Brolloks and Bittergal down to the lower terrace. In a far corner where the trees hid us from the house, we dug two holes in the ground and buried the dogs.

"I've wanted to ask Magnus where he got their names from," I said as I tamped the soil with my shovel.

"The dogs? They're from a fairy tale. My father told me about it when I was a boy. Brolloks and Bittergal, two monsters in the Karoo who ate children. He used them to scare me whenever I was naughty." He touched the mound of earth with his foot. "Poor buggers."

It started to rain again. "Let's go inside."

We were drying off in front of the fire in the living room when we heard the telephone in the study begin to ring. Someone answered it. I glanced at Frederik, and we went out to the corridor. The door to the study opened a few minutes later. Emily looked at us as though she had no idea who we were or what we were doing in her house. Slowly the confusion in her eyes cleared up.

"They've found him," she said.

Coming around the bend in the path, I saw Aritomo kneeling by a hedge of cannas. I stopped and watched him. He plucked and pulled out the vegetation with a practiced hand, his fingers as nimble as the lips of a deer stripping away young leaves from a branch. I thought back to the first time I had seen him, at the archery range. He was the beating heart of the garden, I thought. Without him, the whole place would eventually fall to ruin.

He looked up and struggled to his feet. I offered my hand to him, troubled by how much older he seemed. "Magnus is dead," I said.

His face, even his whole body, sagged. He dropped the crumpled cannas, brushing the bits of leaves and petals from his hands.

I told him how a Chinese vegetable farmer returning from Ipoh had seen something lying in the grass by the side of the road. He did not stop his lorry, but drove directly to the police station in Tanah Rata. As I talked, the tears came, but I kept my eyes open. Aritomo put his arms around me and pulled me to him. We stood like that for a long time, among the stalks of flowers he had broken off and discarded.

The funeral was held on a Saturday afternoon. The planters and their families, the workers, people in the highlands and across the country who had known him, all gathered on the terrace lawn where Magnus used to hold his *braais*. Messages of condolence came from all over Malaya, including one from the high commissioner and his wife. My father sent a telegram from London, asking me to give Emily *pek khim*, the white envelope of money for the family of the deceased. At the funeral service I stood next to Aritomo. Once or twice I reached out to touch his arm, but he was staring into the distance, his body rigid. I forced back my tears when "Und ob die wolke" was played for Magnus one last time. *And if the clouds . . .*

Magnus was buried in the garden behind Majuba House, next to the grave of his daughter. Aritomo slipped away during the wake. From the corner of my eye I watched him leave, but I did not follow him.

He returned to Majuba House with a large cardboard box later that evening, his eyes squinting with fatigue. Inside the box lay three of his paper lanterns, bigger than those he had made for Emily at the Mid-Autumn Festival, their tops covered and sealed. He explained what I had to do, then turned around and slowly walked home.

Halfway through dinner, Emily got up from the table and left the dining room. I made to follow her but she shook her head, loosening the tears from her eyes to slide down her cheeks. Frederik touched my arm, and I sat back into my chair.

We found her sitting at the piano later, her shoulders bent over it. Her fingers moved above the keys, as though she was trying to remember the notes to the piece of music she had been playing. She glanced at us when we came in, and then stared down to the keys again.

"There's something we'd like you to see," I said, but she made no sign that she had heard me. She pressed the keys, the notes discordant in the silence.

"Just for a few minutes, Emily," Frederik said. "Please."

She stood up slowly and we walked her out to the terrace behind the house, all the way to the balustrade. The smell of dew was sharp and clean. There was no moon. The lights of the bungalows and cottages gave a vague sense of shape to the ridges and valleys far below us. I lit the lanterns Aritomo had given me, the candles illuminating the wrinkles in the rice paper. I chose one and raised it high, spilling its glow onto our faces.

In the valleys more points of light pricked out from the darkness, clumped together like luminous seeds in some places, solitary or far apart in others, but taken together, there were so many that it was impossible to count them all.

"What's going on?" asked Emily.

"They're lanterns, like these," I said. "Aritomo made them. For Magnus."

The lantern tugged at my hand. I gave it to her. Frederik took another lantern. I picked up the last one and looked at my watch. At precisely eight o'clock I said, "Let it go, Emily."

She closed her eyes briefly and released her lantern. It hovered in the air for a few seconds and then it began to rise, swaying upward like a phosphorescent jellyfish. Across the valleys, countless lanterns were being set free, light streaking up into the darkness. Frederik and I let go of ours at the same time, and I felt his hand close over mine. Above the dark, formless trees in Yugiri a single bubble of light drifted upward, leaning away from the high winds. Emily acknowledged it with a slight nod, tears shining on her cheeks.

Some of the lanterns soon entered the clouds, flickering like distant lightning. Others sailed farther and farther away, herded by the wind into the far mountains. I made a silent wish that they would never fall to earth.

CHAPTER TWENTY-THREE

In the last four days the words have refused to come to me when I call for them and I can only stare at the paper. When they *do* leak from my pen, I am unable to make sense of them. Only when I work at night am I untroubled by spells of word-blindness. So I go on, writing as much as I can before I fall asleep.

Since midnight I have been sitting at the desk, working over the pages in which I had set down the events in the internment camp, making changes to my choice of words and the structure of my sentences. I am wearing my cardigan, but the study is cold, and my fingers hurt.

I get up from my chair and walk around the room, massaging my neck. My body is sore, but it is a wonderful kind of soreness, resulting from hard, physical work: I have started practicing *kyudo* again. After a few sessions I can feel the old lessons I have learned returning to me.

Going back to my desk, I turn a few pages and read over what I have written. *Even monkeys fall from trees.* Yes, I am quite certain that was what Fumio said to me, before he cut my fingers off.

Memory is like patches of sunlight in an overcast valley, shifting with the movement of the clouds. Now and then the light will fall on a particular point in time, illuminating it for a moment before the wind seals up the gap, and the world is in shadows again.

There are moments when, remembering what happened, I am unable to continue writing. What troubles me more than anything, however, are the instances when I cannot recall with certainty what has taken place. I have spent most of my life trying to forget, and now all I want is to remember. I cannot remember what my sister looked like; I do not even have a picture of her. And my conversation with Aritomo by Usugumo Pond, on that night of the meteor shower . . . did it take place on the day of Templer's visit or did it

294

occur on a different evening entirely? Time is eating away my memory. Time, and this illness, this trespasser in my brain.

The bell at the front gate has been ringing through the house for some time. I am in the study, rearranging the books on the shelves. I call out to Ah Cheong, then remember that he has taken the day off. I wait, hoping that whoever it is will give up and leave. The sign at the entrance has not deterred anyone. The past week has seen an increase in the number of people coming to Yugiri, all of them hoping to be allowed in. A local film crew shooting a documentary on Aritomo's life tried to see me but I turned them away.

Setting down a pile of books on the floor, I massage the pain in my lower back and look around me. It was in this room that Aritomo asked to incise the tattoos on me. The bamboo birdcage is still here, and the same paintings still line the same wall. There is a discolored space where my sister's painting used to hang before he gave it to me.

Voices can be heard from outside, growing louder. I leave the study and go to the front door. Vimalya is talking to two Chinese women just below the verandah. One of them has a shaved head and is dressed in a faded gray robe. Perhaps she is a little younger than me; I find it difficult to tell. A woman stands next to her. Vimalya looks up at me when I come out. "They were at the gate when I got here."

"Thank you, Vimalya."

"Oh, one other thing, Judge Teoh—can you recommend me books on Japanese gardening?"

"I'll lend you some."

She leaves us, and I turn back to the women. In English, the nun says, "My name is Chin Lai Kew." Three round scars in a vertical line mark her forehead, branded into her skin by a joss stick when she took her vows. "Mrs. Wong was kind enough to drive me here today."

"Emily told me about you," I say. "Come and sit inside."

"No need-*lah*." The nun turns to her companion and in Mandarin says, "Can you wait by the pond? I won't take up too much of Judge Teoh's time." When the woman has left us, the nun says, "We've met before, you know, in the Temple of Clouds."

"I don't remember."

"Mr. Aritomo asked me to say some prayers for his friend. You were with him that day."

Like a paper rubbing of the inscriptions on an old gravestone, the memory of the face I saw that morning almost forty years ago slowly takes shape, blurry and ill–defined. "You were—"

"So young then?" The nun smiles, revealing a gap in her teeth. "So were you. But we didn't feel young at all, did we?"

"What do you mean?" An instant later I understand.

The bracelet of jade beads on her wrist makes soft clicking noises as she rubs them. "I was *jugan ianfu*."

I glance back into the house, not certain if I want to hear what she has to say.

"There were twelve of us, captured from all over the country," the nun continues. "I was thirteen years old—the youngest there. The oldest was nineteen or twenty. The soldiers kept us in the convent in Tanah Rata—they had turned it into their base. I was there for two months. Then one day they let me go. Just like that. I went home to Ipoh. But everyone knew what the Japanese had done to me. What man would want me to be his wife? My father was so ashamed of me, he sold me to a brothel. But I ran away. I went to another town, but somehow people knew. They always knew. One day, I heard a woman talking about a temple in Cameron Highlands. The temple had taken in a few women like me. I went up there. I've never left."

Remembering how derelict and abandoned it had looked, I ask, "The temple—is it still there?"

"We look after it as best we can," she says, then falls silent for a while before explaining the reason for her visit. "A few years after Mr. Aritomo had gone, I found out that during the Occupation, he had been to see the regional commander to have all of the *jugan ianfu* in Tanah Rata released. The commander agreed to let four of the youngest girls go."

Aritomo never told me.

"I wanted to tell you this when he disappeared," the nun says, "but you had already left. And you never came back."

"I'm glad you decided to come to see me."

"I had another reason."

"You want to see the garden."

"Garden?" For a second she looks perplexed. "Oh! No-*lah*. No. But Mr. Aritomo once told me that he had a painting of Lao Tzu. I would like to see it, if it is still here."

"It's still here. Like your temple."

I take her into the house, to the ink drawing painted by Aritomo's father. The nun stands before the old sage. There is a tear in the middle of the drawing, but it has been so skillfully mended it is almost unnoticeable.

"*When the work is done, it is time to leave,*" the nun says softly. "*That is the Way of the Tao.*"

I have read the *Tao Te Ching* many times by now, and the words are familiar to me. "Aritomo's work wasn't done when he left."

The nun turns to me, and smiles—not at me, but at the world itself. "Ahhh . . . Can you be certain of that?"

Tidying the study after I have walked the nun and her companion out of the garden, I think of what she told me. There are still so many things I did not know about Aritomo, so many things that I never will.

Pulling out some books from a shelf, I discover a box behind them. Opening it, I find a pair of swiftlets' nests, aged to a treacly yellow. They are the nests Aritomo gave me. I hold one up; it feels brittle when I press it. I do not remember keeping them in this box when we returned from the cave; I never made them into a soup as Aritomo suggested.

"Judge Teoh?" Tatsuji appears at the door. I close the box and replace it on the shelf, then beckon him in. "I have finished my examination of the *ukiyo-e*," he says.

"Use all of them," I tell him. "You have my permission."

It is more than he has expected. He bows to me. "My lawyer will send you the contract."

"There is one more piece of Aritomo's work I want you to evaluate, Tatsuji." I wonder if I should proceed with it; it is not too late to change my mind, but this is the reason I wanted to see him, the reason I called him to Yugiri. "Aritomo *was* a tattooist."

"So I was right all along. He *was* a *horoshi*." The smile on his face broadens. "Do you have any photographs of the tattoos he created?"

"He never took any photographs."

"Sketches?"

I shake my head.

"Did he leave you pieces of his tattoos?"

"Only one."

Realization filters the murk of excitement from his face. "He tattooed you?"

I nod, and Tatsuji's eyes close briefly. Is he giving thanks to the god of tattoos? It would not surprise me if such a deity exists.

"Where is it? On your arm? Shoulder?"

"On my back."

"Where exactly?" he asks, growing impatient. I continue to look at him, and a sudden understanding floods into his face. "*So, so, so*. Not just a tattoo, but a *horimono*." For a while he does not speak. "It would be one of the most important discoveries in the Japanese art world," he says finally. "Imagine: Emperor Hirohito's gardener, the creator of taboo artwork. On the skin of a Chinese woman, no less."

"There will be no mention of this, if you want to use Aritomo's *ukiyo-e*."

"So why did you tell me about it?"

"I want the *horimono* preserved after my death. I want you to handle this."

"That is easily done."

"How?"

"A contract will be drawn up for you to bequeath your skin to me on your death, upon immediate payment now, if you wish," Tatsuji says. His hand draws an elegant circle in the air. "We can discuss the details later. But first"—his hands come together in a silent clap—"*first* I have to ascertain the quality and the texture of the work on your skin. We will do it with a female assistant present, of course. We can arrange to meet in Tokyo."

"No. We do it here. Right here. In this room. I'll only show it to you, no one else," I say. "There's no need to look so embarrassed, Tatsuji. We're both adults. We've seen our share of naked bodies."

"I would prefer to have another person present, so there can be no questions of . . . ahh . . ." His fingers rub his tie.

"At our age? Surely not. Or should I be flattered that you think there's even a possibility that I might . . . change your preferences?"

I give a luxuriant, voluptuous sigh, enjoying his discomfort. "All right, Tatsuji. I'll find someone. A chaperone." I laugh; it feels good. "Such an old-fashioned word, *chaperone*, don't you think?"

"There were things that puzzled me when I was doing my research on Aritomo-*sensei*," he says.

"What sort of things?" My humorous mood flees, to be replaced by a sense of wariness. "Inconsistencies?"

"No. Quite the opposite, in fact. Everything I discovered about his life felt natural yet . . . *manufactured*. It was like . . . well, it was like walking in a garden designed by a master *niwashi*. Take the feud between Tominaga Noboru and him, for instance," he adds. "They had been good friends since they were boys."

"It's quite common for childhood friends to quarrel when they grow up."

Tatsuji thinks for a moment. Telling me to wait, he leaves the study and returns a few minutes later with his satchel. He opens it and takes out a small black pouch. He loosens its drawstring and picks out a shiny, metallic object. For a second I imagined him removing a hook snagged in a fish's mouth. He drops the object onto my palm. It is a silver brooch the size of a ten-cent coin, the quality of its craftsmanship understated and exquisite.

"A flower?" I say, turning it over.

"A *chrysanthemum*. These brooches were given out by the emperor to a select group of people during the Pacific War."

"For what purpose?" I sit down in one of the rosewood chairs.

"Have you ever heard of Golden Lily?"

The brooch glints on the creases of my gloved palm. "No."

"It is the title of one of our emperor's poems," he says. "Kin No Yuri. A beautiful name, is it not, for one of my country's worst crimes of the Pacific War? It was 1937—after we attacked Nanjing. Officials in the palace became concerned that the army was siphoning off the spoils of war. To ensure that the Imperial General Headquarters received its share of the plunder, a plan was conceived. It was named Golden Lily."

The operation was not under the control of the army, Tatsuji explains, but was headed by Prince Chichibu Yasuhito, the emperor's brother. Chichibu was assisted by some of the other princes. "They had accountants, financial advisers, experts in art and antiques working under the direction of these princes. Many of these experts were connected to the throne by blood or marriage," Tatsuji says. "Golden Lily sent its spies out to Asia, to gather information about the treasures that could be stolen. Anything that was worth taking was noted, the information scrupulously recorded."

"As though they were compiling a catalog for an auction house," I say.

"*Hai*. A very exclusive auction house." He shifts on his feet. "When the Imperial Army swept through China . . . Malaya and Singapore . . . Korea, the Philippines, Burma . . . Java and Sumatra, members of Golden Lily followed closely behind. They knew where to look, and they stole everything they could lay their hands on: jade and gold Buddha statues from ancient temples; cultural artifacts and antiques from museums; jewelry and gold hoarded by wealthy Chinese with their distrust of banks. Golden Lily emptied royal collections and national treasuries. It removed bullion and priceless artworks, carvings, pottery and paper currencies."

"They took all that back to Japan?"

Tatsuji's eyes fix onto a point far away in time. "Golden Lily knew that it would be dangerous to transport these items back to Japan once the war had begun. There was also the fear that in the event we were occupied by foreign powers, Golden Lily would have no access to these treasures. It was safer not to move the loot back to Japan, but to hide it in the Philippines. Spies were dispatched to scout for suitable hiding places in Mindanao and Luzon. Once the army took control of these islands, Golden Lily moved in."

"Was Golden Lily operating here, in Malaya?"

"There were factories in Penang and Ipoh that melted down gold and silver stolen from families and banks," Tatsuji says. "They could have been run by Golden Lily."

"Those treasures looted in Malaya were then shipped out to the Philippines?"

"Yes."

"That was a huge risk, transporting the loot across the seas."

"Golden Lily vessels were made to pass as registered hospital ships," Tatsuji says. "Allied airplanes and warships coming across these ships noted the flags, cross-checked the registration numbers and left them alone."

I am rigid with anger. "Thousands of civilians were evacuated from Singapore in a convoy of ships flying the Red Cross flag. Your planes sank all of them. The survivors floating in the sea were strafed or left to drown. The women were picked up, raped and then thrown back into the sea."

Tatsuji looks away from me. "The plan was," he says, "that once things had settled down, once we had won the war, the hiding places in the Philippines would be opened and the treasures shipped back to Tokyo."

"But you *lost* the war."

"*Hai.* The unthinkable happened. And so everything stolen by Golden Lily could still be out there."

I return the brooch to Tatsuji. "Where did you get this?"

"When we were on Kampong Penyu, Teruzen told me that part of his duties was to fly members of the imperial family to wherever they wanted to go, and to organize air cover for their vessels. He refused to say anything further when I pressed him." He stares at the chrysanthemum brooch. "That last morning, after he had flown off, I returned to our hut. I found the brooch among my things." He falls silent. "I have been doing research on Kin No Yuri over the years, just to understand what Teruzen had been doing."

"Was he a part of this . . . Golden Lily?" I feign unfamiliarity with the term.

"A year ago I tracked down an engineer who had worked for Golden Lily," Tatsuji says. "He was in his nineties, and he wanted to tell his story before he died. He had been sent to Luzon, to supervise gangs of POWs toiling in underground vaults built into the mountains. Hundreds of slave workers had worked day and night to excavate the tunnels and chambers. Once the chambers were packed full with the treasures, a Shinto priest was brought in to conduct a blessing ceremony for the site. Ceramics experts from Japan sealed the entrances to the chambers with a mixture of porcelain clay and local rocks, dyed to blend in with the local geology. Fast-growing trees and shrubs—papayas and guava trees worked best, the engineer said—were planted over the entire area to blend it into the surrounding countryside."

"What happened . . . what happened to the prisoners?"

"They were taken to another place a short distance away—a cave or an abandoned mine prepared months in advance. Those who resisted were shot. Once they were all inside, explosives were set off to seal the entrance."

"Burying them alive," I whisper.

"Treasure hunters have tried to locate these sites in the Philippines over the years. Perhaps some of them have been emptied and the loot shipped back to Japan."

"Treasure hunters?"

My skepticism seems to amuse him. "They told journalists that they were searching for the gold bullion hidden by General Yamashita when he evacuated from Luzon. Or they informed the Filipino authorities that they were collecting the bones of fallen soldiers to be properly buried in Japan," he says. "And even if someone did find one of these hiding places, the vaults were armed with thousand-pound bombs and glass vials of cyanide buried in sand. Anyone who tried to open them up, anyone who did not have the proper maps . . ."

I pull myself from the quicksand of memories. "If what you've said really happened, someone would have spoken about it by now," I say. "Maybe one of the Japanese who had worked in one of these underground vaults—like your engineer, or one of the guards."

"The Japanese personnel were buried alive too, along with the prisoners," Tatsuji says. "The man I spoke to was one of the luckier ones—he had been blindfolded when he was brought to the camp. But all his life he was terrified, wondering if someone had made a mistake in letting him go."

"What has all this got to do with Aritomo?"

"I was only interested in his *ukiyo-e*, but the more I found out about him, the more I think he played a role in Golden Lily. I have no evidence of this," he adds hurriedly, "just my own suspicions."

"He was a gardener, Tatsuji." I keep my voice firm so he will not realize how much his words have shaken me.

"He might have come here to survey the topography. He had the necessary knowledge of landscaping and horticulture—remember, the locations had to be camouflaged or concealed. And who better than a master of *shakkei* to do it?"

"But to be party to a thing like this . . ." My voice, even my strength, dwindles away.

"We were heading into war, Judge Teoh. All of us had to play our part, to serve the emperor."

"Even his friend Tominaga Noburu?"

"He was in charge of Golden Lily in Southeast Asia. Eyewitnesses I interviewed—old soldiers and military administrators—placed him in Malaya and Singapore in the years between 1938 and 1945."

"But Aritomo remained here—long after the war ended. He never went home."

"Have you forgotten what the situation in Malaya was like at that time?" Tatsuji says. "According to what I have read in *The Red Jungle*, there was much lawlessness and unrest immediately after the surrender—communist guerrillas taking revenge on collaborators; Chinese and Malays killing each other. And British soldiers were coming back. Maybe Golden Lily thought it was not the right time to move the treasures, but someone had to be here to make sure they were not disturbed."

"So he stayed here, in his garden, waiting for things to settle down." I lay out the pieces in my head to see if I can discover a coherent pattern in the mosaic. "But then the communists started their war."

"If he was a part of Golden Lily, he would have known where the loot was hidden, at least in Malaya."

The thought of the hordes of people that will inevitably come asking to speak to me again should it become known that Aritomo had been involved in something like this frightens me. "If he knew," I say firmly, "then he took that knowledge with him."

"It is not the sort of information he would have left lying around," concedes Tatsuji.

"He didn't tell me anything."

Tatsuji laughs at me, rather unkindly. "A man of his upbringing, and with his background?" he says. "He would have been obligated to carry out his duty properly. All the way to the end."

The new teahouse at Majuba is at the summit of a steep hill and I am breathing hard when I arrive there after a long walk. It is a few minutes before lunchtime, but all the tables have already been taken by elderly tourists in water-repellent jackets and bulky hiking boots.

Looking around the restaurant, I spot Frederik waving to me from the terrace outside.

"You managed to get us the best table in the house," I remark, as he pulls a chair out for me.

"It helps if you own the place," he replies. "I converted it from a bungalow a year ago. It used to be Geoff Harper's. Remember him?"

Our table is at the end of a long, narrow terrace that extends over the valley like a pier, fenced in by chest-high plate glass that provides a vertiginous vista of the mountains and the tea-covered slopes. Wisteria froths down from the trellis overhead, sweetening the air. I close my eyes for a brief moment, going over again what Tatsuji told me about Golden Lily this morning. On the face of it, it is a preposterous story—except that I know differently.

Frederik fills my cup with tea and slides it to me. "Something from our newest range. We're still testing it."

Bringing the cup to my nose, I inhale the steam rising from it. I take a sip and hold the liquid in my mouth, allowing its flavor to bloom on my tongue. "I haven't tasted any of Majuba's teas in years."

He looks insulted. "You don't like them?"

"It's not that." I wonder how to explain it to him. "The tea grown here . . . it has its own distinct flavor . . . it brings back too many memories."

"Whenever I have to travel," Frederik says, "I always bring a box of my own tea with me."

"Magnus once told me about a temple in China he had visited—"

"In Mount Li Wu," Frederik says, a smile sprawling across his face. "I went there a few years ago. It's all there, everything he ever told you—the monks picking the leaves at dawn, the special flavor of the tea. It's still the most expensive tea in the world."

Down in the valley, the brightly colored headscarves of the tea pickers are like petals scattered over a lawn.

He indicates the people around us. "Quite a number of them are here for the anniversary of Aritomo's death."

"I know. They've been pestering me. Some journalist wanted to film me for a documentary she's doing on Aritomo. Another one tried to pin me down for an interview for a news channel."

"You should talk to them, tell them about Aritomo. You of all people knew him best."

"Did I?"

The food arrives and we eat it in silence. "Tatsuji's finished working on the woodblock prints," I say when our plates have been removed. Slowly, working out the sequence of events even as I speak, I tell Frederik about Golden Lily. There is a long silence when I finish talking.

"You think Aritomo was involved?" he asks finally.

"I don't know. But after what Tatsuji told me, I'm sure that I was sent to one of Golden Lily's slave camps. A lot of things he said fit in with what I saw there."

"Did Aritomo know about the things the Japs did to you?"

"I told him."

"But you never said anything to me." Inside his voice is an old hurt, still sharp after all these years. "I could never really understand why you left Yugiri."

"I couldn't live here, Frederik. I couldn't even bring myself to build the garden I wanted for my sister—everything about it would have reminded me of Aritomo. Law was the only thing I knew I was good at."

"You haven't done too badly."

"Strange isn't it? I never considered entering the judiciary when I returned to practice. But I had the sort of credentials a newly independent nation was looking for—I'm not European and I had been so critical of our colonial masters, how they had sold us down the river."

"You've never recovered from being a prisoner."

"Do you know of anyone who has?"

"I'm sorry. That was a stupid thing to say."

Behind Frederik, a hot-air balloon drifts into my sight, bright red and shaped like an inverted teardrop. Frederik follows my gaze, twisting around to look over his shoulder. "Some chap from KL brought it up here a week ago," he said. "He gives rides to tourists. I was told a popular route is the area around Yugiri."

The balloon rotates slowly toward us. Wrapped around its side are the words MAJUBA TEA ESTATE and the estate's logo, an outline of a Cape Dutch house. I groan with mock disgust when I see it.

"Oh come on, it's good advertising!" Frederik says.

"I'll shoot it down if they dare fly over Yugiri."

He laughs, causing several people around to look at us. "Remember that story about the Mid-Autumn Festival Emily used to tell every year?" he says, wiping the tears from his eyes. "Hou Yi who shot down the suns with his bow and arrows? And his wife who swallowed the magic pill and became immortal?"

"Poor, poor Hou Yi, yearning for the wife he had lost to the moon," I say. "He should have made himself forget her."

"Perhaps he couldn't," replies Frederik. "Perhaps he didn't want to."

At five o'clock that evening I change into my walking clothes: a long-sleeved shirt, loose cotton slacks and hiking boots. Ah Cheong is already waiting at the front door. The housekeeper, having realized early on that I have taken up Aritomo's habit of going for evening walks on the trails, never fails to appear with the walking stick for me whenever he hears me getting ready. I have never accepted the walking stick, but it has not deterred him from offering it to me every time.

There are thirteen official walking trails spreading out from the three villages in Cameron Highlands, varying in length and difficulty. There are also many more paths that do not appear on maps, known only to forest rangers and those who have spent their lives in the highlands. One of them winds past the edge of the property. It will take me less than an hour to complete the walk, and at this time of the year, I will be unlikely to come across anyone else.

The heaviness inside me lifts as I walk. Above my head, the overlapping leaves print their shadows on other leaves. The smell of mulch is softened by the fragrance of wild orchids. Aerial roots sprout from the branches of banyan trees; some of the older roots have hardened into stalactites over the years to prop up the sagging branches. Except for the track beneath my feet, there are no other signs that anyone else has been here before me, and within minutes I feel myself being absorbed into the damp, decaying heart of the rain forest.

The path is steep and demanding. At a ridge looking down into the valleys, I stop to recover my breath. The old sense of injustice stings me again: I would have been a more robust woman if my health had not been damaged in the camp. When my neurosurgeon first informed me of the diagnosis, I asked him if it was caused by the deprivations I had suffered, a seed that had been sown forty years ago, slowly burrowing its poisoned roots deeper and deeper into my body. "We don't know for sure," he said, "but it's doubtful."

A part of me cannot help but continue to wonder about it. *Aphasia*. Such a beautiful name, I think as I sit on the stump of a mahogany tree. It reminds me of a species of flower—camellia perhaps. No, more like rafflesia, attracting hordes of flies with the smell of rotting meat when it blooms.

My thoughts return to Tatsuji's theories about Golden Lily. If he is correct and Tominaga Noboru was the head of Golden Lily in Southeast Asia, then I have no doubts that the camp I was sent to was part of it all. But where would that place Aritomo in the entire scheme of things? Is Tatsuji right in thinking that Aritomo was sent here to lay the groundwork for Golden Lily's plans?

A sudden fury against Aritomo grips me. My fingers claw into the sides of the mahogany trunk. The rage subsides after a moment.

I stand up and brush the dirt from the seat of my slacks. It is getting dark. In the low mists over the hills, an orange glow broods, as if the trees are on fire. Bats are flooding out from the hundreds of caves that perforate these mountainsides. I watch them plunge into the mists without any hesitation, trusting in the echoes and silences in which they fly.

Are all of us the same, I wonder, navigating our lives by interpreting the silences between words spoken, analyzing the returning echoes of our memory in order to chart the terrain, in order to make sense of the world around us?

CHAPTER TWENTY-FOUR

A garden is composed of a variety of clocks, Aritomo had once told
me. Some of them run faster than the others, and some of them
move slower than we can ever perceive. I only understood this fully
long after I had been his apprentice. Every single plant and tree at
Yugiri grew, flowered and died at its own rate. Yet there was also
a feeling of timelessness wrapped around it. The trees from a colder
world—the oaks, the maples and the cedars—had adjusted to the
constant rains and mists, to the seasonless passing of time in the
mountains. The turning of their colors was muted. Only the maple
growing by the house remembered the changing seasons in the
expanding circles of its memory: its leaves turned completely red,
flaking away from the branches to drift across the garden; I would
often find the leaves plastered to the wet rocks on the banks of
Usugumo Pond, like starfish stranded by the tide.

Whenever I left Yugiri to go into the village of Tanah Rata, I
would be disoriented by how much time had passed. When I came
to the Cameron Highlands, I had left the world behind, thinking it
would only be for a short time, but one day it struck me that I had
been apprenticed to Aritomo for over a year. I mentioned this to him.

"It was Magnus who first told me the story of the Garden of
Eden. I had great difficulty imagining it," he remarked. "A garden
where nothing dies or decays, where no one grows old, and the seasons never change. How miserable."

"What's so miserable about that?"

"Think of the seasons as pieces of the finest, most translucent silk
of different colors. Individually, they are beautiful, but lay one on
top of another, even if just along their edges, and something special
is created. That narrow strip of time when the start of one season
overlaps the end of another is like that."

He was silent for a few moments. Then he asked, "What happened to the Garden of Eden after the man and woman were forced to leave? Did everything fall to ruin? The Tree of Life, and the Tree of Knowledge? Or is it all still there, unchanged, waiting?"

I tried to recall what the nuns at my school had taught me. "I don't know. It's just a story."

He looked at me. "When the First Man and First Woman were banished from their home, Time was also set loose upon the world."

Kannadasan and his men appeared at Yugiri one morning, and I knew that the monsoon was over. There was much damage to clear up: tree branches had been amputated by storms; leaves and debris had swept down from the mountains, clogging the stream and flooding its banks. I was happy to be able to channel my attention and energies into the garden again. Soon we were occupied with only the lesser tasks—cleaning up the paths, making slight adjustments to the alignments of rocks, trimming the branches, anything that Aritomo felt had been thrown out of harmony.

In the evenings he would collect his walking stick from Ah Cheong, and we would walk in the foothills behind the garden. I enjoyed those moments, when he showed me things I would have missed seeing on my own. "Nature is the best teacher," he said to me.

Requests began to come from senior civil servants and high-ranking military officials, asking to be given a tour of Yugiri. To my surprise, Aritomo agreed to most of them, although he always asked me to lead these tours and show the visitors around. By now my knowledge of garden design was sufficient, but I knew I would require many more years of study with Aritomo.

I was raking the lawn in front of his house one afternoon when I sensed him coming up to me. For a few minutes he observed me silently. I continued with my task; I was no longer nervous when he scrutinized my work.

"How does Yugiri compare to your other gardens?" I asked.

"They have probably been ruined by coarse, unskilled hands," he said. "This one here"—he looked around us—"this is the only one that is still truly mine."

"You can design more gardens here in Malaya. Adapt the principles of the Art of Setting Stones to our climate," I said. "We'll work together, you and I. We can start by creating the garden I want for Yun Hong."

"I had a letter from Sekigawa today," he said. "The bureau has sent him to see me."

I swept the leaves into a gunnysack and laid the rake on the ground. "What will you tell him?"

He looked at me with the steadiness of the sun contemplating its own reflection in the sea. "I will tell him that my home is here, in these mountains."

For a long moment we merely gazed at each other. Then I held up the gunnysack to him. "The garden is now perfect."

Taking the sack from me, he reached inside it and pulled out a handful of brown, withered leaves. He stepped onto the lawn and scattered them, as though he was a gust of wind. When the last leaf had fallen from his hand, he returned the sack to me and stood back to look at what he had made.

That night, when he tattooed me, his hands felt slower, heavier. Once or twice his fingers would rest on my back, like a dragonfly poised on a leaf. It was past midnight when he stopped and sat back on his heels. Outside, frogs belched in the grass. A moment later I felt him touching me lightly on my shoulder.

"It is done," he said.

My eyes took a second or two to focus. I pushed myself off the *tatami* mat and got to my feet. I looked over my shoulder and examined my body in the mirror, searching for the last tattoo he had colored in: the rounded shape of Majuba House, an ark floating on the green swells of tea. The *horimono* faded away into the bare skin around my neck, my upper arms, the sides of my body and just above the swell of my buttocks.

I turned my body until I could see my entire back in the mirror. I looked as though I was wearing an overly tight batik shirt. I moved one shoulder, causing the figures on it to elongate. All of a sudden I was frightened.

"You have a new skin now." He circled me, as he had once done almost a year before, when his fingers had examined my blank skin.

"But it's not complete—there's still this bit here." I touched a rectangle the size of two cigarette packs above my left hip. The emptiness looked unnatural, sickly.

"A *horoshi* will always leave a section of the *horimono* empty, as a symbol that it is never finished, never perfect," said Aritomo, wiping his hands on a towel.

"Like the leaves you scattered on the lawn," I said.

Even though the garden in Yugiri was completed, there was always some maintenance work to be done. Aritomo delegated most of the chores to me, telling me what he wanted done by the gardeners, elaborating on the reasons for each instruction.

Walking past the archery hall one evening after the workers had left, I saw him there, dressed in his *kyudo* clothes. Since I had known him he had never practiced archery this late in the day; there was also something strange in the way he stood that made me stop and watch. My puzzlement increased when I saw him pretend to nock an arrow in the bowstring. He drew the bowstring back, and then released it. There was no arrow, but still I thought I heard the faint sound of paper being ripped, as though something forceful had pierced the target.

He remained unmoving, one arm still stretched out, holding the bow level with his eyes. Finally, he lowered it, bringing a note of completion to the entire movement. He continued to stare at the target, and then he nodded his head once in satisfaction.

I walked along the edge of the gravel bed to stand below him. "Did you hit the bull's-eye?" I asked.

He looked back at the target. "Yes, I did."

"It couldn't have been too difficult, since you didn't use an arrow," I said, masking my confusion in a gently mocking tone.

"But you are wrong. It takes years of practice. When I first started, I always missed," he said. "And there was an arrow."

"There was no arrow," I replied, restraining myself from turning to look at the target to be certain.

"There was." He touched the side of his head. "In here."

He began to spend more of his time in the *shajo*, shooting invisible arrows. And every night he would ask me to let him look at the *horimono*. I lay on the sheets as he studied my skin, his fingers stroking the pictures he had painted on my back: the temple in the mountains, the cave of the swiftlets, the archer shooting down the sun. After a few minutes of this I would turn around and pull him toward me.

It was late in the evening, and Aritomo and I were the only people left in the garden. A silence welled up from deep inside the earth. I remained completely still, hoping that this caul of tranquility would never be pulled away from the world. Then the clouds started moving again, and the mists sagged and squandered themselves over the foothills.

I cleaned my tools and hung them up in the shed. I went past the *shajo*. It was empty. At the front door of the house I found Ah Cheong, the chengal walking stick in his hand. Kerneels sat on a step, licking his paw. Aritomo came out presently. He hesitated for a moment before taking the stick from the housekeeper.

We strolled to the edge of Usugumo Pond, the cat following us, his tail high in the air. Aritomo stopped and stared out over the water. In the shallows the gray heron stood on one leg, trapped by its reflection. Behind us I heard the faint clatter of gravel as Ah Cheong pushed his bicycle out of the garden, one of its wheels squeaking.

The path Aritomo normally took to go up into the hills went past the western perimeter of the garden. At the access to the trail, concealed by the thick wall of ferns and long grass, Aritomo stopped. He bent down and rubbed Kerneels's head. "I think," he said when he stood up, "I would like to be on my own this evening."

He held out his walking stick to me. We looked at each other, and in the end I took it from him.

"I'll leave it in your study," I said.

He nodded and moved past me, touching me once, lightly, on my hand. I watched him climb up the slope, the air tinctured green by the light reflecting off the ferns. At the top of the rise he turned back to look at his garden. Perhaps he was smiling at me, but the spokes of sunlight behind him made it difficult for me to be certain. I lifted my hand to my chest. Was I waving to him? Or was I summoning him to come back?

* * *

The best chance of finding Aritomo was within the first twenty-four hours of his disappearance, Sub-Inspector Lee advised me the next morning when I drove to the station in Tanah Rata. He questioned me about Aritomo's state of mind and asked me what he was wearing. He requested a photograph of him, and it was only then that I realized I did not have one.

The police used Yugiri as their base of operations. One wall of Aritomo's study was pinned with maps provided by the army. Ah Cheong was kept occupied with preparing food for the men who tramped in and out of the house at all hours of the day.

"I found this on his desk," I said, handing a bottle to Lee. "His pills. For his blood pressure."

The large number of people who joined the search parties surprised me. I mentioned this to Lee, and he said, "They are people he saved from torture by the Kempeitai or from being taken to the Burma Railway."

Our hopes weakened when days passed without the search parties coming across any signs of Aritomo. "The rains haven't helped—our dogs can't pick up any trace of his scent," Sub-Inspector Lee said, "and the Ibans have had no success tracking him."

The local newspapers ignored Aritomo's disappearance at first; it was just another hiker who had got lost in the jungle, after all. But after a Japanese journalist writing about the communists in the mountains filed a report with his newspaper in Tokyo, the reporters began to flock to Tanah Rata. They made much of the fact that I was the last person to have seen Aritomo. My experience as a prisoner of the Japanese was brought up, as was my relationship with Aritomo. My father ordered me to leave Cameron Highlands immediately before I damaged our family name beyond repair, but I ignored him.

A week after the search for Aritomo had begun, Sekigawa showed up. I was on the verandah, paging through my notebook, when Ah Cheong brought him to me. I recalled that we had met on the same spot over a year ago—just before Aritomo started my *horimono*.

"You must let me know if there is any way I can help," he said. "I will be at the Smokehouse Hotel for as long as is required."

"What was it you wished to see Aritomo about?"

"It would be better for me to speak to him personally," he replied. "I am sure he will be found soon."

"Of course he will."

Sekigawa's gaze swept across the garden in front of the verandah, and then back into the interior of the house. "Did he leave a note, a letter? For me, or for anyone else?"

"He didn't know that he was going to get himself lost in the jungle, Mr. Sekigawa," I said. "Anyway, as you have said, he'll be found soon."

He did not stay long. I opened my notebook again after he left, turning to the page where I had placed the thin blue envelope. Kerneels came out and rubbed against me. I held up the envelope and looked at it, this letter written by a Japanese war criminal to his son. I set it down on the table, making a mental note to get Ah Cheong to post it the next morning.

My tea had cooled. I threw it over the verandah and poured a fresh cup. Still sitting in the *seiza* position, I shifted my body and turned toward the garden and the trees, to the mountains and the clouds. I lifted the cup, dipped my head once and drank.

CHAPTER TWENTY-FIVE

Late in the afternoon I step into the study. All day long I have been thinking about this moment and I know I cannot put it off any longer. Frederik will soon be here. But still I hesitate. My eyes slide along the bookshelves, to the pewter tea caddy. I pick it up, exposing a circle darker than the rest of the shelf. I wipe the dust off the caddy and give it a gentle shake. Something rustles inside. The cap pulls apart from the neck with difficulty, surrendering with a soft, plump pop when I finally get it out. I peer inside and see some tea leaves lying on the bottom, just enough to fill a teaspoon or two. I bring the caddy to my nose. There is still the faintest smell, like wood fire doused by rain, more a memory of the scent than the scent itself.

"Yun Ling?" Frederik stands at the door. "There was no one to show me in."

I set down the caddy on the desk. "I told Ah Cheong to go home early. Come in."

Kneeling at the sandalwood chest in the corner of the room, I rummage around inside it until my knuckles knock against the object I am looking for. I carry it to the desk and, with a letter opener, lever the cover open. I remember how Aritomo had once done the same. I am an echo of a sound made a lifetime ago.

"Put these on." I give Frederik a pair of white gloves, yellowed with age. They are too small for his stubby fingers, but he pulls them on anyway. I lift the copy of *Suikoden* out of the box and lay it on the table. "Tatsuji spoke about the book that changed the art of tattooing, remember?"

"*The Legend of the Water Margin.*"

The novel, written in the fourteenth century, recounts the tale of Sung Chiang and his one hundred and seven followers who revolted against a corrupt Chinese government in the twelfth century, I tell

315

Frederik. The story of a group of outlaws fighting against repression and tyranny resonated with the Japanese people living under the rule of the Tokugawa regime. Its popularity increased from the middle of the eighteenth century onward, and it appeared in countless editions.

"The best known of all was illustrated by Hokusai." I hold up the book. "This one has Hokusai's original prints."

"And you've left it here all this time? It must be worth a fortune."

Turning the pages slowly, he lingers over the prints, now and again returning to those that he has already seen. The lines Hokusai carved onto wood and then pressed onto the paper are as intricate as an old woman's thumbprint.

"It's quite amazing, isn't it? That a novel could lift tattoos from the common into the realm of art," Frederik says when he comes to the last page.

"This book transformed tattooing. Before it appeared, standards were crude."

The irony was even more striking, I explain, when one considered the fact that the strongest stigma directed against tattooing came from the Chinese, who, since the first century, had viewed it as a practice carried out only by barbaric tribes. The opinions of the Chinese spread to Japan from the fifth century onward, when criminals were punished by being tattooed. Murderers and rapists, rebels and thieves, were all permanently inked with horizontal bars and small circles on their arms and faces. It was a form of punishment that made them easily identifiable and effectively cut them off from their families and mainstream society. Tattooing was also imposed on the "untouchables" of Japanese society—tanners, carriers of night-soil and those who handled the bodies of the dead.

To camouflage those marks, some of the more ingenious offenders had elaborate and detailed tattoos layered over their original markings. By the end of the seventeenth century tattooing had become a form of adornment for couples—whether it was a prostitute and her patron, or a monk and his catamite—to testify to their love for each other. These tattoos were composed not of drawings, but of Chinese ideograms of a lover's name or of vows to the Buddha. It was only a century later that pictorial tattoos became popular, although the practice of tattooing was suppressed, particularly during the Tokugawa regime, when any expression of individuality was punished severely. Restrictions were placed on anything that it considered subversive: theaters and fireworks, books about the Floating World.

"No experimenting on techniques in such a hostile society," Frederik remarks.

"Tattooing was driven underground and gradually faded away, but a resurgence took place, attributed to the popularity of *Suikoden*. Clients started requesting tattoo masters to paint Hokusai's drawings on their bodies."

Some tattoo artists came up with their own designs based on Hokusai's work. Firemen were one of the first groups to have full-body tattoos, to show their affiliation to their guilds. Other guilds soon followed. Writers and artists had themselves tattooed. So did Kabuki actors and the *yakuza*. Even members of the aristocracy had tattoos. The Tokugawa government viewed these developments with horror and tattooing was outlawed again.

"The prohibition against tattooing did not apply to Westerners," I add. "George the Fifth was tattooed by a well-known Japanese master. A dragon on his forearm."

"King George with a Jap tattoo." Frederik shakes his head. "Magnus would have loved that."

"Magnus wasn't the only person Aritomo tattooed," I say softly.

"I'm sure he tattooed others before—"

I look into his eyes.

"You?" He gives me a skeptical smile.

"I wanted Tatsuji to look at my tattoo. That's why I invited him here."

"So it was never about those woodblock prints at all."

"It was." I close the book and place it back in its box. "But I have to arrange to have the tattoo preserved, before . . ." I swallow once.

"This whole business is repugnant. You're not some kind of animal to be skinned after your death."

"A tattoo created by the emperor's gardener is a rare work of art. It *should* be preserved."

"But you *hate* the bloody Japs!"

"That's another matter entirely."

"Well . . . have it photographed if you want to preserve it."

"That would be like taking a photograph of a Rembrandt and then destroying the original," I say. "Tatsuji feels he'd be more comfortable if there was another person with us when I show it to him." I take in a deep breath. "I'd like you to be there."

He is silent. "How large is this . . . this tattoo?"

"I want you to look at it," I say. Frederik saw me naked decades ago and I now feel some trepidation at the prospect of showing him my aging body.

He is taken aback. "What, here? Now?"

"When Tatsuji arrives." I look at my watch. "He should be here soon."

"I don't want to see what he did to you," he says, taking a step back.

"There is no one else I can ask, Frederik. No one."

The room I gave Tatsuji to work in is the same one where Aritomo tattooed me, night after night. For a moment I imagine I can smell the faintest odor of ink and blood, sealed into the walls by the sandalwood incense he always burned when he was working on me.

"Close the shutters." The words sound familiar, and I remember that I had once spoken them, in this room. Or were they just an echo, curving back from across the canyon of time?

For a long moment Frederik looks at me, not moving. Then he goes to the windows and pulls in the shutters, latching them. Tatsuji switches on the desk lamp.

Watching myself in the mirror I placed there this morning, I remove my cardigan and fold it neatly over the back of a chair. I struggle with the pearl buttons of my silk blouse and Frederik reaches over to assist me, but I shake my head. I remove my brassiere, bunch my blouse against my breasts and turn my back to the mirror, peering over my right shoulder.

A glow emanates from my skin, seeming to push back the shadows and open out the space to beyond the walls. Even after all this time, looking at the tattoos gives me a twinge of uneasiness, an uneasiness mixed with pride. I am familiar with every line and curve of his design, but I remember the times when something new would catch my eye, something Aritomo had woven artfully into the patterns.

Frederik has a transfixed expression on his face, a mixture of excitement, awe, and yes, even a hint of the fear I felt a moment ago. "They're . . . they look grotesque," he says in a hoarse voice. "Awful."

On my back stands a gray heron. A temple emerges from the clouds. Exquisite drawings of flowers and trees seen only in the forests of the equator climb up from my hip. Arcane, inexplicable symbols have been sewn in the tattoos, symbols I have never been able to decipher: triangles, circles, hexagons, their strokes primitive as the earliest Chinese writing burned into tortoise shells.

Tatsuji stares at me, like a tree waiting for the wind to stir its leaves.

"Do you want me to catch a chill, Tatsuji?"

He gives a start and apologizes. Swinging the lampshade toward me, he bends over my back, holding a magnifying glass close to my skin. The thought crosses my mind that the light passing through the glass will burn my back. I tell myself I am being idiotic and twist my neck to see what he is doing.

His shadow drowns the patches of *horimono*, the tattoos emerging again when he moves, like coral reefs regaining their colors the moment the clouds peel away from the sun. The cold metal frame of his magnifying glass touches me and I flinch.

"Sorry," he mumbles. "Lift your arms, please."

I obey, staring ahead. The motes of dust floating between the layers of light and shadows are like krill drifting in the sea, and I think of the whales I had seen when I was a girl, standing on the beach below Old Mr. Ong's durian plantation.

"Remarkable," Tatsuji says, his voice breaking into my reverie. "The style is Japanese but the designs are not. The *horimono* could almost be considered a companion piece to his *ukiyo-e*. Did you choose the designs?"

"We agreed to use *Sakuteiki* as the source. But in the end I left it all up to him."

"I recognize the house at Majuba," he says, and Frederik murmurs in agreement. "But what is this tattoo, here?" He touches an area on the hollow of my back. There is no need for me to twist around to see what it is.

"The camp where I was imprisoned," I say.

"And this?" Tatsuji's fingers move an inch to the left, to what I know is a square the size of a postage stamp, almost completely black. "What are these white lines?"

"A meteor shower," I say, half to myself.

His fingers press into a spot an inch from my hip. Tattooed there is an archer, shown moments after he has shot his arrow into the sun, set against a completely white square of sky.

"The legend of Hou Yi," I say, glancing at Frederik. "It's a Chinese myth."

"I know of it. In that story Hou Yi left one sun to shine," Tatsuji replies. "But here, it looks like the archer has shot down the last sun in the sky. And he's dressed not in Chinese clothes, but Japanese. Look at the *hakama*."

"And the sun—it looks just like your flag, Tatsuji," Frederik says.

Tatsuji's fingers glide over my skin again, grazing a temple. The memory of that morning's climb up the mountain with Aritomo returns to me. I am glad that the nun told me the temple is still standing, still wafting incense into the clouds.

"He didn't finish it," Frederik says. "There's a blank rectangle."

"A *horimono* must have an empty area inside it," says Tatsuji. He puts down his magnifying glass. Frederik collects my garments from the chair and hands them to me. The two men move away to the far side of the room.

In the mirror, I see the etchings of age on my face, lines that have never appeared on my back. Turning around, I look over my shoulder at the reflection of the tattoos. Dusk has soaked up the last light from the study, but the lines and colors on my skin continue to give off a glow. One of the figures in the *horimono* appears to move, but it is only a trick of the eye.

Tatsuji comes to speak to me in Yugiri the following afternoon. We sit on the *engawa*. He has brought the contract for the *ukiyo-e* with him. I glance through it: the terms are as we have agreed and I find nothing to which I can object. Nevertheless, I ask him to give me a day or two to study it.

"I spent the morning in the garden," he says.

"I saw you."

He unfolds a large piece of graph paper and lays it out on the table. The paper is covered in his neat handwriting and diagrams. "I made a sketch of Yugiri's plan, with all its major points of interest—the house, the waterwheel, the pond, the Taoist symbols cut into the grass, the Stone Atlas."

It is the first time I have ever seen Yugiri laid out like this, and I take my time studying it. "Aritomo-*sensei* liked to use the principles of Borrowed Scenery in his garden designs," Tatsuji says. "Now, a person in his garden will always be looking outward. I have been studying his *ukiyo-e* for so many days. It made me wonder what I would see, if I were to view his garden in the same way: to stand outside it and look in."

"And what did you see?"

"I have marked out the stone lanterns, the statues, the collection of rocks and the various sites where Aritomo placed the most distinctive views," he says, his finger pointing to various points on the paper. "They are all situated on bends or turns in a path."

"He designed it that way, to make the garden feel larger than it actually is."

"I am aware of that. I have walked through the entire garden many times, but I had no clear idea of how those objects are actually positioned, in relation to each other. Until now."

Taking a fountain pen from his pocket, he circles the symbol of a lantern, then draws a line connecting it to the other objects, to the places where the garden's views are situated, until he comes to the last item, a stone Buddha in a bed of ferns. A rectangle appears, fixed inside the boundaries of Yugiri.

I sit there, looking at it.

"If drawn to the scale matching your *horimono*, I suspect this"—Tatsuji indicates the shape he has created on the graph paper—"would fit into the untattooed space on your back. The lines of your *horimono* would probably join up with the markers and the paths in Yugiri here, on this paper."

I put on my reading glasses and study the graph paper. Since Tatsuji first came to see me—almost two weeks ago, now—I have been thinking about everything he has told me. It has made me reexamine what I know of Aritomo, made me consider what he has said and done in an altered light. This is something I had not expected.

The following night I have dinner with Frederik and Emily at Majuba House. She is animated and alert, chatting with us in the sitting room after we have eaten. It is late when she asks me to help her to her bedroom. I look around the room, trying to remember it from the time when I slept here. The walls are no longer white but a soft blue. A photograph of Magnus in a silver frame, decorated with the spotted feather of a guinea fowl, stands on the bedside table, a shrine among the supplicant bottles of medicine.

Emily lets out a moan of pain as she lowers herself onto her bed. She closes her eyes for so long that I think she has drifted off to sleep. I am about slip out quietly when her eyes open again, brighter than they have been all evening. She sits up and points to a shelf without looking at it.

"That box," she says. "Take it down."

"This one?"

"Yes. Open it."

A rice paper lantern lies on a bed of tissue inside the box. The lantern is old, the woodblock print of ferns on its shade brittle when I give it to her. There is still a half-melted candle stub fixed inside it.

"I thought Aritomo destroyed all of them," I say.

"Oh, I kept this one. It was from one of my Chong Qiu parties, long before you met him," she says, gazing at the lantern. "Remember those lanterns he made for Magnus? What a sight that was, when we set them free into the sky that night. The old people here still talk about it, you know." She empties out a sigh from deep within her. "My memory is like the moon tonight, full and bright, so bright you can see all its scars."

She turns the lantern slowly in her palm, then gives it back to me. I am about to replace it in its box, but she stops me. "No, no. It's for you. I want you to have it."

"Thank you," I say.

Frederik glances at the lantern when I return to the living room. He gives me a whisky and says, "How's Vimalya? Are you happy with her?"

"She's intelligent, and she listens to instructions. Yugiri is starting to fascinate her."

He sits down across from me. "Your tattoos—you've kept them hidden all these years?"

"Apart from my doctors—and my neurosurgeons—I've never shown them to anyone else."

I recall the expression on my own doctor's face the first time he saw the *horimono*, years ago. Over the decades I have suffered from a variety of illnesses, but they have all been minor and have never required surgery. Some days I wonder if the *horimono* does actually contain talismanic powers, as Aritomo claimed. If it does, I am no longer under its protection.

"Your . . . your lovers?" Frederik asks. "What did they say when they saw your tattoos?"

"Aritomo was the last."

He hears what I have left unspoken. "Oh, Yun Ling," he says softly.

I think of the years of solitude, the care I have had to take in my dressing so that no one could ever see what lay on my skin.

"Aritomo gave them to me, and I never wanted anyone else to see them. And I was rising up the ranks of the judiciary—just a rumor of something like this would have ruined my career." I move away from him. "And to be honest, after Aritomo, I never met anyone who interested me."

"Are they the reason you don't want to get treatment?" Frederik says. "You have to. You must."

"Whatever procedures I have to undergo, whatever drugs I take, they won't save me in the end," I reply. The prospect of being locked inside my own mind terrifies me. "I have to ensure that the *horimono* is preserved."

Frederik's eyes sweep the edges of the room. "Make your arrangements with Tatsuji to preserve the tattoos but, please, get yourself treated. There's nothing shameful about a tattoo these days," he says. "So what if you're a judge? You've retired. If people want to talk, then to hell with them! Go for treatment, and come back here to recuperate, to *live*. There's a good nursing home in Tanah Rata you can go to, Yun Ling, people who can take care of you."

"Spend my declining days in an elephant's graveyard?" I say.

"You can move into Majuba House." He attempts a smile, to make what he is going to say next sound irreverent, trivial, but he fails. "I'll look after you."

"I didn't come back here hoping that you'd offer to do that for me, Frederik," I say.

A tear slides down his cheek. I reach over and wipe it away with the back of my fingers. "The *horimono* is a part of what happened to me. It's what Aritomo gave me. I have a duty to make sure it's kept safe."

As I walk out of Majuba House later, holding the unlit paper lantern in my hand, I hear the larghetto from Chopin's piano concerto.

Sometime during the night Emily died, Frederik informs me the following day. She went to sleep and never woke up, drifting away from the shore on the music Magnus used to play for her every night.

Ah Cheong is waiting when I step outside the house. He gives me the box of matches and the packet of joss sticks I asked him to buy. As usual he holds up the walking stick to me. I hesitate, and then take it. If he is surprised, if he feels vindicated by his patience, he does not show it.

"It's late," I tell him. "Go home."

The trees shading the path to Majuba hum with cicadas, like tuning forks that have been struck again and again. The air smells of the earth soothed by rain. At Majuba House a maid informs me that Frederik is still at his office.

I walk around to the back. I stop when I see the pair of statues, Mnemosyne and her nameless twin sister. The goddess of Memory has remained unchanged, but to my dismay, her sister's face is almost worn smooth, her features rubbed away. Perhaps it is caused by the difference in the quality of the stone the sculptor used, but it unsettles me nonetheless.

With the walking stick in my hand, I tread carefully down the slate-tiled steps to the formal gardens. Another sign of age, this fear of falling. How I hate it.

The slave-bell arch, white as chalk, draws me toward it. A starling perched on top of it cocks its head at me. I look up at the bell, into the black iris of its clapper. My body is stiff when I reach up to touch it. The metal feels cold through my gloves, the rust sticking to my fingertips like flakes of desiccated skin.

Vimalya's workmen have been digging up the grounds and removing the exotics, but Emily's rose garden is still there, a bowl in the earth; Frederik has decided to leave it untouched. At the ornamental pond, the bronze sculpture of the girl is still gazing into the water, her face more weathered now. Going behind a stand of bougainvillea trees, I enter a bower of low-hanging branches. The area around the three gravestones is well tended. Wincing at the pain in my knees, I kneel at the oldest gravestone and light three joss sticks for Magnus's and Emily's daughter, inserting them into the soil. Still on my knees, I turn to Emily's grave and do the same for her. Moving over to the last gravestone, I light three more joss sticks for Magnus. Somehow I know that he will not mind me doing this for him.

Levering myself to my feet with the walking stick, I notice a thin, vertical stone further back in the trees, concealed in the shadows. Strange, that I had not seen it when we buried Emily. I go closer to it. The stone is covered in lichen, but what surprises me is the sight of Aritomo's name carved in a vertical line of *kanji*, the calligraphy like a thin, shallow stream flowing its way down the barren side of a mountain. No one has told me about this stone, which marks not a grave but a void.

I light three more joss sticks and plant them into the moist patch of soil in front of it, then watch the smoke rise into the trees.

The shadow of the slave-bell tower lengthens across the lawn as I climb the stairs to the house. The first stars of the evening are blinking to life when I sit down on a stone bench. I look across the valleys and my thoughts return to everything Tatsuji has told me since he first arrived at Yugiri.

Frederik comes out from the kitchen a moment later. "There you are. Come on, old woman," he calls out, rubbing his arms. "Let's go inside. I've made a *lekker* fire."

In the sitting room Frederik throws more pine cones into the flames and I ask him about the gravestone with Aritomo's name on it.

"Emily put it up a few years ago," he replies.

"You should have told me."

He looks at me. "I did."

"I . . ." My voice falters, and I do not know what I wanted to say. "I always thought she blamed Aritomo for Magnus's death."

"I think the older she got, the less she felt that way. I remember she said to me one day, 'I don't care if his body was never found. It's not right that the man doesn't even have a proper grave.'"

Slowly, I describe to him what Tatsuji has shown me in his sketch of Yugiri's layout. For a while after I have finished talking there is only the sound of the fire crackling in the hearth.

"If he's right, if it's a map, I can use it to find where Yun Hong was buried," I say. "But what do I accomplish in the end—assuming that I do find all of Golden Lily's hiding places in Malaysia, assuming I'm still capable of communicating, capable of being understood?"

For years after he got lost in the mountains, I felt Aritomo had abandoned me. The only way to deal with the hurt was to distance myself from everything I had learned from him. Now, I wonder if he left me more than just the garden. Did he also leave the answer to the one question I have been asking? Would I have eventually discovered the connection between the garden and the *horimono* if I had not stayed away from Yugiri?

That sense of abandonment is fading, like water draining from the pond, leaving behind only sorrow for Aritomo, for the way his life was wasted, just as mine in its own way was. I do not want to search for my camp or the mine anymore. Yun Hong has been dead for over forty years. Locating where she was buried will not ease my guilt or undo what has been done.

"No one must be allowed to use the *horimono*, Frederik."

"Change the garden," he says. "Obliterate everything Aritomo created in it. That will render the tattoos useless. Vimalya will help you. And I'll send my men in too."

"You really hate that garden, don't you?" I smile at him, and for just a moment the heaviness in my chest lightens.

"Maybe it's always been a symbol to me of why you will never return my feelings," Frederik replies lightly, but it gives me a pang to realize that he is earnest.

"I made three promises to Yun Hong," I say. "I promised her I would escape from the camp if I had the chance. That was the only promise I kept. I never built the garden we had envisioned together. And I never freed her spirit from wherever she was buried."

Thinking of what Tatsuji told me about Golden Lily and what it did to its slave laborers, I see in my mind's eye Yun Hong and all the prisoners, hardened to clay like the thousands of terra-cotta soldiers discovered in an emperor's tomb in northern China, buried beneath the dust of two thousand years.

Frederik kneels on the carpet in front of me and takes my hands in his. I resist the urge to pull away. "You told me once that Aritomo named the pavilion by the pond after your sister's favorite poem," he says.

"The Pavilion of Heaven," I say, almost to myself.

"The garden for her already exists, Yun Ling. It's been there for nearly forty years."

I stare at him. He releases my hands, but I hold on to his.

"We're the only ones left from those withered days," he says. "The last two leaves still clinging on the branch, waiting to fall. Waiting for the wind to sweep us into the sky."

CHAPTER TWENTY-SIX

*On his last day in Cameron Highlands, Tatsuji arrives at Yugiri ear-*lier than usual, bringing with him materials to pack the woodblock prints. I give him the signed contract and help him cover each of the *ukiyo-e* in plastic wrapping before he places them flat in an air-tight box.

"The work in the garden seems to be going well," he says, when the last of the *ukiyo-e* has been packed away and the box sealed. "Coming in here this morning, I can see how it must have looked when Aritomo-*sensei* was alive."

"There's still a lot to be done. But it will be restored to the way it used to be," I say, "the way I remember it."

"The *horimono* . . ."

"I'll let you know."

Tatsuji takes out the book of Yeats's poems from his satchel. He looks at it, then holds it out to me. I shake my head, but he says, "Please, I want you to have it."

Extending my hands, I receive the book from him. I feel we have known each other for longer than the two weeks he has spent here. We are the same, I realize. The people we loved have left us and we have been trying ever since to go on with our lives. But the one thing we cannot do is forget.

I walk him out of the garden, going past the Pavilion of Heaven by the banks of Usugumo Pond. At the entrance he gives me a deep bow. "Come and visit me at Kampong Penyu, when my house is completed."

I return his bow. "A house on the beach, and time eternal," I say, knowing I will never see him again.

It is while I am practicing my shooting in the *shajo* that the mist comes into my eyes the first time. With no signs, no warning at all, my vision turns opaque, as though words are being murmured into an empty glass bottle. Locking my fingers on the bow, I fight off the fear spreading in my limbs. I want to shout to Ah Cheong, to call for help, but I do not want anyone to hear the panic in my voice.

Control your breathing. I hear Aritomo's voice, so clearly that he could be standing by my side.

I do as he taught me, without any success at first. The span between each breath coaxed in and then expelled gradually lengthens, broad lowlands dividing one mountain range from the next. Slowly the panic recedes and I begin to breathe normally again. Wiping the perspiration from my forehead with the edge of my sleeve, I rest the lower end of the bow on the floor. The sound reassures me.

Complete the shot.

The trees rustle in the wind. The arrows in the quiver-stand behind me shake softly, and I hear the shifting pebbles in the bed in front of the *shajo*; it sounds like someone cracking their knuckles. In my blindness I fit the arrow against the bowstring and pull it, feeling my ribs expand. I see the target in my mind as I wait for the wind to drop. A feeling of tranquility takes hold of me and I know I can stand there in that void forever.

I release the arrow, my mind guiding it all the way to the heart of the *matto* in one extended exhalation. From the song of the bowstring vibrating back into silence, strong and pure, I know it is the best shot I have ever made.

For a long time I stand there. I stand there until the emptiness in my eyes fills with shapeless objects again, coalescing into the familiar forms of trees and mountains and the long gravel bed in front. Lifting a hand to my eyes, I become visible to myself once more.

I return the bow to its stand and walk back to the house, leaving the arrow embedded in the center of the target.

The rice paper lantern Emily gave me rests on a shelf in the study. Late that night, as I am about to sit down at the desk, I stop and look at it. Rummaging in the drawers, I find a piece of paper, cut out a circle and cover the top of the lantern, sealing it with a strip of cellophane tape from a roll Tatsuji left in his workroom.

The pond is a meadow of stars. The frogs' croaking stops when they sense my presence, then resumes a few moments later. I light the candle in the lantern and hold it in my hands. I close my eyes and see Aritomo. A woman's face appears beneath my eyelids and I realize it is Yun Hong. She does not smile. She is not angry; she is not sad. She is only a memory.

The lantern becomes less heavy, and then there is no weight at all. I let it go, and I feel I am releasing a bird from my grasp. There is no wind tonight, and the lantern flickers upward, a buoy of light rising higher and higher. I watch it until it disappears somewhere above the clouds.

Dawn has come when the last line is finished. I have worked through the night, rewriting, but I do not feel tired at all. Holding the sheet of paper in my hand, my thoughts remain far away in that glade of ferns where I last saw Aritomo, almost forty years ago.

There have been times when I blamed myself for not calling out to him: perhaps he would have changed his mind, gone for his walk later or on another day, and not met with whatever befell him. Even after having set down the events of those brief years in writing, and reading them over again, I am still not entirely certain. But I know now, that whether it was an accident or if he did it on purpose, there was nothing I could have said or done to have prevented it.

In the rafters, a gecko clicks. I place the sheet of paper beneath all the other pages I have written, knock them into a neat stack and tie it together with string.

Something is stirring in my memory, and I remain completely still in my chair, so whatever it is that is emerging from hiding will not be frightened off. It takes shape slowly, like clouds forming.

I remember how, for a long time after Aritomo disappeared, the same dream kept recurring to me, staining my waking moments like the faintest of watermarks. I stopped having it once I moved away from Yugiri, and I forgot all about it.

In the dream I watch Aritomo walk on a path in the rain forest, pushing aside the overhanging branches and vines. Here and there the path narrows or crumbles into the river. He is not far ahead of me and I have the feeling that I am pursuing him, quietly, stealthily. Several times he slows down, as though allowing me to keep him in sight. Not once does he look back. The path ends in a clearing, and there he stops. Slowly he turns his entire body around to face me. He looks at me, not saying anything. It is at this point that I realize I am carrying a bow, his bow. I feel it stretch and strain as I take up the stance in preparation to shoot, the stance he taught me to perfect. I raise the heavy bow, pull the bowstring and aim straight at him, my arms, chest and stomach quivering with the effort. Still he does not move or speak.

I release the bowstring. And even though there is no arrow, still he falls. Still he falls.

Leaving the study, I walk past the ink painting of Lao Tzu. Its emptiness glows in the shadows. I stop and look at it, this drawing made by Aritomo's father.

Lao Tzu, the disillusioned philosopher from China, had gone to the west and was never seen or heard from again. Aritomo also set down his thoughts and his teachings before he left: he had recorded them in his garden, and he had painted them on my body.

My decision to restore the garden is the correct one, the only one I can make. I will ensure that Yugiri will remain. For my sister. When the garden is ready, I will open it to the public. I will put up a plaque by the Pavilion of Heaven, describing Yun Hong's life. The garden will also be a living memory of what Aritomo has made. I have told Tatsuji that Aritomo's *ukiyo-e* must be returned to Yugiri. I will put them on permanent exhibition here. The house will have to be repaired as well. And I have to write down as many instructions as I can for Vimalya. I must look for Aritomo's *Sakuteiki* and give it to her. So many things to do. I will be kept busy in the coming weeks and months. I remind myself to ask my secretary—my former secretary—to go to my house in KL and send Yun Hong's watercolor to me. It will be on display to the visitors who come to see the garden.

It is right that Yun Hong will be remembered as I gradually forget and, in time, become forgotten.

The garden must continue to exist. For that to happen, the *horimono* has to be destroyed after my death. I cannot entrust that responsibility to anyone, not Tatsuji, and not Frederik. I will have to do it myself.

The darkness in the sky is thinning when I go out to Usugumo Pond. A bird flies across the sky, returning to the mountains. A memory comes to me of the cave where Aritomo took me to see the swiftlets. I wonder if the aborigines are still harvesting the nests there, if the bamboo scaffolding they used is still pinned to the walls; I wonder if I can find the cave again.

Perhaps the blind old monk Aritomo spoke to on his walk across the countryside when he was a young man was correct: there is no wind; the flag does not move; it is only the hearts and minds of men that are restless. But I think that, slowly and surely, the turbulent heart will soon also come to a stillness, the quiet stillness it has been beating toward all its life.

Even as I am losing myself, the garden will come back to life again. I will work in the garden, and I will visit Frederik. We will talk and laugh and weep like only old friends can. And in the evenings I will walk in the hills. Ah Cheong will be waiting at the front door, holding out Aritomo's walking stick to me. I will take it, of course. But I know there will come a day when I will tell him that I do not want it.

Before me lies a voyage of a million miles, and memory is the moonlight I will borrow to illuminate my way.

The lotus flowers are opening in the first rays of the sun. Tomorrow's rain lies on the horizon, but high up in the sky something pale and small is descending, growing in size as it falls. I watch the heron circle the pond, a leaf spiraling down to the water, setting off silent ripples across the garden.

AUTHOR'S NOTES

With the exception of the obvious historical figures, all characters in the novel sprang from my imagination. The visit of Sir Gerald Templer and his wife to Majuba Tea Estate and Yugiri is fictional.

The Malayan Emergency ended in July 1960, twelve years after it began. With the combined efforts of local security forces, civilians and troops from the Commonwealth, Malaya was one of the few countries in the world to defeat a communist insurgency. Noel Barber in his book *The War of the Running Dogs* called it "the world's first struggle against guerrilla Communism."

Professor Tatsuji's experience as a *kamikaze* pilot originally appeared (in a different and longer form) in the *Asian Literary Review*, Autumn 2007, Volume 5.

The chamber versions of Chopin's Piano Concertos, Nos. 1 and 2 were recorded by the Yggdrasil Quartet in 1997.

The following books were of assistance to me in the writing of *The Garden of Evening Mists*:

The War of the Running Dogs: Malaya 1948–1960, by Noel Barber

In Pursuit of Mountain Rats: The Communist Insurgency in Malaya, by Anthony Short

Prisoners of the Japanese: POWS of World War II in the Pacific, by Gavan Daws

The Journey Back from Hell, by Anton Gill

The Comfort Women: Japan's Brutal Regime of Enforced Prostitution in the Second World War, by George Hicks

Blossoms in the Wind: Human Legacies of the Kamikaze, by Mordecai G. Sheftall

Sakuteiki: Visions of the Japanese Garden, by Jirō Takei and Marc P. Keane

The Japanese Tattoo, by Donald Richie and Ian Buruma
Gold Warriors, by Sterling Seagrave and Peggy Seagrave

I am grateful to Tristan Beauchamp Russell for describing to me what life on his tea estate in Cameron Highlands was like during the Malayan Emergency.

About the Author

Tan Twan Eng was born in Penang in 1972, but grew up in several places across Malaysia. He earned a law degree at the University of London and later practiced as an intellectual property lawyer. He developed a love of aikido at a young age, and the principles of this martial arts discipline have seeped into all aspects of his life; he has a first-dan ranking in the practice. He is also a strong advocate for the conservation of heritage buildings.

Eng's first novel, *The Gift of Rain*, was long-listed for the Man Booker Prize in 2007 and has been widely translated.

Eng divides his time between Cape Town and Kuala Lumpur. His second novel, *The Garden of Evening Mists*, was short-listed for the Man Booker Prize in 2012.

READING GROUP GUIDE FOR
THE GARDEN OF EVENING MISTS

Author's Commentary

Shakkei—the Art of Borrowed Scenery—is one of the main principles in Japanese gardening. When designing a garden, the gardener will make use of the neighbor's trees, or the mountains in the distance; he will even borrow from the clouds, the wind and the mists. The gardener incorporates these elements and views into the garden, making them integral to his creation. He must do it so skillfully, so seamlessly, that visitors to the garden are never aware of it.

Can *shakkei* be a metaphor for creative writing? There are similarities between the Art of Borrowed Scenery and the techniques of fiction. Using the elements of time, setting, and atmosphere, a writer creates a space for the reader to flesh out these characters in his own mind. In the process the reader lends something of his own "scenery" to these characters, making them feel more real to him, more alive.

Yugiri, the Garden of Evening Mists, is also a character in my novel. The garden interacts with Yun Ling and Aritomo. It borrows from their emotions and their responses. Yun Ling and Aritomo—and all who step into Yugiri—react to the garden in their individual ways. Yugiri, Yun Ling and Aritomo are mirrors, reflecting and borrowing from one another. So what is real, and what is only a reflection of a reflection of a reflection?

"Every aspect of gardening is a form of deception," Yun Ling remarks to Aritomo. Writing a novel is similar to designing and creating a Japanese garden: both arts require artifice and lies. Every single object in a garden is carefully selected and placed to create the optimal effect; it's the same with words and sentences in a work of fiction. For a novel—or a garden—to succeed, the lie has to convince, to beguile. Like the gardener, the writer must create a believable world. Yun Ling realizes this when she leads a group of visitors through Aritomo's garden: "The turns in the track disoriented not only our sense of direction, but also our memories, and within minutes I could almost imagine that we had forgotten the world from which we had just come."

But are we ever aware that *shakkei* is part of our daily existence? "A garden borrows from the earth, the sky, and everything around it, but you borrow from time," Yun Ling tells Aritomo. "Your memories are a form of *shakkei* too. You bring them in to make your life here feel less empty."

We borrow not only from our own memories, but also from the memories of the people around us. And it isn't only memories that create the *shakkei* of our lives, but everything we see and hear and experience, everyone we meet and talk to and who talks to us. We borrow from the music we listen to, from the books we read. We borrow from the past and the present. We borrow from the future, those far mountains we will one day reach. We borrow all these into our lives, and they form the ever-changing landscape in which we travel, day after day.

Discussion Questions

1. The author introduces Yun Ling as she is entering retirement, and slowly reveals the key experiences that have shaped her life. What was your initial impression of the main character and how did it change as the novel progressed?

2. As a research clerk in the war crimes tribunal directly after the war, Yun Ling is intimately involved in the national process of punishment and healing after the horrors of the Japanese invasion. Yet, she is hardly healed, and she has her own motives for this work. Can the Japanese crimes be forgiven?

3. Yun Ling tells us on the first page, "[Aritomo] did not apologize for what his countrymen had done to my sister and me." Does he attempt to make amends in other ways?

4. Violence is a frequent presence in Yun Ling's life, from the labor camp to the CT invasion to the destruction of her memory. How does she cope with the trauma of these events? Is she successful?

5. Not just violence, but sexual violence is a factor in the novel. How did you grapple with Yun Hong's experience as one of the "comfort women" in the camp and the shame she felt as a result?

6. Intertwined with the traumatic episodes, art—including literature, painting, and, of course, garden design—appears constantly in the book. Consider some key examples (e.g., Yun Hong's painting, the supposed Golden Lily hoard, Yugiri itself) and discuss their importance to the novel.

7. As the author delves deeper into Yun Ling's memory, the narrative continuously slips from present to past with little warning. How does this structure work to create meaning within the novel?

8. When Yung Ling finally returns to Yugiri and Frederik mentions Aritomo's death, she says, "There are days when I think he's still out there, wandering in the mountains, like one of the Eight Immortals of Taoist legend, a sage making his way home." Discuss the impact of Aritomo's disappearance in the novel, and how he continues to be present.

9. Aritomo's final artistic work is not a garden but a *horimono*, a tattoo covering much of Yun Ling's battered body. What is the significance of this act to their relationship and to the novel?

10. There is a constant struggle between memory and forgetting in the novel. How does the experience of the camp change Yun Ling's relationship to memory?

11. Frederik and Yun Ling have a brief encounter when she first arrives at Majuba estate, and he makes it clear that he has strong feelings for her throughout the book. Why do you think Yun Ling chooses Aritomo over Frederik?

12. Tatsuji is a peripheral character, but he is important not only for the revelatory information he brings. What does Tatsuji's narrative of his relationship with Teruzen and experience as a *kamikaze* pilot add to the novel?

13. Aritomo teaches Yun Ling that "every aspect" of the garden "is a form of deception." How does this aesthetic of deception and mystery become apparent in other aspects of the novel?

14. Why does Yun Ling, after all her searching and striving, choose not to use the possible clues from her *horimono* to try and locate her camp? Is this a hopeful novel?

About Tan Twan Eng's first book, *The Gift of Rain*

The Gift of Rain is the story of Philip Hutton and the haunting tragedies that befall him when he becomes entangled in a web of wartime loyalties and deceits. In 1939, at the outset of World War II, sixteen-year-old Philip is a lonely outsider on the lush Malayan island of Penang. Alienated from his community and family, he at last discovers a sense of belonging through an unexpected friendship with another outsider—a foreign diplomat whose true purpose on the island will ultimately bring unspeakable devastation. When Philip discovers he has been an unwitting traitor to his homeland and its people, he must work in secret to save as many lives as possible, even as his own family is torn apart. At once harrowing and luminous, Tan Twan Eng's celebrated debut novel is a thrilling epic and a true literary page-turner.

Praise for *The Gift of Rain*

"Beautifully written and deeply moving, Tan Twan Eng's debut novel is one of the best books I've ever read . . . Anyone who thinks the novel is in decline should read this one."

—Frank Wilson, *The Philadelphia Inquirer*

"An engrossing story of interlocking worlds . . . this deft first novel by Malaysian writer Tan Twan Eng stands as a lavish demonstration of the truth of William Faulkner's dictum, 'The past is never dead . . . It's not even past.'"
—Alan Cheuse, *The Dallas Morning News*

"Glorious . . . *Rain* is a gift indeed, as robustly absorbing as it is achingly poignant."

—Elysa Gardner, *USA Today*

"A powerful first novel about a tumultuous and almost forgotten period of history . . . *The Gift of Rain* is a war novel with a personal odyssey at its heart, one that complicates the stark lines of right and wrong during wartime . . . drawing the reader into a web of divided loyalties."

—*The Times Literary Supplement* (London)

"Eng's graceful prose evokes a time and place that is little known or remembered now, making it both exotic and familiar, and his beautiful narrative is woven with strong images and characters . . . *The Gift of Rain* is a gift to read."

—Mary Foster, *San Francisco Chronicle*

"Thrilling, introspective . . . Tan Twan Eng's lucid writing carries along the story effortlessly."

—*Milwaukee Journal Sentinel*

"Strong characters and page-turning action make this a top pick for historical fiction . . . Philip's personal drama unfolds against the backdrop of fascinating glimpses into Chinese culture, British imperialism, and the Japanese occupation that eventually claims the lives of everyone around him."

—*Library Journal* (starred review)

"A true saga . . . overflows with mesmerizing beauty and wonder.

—*Star Tribune* (Minneapolis)

"A riveting tale . . . [Tan Twan Eng] writes with deep insight into the history and topography of his native homeland and with deep feeling for its natural beauties."

—*The Washington Post*

"[A] remarkable debut saga of intrigue and aikido . . . Eng's characters are as deep and troubled as the time in which the story takes place, and he draws on a rich palette to create a sprawling portrait of a lesser explored corner of the war . . . measured, believable and enthralling."

—*Publishers Weekly* (starred review)

"*The Gift of Rain* sends the reader back into the world of Somerset Maugham—the waning British Empire, the simmering discord between classes and races, the thick tropical surroundings that are both beautiful and suffocating—but at a different angle. Maugham casts a cynical eye on human nature and its frailties; Tan Twan Eng looks upon them with compassion, like a creator might view the imperfections of his handiwork."

—*The Plain Dealer* (Cleveland)